THE LAST LIE

This Large Print Book carries the
Seal of Approval of N.A.V.H.

The Last Lie

Stephen White

THORNDIKE PRESS
A part of Gale, Cengage Learning

Detroit • New York • San Francisco • New Haven, Conn • Waterville, Maine • London

This is a work of fiction. Names, characters, places, and incidents are used fictitiously and are not meant to state or imply any facts about actual persons, living or dead. Any resemblance to actual persons, places, or events is purely coincidental and unintended.

Thorndike Press® Large Print Core.
The text of this Large Print edition is unabridged.
Other aspects of the book may vary from the original edition.
Set in 16 pt. Plantin.

LIBRARY OF CONGRESS CATALOGING-IN-PUBLICATION DATA

White, Stephen, 1951–
The last lie / by Stephen White. — Large print ed.
p. cm. — (Thorndike Press large print core)
Originally published: New York : Dutton, 2010.
ISBN-13: 978-1-4104-2808-0
ISBN-10: 1-4104-2808-7
1. Gregory, Alan (Fictitious character)—Fiction. 2. Clinical psychologists—Fiction. 3. Widows—Crimes against—Fiction. 4. Boulder (Colo.)—Fiction. 5. Large type books. I. Title.
PS3573.H47477L37 2010b
813'.54—dc22 2010021363

Published in 2010 by arrangement with Dutton, a member of Penguin Group (USA) Inc.

Printed in the United States of America
1 2 3 4 5 6 7 14 13 12 11 10

to Robert Barnett

It is hard to believe that a man is telling the truth when you know that you would lie if you were in his place.

H. L. Mencken

PROLOGUE

Surveillance footage indicated that a woman drove her 2005 Hyundai Santa Fe to the front of the Boulder Police Department at seven forty-five on Saturday morning. The car entered the frame from the south, which meant the driver had turned onto 33rd Street from Arapahoe before she pulled to a stop at the curb opposite the main entrance. The SUV ended up on the wrong side of the road, where the woman sat almost motionless behind the wheel in the don't-even-think-about-parking-here zone for over eleven minutes.

A uniformed officer striding toward his patrol vehicle in the lot adjacent to the building noted the car with the engine running. He tapped on the glass of the driver's door with the tip of his key. The woman at the wheel did not acknowledge him. Not at first.

The officer raised his voice so he could be

heard through the glass, instructing her to move her car. He gestured at the NO PARKING signs. There were so many of them, they could have been part of a public art installation.

Over an after-shift beer he would freely admit to another cop that he had little patience with citizens who acted as though simple rules — STOP, YIELD, NO PARKING — didn't apply to them. He considered the citations he wrote for most misdemeanor violations to be nothing more than comeuppance for violating gotta-get-along karma.

The shift he was finishing that morning hadn't been a good one. Before returning to the department to get some guidance from his sergeant on another matter, he had answered three domestic calls in a row. One right after the friggin' next. A double-wide off Valmont, a decent split-level with a great view below the Flatirons, and a gazillion-square-foot McMansion out near the reservoir.

He hated domestics, especially weekend, middle-of-the-night domestics. Every last one felt like Russian roulette to him. His domestic call mantra was "Knock on the door and fuckin' duck."

A half second before the patrol cop reached

for his citation book, the woman in the parked car lowered her window and turned her head toward him. She did not, however, look at his face. He instructed her to remove her sunglasses.

She hesitated a beat too long before she pushed the shades up onto her forehead. *Lady,* he said to himself, *I've had a bad night. Don't fucking push me.* His usual partner, Missy Abrams, counseled him to have conversations with himself before he had them with citizens. He thought Missy would be pleased when he told her later that he'd been acting on her advice, though she wouldn't be thrilled with the exact nature of the internal dialogue.

"Progress," she would say. "Baby steps."

His first thought when he looked at the woman's face after she pushed the glasses up to her hairline was that someone had hit her in the eye. His adrenaline surged at the possibility that he had just stumbled onto his fourth domestic in a row. That would have been a dubious personal record. But further examination caused him to conclude that the woman looked more like she had started to remove her makeup and had stopped halfway through the process. That's what left her with smudged mascara and half-removed eyeliner. And that's why he'd initially thought she looked so bruised. Some tears were mixed in, too, he thought.

So. This woman had stopped removing her makeup without completing the job, and then she'd driven to the police station. She'd parked in a no-parking zone on the wrong side of the street with her engine running. And then she just sat there, crying.

He tried to make sense of that progression but drew a blank.

He was wishing he had just kept on walking to his cruiser. If he'd kept on walking, she would eventually have gone inside and spoken to Ruth Anne at the desk. Ruth Anne was, like, unflappable.

Or the woman would have just driven away, no one the wiser.

The woman's breathing changed suddenly and audibly. That got his attention. It started coming in rushed little inhales that were paired in twos followed by long silent exhales. He mistook the pattern for hiccups. The officer's ex-wife got hiccup jags that sounded similar.

The presence of the hiccups caused him to lean in a little closer to the open window. He expected to detect the telltale aroma of alcohol on the woman's breath. *DUI? DWI?* Or his recent favorite catchall, DWO — Driving While Oblivious. Texting, iPods, Big

Macs, mascara, whatever. DWO was a small addition to state motor vehicle law that he felt was long overdue.

Had the woman been drinking? *Maybe yes, maybe no.* He wasn't sure. He decided to give her the benefit of the doubt. It wasn't a compassionate gesture. He just wanted her to move her damn car half a block down the street — on the other side, so it was pointed in the right direction.

He said, "You know you can't park here, right?" He gestured again at the signs that were all over the place, not pretending to hide his exasperation. She didn't react. "Tell me this, you waiting for someone?"

The woman considered his question for a good ten seconds, which was out near the frontier of the cop's patience. "No," she said finally. "There's no one."

Either a simple *yes* or *no* in reply would have been fine with him, though he had a bias toward *yes,* because that would have indicated that another human being might soon arrive to spare him this situation.

But the woman had answered with something existential.

In the officer's cumulative experience with Boulder's citizens — a cohort that was more prone to existential retorts than most — eight in the morning was a tad too early for philosophical reflection.

The officer took a deep breath while he admitted that the situation confronting him was not a simple karma violation. He was not that lucky a cop. He thought about what his patrol partner would have said were she with him right then.

Missy — he told her at some point almost every shift when conversation dragged between them — was like the all-time worst cop name ever. Every time he told her that she called him an asshole. "You're an asshole, Heath. Period. End of sentence."

He knew what Missy would want him to say right at that moment. So that's what he said: "Are you all right, ma'am? Do you require some assistance?"

He was hoping she'd reply *yes* to the first question, *no* to the second. But he wasn't holding his breath.

"Assistance," the woman repeated after a perplexed interlude. "Help?" she then said, as she completed some translation of his trailing question. She puffed out her cheeks as though the combination of questions completely stumped her. She finally said, "I'm — There's — Sometime . . . last night?" She punctuated each of the fractured sentences with interruptions of the gasp-gasp-silence breathing melody.

"Take your time," the officer said. It was another useful phrase that he'd learned from Missy.

It was Missy who had convinced him that there was a subset of citizens who were not inclined to speed up their cooperation under insistent verbal pressure from a large man with biceps the size of two-liter Coke bottles, who was wearing a uniform, and who also happened to be armed with a handgun and a baton.

Some citizens, that set of facts motivates. Other citizens, that set of facts flusters.

Missy would say "discombobulates."

That this particular citizen fell into the "discombobulates" category, the officer had absolutely no doubt.

The woman in the Hyundai spread the fingers of her left hand, palm up, so her manicured nails jutted just out the open window. "Last night? Well, yeah, it had to be. No, maybe early this morn — I — That's . . . no. It had to be — No. No. The time part is hard. Why is it all so . . . See . . . okay, okay, I've been —" she said.

She pulled her hand back, curled it into a fist, and shook it like it was her turn with the bones at a craps table. But her expression made clear that she wished she could shake the fist in someone's face. Someone in particular.

The cop noted the absence of a wedding band on her ring finger. Since his own divorce, final only five months before, he had started noticing women's ring fingers. At first, it was the weirdest thing for him, like suddenly discovering women had noses.

He didn't think she noticed him noticing her ring finger. She had something else on her mind. "There's been a —" she said, once again spreading the fingers of her left hand. "I'm pretty sure — Yes, I am, I *am* pretty, pretty sure. I am," she said. "Or . . . I wouldn't be here, right?" She flattened her lips.

He said, "That's not for me to say, ma'am. Why you're here. That's what we're trying to determine."

But his reply seemed to puzzle the woman. "Well, of course. Why would — I didn't . . . No, no, I did not," she said. "I haven't at all, with — Not since, oh God, not since *that* day. *That* very morning, if you can believe it. Lord. But even then I didn't . . . give him —" Her shoulders sagged. "Lord. I wish I had. Even if . . . It wasn't usual for us, far from it. Morning? On a Sunday? On a golf Sunday? But . . . last night? I didn't. I did not. And I certainly didn't give . . ." Her voice trailed off. "But he . . . did. He did it. It's not that I really remember but — I mean, but how else? Right? I can tell. I just can. Other women? Maybe not. I've never had that conversation. Maybe I should have had — But, it doesn't matter, because I can tell." She paused for a couple of quick gasps and one long exhale. She did it one more time. Then she briefly touched the side of her face, on the right side. "I can. I know."

The officer still thought she had hiccups.

She spread all ten fingers, both palms facing up. Her makeup-stained eye went wide. "I was not that . . ." She shook her head. "Not at all. To drive? I wouldn't have, of course. I'm careful about that. It doesn't take that much, but I'd eaten. Tired, sure, but — Not like — Not at all like —

"He did it," she said again. "He did it. To me."

The officer was not hearing alarm in her voice. Most people he dealt with in stressful situations, their demeanors were like I-70 in the mountains — all curves and ups and downs. But this woman's affect and tone were like I-70 in eastern Colorado. On the plains. Heading to Kansas. Other side of Limon. Flat and straight.

By the time she pulled up in front of the department, all of the terrible feelings and all of the momentum that had got her going that morning were spent. What was left of this woman's recent awful experience — whatever that might have been — was blunted. The officer later told Detective Davenport that the woman reminded him of his mother when she was really upset. Not bad-day upset. Holy-fuck upset. Like the morning a couple months before when she got the results of the Pap smear.

She'd managed just one crazy-making call, to her only son. After the call to Heath — there were times he really wished his sister hadn't moved to Tucson to be near her wiseass boyfriend with all the friggin' tats — he had rushed right over to his mother's house in Louisville. He sat with her at the kitchen table for five minutes while she petted a cat purring contentedly in her lap. He didn't recognize the cat.

She finally asked him if he knew that Louisville had been voted the best small town in America.

Heath said he did not know that. He didn't say what else he was thinking, which was that he didn't even remember the question being on the ballot. He waited. He knew more was coming. He spent the dead time trying to place the cat. Was his mother taking in strays? That would be a bad sign.

Minutes later, in the same bland tone she'd used to ask the question about America's best small town, she asked him if he knew that his mother had cervical cancer. Not "Do you know I have cervical cancer?" but "Do you know your mother has cervical cancer?"

His mother's tears didn't actually start flowing for another ten minutes. That's how long it took for her to leave the flat behind.

"Would you like to come inside?" the officer said to the woman in the Hyundai. "Talk to someone about what happened last night — or, or early this morning — maybe? With that man? The one you're talking about who did . . . something? I'm thinking, maybe you could talk to a detective, to help clear up . . . your thinking."

She reacted by reaching over to the center of the car and lifting a big cup of Starbucks coffee from the cup holder on the dash. Her sudden motion caused the officer to take an involuntary step away from the vehicle.

Pure instinct had him getting ready to fall to a crouch, slide to one side, and shift an open palm nearer his weapon. The string of damn domestic calls earlier in the shift had Heath on edge. "Jitter in a jar" is what Missy called domestics. When she said that to him while they were walking up to a house — "Here we go, jitter in a jar" — "Yep, knock and fuckin' duck" is what Heath would say right back at her.

Missy hated it whenever Heath said "fuckin' duck." For some reason he didn't get, that was fingernails on a blackboard for Missy.

"I haven't even had a sip," the woman said. "Of this. My latte? It's pumpkin. I just got it. Over by King Soopers? That Starbucks. I thought of stopping at the one on Baseline — you know that one? — but this one is closer. Maybe not as convenient, though. You think? I had to turn around."

"Ma'am?" he said, not eager to get into a discussion about expensive coffee or how to get from point A to point B in Boulder. Like arguing evolution with his aunt.

She said, "Not one sip. Because . . . I didn't know. I mean, I just did not know. I didn't want it to . . . mess things up? Do you know what I mean? In the lab? Later? I couldn't decide if it would or it wouldn't . . . I tried to remember if I'd seen anything like it on *CSI*. About coffee, after. Or coffee before, even, I guess." She paused to give it some more thought. "I don't think I have seen it. Have they done a show on that? Did I miss it? I must have missed it. Do you know? Is it okay? Maybe it was on *Law & Order.* The sex one. I don't watch that one all the time. I miss a lot of those." She looked in the direction of the officer's bewildered face, not quite making contact with his eyes. "Do you watch *CSI?*"

He did not want to have a conversation with this woman about *CSI.* He hated conversations with civilians about television cops. To his continuing dismay, a surprising number of civilians tried to initiate those kinds of discussions with him. If Missy were in the right mood, sometimes she would go ahead and engage in those conversations. Drove Heath crazy. Missy knew all the fake cops' names, even the ones on cable.

He picked one of the woman's other questions and tried to answer that. "Is it okay to have coffee?" he said. "That's what you want to know? If you can take a sip?" He was once again thinking this must all be part of some complicated domestic. His cop radar was telling him he'd just stumbled onto some potentially toxic jitter in a jar right there in front of the damn headquarters building.

The woman's husband didn't want her to be drinking coffee, or was pissed that she spent too much at Starbucks, or maybe it was the pumpkin she'd added to her latte.

Sometimes it was something nuts like that — the pumpkin she added to her friggin' latte.

Trainers were always telling patrol officers responding to domestics to identify the precipitating event. This time? Heath was thinking the precipitant was a pumpkin latte. Didn't feel right, though. His caution nerves were continuing to fire.

The woman made the most puzzled face before she leaned closer to him and lowered her voice to an almost-whisper. "I haven't even peed yet," she said. "I really, really need to pee. And now, talking about it — about peeing — is making it even worse. I was doing okay about that, before."

Heath guessed right then what was going on. When she said she hadn't even peed.

He spread his feet and he set his jaw. For him, anger always came before sadness. Resolve before compassion. Widening his stance and setting his jaw helped him keep the rage where it needed to be.

"May I have some of my coffee?" she asked. "Do you think that's okay? Or maybe I could pee first. What do you —" She stopped herself midsentence.

His voice was softer when he spoke next. "How about you bring the cup of coffee inside with you, ma'am? The detective I'll introduce you to will know the answer to your question. All your questions. I'm sure about that. Do you think I could see your driver's license? The registration and insurance card, too? Please? Then you can come with me. We'll go inside. Together."

She noticed the name tag on his chest as though it was suddenly illuminated. Locked onto it for a few seconds. She then made eye contact with him for the first time. "Do you have a woman?" she asked him. "Officer Heath Wade."

Oh shit, he thought. His ring finger, like hers, was naked. He closed his left hand. He immediately recognized that the fist could present a problem. He opened it back up. "Ma'am?" he said.

"A woman detective?" she said. "I think I would like to talk with a woman detective."

Officer Heath Wade waited for the woman to find the papers he requested. He waited for her to open the car door. Even in trying circumstances, he was a meticulous cop. Anything he didn't have to touch, he didn't want to touch. Another one of Missy's favorite sayings on patrol was "You never know." He tried not to touch things he didn't have to touch because "you never know."

After the woman had climbed out of the

driver's seat, he took the license and registration and insurance card from her hand and slid them into his shirt pocket. He directed her to stand on a spot on the sidewalk about ten feet out in front of the car. "Please wait there, right there," he said. She didn't move. He had to guide her to the spot.

He pulled a latex glove from a pouch on his belt, stretched it onto his right hand, reached inside the car, switched off the ignition, and removed her wad of keys. He kept an eye on her the entire time.

He used his gloved hand to shut the car door. He found the button on the key fob that locked the doors. He said, "Talk about what, ma'am?" not really expecting a straightforward answer. "Do you want to talk with a woman detective?"

"The rape," she said. "The . . . rape. What else?"

1

The damn housewarming took place in Spanish Hills on the Friday evening just after Halloween.

I had no way to know it at the time, but a strand of silk from the tangled web of that party had begun spinning my way long before the first guests arrived.

A psychotherapy supervision session I'd had a few days before the party had been far from routine. I remembered many details. Topics had included vacation time, desert rituals, plastic surgery, an eighteen-foot-long bridal train, naked breasts, fluorescent Crocs, and quality embroidery.

Supervision? I've been practicing my craft in Boulder, Colorado, for so long that my longevity alone had qualified me to enter the realm of experienced clinicians who attract the attention of young psychotherapists eager for professional guidance. Occasionally, I succumbed to a plea for help.

I've never thought that *supervision* was the right word for the complex professional relationship during which most of the actual training of psychotherapists occurs. But supervision is what it's been called as long as I've been in the business.

I first heard the word used in that context during graduate school. I was a first-semester graduate student in clinical psychology when my academic adviser informed me that the time had arrived for me to begin psychotherapy.

I was initially taken aback at the presumption of his suggestion, even suffering a transient how-dare-he moment of personal offense. As my defensiveness waned and the reality of my questionable mental health seeped into my awareness, I thought, *I could probably use the help.* I nodded to my adviser. I said, "Okay."

He stared back at me with an expression on his face indicating that he had not been seeking my assent about anything. He then proceeded to inform me who my supervisor was going to be at the start of the coming semester.

My *supervisor.* The psychotherapy my adviser wanted me to start involved my functioning in the therapist role, not the patient role. I had a little trouble with the concept. *Seeing clients? Me? Already?* He told me that some unsuspecting freshman English major would probably be cast in the patient role.

I could hardly have been more surprised at the news that I was about to start being a *therapist.* I could only guess how the freshman English major was going to feel.

My guide on the perilous journey to becoming a functioning psychotherapist was my "supervisor," a well-practiced clinician who would educate, guide, inform, instruct, confront, critique, cajole, explore, and do whatever else he or she determined was necessary in order to help me develop the knowledge, the skills, the maturity, the self-awareness, and the sensitivity necessary to be an effective therapist.

I thought it then and I continued to think it: *supervisor* is not the right word for the role. Not even close. But it's the label we have.

For the next ten years or so — five more in graduate school, a year of clinical internship, a couple of years prelicensure, a few more postlicensure — I had supervisors. A few were good; a couple were very good. One was so skillful that he elevated the game to another level. Two or three others? I could have learned as much about psychotherapy by talking with a random customer about snow tires in a 7-Eleven.

I'd become an experienced therapist. I was a supervisor. One of the clinicians I was supervising was a young Boulder psychologist named Hella Zoet, Ph.D. We'd known each other professionally for a while. She had been one of the advanced graduate students from the university that I had supervised in previous years. After graduate school she'd gone off for her internship year in L.A., then had worked briefly in Grand Junction, across the Rockies on the Western Slope, before returning to Boulder as a full-fledged Ph.D. Hella had a freshly framed Colorado psychologist's license hanging on the wall of her private practice office a few blocks from mine.

Hella had asked me to supervise her practice while she established herself professionally in town. She wasn't required to seek postlicensure supervision. It was something she'd chosen for professional development.

Hella was a wisp of a woman. She was maybe five feet tall, with bright blue eyes and straight, fine blond hair that she wore mostly down. Her ears always poked through the hair on each side of her head. I'd never asked her age, but during her student years I had guessed she was a few years older than most of the department's clinical graduate students. I guessed that she was older because of her maturity, not because she looked anywhere close to her actual age. She was doomed, or blessed, to be carded by bartenders until she was forty.

Hella was skillful, smart, intuitive, imaginative, and compassionate. I had no doubts about her diagnostic acumen or her therapeutic talents. If she ultimately decided to set down roots in Boulder — I wasn't sure she would; my gut told me that Hella had some vagabond in her — I expected to be referring cases to her for years to come.

Hella favored long skirts. She also favored sitting during supervision with her legs crossed or folded beneath her. So those long skirts served a purpose.

As we walked from the waiting room to my office, she greeted me with a caution. She said, "We have some things to talk about today."

I said, "Okay."

She crossed her legs beneath her and arranged her skirt. She made a face I couldn't interpret as she said, "Do you remember when I told you about running into that patient at Burning Man a while back? In September?"

I nodded. Hella had mentioned an encounter with a patient at Nevada's Burning Man festival in passing. That was all. I had followed up by asking her if it was something she and I should discuss. At the time, she had chosen to wait to see how the issue developed with her patient in treatment. I hadn't challenged her. We'd moved on to another topic.

Just as every coach coaches differently, every psychotherapy supervisor supervises differently. Some supervisors focus more on process issues between the therapist and his or her patient; some supervisors will pay more attention to the content — facts — that are revealed during the treatment. Some are rigorous proponents of a treatment model or theoretical approach. Some supervisors are big-picture advocates; others sweat the smallest details of what happens in the treatment.

My own style was to let my supervisee lead me to areas requiring my attention. That's what Hella did that day. I considered it my responsibility to keep peering over her shoulder to see where she was headed.

"Now, I think we should talk more about me running into her that night," she said. "It's come back up."

The patient Hella had crossed paths with

at Burning Man was a thirty-four-year-old systems analyst whom Hella had been seeing for individual psychotherapy since late that same spring. The patient's presenting problems were unresolved grief issues, depression, and anxiety. The immediate precipitant for the therapy was the sudden death of the woman's husband on a Sunday morning the previous April. He had been playing a round with some friends in a foursome at a Denver golf course. He collapsed a second after he released the grip on his three-wood at the apex of his tee shot on the fifth hole. He had died in the ambulance on the way to the hospital. Cause of death was an M.I. Terrible family history, it turned out.

An enduring mystery of his death was the flying three-wood. The other members of the foursome said the club left his hands like a rocket. It had never been located.

From the beginning of the treatment, Hella considered her psychotherapy with the golfer's widow to be progressing uneventfully. The woman was committed to the treatment, was motivated to do some work, and her presenting symptoms were beginning to remit. She was tentatively examining underlying issues in the marriage, a relationship that she had begun to acknowledge had been less than satisfying for a long while.

When Hella initially presented the case to me, I wondered aloud, as I usually do with supervisees, about her diagnostic impressions of her patient.

Hella had prefaced her reply with some insight into her countertransference. "I really like this woman," she said. "She's funny, she's self-effacing. She has a deep soul."

I said, "Noted."

"Diagnostically?" she went on. "I think she's half-lost."

I was unfamiliar. "Is that one of the new diagnoses I should expect from *DSM-5?*"

She said, "When I was an intern in L.A., I did outpatient work in a clinic in West Hollywood. Many of my outpatients were in therapy because they were half . . . lost. It's a descriptive diagnosis I like to use. Serves me well clinically, too. In addition to being half-lost, this woman also meets criteria for reactive depression and for an anxiety disorder. But the truth is she is in therapy because she lives in Boulder, not in Boise or Biloxi, and because since her husband's death she's been feeling . . . half-lost."

In supervision, as in life, the squeaky wheel tends to get the grease. A good supervisor is the mechanic who can hear the telltale squeak even when the supervisee thinks everything is running along fine. But that hadn't been the case with the Three-Wood Widow — which was the shorthand name that Hella used to provide instant context for me when she wished to discuss the young woman. It had been my impression that Hella had the case under control. She and I had been paying it only passing attention in supervision.

Hella began relating her fresh concerns about the extracurricular encounter with her patient by revealing that she was a Burning Man veteran, a factlet that surprised me not at all. The previous month's celebration in the Nevada desert, it turned out, had been Hella's ninth consecutive in attendance. I, on the other hand, hadn't even been aware of the existence of Burning Man for anywhere approaching nine years.

Those facts said something important about both of us.

Since Hella had initially mentioned the festival, I'd done some reading to flesh out my understanding of a celebration that, frankly, didn't sound particularly understandable to an outsider, which I was. Burning Man is an annual festival of experimentation, expression, and self- and community reliance that takes place for a week each September on a remote playa in Nevada's Black Rock Desert wilderness. Once an intimate affair, it has grown into a gathering of almost fifty thousand people.

Hella identified herself as one of the founding members of a Burning Man theme camp — she explained that her theme camp was composed of a cadre of like-minded souls who met up annually during the festival in Nevada. Her group lived together under the stars while they created a complex, intentionally interactive art installation for a onetime performance during the festival.

Hella's recounting of the patient/therapist extracurricular encounter at Burning Man began with particular bemusement in her eyes and in her voice. "The final performance put on by our camp traditionally involves fire. I mean, it's Burning Man, right? Fire, for us, is . . . a force of rebirth. We — the group, the camp — have always strived to play with perception, to maximize the use of shadows, to contrast the interface of light and dark. Destruction and construction. Good and evil. Life and death. Positive and negative space. Integration and conflagration. We are attempting to control the ultimately uncontrollable. To freeze movement that can't be frozen. And always, always, to succeed by failing."

Hella's tone changed not at all as she continued. "During that one grand performance each festival, we encourage participation from attendees outside the theme camp. Although it's not a requirement, and we have never attempted to design the performance that way — not consciously anyway — inevitably some of the people from inside the camp and others who join with us in the performance and in the celebration that follows participate while in various stages of . . . undress. Depending, of course, on the weather."

I'm not completely sure that Hella paused between the *of* and the *undress.* It's possible that my ears added those ellipses.

I did endeavor to be a self-aware supervisor.

I reminded myself that the dialogue I was having with Hella was, in fact, supervision and not psychotherapy. And that the events she was describing had taken place during her vacation time, in her personal life, in a land far, far away. With that spirit in mind, I continued to swallow the many questions I had about light and dark and shadows and theme camps and freezing movement and positive and negative space and the demographics of the group and controlling the uncontrollable. I particularly withheld comment about integration and conflagration, and about the various stages of . . . undress of the participants.

I also swallowed a few *whys*. Six or seven, at least. I was wishing they were relevant — I was that curious — but they weren't. Not yet.

Hella went on. "What I'm about to tell you next is more information than I would like to share with you, and I hope it's more information than you would like to learn about me, but . . . this is supervision, and I think you need to understand the context of my run-in with my patient. In the event it is becoming relevant in the therapy. Right?"

I suspect that Hella was hoping I'd say *Not really.* But I didn't. I said, "If it's becoming relevant, I think I do need to understand a little more."

She looked at me and smiled an okay-here-goes smile with her bright eyes wide and her ears poking through her blond hair. At that moment, she appeared elfish. "That particular night, for that particular part of the performance — it was during the final half hour, near the finale — I was wearing" — she poked a shoe out from beneath her voluminous skirt — "these boots."

The boot she exposed was of scuffed black leather, had two-inch heels, and extended up to near her knee. It was closed with a long zipper on her inner calf. I had seen the boot before. It did not appear to be a special boot.

I was waiting for Hella to complete the description of her outfit.

Although my wife would argue to the contrary, I'm not as naïve as I appear sometimes. I knew Hella well enough to predict that the costume she was wearing at Burning Man was unlikely to be an ensemble out of an Ann Taylor catalog. And she knew me well enough to know that the peculiarities of her outfit, whatever they might be, would not become an issue for the supervision unless they were an issue for the therapy.

Hella added, "And I had this gorgeous — fabulous — eighteen-foot lace wedding veil that I found on eBay. Never used. The woman had called off her own wedding. There was some special meaning there."

I allowed myself a moment to digest the image that Hella was painting. Of the boots and the veil and . . .

"I'd woven a pattern into the length of the veil with some grosgrain ribbon. It evoked shadows in the desert near a roaring fire. Fire climbing from below to the earth's crust, and from the earth to above."

I nodded then, not because I understood the evocation of ideas of shadows in the desert and climbing and descending fires. I nodded because I realized that Hella had completed the description of her outfit.

2

I started doing my best to try to stop digesting images, though I wasn't completely successful.

Hella smiled an unself-conscious smile. "It's a great week, Alan. Burning Man is. Every year. Although in many ways I preferred it when the festival was more obscure and smaller and more intimate, each time I go, I find it's medicine for my heart and my soul. I've grown up there in some intrinsic way."

I didn't want Hella to feel she needed to rationalize her attendance at Burning Man or apologize for the costume she'd chosen for her performance. I said, "And for your patient? How were her heart and soul doing?"

Hella recognized that I was redirecting her. "Thank you. I see what you're doing. It's kind, but what I was wearing is significant, Alan. I'm not embarrassed. The thing is, it's not a gratuitous detail."

I waited. To myself, I said, *Prurient detail, certainly. Gratuitous detail, not.*

Hella pressed on. "Like I said, I saw her there near the end of our big performance, which took place near the end of the festival. I didn't run into her at all earlier in the week, and I didn't see her during the beginning of the performance. She says she didn't see me earlier, either. When I did finally see my patient, really when I recognized her through the smoke — I'm pretty sure I saw her before she spotted me — she was one person out of a large group . . . dozens, scores, even hundreds . . . who were observing or participating as part of the . . . event." She narrowed her blue eyes and asked me, "You've never been?"

"No," I said.

"It's hard to describe what it's like."

"Yes," I said, agreeing. "It's hard for me to imagine."

"What she was wearing is important, too. It's why I felt I should describe my own . . . attire." For the record, those ellipses *were* Hella's. "My patient was wearing a tiny, very tiny, jean skirt with intricate, embroidered black suns — one rising, one setting — on each of her butt cheeks, and she was wearing a pair of fluorescent green Crocs.

"She also had a three-wood that was fashioned in a way that made it appear to impale her skull above one ear and exit below the ear on the other side."

I waited a suitable length of time for more clothing details before I said, "A lot of symbolism in that outfit."

Psychotherapy supervision is not a time when it pays to ignore the obvious.

"A little overt for my taste," said Hella. "But gosh yes. The suns? The three-wood? Definite symbolism there."

"Her outfit?" I tried to restrain a smile. "What you've described? I assume that's all?"

"Maybe some jewelry," Hella replied.

"Okay then," I said.

Hella said, "You know, until that moment, I had not even known she embroidered."

I laughed. Hella laughed, too. She was not unaware of the absurdity of the events that had taken place that night in the Nevada desert.

"My countertransference? This is probably important: If fate determined that I was to run into one of my patients that night, in those circumstances, I would never have guessed that it would be her, that she would be the one who would be at Burning Man. But I might have chosen . . . that she be the one who would be there. Of all the patients in my caseload — if it had to happen — I'm glad it turned out to be her."

"That helps," I said. A therapist's feelings about a particular patient tend to become more of an issue, and an influence, when they are unacknowledged.

Hella pulled the disparate pieces all together for me, just in case I had missed anything crucial. She said, "So, basically, she and I run into each other completely by chance in this crazy, ephemeral, transient city of fifty thousand strangers and seekers and gawkers in a dry lake bed on the Nevada desert. It's the middle of the night, I'm naked for all intents and purposes, my patient is topless, and in the interest of full disclosure, should it turn out to be relevant, I should probably add pantyless, and we're both completely, totally, absolutely involved in the performance of this wonderfully elaborate interpretative piece about the collision of primitive life forms in the earliest moments of the survival of carbon-based life on earth."

"I'm with you," I said. Though I'm not sure why I said that. The circumstances she was describing were as foreign to me as string theory.

"Two minutes after I spotted her for the

first time, the dance we were doing brought us side to side. She completed a spin, and her eyes showed just a flicker of surprise as she recognized that it was me dancing beside her. I watched her glance flit from my face to my boots to my veil, and down my train, not really ever pausing too long anywhere in between. Finally, she took my hand. Softly. She said, 'Hello, Doctor Zoet.' Just like she might be greeting me in the waiting room."

Hella narrowed her eyes at me. "You told me once during supervision back when I was still in graduate school that when a therapist runs into a patient in public, out of the office, the safest thing to do is to follow the patient's social lead. Allow the patient to say hello, or not, to make introductions, or not, that sort of thing. So that's what I did right then. I said, 'Hello,' back to her. I didn't even use her name, you know, just in case she wasn't using it while she was at Burning Man."

"Good call," I said. "Considering the circumstances." And the event. And the wardrobe.

Hella said, "There's an underlying expectation of anonymity out there. At Burning Man. Certainly at our theme camp. Absolutely during a performance like that one.

No cameras, no recording. It's made clear to everyone who attends."

"I can imagine," I said. Actually, I was taking Hella's word for it.

Hella continued. "She and I were tugged in opposite directions. Literally. By the dance. We parted, danced away. The performance brought us back together a few minutes later. Maybe five, ten.

"Her presence was a distraction for me, I have to admit. I would have preferred she not be there. I think it's important that I say that. Burning Man is a place I go to get away from . . . my work. My life."

"Understood," I said.

"When she saw me again, almost immediately she said to me, 'In case you're wondering, they were Dan's idea.' "

My expression made it clear that the name Dan wasn't ringing a bell.

Hella reminded me, "Daniel was her dead husband, the golf pro. The man without the three-wood?"

"Got it," I said, grateful for the information. In my professional life, the names of patients, my own and those of my supervisees, not to mention all of their numerous significant others and friends and family members and adversaries, and colleagues, and neighbors, tended to run together for me. Contextual nicknames helped me keep important people distinct. Hella's patient had always been "Three-Wood Widow." Her dead husband, Daniel, had been "the golf pro" or "the dead golf pro."

Hella had a new name for him, apparently. "The Man Without the Three-Wood."

"Go on," I said. Few stories in therapy, or supervision, interest me from a narrative point of view. I have, literally, heard them before. However, I definitely wanted to know how the Burning Man vignette turned out.

Hella said, "I didn't know what she meant with her reference to her husband; I didn't know what exactly had been Dan's idea. Was she talking about being at Burning Man? Was she a return visitor? Or had she made the trip to the festival as some kind of tribute to her dead husband? And why did she say 'they' and not 'this'?

"Frankly, Alan, I wasn't even sure whether to respond to her at all. I didn't want to be her therapist right then. You know what I mean? I didn't. I had other things in my head. Her presence was . . . distracting. By introducing Dan she seemed to be inserting the psychotherapy into the moment, which did not make me happy. But, on the other hand, I didn't want to ignore her. That would be rude. Right? Even unprofessional."

"Tough situation," I said. I meant it.

Hella said, "You've always told me that I have to be prepared to take control at moments when reality and therapy collide outside the office."

It was one of my standard supervisory prompts, though I would have admitted that I had never imagined a moment precisely like the one that Hella was describing.

"What should I have done, Alan?"

"Finish the story, then we'll talk about that." I hoped by the time she finished the story I might come up with an answer to her question.

Hella said, "Well, I turned to face her, and I said, 'They?' You know, to clarify?

"She turned her body to face me. She lifted both her hands so they were floating in front of her abdomen, palms up. She said, 'These. The C-cups. The girls.'

"I'm not surprised by much that goes on at Burning Man, Alan. I've been going for a long time. I've seen a lot. Most of what happens there now is evolution, not pure inspiration. But she must have noticed the bemusement on my face right then because she began to dance in front of me, pulled her shoulders back, bent over a little at the waist, and she shook her chest at me in a shimmy that was so well executed that I'm pretty sure she'd been practicing . . . the move."

I shook my head slowly, in amazement. It's not something I would have done in psychotherapy, but in supervision, it seemed okay to express my wonder.

"I'm little, Alan. She's not — she's like five-eight. A lot of curves. Very pretty, in a *dolce vita* way. You know what I mean? Anyway, with the dance, and the lean, at that instant her shimmying breasts were right in my face." Hella held her open hands inches from her eyes. "And I swear those boobs of hers were so well packed they didn't move a millimeter on their own during the shimmy. It was like the damn plastic surgeon had bound those puppies in shrink wrap."

I'm rarely speechless in psychotherapy, except by choice. In supervision? Before that moment? Never that I could remember.

Hella continued. "She says, 'See, Dr. Zoet?' And she shimmied again. 'This is just the way Dan wanted them.' "

Despite more numerous potential side roads than I could count, I managed to stay in the supervisory moment.

"She hadn't mentioned the augmentation

previously?"

Hella said, "No."

I said, "Well, it has always been your impression of this woman that she's a man pleaser."

"Exactly," said Hella. "Exactly what I was thinking."

"And the golf club through her head?" I said. "Thoughts?"

"I kept thinking it would come up. But she didn't mention it until this week's session."

3

As things developed, I discovered that I knew more about almost everything and everybody involved with the allegations that emanated from the damn housewarming than I should have known.

At no point would it turn out that I was pleased about that.

I wasn't aware, for instance, that the precise time the caterers left the gathering would become important.

It was one of many things that the authorities could have just asked me, had they ever gotten around to treating the events of the evening as an actual criminal investigation. Which, from my perspective, they never did.

It's also one of the few things I knew, or had learned, that I would have been comfortable telling the authorities.

What I came to know about the damn housewarming and at least some of the people who attended it and how I learned all of it became crucial as the days passed; it also made it difficult to keep the various categories of facts straight in my head.

There were some things I didn't want to talk with anyone about.

Other things that I couldn't talk with anyone about.

But right from the start I did know the time the caterers left the event because the damn catering van had almost run me over on the way out the lane.

Had I looked at my watch? No, when I'm not at work I don't wear one. Had I checked the time on my phone? I didn't, but it would have been convenient. At the moment when the big van came barreling out of the blackness I was staring at the phone rereading one of the day's e-mails. I dropped the phone — actually what I did was more akin to launching it — as I leapt out of the way of the blunt front fender.

The time of the caterers' exit didn't seem important to me right then. Not even remotely. What seemed paramount to me was the safety of my dogs.

Emily, a getting-on-in-years Bouvier des Flandres as black as a new-moon night and a protector as relentless as white water, was nearby, somewhere within a four- or five-acre perimeter, methodically conducting her last patrol of the day on the hillsides that rise gently on the southeastern rim of the Boulder Valley. Emily was the unofficial sheriff of Spanish Hills. Leashing her while she was running her beat was no longer even a consideration for me. A lifetime of responsible service and unwavering friendship had earned her the privilege of making the nightly rounds of her protectorate not only solo, but also untethered.

The alternative would have been an insult to her.

Only minutes earlier, Emily had been first out the door of our home. She always was. Her initial stop had been directly across the lane at the house that I'd probably always think of as Adrienne and Peter's. They had been my longtime friends. Each had died a violent death, their passings separated by many years. In the months since Adrienne's more recent death in a bombing at a Mediterranean resort in Israel, the house and its nearby barn had been vacant.

Even though I had told myself I would never adjust to her absence, the dogs and I had slowly grown accustomed to the quiet that had begun to shroud our life at the end of the lane.

But the house had recently been sold, and the new owners had begun what promised to be an extended process of moving in. That night they were throwing some kind of celebration to introduce their old friends to their new digs in Spanish Hills.

Given the extended inactivity at the property prior to the sale, I wasn't at all surprised that the sudden presence of a couple dozen vehicles near the long-deserted farmhouse would warrant some of Emily's attention. From the moment the new owners' moving truck had arrived to begin the moving-in process a couple of weeks before, it was apparent to me that Emily wasn't entirely pleased at the increase in commotion in our quiet corner of Colorado paradise. I was thinking that the fact that our new neighbors were so clearly not dog people had something to do with Emily's disappointment, too.

Mattin Snow, the male half of the new couple, had introduced himself to me only a week or so before, the evening after a big truck had arrived to deliver an initial fraction of their stuff. Before Mattin found me outside with the dogs that day, I had already knocked on the door a couple of times to formally introduce myself, but neither of those attempts to meet the neighbors had been successful.

The introduction, when it finally occurred, seemed solely intended to provide an opportunity for Mr. Snow to inquire if it was my habit to allow my dog to run free. He meant Emily, the big Bouvier.

He'd said, "Hello, Matt Snow." At that juncture he did not, I should note, allow a pause for me to insert my name. I offered my hand. He didn't offer his. A quick glance revealed his right hand was absent the ring finger. Burn scars raked the top of his hand, disappearing under the french cuff of his shirt. "You allow that big dog to run . . . wherever it wants?"

I thought my new neighbor had said *Matt.* But he may have said *Mattin* and swallowed the final syllable. I also thought I heard a British Empire accent playing in his speech in a minor chord. I couldn't quite place it, but when faced with empire accents, I inevitably embarrass myself guessing the country of origin.

I'd forced a smile and said, "I'm Alan Gregory. We live across the lane. My wife, Lauren. Our kids, Jonas and Grace. I think you'll love it out here. Welcome." At that point, my neighbor took my hand reluctantly, the way I agree to smell a piece of halibut after Lauren has asked if I think it's still good.

We lived on the upper slope of a hill. On a

different hillside, one not low-single-digit miles from Colorado's Front Range, I probably would have said "up here," not "out here," to indicate the location of our house. The hill we live on is modest. Seventy blocks or so to the west loom the foothills of the Rocky Mountains. Ten miles or so beyond that is a line of fourteen-thousand-foot peaks. So, up is relative.

Mattin's face was familiar to me the way that local media personalities' faces become familiar from repeated exposure on advertisements on billboards and on the sides of buses. I couldn't have pointed to a particular way that I'd come to know what Mattin Snow looked like, but I definitely knew what he looked like before I met him that first day. He had fine silver hair — not old and gray, but silver and distinguished — that was just long enough to be interesting, eyes that hinted at a gene pool worthy of a long story or two, and skin that was solidly in the range of Mediterranean tones that looked good on the beach after a few hours. I thought he appeared more ruddy and real without powder on his face and without the earnest, toothy half smile that I'd come to associate with his public persona.

I proceeded to welcome him and his wife and their family to our shared remote dead-end lane in the already remote corner of Boulder County called Spanish Hills, and I offered any kind of help they might need getting settled.

He didn't acknowledge my offer. He merely repeated his inquiry about Emily running free. "My wife? She's frightened of dogs," he said. "Especially big dogs."

The Bouvier qualifies as a big dog. Or a small bear, depending on one's level of trepidation about big, husky black, four-legged mammals.

I could have used that moment to clue Mattin in about the multiple red fox dens nearby, or about the wandering pack of coyotes that lingered menacingly in the vicinity of our homes. Certainly, he must have already known about Boulder's troubled history with quick brown bears and even quicker predatory cats.

I was prepared to mount an argument that my dog was the least of his wildlife problems. That, in fact, she was an integral part of the solution. But I decided that such an argument wasn't a good place to start on day one of our relationship as neighbors. *Mattin and his wife must,* I thought, *be exhausted from the stress of the move,* and I silently allowed him the benefit of the doubt.

I also reached a hasty conclusion that it

was preferable to begin our relationship as neighbors with an unpleasant truth rather than with a lie. So I told him that it was, indeed, my practice to allow the big dog to roam at will, at least late in the evening when most everyone was inside. I could have added my certain confidence that Mattin and his family would come to appreciate Emily's services. Or I could have told him tales of how she had come to earn her off-leash privileges the hard way. But the tenor of our interaction did not leave me feeling that stories of Emily's exceptional canine bravery in service of the homeowners in Spanish Hills would have been welcome, or even tolerated.

"Really?" he said in response to my admission that I allowed Emily off leash. "Is that legal out here? I didn't know that it was acceptable to allow dogs to run free in the county."

I opened my mouth, but nothing came out. Boulder has a complex history of dogs and leash laws in open space. The history involves the Internet, GPS mapping of canine feces, and other indications that the people involved haven't always been either considerate or mature.

He took advantage of my temporary apoplexy. "Legal, I mean. That kind of acceptable. I could look into that. Maybe I will." I was going to say something in reply. But before I had a chance to come up with something witty, he continued. "Just to clarify. Alan? It's Alan? Are you talking on our land, as well as . . . your land?"

From California to the New York islands . . .

Suddenly I couldn't get Woody Guthrie out of my head. I like Woody fine, but, I mean, *damn.* "This Land Is Your Land" was one of those songs that could stick to my dendrites like a wad of gum adheres to the sole of my shoe.

Mattin Snow, our new neighbor, and my apparent new adversary, at least in matters canine, was a highly regarded attorney. A hugely popular attorney with a fan base that extended from Woody's redwood forests all the way to his Gulf Stream waters. When Lauren and I initially learned that Mattin and his wife had bought Adrienne's house, my wife, also a lawyer, had told me that in her opinion he was in the process of doing for her ever-misunderstood profession what Mehmet Oz had done for medicine.

At the time of that conversation with Lauren, I didn't know who Mehmet Oz was or what the hell he had done for medicine. But, fortunately, Google did. I learned that Mehmet Oz, M.D., was America's favorite daytime doctor, a surgeon with magic hands, endless wisdom, an extra dose of charisma, a nonjudgmental ear, and apparently, always sound advice for the masses.

Mattin Snow was a J.D., though, not an M.D. Google links made clear to me that he was teaching his ever-expanding television and Internet audience — primarily women — how to use the law to their advantage. His first book, *This Law Is Your Law,* was due out just before Christmas. One of the Googled links I'd followed informed me that it was already a national bestseller in preorders on Amazon. I was impressed.

I was also very aware that it was *that* Mattin Snow, the attorney Mattin Snow, who was asking me if my big dog, Emily, on her nightly prowls, might have been crossing invisible boundaries between his land and mine. Which meant that my new neighbor was a lawyer hinting at instigating a quarrel with me about leash laws.

I thought, *Oh damn.* The truth? I couldn't have identified the property line between Mattin's land and my land — hello again, Mr. Guthrie — even had there been a knife at my throat and a psychotic threat spelled out in neon spittle on the knife-wielding surveyor's lips. I did know that of the twelve acres of ranch land that remained of the expansive homestead that was anchored by Mattin Snow's newly acquired house, my ranch hand's shack sat on a cropper's share that was a skosh more than a solitary acre.

In Boulder proper, if Boulder has a proper, an acre-plus-sized piece of land would be a rare treasure for a homeowner. But out in rural Boulder County, where we lived in the country on the side of the valley that looks *at* the Rocky Mountains but isn't *in* them, ownership of an acre or so would not peg me as an astute real estate operator, but rather as an interloper. An acre was barely a homesite out in this part of the valley, certainly a parcel not significant enough to qualify as a ranchette.

Many years before, early in our relationship, Peter — the first of my Spanish Hills neighbors and friends to die a tragic death — had educated me about how little of our shared hillside I actually owned. As was Peter's proclivity in such matters, he had gone to great lengths to determine that my legal domain was, in fact, just shy of half a hectare. A hectare, he explained to me, is itself just shy of two and a half acres. We were in his wood shop at the time. Like a professor schooling a recalcitrant pupil, he used white chalk on the not-money side of a full sheet of walnut veneer to show me the arithmetic that proved that the plot to which I held title — one that had been carved out of the larger ranch when the lovely woman who had been my landlord of many years agreed to sell me the caretaker's home I'd been renting — was scant a true half hectare by a couple of dozen square meters.

I wasn't as fascinated by the lesson as Peter had wanted me to be.

To memorialize my minority landowning status — and to taunt me with the reality of my comparatively diminutive holdings — Peter had carved a sign on a big hunk of scrap mahogany from his shop's stash. Peter was a woodworker extraordinaire; the woodcarving that commemorated the limits of my stewardship was a fine piece of art. He had proceeded to anchor the sign proudly, with dowels and marine glue, to the mailbox post at the end of the lane.

The placard read: ALAN'S AHAH.

It stood, of course, for "Alan's almost half a hectare."

Until the day he was murdered on the stage of a downtown theater, Peter loved the fact that no one had ever guessed the meaning of the acronym.

4

My brief meeting with Mattin Snow during the week before the big housewarming they were planning to show off their new digs — or at least the "before" version of their new digs — proved an inauspicious start between new neighbors.

I think Emily was aware that I shared her sense of impotence about the state of affairs that was developing across the lane. Peter and Adrienne had been almost perfect neighbors. Whoever followed them into that house had a high bar to vault. I was determined to offer Mattin and his wife, Mimi, whom I had not yet met, as much latitude as I could muster while they settled into our remote Spanish Hills neighborhood and assimilated into our odd part-of-Boulder-but-not-part-of-Boulder culture.

I reminded myself that I didn't really know Mattin. But Boulder is, despite its geographical size, a small town. Our good friends Diane and Raoul knew Mimi and Mattin well and considered them friends.

Diane, in fact, was the one who told me who had purchased Adrienne's house. She'd explained that she'd only known Mattin for a few years, but that she'd known Mimi, Mattin's wife, and her ex-husband since Raoul's heady NBI days in the eighties. Diane, who knew more about other people's family histories than the average ancestry website, also informed me that Mimi had a couple of kids who wouldn't be around much — a daughter, currently studying in Prague, who was a cheerleader at the University of Iowa, and a son who was at a boarding school in the mountains perfecting his skiing, or something.

Diane thought we'd all become fine friends. Lauren seemed to agree. It was increasingly clear to me that my wife was a fan of Mattin's work, and perchance even a fan of Mattin himself. Lauren, I knew, had good radar. So, except for the part about maybe being a jerk about Emily running off leash for ten minutes each evening, I was working to keep an open mind about my new neighbor.

Emily's late rounds the night of the big housewarming began only after she completed a careful reconnaissance of the few vehicles that remained parked across the lane. Her quick appraisal — she's a nimble beast — ended with a head-shake and a loud huff. I could relate. She then dashed through the narrow gap between Peter's old barn and our house in the direction of the distant dark vertical gash in the Front Range that was the entrance to the wonders of Eldorado Canyon. When she reemerged in my sight she was halfway down the hill, hopping at an angle in the Bouvier-as-jackrabbit motion of hers that I have never tired of observing. In seconds she bounded over the nearest mini-ridge — okay, it was more like a berm — and disappeared from view.

Our other dog was by my side.

When Adrienne died the previous year, she left behind her wish that Lauren and I raise her son, Jonas. Our second dog was her posthumous gift to Jonas. Fiji was a Havanese, a breed I hadn't known existed. It took Jonas a while to settle on a name for the puppy — she'd come to us as Callie, a moniker that he announced wasn't going to last. Befitting her heritage, Jonas had eventually named his new dog after a tropical island. Jonas being Jonas, he'd chosen an island about as far from the puppy's ancestral homeland, Cuba, as was possible.

Fiji had no choice but to stay with me while Emily took off down the hill. Because she hadn't yet proven herself qualified to act as Emily's deputy, Fiji was haltered and leashed. Truth be told, Fiji wasn't even yet Girl Scout material. The Havanese was still a puppy, if not in size — the vet assured us that she was approaching her full weight of a dozen pounds — certainly in temperament.

She was a bit of a nut. Intellectually, we hoped she still had some maturing to do. Though we were no longer holding out hope for a canine Einstein, we were praying for something more cognitively complex than what we'd seen so far. Jonas kept telling us that the dog had hidden smarts. I kept hoping he was right.

For almost a month, Fiji had spent every determined moment of our daily late evening walks sniffing for prairie dogs. After a solitary surprise encounter in the open with one of the critters — the two mammals, Cuban puppy and Great Plains prairie dog, had a precious moment nose-to-nose before the prairie dog went all subterranean on her — Fiji reached a couple of impetuous conclusions about life in the Boulder Valley. She decided that prairie dogs were as ubiquitous as dirt and that they were as dangerous as the devil.

The first conclusion had some truth to it. There were plenty of prairie dog colonies in our neck of the nonwoods of Boulder County. But dangerous? Not so much, at least not to humans. Well over a century of Western history had proven that livestock legs and prairie dog tunnels were most definitely not a match made in heaven. Occasional plague was another small risk from the colonies, sure. But from my perspective of many years in the valley, prairie dogs were more of a nuisance than they were a danger.

Our little Havanese, bred to protect Cuban chickens from Cuban foxes, begged to differ. That evening's search-and-destroy mission had Fiji checking at the roots of some dry grasses at the base of the accumulated loose dirt that multiple passes by graders and snowplows had left piled on each side of the lane. Since I was significantly more copacetic about burrowing rodents than was the dog — but please don't get me started on wasps and yellow jackets — I was content to meander along the edge of the eastern rim of the dirt and gravel path while catching up on my e-mails.

Fiji's retractable leash dangled from one

of my hands. The dog's lead was at maximum extension, stretching across the lane between the amusingly paranoid Havanese and me. My other hand held my cell phone.

I was walking north. An hour or so before, a solid wind had begun blowing out of Wyoming. One of the perks of living in the vicinity of Colorado's Front Range is that compass directions are easy to discern. If the Rocky Mountains are on your left — as a landmark, they are nigh on impossible to miss from a distance of seventy blocks — north is the direction you're walking. Since north is also where Wyoming is, the insistent gusts from the Wind River Range were blowing into my face. I was forcing my chin down near my chest in a futile effort to keep dust from my eyes.

I was already thinking that night's walk with the dogs would be abbreviated. Although the sky was clear above the Rockies, the harsh chill in the wind and the unpleasant tang in my nose — northern gusts carried the unmistakable scent of the big stockyards near Greeley — suggested we might have a dusting of snow by morning.

Because the northern wind was so boisterous, my ears didn't even register the advent of the siren crackle of tires rolling on gravel behind me, from the south. The first thing I heard that announced any impending danger was the scream of a woman's voice: "Eric! Oh my God, there's — Your lights! Lights! Lights!" Then, as the van passed, "Oh my — Did you —"

The driver of the van — Eric, I presumed — didn't flick on the lights until his vehicle was almost fifty yards farther down the road, a fraction of a second after he was into the kind of not-so-subtle bend that drivers typically don't like to be surprised by in the dark on unfamiliar, unlit, unpaved roads in rural neighborhoods on hillsides. The sudden illumination of brake lights, followed by the even more sudden shift of those bright red squares to the right, confirmed what my ears were telling me — the van's rear tires had lost purchase on the first sharp curve that lay dead ahead.

I knew from ample personal experience that there was not much margin for driver error in that particular location. If the back of that big van slid even a few feet off the center line of the narrow lane, the van's right rear tire would cross the laughably small shoulder and then it would immediately succumb to gravity's will.

Gravity's will was, of course, reliably down. *Down* in that location meant an immediate slide of eighteen inches at about forty-five degrees, followed by a quick dozen feet at about thirty degrees. Once the van's tire scooted down the first foot and a half, those next dozen feet were almost guaranteed to follow. The odds of a vehicle with the van's center of gravity staying upright during that kind of sudden detour? Let's just say they were much worse than the odds of Fiji finding her prairie dog. The immutable truth was that if the right rear tire crossed the shoulder and completed the first little slide, the van was going to start to roll. And once it started to roll, it wasn't going to stop for a while.

If the van does go off the lane, I thought, anticipating the aftermath of the almost certain disaster that was coming, *maybe I'll consider going over to help after I corral my dogs.*

I had all those thoughts from the sitting position that I'd ended up in as I avoided the fender of the van. As I tried to regain an upright posture, my balance, and my bearings, the wind carried a cocktail of obnoxious fumes to my nose. Three components dominated the aroma: cow shit from Weld County, overheated motor oil, and burning tobacco leaves.

Two conclusions were instantaneous for me. The van needed a ring job, or worse, and someone in the van — Eric or the woman in the passenger seat — needed a nicotine patch. The stockyards? No conclusion was necessary.

The woman hadn't lowered her voice at all. The passenger-side window, open, I assumed, to release the cigarette smoke, permitted me to hear her continuing play-by-play: "The dog! Eric, stop! Stop! Go . . . back. Stop! Eric! Did you even see the little —"

The dog?

From my vantage, it appeared that Eric wasn't stopping. Eric didn't even seem to slow. He had instead decided to chance the application of brute horsepower to try to keep his vehicle on the lane. The van's engine roared and whined as the RPM climbed. The back wheels continued to spin faster and slide sideways in mockery of Eric's strategy.

I suspected that Eric wasn't aware that he had yet another unwelcome surprise just ahead of him. The curve he was currently navigating, not very successfully, was only the first C-bend of an S-curve.

S, like in *shithead.* I muttered, "Asshole," as I scrambled toward the other side of the lane on my hands and knees after Fiji.

I had already tugged on the lead. I had

tried to call out to the puppy but failed both times to get past the *F.* My vocal cords were coated by dust and smothered by pressure from my suddenly swollen heart. The rest was beyond my capability.

I'd felt dead weight when I yanked on my end of the leash.

Jonas doesn't need this, is what I was thinking. *Jonas can't take this.*

Please. Please. Please.

5

Lauren and I were worried about Jonas's reaction to the sale of what had been his family home.

Weeks before, on the afternoon before the sale of the house became final, I asked Jonas if he would like to spend one last night in the room where he'd slept while growing up.

"Maybe," he said after a moment's contemplation. Way too much trauma and loss had left Jonas a tentative kid.

"Dogs or no dogs?" I asked.

He said, "Didn't have a dog then. So, no dogs. If . . . I decide to do it."

Jonas was growing more cryptic as he aged. I associated his parsimony with his father, Peter. But I was concerned that it might simply be a response to all he'd suffered.

"Not by yourself. I'll be there too, you know," I said. "If you decide to do it." One of my guidelines for myself as a parent was that I always wanted my children to know what options they had and what options they didn't have. My "I'll be there" was my way of making certain that Jonas understood his degrees of freedom in that particular situation. If he chose to spend another night in the house, he would have my company.

Jonas, I thought, was relieved. I assumed he wouldn't want to let me know that he'd feel safer with me close by.

"You can sleep in Ma's room," he said. "If I do it."

Maybe not, I thought. I didn't believe in ghosts, but if I knew anyone who would be eager to haunt me playfully from the afterlife, it would be Jonas's mom, Adrienne.

"I'll stay out of your way, if that's what you want," I said.

Jonas's aunt and uncle had recently flown out from New York and offered a big assist in helping to sort everything that had been in the house. Some special items had been crated and stored away for Jonas, a few coveted things were distributed to other family members on both sides of Jonas's family, and the rest was tossed or put up for bid at an auction that I didn't attend. What didn't sell went to charity.

Jonas was an eleven-year-old kid. Although

he was precocious in some ways, he was immature in others. His sense of value, monetary or sentimental, was undeveloped. He had asked for very little from the house. But he had requested his father's tools. Because the barn that had been Peter's shop and studio had been vacated for the new owners, too, the precious stash of professional woodworking paraphernalia now filled a big rented storage locker down on 55th near Arapahoe.

Jonas had also asked for his mother's music collection, which included a couple of boxes of vintage vinyl that Adrienne had stashed in the cellar — she'd apparently once had a serious disco jones she'd kept completely secret from all of us — and a gazillion CDs. Jonas locked on to what he said was his mom's favorite band, an indie folk group named Girlyman. Their multitonal harmonies proved so easy on Lauren's difficult-to-please, MS-irascible ears that we began listening to a lot of Girlyman in our house. Jonas knew all the lyrics and could sing any harmonic line. Gracie started to join him in duets.

During the first weekend after the autumnal equinox, while we were enjoying a Sunday supper of panko-crusted salmon to the sounds of "Tell Me There's a Reason,"

Grace asked, "What is a girlyman, anyway?"

Lauren and I locked eyes — each of us was begging the other to jump in. Jonas saved us. He said, "My mom was a girlyman." I was shocked by Grace's response: she asked him to pass the creamed corn.

The departed stuff left the big house empty in the way that only well-lived-in houses are ever empty.

Some furniture — almost all of it, save the upholstered pieces, had been handmade by Jonas's father, Peter — had left literal footprints behind. Indentations in the carpet. Scratches on the hardwood. The fingertips of ten thousand hands had darkened the lacquered or polished wood in those places that humans are drawn to touch by instinct or habit. In the master bath upstairs, I spotted a fossilized mosquito frozen in three dimensions, four if you count time, on the vanity mirror. In the scenario in my head, I guessed that it had been squished by Adrienne's hand only hours before she boarded the airplane flight that would take her to Israel and to her death.

I found the empty house eerie yet comforting. I could still feel the human energy in the space that had long been occupied by Peter and Adrienne and Jonas, and a seemingly endless parade of nannies. When I walked the house, I could still hear the echoes of Jonas's laughter ringing through all of his earlier developmental phases.

Jonas's bedroom had been in the middle of the eastern side of the second floor, down the hall from the master. I suspected — if he chose to spend an additional night in his room — he would sleep in his bedroom's peculiar loft.

The loft. Peter created the nook as a gift for his infant son. He called the private space "the knothole." Adrienne had always called the quirky space "the cubby."

Peter's creation was maybe six feet long, four feet deep, and four feet high. The recess started a good five and a half feet off the floor of the back wall of Jonas's bedroom. A low rail extended across the front opening. It was not there to keep Jonas from tumbling out. Peter, a master rock climber, had always presumed that any kid who carried his genes would be able to intuitively sense gravity's inclinations and would be able to amble short distances with the agility of a cat, if necessary.

The rail was there to assuage Adrienne's tendency to fret.

And then to kvetch. Adrienne had never been one to suffer her nervousness in silence. When Adrienne fretted, she then kvetched. Sunrise/sunset. Inhale/exhale.

Everyone who loved her knew the best cure, perhaps the only cure, was prevention. Fret prophylaxis equaled kvetch abeyance. Peter knew it better than anyone. And that is why a low rail extended across the opening of the knothole.

The base of the odd nook was lined with a thick slab of corduroy-covered foam. The walls and ceiling were an intricate chevron pattern concocted of zebrawood veneer. The lines — the natural grain of the fabulous wood and the father-made lines of the angled chevrons — went every which way.

The little space was a marvel. On one end of the knothole Peter had recessed shelving and drawers for Jonas's books and his little-boy treasures. The nook had two built-in reading lights, dual outlets for future electronic desires — Peter was a visionary — and a disappearing curtain system that could, at Jonas's whim, transform the space from his private retreat into his public stage.

What the knothole didn't have was any visible means of entry. Peter, who overlooked nothing when he designed and built furniture, had intentionally omitted a ladder, or steps, or handholds, or ledges, or any other way for a small child to enter the high sanctuary of the knothole.

I had always thought that Peter had omitted an entrance because he wanted to be his son's personal elevator. The space was constructed high enough off the floor that Adrienne — she had an excess of many things, but height and upper body strength were not among them — wouldn't be able to lift her growing child, or herself, up into the space. Peter knew all that. By building the knothole so high off the floor, Peter had ensured that it would forever be a special father/son place. That was my theory.

It would turn out that I was wrong about that. If I had been at all prescient about the damn housewarming and what was to follow, it would have been a good place to begin keeping a list.

Of the things I was wrong about.

"Turn your back, Alan," Jonas said.

We had carried sleeping bags over to spend the night.

I did what he asked. After I rotated, I found myself looking out his bedroom door, through the open door of the room across the hall, out the far window, and across the lane. I was seeing the shingled roof of the modest house that had originally been constructed as a domicile for the caretaker for the big ranch house. I'd bought that caretaker's shack from the woman who had owned the ranch before Adrienne and Peter.

The now-renovated shack was Jonas's new home, the house that, since his mother's death, he shared with Lauren and me and his sister, Grace.

Behind my turned back, I heard the squeak of a hinge. Once, then again. The brief, hushed hum of a motor. A few seconds passed. I heard the hum of the motor one more time. Then a click, and another.

"Okay," Jonas said.

I turned around. Jonas was in the knothole.

Had he jumped up? I didn't think he could do it without making some kind of racket as he jumped up and scrambled in. I wondered, of course, about the squeaks and the motor. I assumed the squeaky hinge was on the door to the closet that shared a wall with the knothole. The motor? No idea.

"I heard a motor," I said.

He shrugged.

"Can I look?" I asked, nodding at the closet.

"You can try," he said. It was a bit of a dare.

I opened the closet. Heard the telltale

squeak from the hinge on the door. The tight space was wainscoted with rough cedar planks, cut and installed on a bias. I tried to spot something that would indicate the entrance to a passageway that might lead from the closet to the knothole.

Nothing was apparent.

Jonas seemed pleased at my failure. "Closets should have closets," he said.

"Closets should have closets?" I said back.

"That's what Ma said Dad always said."

Your mom lied a lot, is what I was thinking. "Does this closet have a closet?"

"Closets . . . should have closets, Alan." He smiled.

Jonas called me "Alan." Every once in a while he called Lauren "Mom." He'd always called Adrienne "Ma." Peter was "Dad."

After he'd shown off his cubby, Jonas told me he didn't want to spend the night after all.

6

When I finally got to her after the van passed, I found Fiji's nose buried in the foyer of a prairie dog den. Her leash was completely tangled in the dry grasses nearby.

I picked her up, which wasn't her favorite thing. She wasn't a dog who liked to be restrained, no matter how affectionate the restrainer's intent. She wriggled to try to get out of my arms. I didn't care.

When I finally put the puppy down, I picked up a stick a couple of feet long and stuck it in the dirt where I'd tumbled to avoid the truck. My plan was to use the marker as a guidepost the next morning to begin the search for my damn cell phone. Then I clenched my hands together and blew between the bent knuckles of my thumbs. The sound I made with my hands cupped that way was a bass-horn-like bellow. It was my signal to Emily that her evening rounds were complete.

The first blow was an alert. With the second — it was a two-note, low-high melody — the big dog knew it was time to come running.

In seconds she was by my side. "Let's go home," I said to her more than to the puppy, whose English-as-a-second-language skills were still in development.

Emily knew the drill, but she was hesitating. She lifted her twitching nose into the wind from the north. She turned her ears due north, as well.

"It's some idiots in a van," I explained to her, but she wasn't mollified. I inhaled but by then I couldn't smell anything other than the distinctive perfumes of Greeley.

And maybe some smoke. I inhaled again. No, no smoke.

Emily finally took off down the lane. The puppy tried to chase after her. But I tightened my grip on the lead. Emily stopped once more on the way home, again sticking her nose into the north wind. Again tuning her ears to capture sounds from down the lane.

She mouthed one deep "woooo" bark. I translated that particular sound as one of general disfavor, not danger or alarm.

She and I were, I thought, on the same

page. "Good girl," I said.

When we arrived back between the two houses, it appeared to me that almost all the guests had departed our new neighbor's party. A solitary car remained.

I'd kissed the sleeping kids good night before I went out with the dogs — Jonas in his room in our west-facing walk-out basement, Grace down the hall from the main floor master. I brushed my teeth and climbed into bed.

Lauren was restless, which was nothing new. I touched her shoulder with my dry Colorado lips. She said something about my lunch with Raoul, which reminded me about my other commitment.

I checked the alarm. Set it.

I sighed. I had to be up in time for dance class.

Lauren's prompt shouldn't have been necessary. Raoul had already reminded me about our rendezvous when he and Diane had arrived at the housewarming.

"Well, this is awkward," was what Diane had said to me after she'd climbed out of the passenger side of Raoul's Range Rover. She was looking me over the way a skeptical father might appraise his young teenage daughter's outfit minutes before she departed on her first-ever date.

It was apparent that Diane didn't like what she was seeing. I was feeling as though I was displaying too much décolletage and was about to be directed back inside to pick something a tad more modest, even though the actual problem was that Diane was dressed for a night out while I was dressed to walk dogs.

Diane Estevez was my oldest friend in Boulder and my longtime partner in business. We were both clinical psychologists. I worked full-time at my craft, Diane a little less than that. Our business was, of course, mental health. We both had long considered it our good fortune that the success of our business endeavor was dependent on our abilities to boost the mental health of others, not ourselves or each other.

Diane's husband, Raoul, was a brilliant Catalonian with an electrical engineer's training, a hound's nose for business opportunity, and an unmatched two-decade-long résumé of venture capital success in Boulder's fertile entrepreneurial soil. Raoul's well-placed bets on incubating businesses and his knack for stewardship while the companies were young had earned Diane and him significant wealth. How wealthy were they? I didn't really know, which was fine with me and was typical of the way accumulated wealth tended to work in Boulder.

Boulder had just turned one hundred and fifty years old. Originally born of humble mining and ranching roots, it had long since transformed itself into an academic and scientific powerhouse. Most would agree that it had managed to remain humble, despite its striking good looks, until the last few decades of the twentieth century.

That's when Boulder began an evolution, dubious or not, and became cool. Then seriously cool. Followed in short order by something suspiciously resembling trendy. Despite the evolution, Boulderites took some pride in the fact that their burg had never become the kind of commercial oasis that was Aspen or Vail, which were both nearby safe cradles for the ostentatiously rich, either native born or merely visiting.

Although Boulder was, by almost all standards, a town of much-greater-than-average affluence, the town's wealthiest citizens tended to keep the evidence of their fortunes on the down low. People drove themselves around Boulder. Although very nice cars were commonplace, exceptional cars were rare. The determined, at times even overdetermined, egalitarian ethos in

Boulder limited exclusive clubbing — either the country kind or the night kind. Restaurants that catered only to the I-don't-care-what-it-costs set weren't part of the town's fabric. The fabulously wealthy ate at the same few fine restaurants — Pain Perdu, Frasca, L'Atelier — as the merely well-to-do. If their tabs reached from oh my to the stratosphere it was only because of the wine they'd chosen to sup.

To drop serious money on a designer-label gown or an outrageously bejeweled necklace, or to pick up something for the house that was exceedingly precious, required that Boulderites make the hop down 36 to Cherry Creek in Denver, endure a flight to one of the coasts, or at the very least carve out a shopping detour during a ski weekend in one of the mountain resorts.

Boulder is a community where social mores dictate that the very rich limit their public displays of consumption to a stunning home on an exceptional piece of land; a nice set of wheels, or maybe two; and perhaps a solitary piece of oh-really bling. At least at a time. The second and third houses, the private aircraft, the daring Rothko or the da Vinci drawing, just weren't mentioned in general conversation in town.

It's not that it was considered bad form.

It just wasn't considered.

In Boulder, if one boasted in public to raise someone's eyebrows in a good way, one talked not about one's money but about one's handcrafted bicycle, or hot new skis, or even better, one's new personal best in the previous month's 10k, or the completion of that summer's Triple Bypass, or a successful training regimen for the upcoming Leadville Trail 100.

Knowing all that, I still assumed that our new neighbors were counted among Boulder's wealthy. Somewhere, I guessed, in the same neighborhood of rich as Diane and Raoul. On the day that the sale was finalized, Jonas's uncle had informed me that the buyers of his sister's home had brought cash to the closing table. To afford to buy Adrienne and Peter's prized digs and its many surrounding half hectares, especially with cash, required some significant financial resources.

By the time Diane and Raoul arrived at the housewarming, there were a couple of dozen vehicles lining the lane — a typical high-end Boulder mix, which meant primarily SUVs and hybrids. The big Mercedes and the little BMW coupe that were parked near the house beside Raoul's shiny Range

Rover announced to me that for Diane and Raoul, this was a night for socializing with at least a few of their wealthy friends.

A vintage Camaro, pristine but for the thin layer of dust deposited from the jaunt down our unpaved road, was fifty feet farther away, near a caterers' van at the southern end of the property. The Camaro told me that a classic car aficionado — an acceptable local affectation — was among the guests, too. Between the Camaro and the Euro collection was a small SUV — a Hyundai, or a Kia, or something. I can't keep track of all the small SUVs that dot Boulder's roads. In my head, I assigned the pedestrian ride to catering staff.

Raoul had one bottle of wine cradled in the crook of his left arm. He gripped a duplicate by the neck in his left hand. The label confirmed for me that the housewarming gift was most generous. The wine selections were from a prized case that Raoul had purchased at a recent online auction. He had shown me a solitary bottle the last time I was at their house. I hadn't recognized the label. I'm not a wine expert, but I can tell a Burgundy bottle from that of a Bordeaux. His prize was the former. I did remember that even though he was trying to convince me he had gotten a bargain on the case, the price revealed that each bottle had cost half as much as my bike.

And, even though I was far from wealthy, I didn't ride a cheap bike. That wasn't an anomaly in Boulder, where having a bicycle, or two, much grander and more expensive than one's car is not an unusual occurrence.

Raoul took one look at my old polo shirt, glanced at my even older jeans, and offered a grin at the pair of running shoes I'd bought on sale at Gart Brothers when Bill Clinton was still president, and when Monica was still an acceptable name for a female infant. Then Raoul chanced a restrained smile at his lovely wife — Diane looked gorgeous in the kind of dress rarely seen in Spanish Hills; she cleaned up good, always had — and said, "I thought you told me that Alan and Lauren would be invited to this party."

He said it with a warm tease in his tone.

Diane shrugged the shrug of someone who expects to be right even when she clearly isn't. She lifted an airy shawl from the upper reaches of her bare arms to the rise of her shoulders.

Raoul said, "Alain, non? You are not part of the festivities?" Raoul blended languages like a talented bartender mixes spirits in a cocktail. The result was almost always interesting.

"No, not this time," I said. "I'm sure there will be plenty of opportunities in the future."

Diane shrugged again. "Maybe it's the theme," she said.

"I thought housewarming was the theme?" Raoul said.

"Mimi's parties always have themes. You never read invitations, Raoul. This event is called Two Cents. She wants all of her friends to give our opinions about how we think they should renovate the house."

Raoul said, "I just assumed that Mimi would take this opportunity to meet the —"

"No, no. It's fine," I said, trying to short-circuit any discomfort. "I think it's better that we skip this one. I'm actually yet to meet Mimi, Diane. I've only spoken to Mattin, Matt, once. He seems to be out of town a lot," I said, offering an easy rationale for why our new neighbors excluded us. "Absolutely no hard feelings. We're probably not the best people to participate in a group activity about remodeling Adrienne's home, anyway."

Raoul said, "Mattin's his TV name. His friends call him Hake. I don't think anyone calls him Matt."

Raoul pronounced *Hake* like *rake.* Not *Hak-e,* like *Rock-ay.*

During our brief conversation about rogue dogs, my new neighbor did not once suggest I should call him Hake. On television, he was Mattin Snow. But, when discussing my wayward dog, I really thought he said he was Matt.

I said, "Come on, it makes perfect sense. I'm sure they're eager for their old friends to get a chance to see the new . . . place, without the neighbors looking over their shoulders." Lauren and I had heard from the real estate agent who had listed the house — he lived at the other end of the lane — that both of our new neighbors had referred to Peter and Adrienne's place not as a home, not as a house, but as a "wonderful opportunity." We knew change was coming.

Diane took her husband's arm. Over his shoulder, Raoul said, "We're still on for tomorrow, right? To discuss the Walnut thing?"

Diane shook her head. At the thing, or at her husband's mixing of business with pleasure, I did not know.

"I will be there, Raoul."

"A bientôt."

7

I woke first on the morning after the damn housewarming. The wind had stopped blowing but had left in its wake an unwelcome gray sky and a blanket of cold, damp air. Just before six forty-five, when I took the dogs out for their morning stroll, I could see my exhaled breath. I wasn't ready for a regular diet of visible exhalations. Within ten steps of the front door, I had already begun awaiting the next interlude of Indian summer — the Front Range usually gets a few before the determined chill of the dark season takes over.

November is way late for Indian summer, but Colorado is home, almost exclusively, to weather optimists.

Across the lane, only one car remained from the party the night before. It was that little SUV, or crossover, parked near the very end of the lane.

Japan, Korea. Honda, Toyota, Kia, Hyundai. Gray, brown. Few cars made an impression on me. It was one of the many that didn't. Since it wasn't a classic Camaro, or a Mercedes or BMW or Land Rover, and since the caterers were long gone, I considered that it might have belonged to a housekeeper who had stayed over to straighten up after the previous night's festivities.

The dogs and I ambled down the lane to search for the mobile phone I had launched while dodging the caterer's truck. I had Lauren's cell with me. I hoped that dialing my own number from her phone would cause mine to ring, ending my treasure hunt. That is, if a prairie dog hadn't filched it.

I called myself. I located the phone. The day began to look auspicious.

I heard the engine of the nondescript SUV come to life behind me as I was herding the dogs back in the front door. I turned to look at the occupant, but the car's glass was rendered opaque by a thin covering of frost.

Inside the house, Gracie was in bed reading, while Jonas was sleeping the sleep of preadolescence. Lauren had suffered through a difficult night but was finally asleep, so I tried to be as quiet as I could be as I urged Gracie to get ready for dance class.

She had just started taking tumbling and jazz/contemporary. This would be session number three. I'd watched the first two classes — they involved little girls alternating between being precious while they pretended to dance and then being tomboys as they did cartwheels and somersaults.

Grace was loving the experience. She'd always been a tough kid, but it was becoming clearer every day that she was also being influenced by tidal estrogen flows. I watched with parental wonder as she balanced on the developmental fence between tomboy land and the princess castle. Lauren thought she would fall to one side soon. I was thinking that she might keep her balance on the fence for a while longer.

A more immediate crisis loomed. She wanted to wear her purple tights to class. I could find only her pink tights. She wanted to wake her mommy to find the purple tights. I thought that was particularly unwise.

We worked it out. Grace almost always knew when to push and when to retreat. I envied the kid's radar.

I got toast, juice, and a banana in her and we hustled to the car. On our way out the lane, just beyond the spot on the S-curve where the caterer's van had almost taken a tumble, I pulled over to allow a black limousine to pass. I sighed. Traffic near my home had never before been much of a concern. Limos, in particular, were as rare as comets.

"Who's that for?" Gracie asked.

"Not us," I said.

"The new neighbors then," she said with a bit of a tone.

My attitude about the new neighbors, I sensed, was infectious, and not in a good way. I promised myself I would watch it, at least around the kids.

"I guess."

"Are they on a reality show?" Gracie asked.

God help us. "I don't think so, honey. The car is just here to pick someone up."

"Cars like that come once you've been eliminated. Maybe they got voted off."

"Off what?"

Gracie gave my question some serious thought. She shrugged. "Our mountain, I guess. They got voted off our mountain."

I wish we could vote people off our mountain. For the time being, we had them outnumbered. "People can't get voted off our mountain," I said. "Cars like that come for other reasons, too."

"Limos never came for Adrienne," my

daughter pointed out.

The limo driver tipped an imaginary cap at me as he passed. The back of the vehicle was unoccupied. I gave the driver a thumbs-up in response. Life with our new neighbors promised to bring many changes to our corner of Spanish Hills.

Lauren's last thoughts when I climbed into bed late the night before had been, "Hear Raoul out, tomorrow. Please? We need to be open-minded."

Maybe Lauren was right. Maybe the environment was ripe for change.

She hadn't said it out loud yet, but every time that Lauren encouraged me to open myself to change, I was hearing her preparing the soil for a single crop: she wanted to discuss leaving Spanish Hills.

I knew the arguments. *We live too far from town. We're always schlepping the kids somewhere. Lauren and stairs no longer get along. Peter and Adrienne are gone. Jonas needs a clean break.*

It might indeed be time, is what I had started thinking.

I planned to skip dance class number three. My cop friend Sam Purdy was going to meet me at the Village for breakfast while Grace danced and tumbled. Seconds after I pulled into the strip center parking lot on Folsom, my phone chirped with a text. I bet it was from Sam, but I had to wait to check while a guy the size of Paul Bunyan pulled his considerable mass into a Tahoe the size of an Abrams tank. The tires he'd mounted on his elevated rig were shaped like Krispy Kremes on steroids. The truck filled two spots in the tiny lot. It didn't have to, but the guy had parked so that it did.

I wondered if he could be voted out of the parking lot.

The driver spotted me waiting for him to depart, which is never a good thing. I waited while he checked his phone. Straightened his sunglasses. Played with his radio. Pulled on his seat belt. Looked in the mirror while he practiced chin thrusts? *What? Who does that?* Finally, he backed up slowly, as though he were practicing docking the space shuttle to the International Space Station and he didn't trust his instruments. I was not at all surprised to learn that the truck's exhaust was tuned to approximate the sound of repetitive sonic booms.

I pulled into one of the two spots the truck vacated. A Smart car immediately took the other. The line was out the door at the Village.

Sam's text read: **Luce needs me. Sorry.**

Off to 33rd.

"Luce" was Lucy Davenport, Sam's detective partner in the Boulder Police Department, and "33rd" was 33rd Street, home of the Public Safety Building.

Hope it's nothing is what I texted back. But I knew that if it were nothing, Lucy wouldn't have called Sam in on a Saturday morning. A senior detective pair catching a routine call on a day off? Not a chance. Either something big had happened, or Sam and Lucy were being punished for something.

Although I couldn't rule out the latter hypothesis — neither cop was renowned for rule-following inclinations; Sam's recent history of transgressions was much worse than Lucy's — I was wondering if Boulder had suffered a rare homicide.

Ha was Sam's texted retort to my good wishes.

Breakfast at the Village had been Sam's idea, not mine. I gave up my parking spot and headed up Canyon to 14th Street in the direction of Lucile's.

I knew that the line would be out the door at Lucile's, too. But my kid was doing interpretive dance and cartwheels, so I had time to waste. I lucked into an angled parking spot near my lawyer Cozy Maitlin's office across from the Colorado Building on the other side of the Mall. I hoofed it from there. What breeze was left from the night before was still from the north, so I could smell chicory and beignets wafting in my direction the moment I opened the car door.

I grabbed a seat at the communal table and ordered eggs and grits and toast and coffee. And a beignet. While I ate, I read an article in the *Daily Camera*'s sports section about how the Buffs were about to rescue their disappointing season by surprising some ranked football foe. I was thinking I'd read an annual version of the same story every fall for at least a decade.

I stayed in town all morning. Soccer practice followed dance class for Gracie. I had her back home, as I promised Lauren I would, in time to get her ready for a one thirty birthday party. Gracie had a full social calendar.

Jonas, on the other hand, was still looking for his social niche. Through no fault of his own, his path in life was a difficult one. He'd lost his father to a homicide when he was still too young to realize what had happened. Then, only the previous year, he had lost his mom to a bomb in a cowardly battle in a decades-old foreign war. Jonas had taken shrapnel in his leg from the same explosion that took his mother. His emotional wounds were more visible to me than were his permanent physical scars.

From the moment I flew to Israel to retrieve him after the terrorist bombing, I was determined to be a good card in his bad hand. I didn't know how I was going to do it, but I was determined to succeed as his parent.

He and I had plans to go to a movie later that afternoon. Jonas and I went to a lot of movies, often late on weekend afternoons. He tended to choose adolescent fare that I considered too lurid or too lusty for him, or childish flicks that seemed to provide some regressed comfort. I assumed he was working out something with his attraction to the violence. I usually went along with his choice. With the blood and guts, my consent was usually reluctant. On the lusty side? I didn't care if he saw an exposed breast or two.

I wasn't sure about many things as a parent, but I was completely certain that no child had ever been harmed by gazing at a boob.

On rare occasions, Jonas would ask me to pick the movie. Those times, I'd take him to a film at the university or to a theater playing classics I'd really liked — movies I wanted to share with him. He had loved *The Sting*. And the first *Indiana Jones. The Great Escape. The Godfather. Butch Cassidy and the Sundance Kid.* He'd thought *Bridge on the River Kwai* was "weak." I defended it, but I couldn't bring him around to my way of thinking.

I had no idea what that afternoon's choice would bring.

But first I had that meeting with Raoul. He had an investment opportunity he wanted Lauren and me to consider. Something about Walnut.

8

Lauren called me into our bedroom while the kids were eating lunch. "Close the door," she said. There had been phases in our marriage when a magical moment might have ensued. We weren't enjoying one of those phases.

She sat on the edge of the bed up near her pillow. She sighed.

I said, "Gracie still loves dance. She may stick with it this time. She even likes the girly parts. Something is changing for her, you know."

"I can tell," Lauren said. "She talks about it all the time." She smiled. Then she stopped smiling. "Sam was here this morning along with a sheriff's investigator."

That was news. I sat down on the upholstered chair across from the bed. I figured the cops had stopped by for something to do with Lauren's work. It was not an unheard-of occurrence. My wife was a deputy DA for Boulder County. I surmised that she was going to have to go to the office, which meant that I was going to have to get Grace to the birthday party.

God, I hope we have a present already. And that it's wrapped. I asked, "Do you have something that's breaking at work?" Sam was the Boulder PD detective who had stood me up at breakfast. His jurisdiction was the City of Boulder. Boulder County, which included the rural enclave where we lived, was the law enforcement purview of the Boulder sheriff. That representatives of both departments had been out our way together was an anomaly; the agencies rarely rolled together.

Lauren said, "They weren't here to see me. They were across the lane for something. Neither of them would tell me why.

"The sheriff's investigator was Courtney Rea. She recognized me from court. She asked me if I knew where our neighbors were, or when they'd be back. I said I didn't."

"That's it?"

"Pretty much. Do you know Courtney?"

I shook my head. I'd met many of Sam's police colleagues over the years but wasn't well acquainted with the sheriff's department staff. Through the DA's office, Lauren got to know all the investigative players for both departments.

"She asked me how well I knew our neighbors. I told her they had just moved in — I don't think she'd known that; she wrote it down — that I'd met them once, casually. She asked if I was aware of a gathering at their house last night. I said I saw a lot of cars over there before I went to bed and that some catering people had arrived earlier in the day. Sam stepped over and whispered something to Courtney. Courtney said that was it. She didn't have any more questions."

I said, "Gracie and I saw a limo coming in the lane this morning when we were on our way to dance class. Mattin and Mimi must have had a car taking them someplace."

"I missed all that. I didn't get out of bed until late."

That was her way of letting me know it had been another difficult night for her. She looked like she could use a smile. I told her about Gracie's reaction to the limo and her theory about someone being voted off our mountain.

The story earned the smile. Lauren added, "I find it odd that Sam never offered a hint to me why he was out here. He played it cool, professional. I don't think Courtney could have guessed that Sam knew me in any way other than through work. After she got in her car and took off, Sam backed up, leaned out the window, and said, 'Leave this alone. The less you know, the better.'

"I saw nothing to indicate that anything special was going on. Their house has been quiet all day. No emergency response on the lane. No fire, no rescue. Just Sam and Courtney."

"Why a cop and a deputy?" I asked. "That part makes no sense."

Lauren didn't know that either.

I hadn't had a chance to tell Lauren about my run-in with the catering truck the night before. I filled her in.

"Idiots," she said. "But it didn't actually crash, right? You didn't call it in?"

"I didn't."

She shook her head. "None of it makes sense."

I asked, "Who was catching this morning at your office? They would know what's going on." A deputy district attorney was always on call to respond to the police department or the sheriff's office regarding developing law enforcement situations. Occasionally, a crime scene or a fresh development in an ongoing investigation might require immediate consultation from the

DA's office.

Lauren didn't reply. Since her last MS exacerbation, she hadn't been taking much call time. It was a sensitive subject for her. She stood up, shifted her weight onto her cane, and began the laborious process of walking down the hall toward the kitchen. She hated the cane. Hated the weak leg.

"How are you doing?" I said as I examined her gait for signs of change. Her recovery from a serious exacerbation that had left her temporarily unable to walk had been agonizingly slow. Although we rarely talked about the future of her illness, we were both concerned that her recovery from the recent event had reached a plateau, which might indicate permanent damage to the affected nerve.

Permanent damage could mean permanent disability. A long relationship with the cane. We were both scared.

"It's getting old," she said without turning her head. "I had trouble with the lift on the stairs again when I went down to check on Jonas this morning. We have to get someone out to look at it again."

After she regained enough strength to get around with the cane, I'd had a lift installed on the stairs that led to the basement so that she would be able to get down there to check on Jonas.

"I'll take care of it," I said. "First thing Monday."

9

In my personal-life lexicon, *walnut,* as a noun, typically referred not to the hard-shelled nut essential to a Waldorf salad, but rather to the unremarkable Victorian house that had been home to my clinical psychology practice, and that of Raoul's psychologist wife, Diane, for many years.

Diane and I jointly owned the century-old building on Walnut Street. Our utilitarian workspace on the first floor included our two consulting offices, which faced the backyard; a shared waiting room fronting the street; a tiny kitchen; and a solitary bathroom.

We rented out a minuscule second-floor office suite. Over the years, the upstairs space had successfully incubated the businesses of a half dozen or so budding entrepreneurs. We gravitated toward tenants who didn't seem inclined to require us to act like landlords. The rental suite was currently occupied by a woman about my age whose stated business purpose was "independent product enhancement."

Diane and I didn't know what that meant, but we hoped she wasn't hooking. At the end of the day, we didn't really want to know. The fallout from a revelation that we were leasing space to a sex worker would undoubtedly force us to act like landlords. Neither of us wanted that.

We had originally purchased the house on Walnut just before downtown Boulder began its gradual transformation from Rocky Mountain cool to oh-so-trendy hot, and quite a while before our questionable neighborhood on the wrong side of Ninth Street began its conversion from being a desolate haven for body shops, bail bondsmen, crappy student housing, scrap metal shops, and light industrial warehouses.

Diane and I didn't buy the old house because it sat on thirty-nine one-hundredths of an acre — almost an entire sixth of a hectare — that happened to be situated less than three blocks from Boulder's commercial heart at the corner of Broadway and Pearl. Buying a decent-sized chunk of desirable, developable real estate in such a prime location in the depths of a soft market would have demonstrated investment acumen, a trait that Diane and I lacked equally.

We bought the Walnut house because it was the best property we could afford within easy walking distance of town, my requirement, that also had at least one off-street parking place, Diane's nonnegotiable condition for her Saab convertible.

The house had been nearly derelict at the time we purchased it. The real estate agent assumed we planned to scrape and rebuild — during the initial showing she made a point of telling us that the purchase price did not include demo costs. We had no plans, or funds, to rebuild. I was fresh out of school, and Diane and Raoul had not yet made the transition from the middle class to the we-don't-think-about-money class.

We slapped a much-needed new roof on the old house — vegetation was growing out of the old one in places, which we agreed couldn't be a good sign — and did the minimal renovations necessary to convert the space for our therapeutic purposes. Over the years we had added some creature comforts, like insulation and windows that not only opened but didn't leak like sieves. More recently, Diane had overseen an overhaul of the waiting room décor to spa-like standards. I remained almost cool with that.

It turned out that buying the Walnut Street house had been an inadvertent act of business genius. As Boulder's Pearl Street Mall became a success, and a decade later as hip migrated west and hopped across Ninth Street, our property appreciated like mad. Complete strangers made us blind offers to sell at exorbitant profits. We were in no rush; the bland little Victorian building had served our clinical needs perfectly for the many years we had practiced within its undistinguished walls.

I considered the place my retirement plan. In my mind, my work address was 401(k) Walnut Street, Boulder, Colorado 80302.

Raoul had asked me to meet him on Walnut. To discuss the future.

His Range Rover was already there when I arrived. He'd parked in the location where a ramshackle garage had once stood.

"Alain," he said as I climbed from my car. "Howdy."

Howdy? The cowboy touch was novel. "Hello, Raoul."

I got kisses to each of my stubbled cheeks along with a casual embrace. Immediately, he placed an arm on my back and began to urge me toward Ninth. Emily, our big Bouvier, often used her stout mass to herd me the same way. Turns out that I'm a relatively docile mammal; I usually do what the herding animals want.

Raoul said, *"Allons."*

"Fine with me," I said. "It's a pretty day." The gray skies had become partly cloudy. A little cool, but the air was fresh.

His route took us down Walnut toward downtown. We waited on the curb to weave through weekend cross traffic on Ninth. I asked, "How was the Two Cents thing last night?"

"Surprisingly lovely," he said. "Preston Georges did the food." Raoul pronounced the first name *Press-tone,* the *n* existing mostly in my imagination, and the last name *Jorge,* turning the *G* into a so-soft *J.* I knew the name from somewhere, but I couldn't place it. Raoul kindly offered a clue. "The chef from Pain Perdu? The one who left after that dust-up in August?"

Of course, Preston Georges. "I didn't know there was a dust-up at Pain Perdu in August. They changed chefs? Preston Georges left?" My pronunciation was *Press-ton* with a hard *n, George* like Washington. "What happened?"

"Chefs? Doesn't matter. I don't know how Hake got him to do the party, but he cooked for us. The man is a huge talent. It is like convincing Placido Domingo to sing at a birthday party. He did six, eight appetizers. A few entrées served buffet style. The food?" Raoul made a gastro-orgasmic noise before he continued. "The *amuse-bouches?* One was a perfect scallop, one a perfect quail thigh. Some wilted greens and some cabbage that . . . wasn't cabbage. There was a grilled crawfish salad. Simple but . . . how it was flavored? Some tamarind, perhaps. Asian and Latin all at once. African? I'm not sure. Then roast pheasant — freshly dressed — with turnips and beets. The turnips were a revelation. And usually, I don't like beets, but . . . And the sauce, oh, Alain. For the vegetarians" — Raoul raised his eyebrows at Boulder's vegetarians — "an umami terrine of mushrooms and julienned brussels sprouts topped with shaved white truffles. For desert, poached pears on blood orange *sabayon* with vanilla and caramel ice cream. Almond *tuile.*"

"And the company?"

"Oh, and chocolat, after. The pastries? He has this pastry chef. . . . My lord. It was a good crowd. Some of our oldest friends were there, Alain." He moved his head from side to side. I recognized the gesture as a modifier. I thought Raoul was indicating that some of the members of the group were older friends than others. "Like us, you and me? We finish each other's stories. You would like them, I think. These old friends. Diane and I will host a dinner soon. Maybe early in December before the holidays get all American on us. Oui? We will include you and Lauren. I promise." He smiled.

I could have warned Raoul that tension seemed to be building between Lauren and me and the new neighbors, his old friends, over the dogs. I suspected that whatever plans Mattin and Mimi were spawning to redevelop Adrienne's farmhouse and barn would serve to aggravate the nascent canine disagreements.

I changed the subject. "Mattin's accent? What is that? Is it British?" I asked. Raoul had a savant-like talent for matching accents and geography.

"Not British. He lived in South Africa, Johannesburg, when he was young. That's what you're hearing."

I never would have guessed. Raoul and I crossed Ninth and continued past the St. Julien Hotel until we reached a little pedestrian alley connecting the sidewalk on the thousand block of Walnut, adjacent to Brasserie Ten Ten, with the sidewalk on the thousand block of Pearl. I didn't know the official name of the passage — or even if it had one — but I always thought of it as the Tenth Street alley, because if Tenth continued south from Pearl, which it does not, it would run where the alley is located. We took the walkway to Pearl. Raoul stopped me right in front of the patio of Centro.

I was aware that we had officially left Walnut — not only the building, the purported focus of my discussion with Raoul, but also the street — behind. Raoul is rarely disingenuous, so I found myself curious about the connection between Walnut and Pearl, or at the very least, between Walnut and the Tenth Street alley.

Raoul faced east. In Boulder, that reliably puts the Rocky Mountains at one's back. He stuffed his hands in the pockets of his khakis and adjusted his posture — shoulders back, chest out. Raoul was a much more impressive physical specimen than I. I put my shoulders back too, even though I don't have a chest that thrusts out very far no matter what the hell I do. I put my hands in the pockets of my sweatshirt.

"What do you see?" he asked.

It sounded like a trick question. "Literally?" I asked. "Or are you hoping for . . . I don't know, vision?"

He chuckled. "Let us begin literally. There is always time later in the day for metaphysics. With cocktails, I think is best."

I smiled. "I see downtown. The Mall. A lovely late-autumn day."

"Closer."

I adjusted my frame of reference. "The Kitchen, Salt, Juanita's —"

"What? You see food only? I'll buy you something to eat when we're done. You are leaning too far left." Raoul laughed at his own joke. His politics were difficult to discern — I blamed that on his youthful experience with Franco — but his bias toward protecting business interests at all costs was not much of a secret. I suspected he and I would not agree about much. "Now look straight ahead. That way." He pointed due east.

"If I must. I see the *Daily Camera* building, and its always alluring parking lot."

The *Daily Camera* was Boulder's legacy newspaper. The structure was a two-story, unimaginative brick rectangle that had been plopped into the heart of what was otherwise a nineteenth-century, pioneer-heritage, Victorian-accented, vibrant, pedestrian-friendly downtown. It is hardly one of the area's architectural treasures. If some rogue state — or, more likely, another Colorado county — decided to bomb downtown Boulder, the *Camera* bunker might be a good place to seek shelter. That is the extent of its charms. A couple of significant renovations over the decades I'd been in town had somewhat improved its looks, in much the same way that a trip to Maaco improves the prospects of an '82 Plymouth Reliant.

Raoul said, "You see *le Camera.* Bueno. Now, let's try vision."

English, French, Spanish, English, I thought. One of the reasons I loved talking with him was to get an opportunity to hear all the instruments he used in his orchestra. Then it hit me. *Really?* I let my jaw drop. "Raoul, did you buy the *Daily Camera?*"

He didn't respond to my question. I persisted. "Have you somehow discovered a business model that will permit you to make money printing out copies of yesterday's news and delivering those printouts to people's residences by throwing them out the windows of moving cars?"

He smiled at me warmly. He said, "You know confidentiality? Sí? We call it nondisclosure. Whatever I tell you next is nondisclosure. *Agreeable?*"

The last word, from Raoul's mouth, was *ag-ray-ahb-la.* "My forte," I said, placing an open palm on my chest. It was true. Confidentiality was one of my strengths. Secrets were my thing. I kept my mouth shut with the best of them. Better than most of them. I said, "I have to tell Lauren. She has an interest in all of this. What I own . . ." I shrugged.

"Mais oui."

"May I talk to Diane, too?"

He made a face that said, *Are you kidding?* He added, *"C'est tout? Avec les questions?"* I nodded. "I am part of a syndicate that has just optioned the buildings and the land. No, not the newspaper, not the business — only the land, for redevelopment purposes. We have formed an LLC. You know about LLC?"

I nodded. Limited liability company. A name that put the ass-covering in front of the venture, precisely where business thought it belonged.

"We are in due diligence. Back to that vision — what do you see in front of you?"

"I assume you are planning to knock it down."

"Oui. Sí. Yes. The Pearl Street building, definitely. The Walnut side? *Peut-être.*"

In recent decades, the *Daily Camera* had constructed a modern office structure across the alley, behind the main building. That structure faced Walnut Street, not Pearl.

"My vision for the land on Pearl? Given

that A, you and your partners want to make money, and B, that you need to come up with something that the planning board and the city council will approve, I would say that . . . you'll dig a big hole for parking, of course. A big, big, hole. First floor retail — the planning department would insist. On the upper floors? Offices? Condos?

"Design? Probably the same kind of inoffensive stuff that was done on the stretch of Walnut that's east of Broadway. Or the new stuff on Canyon west of Ninth. That would be the easiest to get approved." I was thinking and talking simultaneously. "Red brick, and glass. A contemporary feel, but with just enough Victorian brickwork to keep the preservationists from cardiac arrest. Something, ultimately, forgettable."

I was just getting started. "Your syndicate will have to make money, so you'll probably put in more square feet than anyone really believes should be squeezed onto a piece of land this size." I turned to look at Raoul. "How am I doing? Is that what you have in mind? An inoffensive monolith?"

He rolled his eyes but nodded an acknowledgment.

I asked, "Tell me something. You don't do real estate, you do engineering, and you do tech. You do them better than anyone. Why this? Why now? Somehow you've convinced yourself that a speculative real estate development is prudent in this economic environment? Can you actually make money building a big, expensive multiuse project? On spec, I presume? You don't have a tenant, do you?" He didn't. "This land has to be terribly expensive. I heard that somebody spent two million bucks for the Tom's Tavern building to renovate it for Salt."

The legendary Tom's Tavern was right across Pearl Street from the *Camera.* The prime corner restaurant had dished burgers and beer to generations of Boulderites from a storefront parcel that was tiny compared to the land Raoul was eyeing.

Raoul corrected me. "A developer redid Tom's Tavern. Brad Heap is food, not bricks. Although it's only a guess — these things are blind — I suspect we've been bidding against the same developer for the *Camera.* He's probably waiting for us to stumble so he can sweep up the crumbs. But sí, the land is expensive," he said. "My partners in the LLC, most of them at least, are in development. This project will take years to bring to . . . fruition. *Fruition* is the right word? *Fruition*" — *fru-i-see-on* — "yes? So we are confident that the building will come online during the period of the coming economic recovery, not during the dark days we are in now."

Over the years, Diane and I had listened to more than a few proposals from developers eager to flatten the Walnut Street property and do something else with the land. Because the dollars we were offered for our nest egg often took our collective breaths away, we always considered each proposal's merits seriously before rejecting it. For me, the process had been an ongoing education about urban planning, development, and the nature of developers' hope. The experience that I gained examining the proposals had also left me with more than a passing acquaintance with the hurdles involved in bringing redevelopment endeavors to a conclusion in downtown Boulder.

I said, "I'm sure you know all this, Raoul. But there are height restrictions downtown. You can blame those rules on the Colorado Building." I pointed at the Colorado Building, which was four blocks due east of us. And I growled.

Raoul had heard my rants about the Colorado Building before. In unaccented English, he said, "Don't go there, Alain. Please? Not again."

I demurred. "The *Camera* block on Pearl? There are setback restrictions. Historical guidelines. God knows how subjective that will turn out to be. And off-street parking requirements. Off-street *bicycle*-parking requirements. And if you're including residential in your building? There'll probably be off-street *kayak*-parking requirements. Maybe ski-storage lockers. Who knows what else? You have to be ready for view plane controversies. Solar easement problems.

"When you start digging, you may find undiscovered archaeological treasures under that parking lot from the storefronts that fronted Pearl before the last big flood." Boulder's last hundred-year flood had filled the downtown basin with silt in 1894. The thick muck from Boulder Creek had buried treasures from Boulder's pioneer past. Subsequent development was built right over it.

"Flooding, Raoul?" I hit myself in the forehead with the heel of my hand. "The floodplain. This land is in the Boulder Creek floodplain, right? Is it the fifty-year boundary? The hundred-year boundary? God knows what the flood-management people will require of you. Every activist in town — and that's at least half the population — is going to want a say in what happens to this land. The planning meetings for this project will be standing-room only. They'll have to hold them in Macky."

Raoul looked at me with infinite patience in his eyes. I envied his graciousness much more than I envied his attractiveness to women. Okay, I envied both.

He said, "Yes, all of those things you mention will be complications. But you know what they say about real estate, Alain? Location, location . . ." He spread his arms toward the depressing parking lot in front of us. "Well, this is . . . location."

He sighed the contented sigh of an investor who was not interested in discussing risk after he had just been offered ten thousand shares of Google's IPO. "It doesn't get any better than this in Boulder. Not downtown. Try to assemble this amount of land within a mile of here. Not this quality of land — the quality can't be duplicated — just this amount of land. Maybe with enough money, the Ideal Market site could be assembled — *peut-être* — but that fronts North Broadway, not Pearl, and it's blocks from downtown. The Liquor Mart block? Nice, but too far from *le coeur.*" He placed his hand over the center of his chest. "Not the same. You can't assemble land like this near the Mall. Remember what it took to get the St. Julien built? That was perimeter, and that land was vacant for years. It will never happen again.

Jamais.

"If you ask the experienced developers on our team to identify the single best location for a high-end multiuse development in Boulder, every last one would point to this block. I know. Because we asked almost every one of them."

Raoul didn't need my help doing due diligence on his redevelopment dreams. I refocused my attention on my tiny corner of the Boulder redevelopment universe. "Where does Walnut fit into your grand scheme? Walnut is what, a block and a half away? I don't see the connection."

He turned to me and smiled his best gender-neutral, seductive, Casanova smile. A young woman walking down the alley toward Walnut noticed and assumed Raoul's irresistible grin was intended for her. She smiled right back at him and added a definite arc to the curve of her hips as she sashayed by us.

Raoul winked at her. She dropped her chin as she tucked her long hair behind her ear. My mouth fell open in more than mild disbelief. If I had winked at her, she would have hit me. Literally, verbally. Somehow. One way or another, I would be in pain.

Raoul said, "You are wondering why are you here, Alain? Sí?"

"Other than to be humbled, yes."

He ignored the compliment. "We may need Walnut to make the deal work."

"I don't get it."

"Long story. Trust me. For later."

I considered pressing him but realized that my effort would be in vain. "But the end of the long story is that your LLC wants, or maybe needs, to purchase Walnut Street? If Diane and I don't sell, the redevelopment of the *Camera* property is in jeopardy?"

"It's all a little more nuanced than that, but yes."

"Diane knows about this?"

He made a dismissive noise. We had both known Diane for a long time. That meant we each knew that keeping secrets from Diane was like trying to keep news of your misbehavior from Santa Claus.

Raoul turned and began walking. I followed him around the corner so that we were heading west on Pearl, toward the mountains that stretched toward the sky ten blocks away. After a hundred feet or so, Raoul stepped inside the door of the West End Tavern, a destination I knew well. We climbed the stairs to the rooftop deck.

The West End's outside space was packed with the late lunch crowd. Tourists and locals. On pretty days, and even days that aren't quite pretty days, the rooftop deck of the West End was packed. Why? Because of the remarkable views.

From the deck of the West End, patrons can see the gentle rise of The Hill as it climbs from the edge of the flagstone Italianate buildings of the university campus. The backdrop of the foothills. The luxurious expanse of Chautauqua's unspoiled acres below the vault of the Flatirons. The miles of protected green space.

"You remember this view?" Raoul said. "Before?"

Raoul meant before the recent construction of a new building to the west. "Yes. Before they built the monster wall next door."

"Well, my Diane wants that view. For herself. In perpetuity," he said. "The one from up here, from before."

"Ah," I said. "I think I'm finally getting this. You are not only developing a massive real estate project that promises to make you a ton of money you don't need and promises to change the public face of Boulder's West End forever. You are also buying a condominium in your new building? A home, a real home, for you and Diane."

"The top floor. Facing south and west.

With a big, big terrace" — *tear-oss* — "for the sunset. A lap pool for me. A fire pit. An outdoor kitchen. A fountain. Diane is hoping for a gazebo too, with curtains. Like Morocco? She dreams . . . I think the architects will say no. A gazebo on top of the building? With the chinooks? But she is hard to refuse. We will have a hundred square meters of terrace overlooking the Rockies. Maybe more."

I considered asking him to translate that hundred square meters into hectares. "So this project is personal," I said.

"Sí. *Amor.*"

10

The dogs and I went out for evening rounds.

For a while after Jonas's puppy joined our household, we'd had three dogs. The second was a miniature poodle foster dog we were caring for as a favor to an enrollee in the witness protection program, WITSEC.

Over the previous Labor Day weekend, a federal marshal had knocked on our door and told us that he was there to collect Anvil, the foster dog. Just like that. Anvil had been ours for so long, I'd stopped believing that his aging mafioso owner would ever return to claim him.

"Carl is okay?" I said to the marshal. I knew the protected witness as Carl Luppo. I also knew it wasn't his real name.

"Don't know," the marshal said. "I was told to get the dog. To tell you thanks."

While the kids and Lauren said a sudden good-bye to our little tough-guy poodle, I packed up his crate and toys and food, and worried about the effects of the loss on the kids, especially Jonas.

Minutes later we were again a two-dog family. Our poodle had returned to witness protection. I hoped Carl was okay.

Emily had a destination in mind for that night's walk. She had taken off uphill, on the path that ran near the basement walk-out on the south side of Peter and Adrienne's house. I thought I'd take advantage of the fact that our neighbors seemed to be gone, and I took the same route with the puppy.

I guided Fiji uphill toward the ridge at the top of the Boulder Valley. Fiji, of course, started searching for prairie dogs. I phoned Sam. The top of the hill was five-bars country.

He answered with, "Sorry about breakfast. You catch the way the Avs lost this afternoon? Pitiful. Defenseman has to slow that guy. Goalie has to stop that shot. Has to." He sighed. "I know they're young, but I don't care. Defenseman has to slow that guy."

Sam had been, was, a defenseman. He took certain failures personally.

"Happens," I said. I was talking about the missed breakfast, not the bad hockey. I added, "No worries," mostly because I had kids in the house and needed practice employing their always-ephemeral vernacular. *No worries* was one of those phrases that would finally begin rolling off my tongue about two weeks after my children had officially started considering it lame.

Gracie, though a child in all ways, would be the first to note my bad timing. She would find it hilarious that once again I'd caught on to some fleeting social idiom a smidge too late. When I'd recently stumbled into a similar swamp, she'd announced deadpan at the dinner table, "Dad just hit another three-pointer right after the buzzer."

Although I knew Grace was repeating something she'd heard from her brother, it stung me even more that my barely six-year-old daughter had zinged me with an almost perfect use of a sports metaphor.

"So you were home last night?" Sam asked me.

Interesting, I thought. Last night would have been Friday, the night of the damn housewarming. I was giving him some latitude to see what he was going to reveal about his morning visit to Spanish Hills in the company of the sheriff's investigator.

"I was," I said. "I think I'm getting boring."

" 'Fraid that ship has sailed," Sam said.

I waited for a good fifteen seconds to see if Sam planned to continue the conversational thread. When it appeared he didn't, I said, "Heard you came up this way after you ditched me at breakfast. Lauren saw you."

"She's still using the cane? Yes?"

I recognized Sam's attempt to hijack the conversation. "Why were you here? Must have been some kind of big deal to bring both you and a sheriff's investigator out on a Saturday morning."

"Don't make assumptions, Alan. The less curious you are about my visit this morning, the better."

"I'm already curious."

"You're not listening. You don't want to know why we were there. Understand?"

I let the air go dead between us. I still had questions. "I need to ask a question before I take your advice."

"I wish I was surprised."

"I'm a father and a husband. With responsibilities. Is there something that a couple of detectives know about my new neighbors that a father and a husband with responsibilities would want to know, too?"

Sam hesitated again. Only seconds, but still. *God damn,* I thought.

No more than three seconds later than he

should have, he finally said, "You're good . . . on that."

Sam lied to me. What the hell happened during that party? "But your visit here today had to do with last night. I'm basing that assumption on your question about whether or not I was home."

Sam didn't reply. "Diane and Raoul were at the party, Sam. Diane will tell me every last detail. You know her. Once I ask her how the housewarming went, the only way I won't know what happened is to put fingers in both my ears and sing *la-la-la-la-la* until she stops talking."

"Diane and Raoul were there?"

Sam hadn't known that? *Huh?* "They're friends with our new neighbors."

He said, "Doesn't matter. I think you'll find that Diane's natural inclination to gossip is on hold. Let it go, my friend. You don't have the finesse to play in this league."

"Should I be insulted?"

"No," he said. "It's not a nice league."

"I'll consider your advice. As a friend." Sam laughed. "You were a little out of your jurisdiction up here," I said.

"Things get confused sometimes," he said. "Police work isn't always science."

"What is it? Art?"

"Some art. Mostly just not science."

"What about forensics?"

"That's the part that's science. But they don't pay me to do the science. They pay me to do the analytical part, the art. They don't pay me much, but . . . hey, I got work."

"Even, it turns out, when the work is out of your jurisdiction," I said.

I didn't expect to get any more of an explanation from Sam about the jurisdiction issues beyond his "things get confused" headline, but it turned out that he was willing to add some detail. "Complainant came into 33rd. Thought the events in question took place in Boulder. Almost nobody in Boulder knows where Boulder begins and Boulder ends. People think Boulder's bigger than it is. Gotta be a metaphor there." I was tempted to chime in, but Sam was on a roll that I didn't want to interrupt. "But since the person in question didn't know the city limits and didn't have a street address for the residence . . . we didn't know to hand off to the sheriff. By the time Lucy got it sorted out — and discovered that the cul-de-sac in question is in the county — I'd already screwed my Saturday."

"I prefer to think of our lane as a dead end. Not a cul-de-sac."

"Call it whatever you want. But I did get a chance to see your lovely wife." Sam paused right there. "She's still moving . . . I don't know, slowly."

"She's kind of plateaued, Sam. Mobility-wise. The recovery has been more gradual than we'd like."

"Give her more time. Healing? It's about time."

Sam knew a little about the slow healing of significant others.

"I want to make sure I get it — you and Lucy are off this case? It's the sheriff's?"

"You got it."

"Just tell me why I don't want to know what happened. Why all the secrecy?"

"Ever noticed we don't say a whole lot about active investigations? That includes to neighbors, in case you're feeling special. Trust me on this — you're better off not knowing any more than you know."

"Lauren will find out, Sam. Someone in her office already knows."

"If she finds out, she finds out. But she's too smart to tell you."

"Sam, I have kids," I said. "A wife who's home a lot. By herself. I need to know if I should be concerned. You hesitated earlier."

"How well do you know your new neighbors?"

"Barely. Not at all. I know him like you know him. From TV."

"Lucy told me he's a daytime TV darling of some kind. I don't watch a lot of daytime TV. I never, ever watch television darlings."

"Okay."

"Keep things the way they are. Your family will be fine. Understand?"

"No."

"Tough shit."

11

At supervision on the Monday morning after the housewarming, Hella Zoet began by telling me she needed to talk, once again, about Burning Man Lady.

The patient formerly known as Three-Wood Widow.

"This is an awful story," she said. She swept her hair back with her fingers and hooked it behind her ears. "I feel so sad for her. I saw her for an emergency appointment on Saturday night, Alan. If you had asked me who in my caseload would be least likely to make an emergency call to me, she would have been near the top of my list. She called me Saturday, late afternoon, and left me a despairing-sounding voice mail asking me to call her back as soon as I could. I was out on the Mesa Trail with friends, but I got back to her within the hour, as soon as I got back to my car.

"She said — I wrote this down — 'I think

I need . . . Maybe if we could meet, I think. Dr. Zoet, I've been . . . raped. Last night, I was raped.' Then she paused, Alan. A good five seconds before she added, 'I think I was raped.' "

I took a metaphorical deep breath. I said, " 'I think'? She said, 'I think'?"

"Yes. We talked for only a couple of minutes on the phone, long enough for me to be sure she was okay physically, that she had done what she needed to do to take care of herself. She said she'd driven herself to the police and that a detective had accompanied her to Community, to the hospital. She met with a rape crisis counselor there, too.

"I canceled my plans for the evening and met her at my office a few minutes before seven o'clock. I have never done that before, Alan. Met a patient for a session on a weekend night." After all my years of practice, I could still count on the fingers of one hand the number of times I had done something similar. "She said that one of the cops she talked to earlier that day — a woman detective, she said" — Hella consulted her notes — "Detective Davenport, told her at the hospital that no matter what happened during the rest of the day she should think about getting her own attorney as soon as she could. She even gave her a name."

"Really? I don't think that's routine advice for rape victims. Do you know why the detective advised that?"

"I don't. During that call, whenever I asked a question like that my patient kept saying, 'This is going to be a big deal. This is going to be a *big* deal. Oh my God, this is going to be such a big deal.' Like it was a mantra. I figured she was talking about the rape, but who knows? I was hoping you might be able to help me understand."

"What kind of big?" I asked.

Hella pondered my question. "Ominous? That kind of big."

I said, "Let's go back to the beginning. Tell me what happened. Let's see if we can puzzle this out."

Hella began the story by saying, "She's calling what happened to her 'acquaintance rape.' I think that's important. It's one of the first things she said." She looked at her notes again. "I think I have her exact words: 'I know this man, the one who did this. He's my friend. He's not someone who — I know him.' "

I listened carefully as Hella continued to talk, trying to ascertain if she was using the *acquaintance* descriptor as a diminutive.

Hella, it turned out, wasn't. She was telling me only that her patient knew her rapist. Thus the word *acquaintance.*

She said, "The fact that she knew the guy so well is important to her. I think she was expressing shock that he could do this to her — that's why she kept repeating it. That's the only reason that I am emphasizing it with you."

"Betrayal?" I asked.

"Definitely. She doesn't remember the assault. What she was feeling at first was . . . bewilderment over the betrayal."

Hella's patient had been at a big party that included some friends. She drove herself to the party — it was at a home she'd never visited before in "east Boulder, out Baseline" — from her house in North Boulder. Since she has a reputation for getting lost when she goes anywhere unfamiliar, she first drove to meet a couple who live below Chautauqua, and she followed them to the location of the party.

She drank more than she intended but maintained to Hella that at no point did she consider herself drunk. Still, as the festivities were winding down she thought about accepting a ride home with the friends she'd followed to the party. She would then return the next day to retrieve her car. But Burning Man Lady ultimately decided to stay at the party to sober up. Her plan was to drive back home after a cup of coffee or two.

At some point shortly after the last of the other guests headed home, the hostess invited her to spend the night in the guest room and drive herself home the next morning.

Staying over in her host's guest suite quickly became the plan.

The host and hostess poured some more wine. The three of them sat in front of the fireplace.

At that point in Hella's story, I said, "I think I'm going to need some names. I'm having trouble keeping everyone straight. The host? The hostess?"

Hella said, "I don't know anyone's names. She wouldn't tell me."

"What?" My *what?* was puzzled, not challenging.

"The lawyer? She met with one Saturday before she met with me. He instructed her not to reveal the name of anyone who was involved in the rape in any way. The other people who attended the party. Anyone. He doesn't want anyone to learn those identities. She said he stressed the need for discretion when she spoke with him on the phone, and then again when they met in his office. No names, no addresses, no directions, no license plate numbers, no vehicle makes and models, nothing that could identify anyone who was there."

"Do you know the lawyer's name?" I asked.

"No," Hella said. "Only that he's really tall. And very formal."

She was describing Cozier Maitlin. Cozy was six-seven. He dressed like a lord. At various points in his career, Cozy had defended both Lauren and me, and he'd once defended Sam's detective partner Lucy Davenport. Although I couldn't understand why Lucy felt the rape victim needed a personal attorney, it wasn't surprising that she'd given out Cozy's name.

Cozy could be bombastic. But I knew from experience that he was a thoughtful advocate who had a purpose for everything he did during any case he was litigating. If he told his new client to keep her mouth shut, the advice wasn't pro forma. Cozy had to be concerned about something specific.

But I didn't know what it was. I couldn't figure out why Cozy had directed his client not to use the name of the alleged rapist, and was even more puzzled that he was adamant that she not reveal the identity of anyone who'd been at the party. Regardless of Cozy's legal rationale, because communication between his client and her psychologist was privileged, and thus protected from discovery, I was certain that he didn't intend that his instructions to his client extend to her psychotherapy relationship. And although Cozy would have no way to know that Dr. Zoet's practice was supervised, the privilege that the patient enjoyed with her therapist also extended to the relationship between the psychotherapist and his or her supervisor.

I began to explain all that to Hella. She stopped me; she already knew it.

"I told her the same thing, Alan — except for the supervision part. She said she explained to the attorney she was in therapy and she made it clear to him that she wanted to be able to talk to me about what happened. He told her that wasn't a problem, he encouraged her to talk to me about what happened, but he also made it clear to her that even with me the safest thing was not to use anyone's name."

"*Safest?* Cozy used that word?"

Hella hesitated. "I think that's the word she used with me, Alan. I could be wrong. Maybe *prudent.* I wasn't taking notes at that point of the conversation. That's the connotation, though. I'm sure of that."

I remained puzzled. "You said she went to the police. Have charges been filed?"

Hella shrugged. "I don't know. She went straight to the police when she woke up and realized what had happened. But as of yesterday afternoon — she and I met on Saturday, and talked on the phone for about ten minutes yesterday — no one had been arrested. Charges had not been filed. Since then? Maybe that's why all the secrecy? Would that matter? If an arrest was pending?"

I shook my head. "I don't know."

"I may find out more later today. She's coming in again after she gets off work."

I said, "I haven't seen anything in the news about this."

Hella said, "There is nothing in the paper or online. I checked."

Colorado has a rape shield law that protects accusers' and victims' identities by shielding their names and likenesses from public/media scrutiny. I wasn't aware that Colorado had any kind of restrictions on reporting the names of alleged assailants, or of witnesses who might have been present around the time of the alleged crime.

"Why don't you tell me what happened?

Maybe the need for all the secrecy will become clear."

Hella resettled on the sofa. "The way she told the story is important, I think. She was determined to remember everything she could, even little details that are probably irrelevant. I'm going to try to give you all her little details, just in case they turn out to be significant. This is my first real, big legal case. I don't want to screw this up."

I said, "Sounds good, Hella."

"The three of them were drinking wine. Everyone else was gone. The housewarming had been catered by some famous chef. He had left. The bartender had left. The caterers — the servers — had left."

The vague discomfort I was feeling about the story suddenly jumped up and barked in my face. I exhaled twice in a row, with no inhale in between. I thought, *Did those caterers leave in a big white van, maybe?* I was telling myself, *No way. Can't be.*

"At one point, the woman — the hostess — got up to check on something. The host kept insisting she have some more wine. She agreed to have one more glass. The hostess came back. The three of them — the host couple and my patient — sat and talked. She said they eventually finished a bottle.

"My patient admits that she was a little

drunk by then. She said she definitely would not have gotten behind the wheel of her car after they finished that bottle of wine.

"The hostess excused herself again to check on the linens in the guest suite. My patient offered to help her out. The hostess said she wouldn't think of it — she said something about being so excited that they were having their first overnight guest in their new house."

Shit, I thought. *Oh shit.* "First guest?" I said.

"They'd just moved in. It was a housewarming-type gathering. The couple wanted their old friends to see their new place. Want more details?"

No, I thought. "Yes," I said. "Whatever you have."

"The couple is planning to do extensive renovations and they wanted to show everyone the house and hear their friends' thoughts so they could pass along any good ideas to their architect. The architect is apparently busy designing the remodel.

"They had set up a couple of drafting tables and had copies of the floor plans and pencils and rulers and things. They wanted everyone to sketch out their best ideas.

"My patient said the house has an amazing view of the mountains and the city that is partially obstructed to the west by an old shed or barn of some kind, and by a nearby neighbor's house, which my patient said is not very attractive, and by the neighbor's garage, which everyone agreed is out of scale and an eyesore."

Not attractive? Out of scale? An eyesore?

"The people who threw the party own the shed, which they said they're planning to knock down as part of the renovations. The host and hostess are worried that the neighbors might object to the demolition on historic grounds — the structure is apparently pretty old, original to some . . . ranch."

It's not a shed, it's a beautiful old barn, meticulously restored by the previous owners.

Hella hooked her hair behind her ears. "One couple at the party knows the neighbors across the way, the ones with the ugly house and the big garage, the ones who might object to the demolition and the renovation. The woman in that couple said she wasn't comfortable talking about their friends' home. My patient said that the discussion became kind of awkward at that point, but that the hostess sensed it, handled it well. She moved the conversation on and got everyone talking about the addition they were planning to the main house. How big a footprint it should have. Where to put a new powder room on the main level — there isn't one currently, the guests had to use the bathroom in the guest suite. What kind of traffic flow they want. What walls to take down. Stuff like that."

I was hit by an instant wave of grief. I had thought that after many months and many tears I was getting over Adrienne's death, but the fresh sadness that she was gone, really gone, almost knocked me out of my chair. It sounded as though my new neighbors were determined to erase every trace of her.

My heart was ripping for Jonas.

"Are you all right, Alan?"

Rape, I reminded myself. *There was a rape.* I composed myself enough to say, "Yes, fine. I'm fine, Hella. This is a tough situation you're describing, that's all."

Hella nodded as though she understood. She didn't, of course, which was the way I preferred it.

I said, "I interrupted your story. You were saying that the hostess had left to check on linens?"

"Yes. My patient thought she'd been gone quite a while, but she came back carrying some pajamas and some fresh towels. Later on, she led my patient to the guest room.

It's on the back of the first floor, off of a family room addition. Sort of off by itself, she said. My patient thought it was probably originally a maid's room. She said that the other bedrooms are upstairs. Three, or four, she thought. They got a tour at the beginning of the evening. One of the upstairs bedrooms was used as an office. One as a kid's room. I hope I have all this right."

She did. All of Hella's patient's architectural descriptions about the house were correct. Peter and Adrienne had added a two-story addition to the back — east side — of the house immediately after they moved in. On the first floor of the addition was a family room. Above it, an extension of the master suite. Peter had also lined one of the small upstairs bedrooms with floor-to-ceiling walnut bookshelves so that his wife, Adrienne, a urologist, could have a proper office.

"My patient thanked both of her friends for the party and said good night. She went to the guest room, shut the door, used the bathroom, changed into the pajamas, and climbed into bed."

"She said everything about the guest room — the pajamas, the linens, the mattress, everything — was so much nicer than what she was used to. They left bottled water for her, a fresh toothbrush. New soaps, everything. She said she felt completely pampered in that guest suite. It was as though she was staying in the kind of hotels she saw pictures of in magazines."

I had been in the suite Hella was describing before. I'd followed Adrienne in there once as she was preparing the space for a new nanny after the previous nanny had departed in a huff. Adrienne's nannies mostly departed in huffs.

The nanny/guest suite at the back of the original house was a nice space, but I never considered it opulent. It sounded to me as though Mimi and Mattin might have spruced it up a bit.

I was impatient to get to the ending. I was waiting, almost literally on the edge of my seat, for the unknown acquaintance rapist to enter from the wings.

Hella said, "Oh my God, we're out of time! I have an eleven o'clock." She looked at me, then at her watch. "I'm not sure I can get back to my office on time. I may be late." Her eyes revealed an emotion I had never seen in her face before — mortification pureed with disbelief. "I am *never* late, Alan. Never."

It was true, at least with me. Hella was never late.

"Hella, that's fine, I understand if you need to go. But I absolutely need to hear the rest of this story. I need to know what's going on with your patient, both psychologically and legally, in case something comes up. I can't be in the dark on this. What time are you done tonight?"

She hit some buttons on her phone. I assumed she was checking her calendar. "Six fifteen," she said. "By the time I actually walk out to my car though, it'll be closer to six thirty."

I would still be with a patient at six thirty. "Can you come back here at seven?"

She was pulling on her jacket as she took two tentative steps toward the door. "I will really have to get something to eat. Blood sugar? Sorry. How about eight o'clock?"

That would mean I wouldn't get home until well after nine. Lauren was going to be exhausted by then. Asking her to manage the kids and get them fed and ready for bed wasn't fair to her, especially on an infusion day.

I said, "Do you have any breaks during the rest of today? Any brief windows when we could meet?"

Hella was at the door. Her purse was on her shoulder. Her keys were in one hand. Her phone was in the other. She said, "She is such a sweet woman, I want to go over and give her a hug and tell her she'll get through this. But don't worry, I won't. I'll check my calendar, and I'll text you about possible times. Sorry, but I really have to go."

12

The time between appointments for me can be brief. Seconds, literally. One patient leaves. The door closes behind her. I step down the hall to greet the next patient in the waiting room. Sometimes I'll schedule three sessions back-to-back-to-back. Three is about all my bladder will permit.

Shifting gears becomes second nature. I've grown accustomed to leaving the intensity of one patient's life behind as the door closes behind him so that I can permit the intensity of the next patient's life to enter my awareness and become the focus of my concentration. Somehow in the short, solitary walk I make from my office to the waiting room, I am almost always able to clear my head and set aside whatever insistent emotional pressure I was feeling from the affective undertow of the previous session.

That morning, my ability to compartmentalize failed me. I couldn't stop thinking about my supervision appointment with Hella Zoet and what had happened to Burning Man Lady shortly after she mused that the linens in my neighbor's guest bedroom were the quality of a five-star resort's.

Before work that morning, I had dropped Lauren at an infusion center near Community Hospital so she could receive her monthly dose of Tysabri. The IV-only drug was a monoclonal antibody intended to prevent an acute exacerbation of her multiple sclerosis.

An MS exacerbation — the formation of scarring caused by an acute loss of myelin somewhere in her central nervous system — can be a small thing to an MS sufferer, or it can be a big thing. Many exacerbations are silent; a patient like Lauren wouldn't know she'd had one of those until a routine MRI indicated a plaque in her brain that hadn't been visible on a prior scan. Other new lesions — plaques — cause immediately apparent symptoms like vision loss, numbness, weakness, pain, or bladder problems. The list of possible new symptoms from an MS lesion is almost as long as the human body is complex.

With each new MS symptom, dice get rolled on the craps table that is multiple sclerosis. How those dice come up determines important things for the person with the disease. The new symptom, or symptoms, caused by the newly faulty neural wiring, might be transient — days, weeks, or months in duration — or the new symptom might prove to be permanent. Any recovery from the symptoms, if recovery occurs at all — that's not a guarantee — might be complete, or the recovery might be only partial.

Partial may mean 90 percent resolved or only 10 percent resolved.

The remission that follows the fresh exacerbation may extend for years. Or the next relapse may come the same afternoon.

With MS, the dice are always rolling.

The major exacerbation Lauren experienced in Holland had robbed her of a lot. For weeks she was almost paralyzed in her lower extremities. These many months later, she was still too weak to walk without a cane. The prophylactic drug that Lauren had been taking before the switch to Tysabri knocked her off her feet for a day or more each week with severe side effects. Despite the fact that the new drug required her to schlep across town to get the IV, Tysabri was proving to be much less intrusive to her life. Once she left the infusion center Lauren usually felt as well as she did going in.

The Tysabri that was pumped into her vein that morning would do nothing to undo the damage from the last truck that hit her. The drug's sole purpose was to keep Lauren from being hit by the next truck, from suffering the next exacerbation. Because every MS preventative medicine — each more profanely expensive than the next — was nothing more than prophylaxis against a rare event, it was always an act of faith for me to believe that any of them was more than god-awfully expensive modern sorcery.

Although scientific data revealed that the drugs reduced exacerbation frequencies and disability profiles across a sample of MS sufferers, there was no way to be sure that any particular medicine was at all salutary for a specific individual. Like my wife. With Lauren's MS, I had days I believed in Tysabri like I believed the earth rotated around the sun, and I had other days when I believed that MS was in the hands of a god whose portfolio included folly and fate.

Even during days when I believed in science, I had moments when I was sure I could hear the dice tumbling after they'd been tossed by that god, as he laughed.

When I arrived to pick Lauren up at the infusion center after my supervision appointment, she responded to my "How are you doing?" by telling me she was feeling "okay." Between us, the word had a certain meaning. It didn't indicate "fine." It meant "tolerable." Or "how I expect to feel." It almost always meant *Don't inquire further, please.*

I knew the dialect. I didn't inquire further.

Lauren then asked me to take her to work, not back home, which had been the original plan.

"Do you have time for lunch first?" I asked. "I'm free until one thirty."

"I'd love to," she said.

I turned onto Ninth, the mountains to our right. "Do you feel up to walking a couple of blocks?" I was hoping to park at my office; midday parking near the Boulder Mall was always a bitch.

"What are you thinking? Brasserie Ten Ten? The Kitchen?"

Not quite. I'd been thinking I had a nonintrusive way of discovering how strong she was feeling. But I said what else I was thinking. "Actually, I was thinking Salt."

"That sounds great. You want to park at

your office? Why don't you drop me off at the restaurant first? I'll get us a table."

I dropped Lauren off on the west edge of the Downtown Mall before I weaved over to Walnut to park at my office. By the time I hustled back to Pearl Street, Lauren was seated at a table by the windows that fronted 11th. I leaned over and kissed her on the lips. As I pulled away from Lauren's face, I thought I noted a novel scent on her neck, perhaps the slightest trace of a new perfume.

At another phase of our relationship together I would have told her that I liked the fragrance — in fact, I did like it; the new scent was alluring. But in the wake of the revelation of her infidelity in Holland, the novelty of my wife wearing a new perfume could be cause for fresh suspicion. Or it could be a subtle plea on her part that she wanted us to turn the page to something new.

Or it could be she just wanted to try a fresh scent.

Only a week before, as I made our bed, I'd spotted Lauren's handwriting on a solitary sheet of paper on her bedside table. The paper had been torn from a notepad from the Boulderado Hotel. The note she'd written said "Elliot," and was followed by

"303" and seven more digits in an unfamiliar cadence that likely indicated a Colorado mobile number. I knew the odds were high that the Elliot in question was Elliot Bellhaven, one of Lauren's superiors at the DA's office. I assumed the number was for Elliot's cell.

What I didn't know was why the Boulderado Hotel notepad was the location that Lauren had chosen to write down the number. Most likely, she'd used it because it was handy. I could think of ten benign reasons why hotel stationery had been handy at the moment that Lauren had needed to jot down the number.

I could also think of one malignant reason.

It had taken me most of two days to reject the malignant option. I'd ended up exhausted by the emotional effort. I could not stand how much work it took at times to tamp down my doubt.

"This is a nice treat," she said as I sat down, my thoughts about her new perfume still my own. I feared that the labor that would be required to move the mystery of the new perfume onto the neutral shelf alongside the Boulderado notepad would psychologically annihilate me.

"Yes, we should do this more often," I said.

The perfume found my nose again. I needed a distraction. Our lunch would be only my second meal at Salt, which hadn't been open long. I looked around the compact restaurant, which I was seeing for the first time during the daytime. I couldn't help but notice the narrow confines and recognize how little actual physical space almost two and a half million dollars had purchased on this prime corner in downtown Boulder.

Salt's footprint was a tiny fraction of the size of the *Camera* property across the street. The value of the land Raoul was considering buying? Had to be astronomical.

I couldn't tell Lauren about what I'd learned during my supervision with Hella. As an alternative, as casually as I could, I asked, "Have you heard anything from your office that might explain why the detectives were at our house on Saturday? I still haven't figured that out."

She sipped some water. She straightened the napkin on her lap. She seemed uncomfortable with my question. I also thought that she seemed like she didn't want to appear uncomfortable with my question. She said, "Nothing I can talk about. Sorry. You understand, right? Sometimes, I just can't discuss . . . things . . . that happen at work. Same thing with you and your patients." She shrugged, mostly with her left shoulder.

She had no way to know that our many years together had taught me to trust her one-shoulder shrugs just a little bit less than her two-shoulder shrugs. The one-shoulder shrugs had reliably proven to be less sincere.

On another day, a day when I hadn't heard the recitation of facts, once removed, from one of the alleged participants in the events of Friday night, I probably would have simply nodded agreement to my wife — what she'd said was certainly true, although I was withholding judgment about how honest it was — and allowed my line of inquiry to expire.

Because of what I'd learned in supervision, that wasn't another day. I said, "But you do know why Sam and the sheriff's investigator were there?" She didn't answer me right away. I said, "You can at least tell me if there is an investigation ongoing, can't you? That can't be a secret."

"I do know some of what's going on. But it's being handled higher up the food chain, so I'd really prefer not to say anything about an investigation. Or not."

"Why all the secrecy? I mean, it can't be that big a deal, right? I haven't seen anything in the news."

Lauren's eyes went wide. "So much happens in our office that never hits the news, Alan. God, what our lives would be like at work if the public actually knew what we did every day. Innocent people can be damned by the taint of our attention. It wouldn't be fair if we talked about . . . everything."

The public — that includes me — typically knows only what leaks from the district attorney's office, or what goes to court, where a public record is created. Investigations that don't lead to charges? We never know.

"From where I sit," I said disingenuously, "it seems like it's blown over already. No one from the sheriff's office has been back out to Spanish Hills. Mimi and Mattin seem to be out of town. Am I missing something?"

She made a cute face, wrinkling her nose. "Things aren't always as they seem."

A waiter came by. Lauren ordered iced tea. I asked for lemonade and iced tea. I refused to call the drink an Arnold Palmer.

The waiter said, "An Arnold Palmer?"

I said I would just have lemonade. He left. "Please?" I said to Lauren. "Just give me a hint."

"This isn't like you, Alan. Usually when I

tell you I can't talk about something, you let it go."

True. "Usually, it doesn't involve my neighbors. I think I have reason to be concerned about something so close to our home. If something significant happened across the lane, I want to know about it. We have kids to worry about."

Lauren gazed out the window. I had intended for it to be a hard argument for her to counter.

"Okay," she said. "Some allegations were made. The facts are in dispute."

"Allegations of . . . ? What? Poor seasoning? Watering down the booze? It was a housewarming."

"Please."

I lowered my already quiet voice to a whisper. "Sam was there on his day off. Is it a felony, Lauren?"

"There are lots of different felonies." Lauren was a polished litigator; she had great skill at obfuscation.

I knew I was getting near the end of any license I had to continue to press her. "Are our kids . . . in any jeopardy? Are we? Tell me that."

Lauren hesitated. Her hesitation, more than anything else she'd said, confirmed for me that Burning Man Lady's recitation of the events on Friday night might have some approximation to the truth.

"It's better that you don't know any of this, Alan. Trust me. It's become . . . involved. You know what lawyers can be like? Well, in this situation we're talking big-time lawyers. If any of this leaks it will get ten times worse."

"Is Mattin one of the big-time lawyers?"

She lowered her voice to a whisper and opened her purple eyes wide. "I expect all this to blow over. Okay?"

"Really?" I said. I was very surprised.

"Yes. Now will you leave it alone? Please? I've already said more than I should. Let's enjoy lunch."

I was in the strange circumstance of knowing way too much, and altogether too little, to stop with what I had so far. I really wanted to know what Lauren knew that caused her to believe that an allegation of rape would evaporate like the aftermath of a routine July thunderstorm.

I pushed just a little more. "Does Diane know what happened? Were she and Raoul there when whatever went down, went down?"

"Can we talk about something else? Please?"

I would have to go to Diane for more

information. For me, going to Diane for information was like going to Tiffany for diamonds.

Lauren and I hadn't had a chance to talk about my meeting with Raoul over the weekend. Every time I'd started to bring it up with her, it seemed that something had intruded. The phone rang, the kids — something.

I said, "My meeting with Raoul? Did you know the *Daily Camera* property is for sale? The whole thing?"

She immediately looked down the length of the narrow dining room toward the restaurant windows that fronted Pearl Street. She looked back at me. "I heard rumors a while ago that some Denver developers were interested," she said. "The guy who did that high-rise condo near the convention center? You know the one I'm talking about? Him. But I thought that deal fell through."

I lowered my voice. "Raoul wanted to talk to me about the *Camera,* indirectly. He told me he's part of a cabal that's made an offer for the whole site, with plans to redevelop the Pearl Street side. They're in due diligence right now. Everything I'm telling you, by the way, is covered by nondisclosure."

"And is that also why he wanted to talk

with you about Walnut?" Lauren is smart. She has a prosecutor's eye for the faint threads that tie seemingly unrelated events together.

I said, "One of his partners wants to include the Walnut building in the deal. Raoul said he thinks it may end up being a crucial component to make everything work."

"I don't get that part."

"Nor do I. But get this — he did tell me that if they can make this happen, he and Diane are buying one of the condos in the new building."

Her face brightened. "Really?"

"The best unit, of course. Top floor, facing the Flatirons. The old West End Tavern view? They want a big terrace for entertaining. Diane wants a friggin' gazebo."

Diane wanting a gazebo in the middle of downtown Boulder made Lauren smile. She said, "I know they talk about moving all the time, but I never thought they would really leave the mountains. I always thought they loved the Lee Hill house."

"Raoul's tired of the long winters up there. They want to travel. They'd like someplace that's easier to leave behind."

The waiter returned to take our lunch orders. Lauren was having trouble deciding between the pastas. The waiter was a chatty man who seemed like a guy who would have been content to talk the wonders of a fresh Bolognese sauce all afternoon. I learned much more about the lineage of the meat and the provenance of the milk than I wanted to know.

Lauren indulged him for quite a while. I zoned out. My thoughts drifted to Burning Man Lady and the guest room. Ultimately, Lauren went with the mushroom fettuccine. I interrupted the waiter with my choice before we learned about the forest where the fungi had grown strong and prospered. He left in search of another patron to school about the menu.

We sat silently for a while. It's possible that Lauren and I had always had long interludes of silence when we were out alone as a married couple, but I didn't think so. We were certainly having them with some frequency since Holland.

The circumstances of Lauren's MS exacerbation in Holland had wounded our marriage in ways I was determined to keep from being fatal. Those circumstances? The exacerbation caused paralysis of her legs that struck, almost biblically, while she was in the bed of the man who had fathered her first daughter sixteen years earlier.

That man, father of a stepdaughter named Sofie whom I'd never met — his name is Joost — was the one who called to tell me that my wife was very ill.

I had tried to convince myself that the silences that hung between Lauren and me in the wake of those events were a form of scar tissue from the serious marital wound we'd suffered. I feared at times that the evidence of the injury to our relationship would never really go away. I believed we could heal, but that the scar tissue would linger and remind. Could we deal with it? Survive it? Most days I believed we could.

Most days are not all days.

Lauren leaned forward. She took one of my hands in both of hers. "I have an idea. Don't go all — It's just an idea. I'm thinking . . . maybe we could do it, too. Buy a condo in the building across the street. I mean, if they can get it done. What do you think?"

"You're serious?"

"Elevators?" she said wistfully. "For me? I know that's selfish, but . . . I would love to live someplace that has an elevator. And us and the kids all on one floor? No maintenance. No snow to plow or shovel or rake off the roof. No lane to level. No critters to fence out. Even if it turns out that you had to sell Walnut, you and Diane could always find another office downtown, and if we were living on Pearl, you could walk to work. Think about that. The dogs would be close to the creek. When my leg gets stronger, I could start walking to work, too. It'd only be four blocks.

"All the restaurants we go to anyway would be right outside our door."

Lauren had obviously given the idea of moving to a downtown condo some serious thought long before I mentioned Raoul and Diane's plans at 11th and Pearl.

The possibility of us leaving our current Spanish Hills house had come up before. After I got back to Boulder from Israel with Jonas, and we learned that Adrienne wished for us to become his parents, Lauren and I briefly considered trying to swing a deal to move into Peter and Adrienne's farmhouse to accommodate our suddenly larger family. We quickly realized that financially it would be a monumental stretch. Even if we could find a way to make the numbers work, the big house was on three floors, with a laundry room all the way down in the walk-out basement. Given Lauren's mobility problems, a three-story home made no sense for us as a family.

"I'm sure that whatever Raoul and his

buddies will end up building across the street is way out of our league, Lauren. Financially. You know what the new condos sold for on Walnut and on Canyon. We can't manage that. And this location is even better. And we would need three bedrooms. Or four. I don't see how it could happen."

"Even if we sold Walnut and Spanish Hills?"

"We own only half of Walnut. And we have a healthy second to pay off in Spanish Hills." I reminded her that we did the remodel and the garage with borrowed money.

I took my own temperature. I thought my voice sounded normal. I considered that quite a feat considering that I could feel my heart galloping — the hooves of a passel of horses pounding against my chest wall — at the mere thought of selling my sanctuary in Spanish Hills. Spanish Hills was home. For me, it was special. I'd rented it long before I bought it. Apparently not so much for Lauren. I fought to keep my panic from infecting the conversation.

She released my hand. She looked away briefly. Sipped some tea. Fiddled with her silverware. "What if we sold the rental house, too? The current tenants have been wanting to do a lease/purchase. Could we make it work then?"

The rental house was the bungalow Lauren owned when we met. It was on a quiet street on The Hill, the neighborhood tucked between the university and the sudden rise of the Rockies on Boulder's western boundary. The house was small but in reasonable repair. The block was quiet and far enough from the university that the street wasn't attractive as student housing.

From the time we started living together, we had used the little charmer for rental income. In the intervening years, Boulder's real estate values had skyrocketed. Although prices had stabilized during the grand recession, the housing shock hadn't taken as much of a toll on prime real estate in Boulder as it had in other areas of the state. The financial bottom line was that, despite a small remaining mortgage, there was a lot of equity waiting to be tapped if we sold the house on The Hill.

"You are serious?" I said.

She sat back, folding her hands in her lap. "Our house has become difficult for me. With the stairs especially, the laundry in the basement, and the garage being separate from the house. Grace has started making noises about wanting to move to the other room in the basement to be closer to Jonas.

Having both kids down there will make things even harder.

"The kids are growing up. They don't run out to play in the fields anymore. They are doing more and more things at school and in town. We're on the road with them constantly because we live so far out. It would be so much more convenient to be in town."

My most compelling counterarguments, I knew, were sentimental and personal. And they were, ultimately, selfish. I swallowed them. Lauren was telling me something important. I told myself to try to hear it.

Instead of arguing, I said, "This is a lot to consider, Lauren. A lot. You're suggesting we sell everything? The Walnut office, Spanish Hills, your place on the Hill?" We still called it, all these years later, her place. "And then we would use all the money to buy a condo downtown? One we've never seen, that doesn't really even exist except in a developer's imagination." She smiled. I said, "You're talking changing everything at once. New schools for the kids. A completely new lifestyle. Everything . . . would change."

"Not everything," she said. "Just some things. Okay, you're right, maybe most things. A fresh start, Alan."

The prospect didn't cause her the vertigo

I was feeling. She was able to consider the upheaval that was on the table without any apparent trepidation. But trepidation is all I felt at the prospect of those changes.

I realized at that moment that Lauren's grand plan wasn't a series of real estate moves. Or a simple change of lifestyle. Or even a practical plan to find a home that acknowledged her disability.

The most important thing she was trying to do was create a fresh start.

For us.

13

When I got back to my office after lunch, I left Diane a note. The old-fashioned kind, in an envelope, affixed to her office door with tape.

It's how she rolls.

E-mail and Diane had been acquainted for years, but they had never become friends. She had gone far out of her way to make certain she was never formally introduced to the convenience of texting. The cell phone she carried was a vintage brick with large buttons. She maintained she liked the big numbers and the substantial feel of the thing in her hand. Any lack of modern features was irrelevant to her.

Her office answering machine was exactly that — a machine. It took up almost a square foot of real estate on her desk. To pick up messages from home she called her office number and punched codes into the phone she was using, codes that would cause the device to erupt from slumber and then to begin to beep incessantly. And non-melodically. That beeping, in turn, resulted — if things went well — in convincing the black box to start playing back her recorded messages from afar.

Despite copious soundproofing between our offices, I could always hear the infernal beeping whenever Diane would communicate with her machine and it would begin its responsive mating chirps.

Ironic as the thought sounded to my children — keeping up with the two of them was solely responsible for my recent transition to twenty-first-century digital life — I was Diane's resident IT guy. The previous week, Diane had cornered me after she finished a psychotherapy session with a young woman she was treating. She said she had an urgent tech question for me. She didn't actually say she had a tech question. She said, "You need to explain something to me about the Internet."

It wasn't an uncommon occurrence; my IT role meant that I did curbside tech supervision on the fly with Diane with some regularity. I could reliably count on the fact that whatever Diane wanted to know was entry-level stuff. Which, fortunately, was my tech area of specialty.

Recently, since she adores Christopher Walken — were she sufficiently inebriated, I actually think she'd risk all the glorious aspects of her marriage with Raoul for a single night of bliss with the god Walken — I had tracked down a YouTube video of the man preparing a dinner of, well, salt supported on the framework of a vertically roasting chicken.

As I suspected she might be, Diane was enamored with C. Walken, chef. "Wouldn't you like to be able to find videos like that yourself, whenever you want, on your own phone?" I asked.

"Nice try," she'd said. "You know I don't play video games." Everything online that Diane didn't understand was a "video game." One, of course, she didn't play.

The old-school note I'd left taped to Diane's door listed the breaks I had in my afternoon followed by "Free to chat?"

She marched into my office shortly after three thirty. She plopped on the sofa, put her feet up on the coffee table, and pushed her skirt down between her spread legs. To my dismay, she asked me how Twitter worked. Despite my better judgment, I began to explain what I knew. She put a quick end to my soliloquy at the moment she was convinced I had moved into dead-pan ridicule — she thought I was actually saying *retreating* instead of *retweeting* and accused me of speaking in cartoon voices in an attempt to mock her.

It took me a few moments to clarify my intent. And to convince her that I was not talking in Tweety Bird tones. She recovered quickly, which is one of her strengths. "So what's up? You ready to talk about you and me selling this pop stand for a whole mess of money so that I can start designing my penthouse in the sky? I'll give you fifty-one percent. My final offer."

She was talking about selling the building in which we sat, so that she and Raoul could buy the prime condo on top of the yet-to-be-built structure on the *Daily Camera* site. I did indeed want to talk about those things with Diane, but not urgently. I had already decided that in order to get what I really wanted from Diane, I would employ a give-a-little, get-a-little strategy.

I said, "Did you hear that the Boulder police and the county sheriff were out at your friend's new house on Saturday morning? After the housewarming? The one we weren't invited to."

Diane winced. "I know. I know."

"And?"

"Don't worry. It's going to go away."
"You know that for sure?"
"It doesn't involve you. Believe me, you want no part of it. Forget you know anything, forget what you saw. Everything, anything." She lowered her face so that she was looking down. Then she shook her head again, frantically, like her face was the screen of an Etch A Sketch that she was urgently trying to erase. "God, I was so wishing you didn't know about any of this. You saw the cops?"
"Lauren did."
"I want to curse."
"Then curse."
"I'm trying not to. Self-improvement."
"What's the big deal, Diane? The cops came, they left. They haven't been back. How big a deal can it be?"
I was being disingenuous of course. I knew what the big deal was. I just didn't know the details or the truth. I was determined to learn the details, under the assumption that they would reveal the truth, and I was determined to understand why there was so much secrecy.
My personal stake in the mess was clear, at least to me: if there was someone capable of committing acquaintance rape living or visiting across the lane from my children

and my wife, I wanted to know the details.

"I can't tell you why. It'd be the same as telling you what. And if I told you what, you would immediately wish I hadn't told you. Trust me."

I didn't get it. I knew enough to know that I wished what I knew wasn't true, but I wasn't feeling at all as though I wished I didn't know. I said, "You're sure I wouldn't want to know?"

"What I'm sure about is that even if you thought you wanted to know, after you knew, you would immediately see the error of your ways, and you would agree with me about it being better not to know. But then it would be too late. I'm doing my part to save you from all that regret."

Diane smiled. At rare times, she could be as charming as her husband. Most other times it wasn't a contest.

She knew me well. I have more than my share of anxieties and other garden-variety mental health vulnerabilities. She also knew that regret isn't one of the psychological albatrosses I typically lug around. I'm not someone who wastes hours gazing longingly at water that has passed beneath the bridge. I said, "If what happened was insignificant, we wouldn't be having this conversation. I assume the opposite is true. What you're telling me is that what happened is extremely serious."

The game we were playing felt awkward. She thought she was keeping a confidence, I assumed, for a friend. She didn't know that I already knew the critical letters in her Scrabble tray. All I was trying to ascertain was what word she was planning to construct with those letters. I was continuing to hope it wasn't R-A-P-I-S-T.

Diane chose her next words with atypical care. She seemed to be examining each one for bruises, as though she were selecting Palisade peaches for a tart and wanted to be certain each was unblemished. "There is a dispute, a serious dispute — a conflict of opinion, really — between . . . friends. These things happen."

Acquaintance rape is a dispute? A conflict of opinion between friends? In what universe? I had an uncomfortable thought. *Has Diane taken sides? Does she believe that Burning Man Lady is making a false accusation? She said. He said. And he's right?*

I wondered why Diane would come down on that side of the fence. If I knew no other facts, I would guess that Diane's instinctual inclination would be to support the woman's point of view in a rape allegation.

I went fishing. "These 'friends'? They're

all old friends of yours and Raoul's?"

"Kinda . . . sorta. It was a big party, but there's a core group of couples who have been friends forever, one couple and us go all the way back to Storage Tech. Long time. Mimi and her ex-husband divorced five or six years ago. Nasty, nasty. Tough on Mimi and the kids. Terrence is now living with a trophy on Grand Cayman. Mimi and Hake have been married . . . eighteen months or so. One of the other couples has been part of the group for a . . . much shorter time. He is, was, a golf pro in Denver. He died not too long ago. His widow was at the party alone."

That, I figured, was Hella's patient. It sounded as though Diane's true friendship allegiance was with Mimi, Hake's wife. Perhaps Diane's defense of Hake had been reflexive. It also seemed likely that Hella's patient, the recent widow, sat at the newest place setting at the table. It was possible Diane hadn't connected with her. Or had a reason to doubt her honesty. I put a lot of weight in Diane's judgment. She had a good eye, little narcissism to color her impressions, and she kept her scales of personal justice in reasonable balance.

"A conflict of opinion? Like an argument?" I said. "What's the big deal? Why would an argument between friends involve a police visit? And all this secrecy?"

She stomped her right foot. She didn't pound it; the move was theatrical. In another circumstance, I might have considered it cute. "See, there you go. Alan, you've proven a dozen times — a hundred dozen times — that you can't leave stuff alone. I'm right, aren't I? You'll stick your nose — I don't need to tell you this — in anything. But this time has to be different. You have to leave this alone."

She took a moment to examine my face for signs of my acquiescence. I was pretty sure that she didn't see what she was hoping to see. "Promise me you won't talk to anyone — I mean anyone, Alan — about this."

"About what?"

"About the cops visiting. About what you think."

"I think I have a right to know if there is something going on with my neighbors that might impact my family's well-being."

"See? *Exactly.* You'll just keep fishing and fishing and fishing. I know you will. The cops were there. So don't talk about that. To anyone, okay? Is that so much to ask?"

"Are you and Raoul involved?"

"Alan." Diane brought her hands together

in front of her chest in schoolgirl prayer position. The posture looked as foreign on her as would a tattoo of dripping blood on the side of her neck.

"This isn't like you, Diane. You love telling me shit. *Especially* shit no one else knows. And you know better than anyone that I can be trusted to keep my mouth shut. When I say I won't say anything, I don't say anything."

She stood up. "The stakes are too high. I am protecting people I care about. Okay? This time, trust me. And, just so you know, one of the people I'm protecting is you." She stepped toward the door. Spun back to face me. "Hake played pro football. Big-time. When he was younger. He was a kicker for, like, four games or something at the end of one season for . . . Buffalo, or Cleveland, or Milwaukee — someplace really cold."

"Milwaukee doesn't have a team. You must be thinking Green Bay."

She glared. "Don't correct me. You wanted gossip. I'm giving you gossip."

"That's not gossip," I said. "You're leaving?"

She smiled over her shoulder. "I have to pee."

"I've already talked to people," I said to

her back.

She spun again. "You what? About what? With whom?"

"Sam. Lauren."

"I don't know what either of them knows, really. They're not going to tell you anything. They've both already had the fear of God put in them."

"What does that mean?"

"I really have to pee. And then I have a three forty-five. Listen to Mama, Alan."

I thought it was likely Diane really did have to pee. Her bladder was the size of a plum. I decided to take advantage of the fact.

I asked, "What happened to Mattin's hand? His missing finger?"

She lifted her chin so she could look down her nose at me, just a little. "Years ago he drove up to an accident where a car had flipped. He was helping to pull a kid from the backseat when another man yanked the door open. The metal pinched his finger. Crushed it. There was a fire. He was burned."

"Heroic," I said. "The kid?"

"They saved the kid. Is that enough gossip to shut you up?"

I knew I'd pushed Diane as far as I could. I said, "I talked to Raoul about selling the building. He never got around to telling me why it was necessary."

She rolled her eyes at one of us. Or both of us. "One of the partners," she said, shifting her weight, "who shall remain nameless, has his eye on my penthouse. The one I . . . will have. Raoul says the man is open to an alternative. His wife would prefer to own a duplex downtown, with some yard. Something urban and central but with just a little . . . more of a residential feel."

I saw where she was heading. "This building? Really?"

"Hardly," she said. "This location. The idea is that they would scrape and build a duplex — the wife's sister is a single mom and would take the smaller unit. They would end up with an urban town house with incredible views from the top floors and the rooftop deck, and they would also have two things the condo on Pearl would never have: a private garage, and a yard."

"If we sell," I said.

She frowned. "We're not in the business of spoiling dreams, Alan. Anyway, the city is insisting the partnership have control of some nearby land for construction parking and for staging materials for the project. Our land would be perfect."

"You've thought this all through?"

"Uh . . . yeah. We're talking about my dream home."

"I thought Lee Hill was your dream home."

"A girl's only allowed one dream?"

14

In Colorado, it's hard to lose track of the sun. It rarely goes into hiding for more than two or three days. On most days, I am blessed with the view of the pastel wonders of sunrise as I drive to my office. A half cycle later, the sunset from our Spanish Hills perch is a predictable glory that feels more gorgeous every time I see it.

But the moon? Sometimes I lose the moon for the longest time. I don't know how that happens. I'm either too ignorant about lunar phases to know where in the sky to look, or the thing plays lunar peekaboo during times of the day or night that I don't expect it.

In the nights before and after the damn housewarming, I'd managed to completely lose the moon.

I was out with the dogs for their Monday evening constitutional. A lovely pattern of interlocking lenticular clouds was beginning to rip apart under the insistent force of invisible shearing winds. As I watched the celestial shredding, a telltale light emerged behind the clouds. I waited for the high-level winds to finish turning the clouds to ribbons. Sure enough, behind them was the damn moon. Or at least about a third of it.

My universe felt more ordered. My cell phone vibrated.

Hella Zoet. She had texted me over the lunch hour, while I was at Salt with Lauren, to let me know she didn't have any time she could meet that afternoon. In the text, she said she'd call to try to find some free time to continue the supervision so that I didn't have to wait until the next week's appointment to be brought up to speed on Burning Man Lady. I assumed this was that call.

"Hella," I said. "Hi."

"Is this an okay time?" she asked.

"Sure," I said. "I'm out with the dogs. Be warned, I have only two bars. Now . . . one bar. But my calendar is on my phone. Let's see what we can do."

"Somebody broke into my patient's house today."

"Which patient?" I asked. But I knew.

"Burning Man Lady."

"Was she home? Is she okay?"

"She was at work; she wasn't home. She's okay, but she's nuts about it."

I fell back on my favorite all-purpose therapeutic prompt. I said, "Tell me."

The evidence for the burglary was, I thought, less than compelling.

Hella knew a lot about her patient's coping style. She'd watched her efforts to manage intense loss in times of intense crisis. In those times of emotional upset and potential chaos, Burning Man Lady had shown a predilection for finding some peace by creating order wherever she could create it. After her husband's death, she had reorganized their home, cleaned every nook and cranny — she used a toothbrush on the cabinet hinges — and come up with a new filing system for her financial records.

Before work that Monday — after a third consecutive night with too little sleep — she'd cleaned and vacuumed all the floors in the house, even raking the shag carpet her husband had installed in the master bedroom because he thought it would be romantic.

It was to a completely clean, reordered environment that Burning Man Lady had expected to return home from work a few minutes after six that evening. And with one exception, that is what she found.

The exception was a short series of indentations in the freshly raked shag that she was convinced were footprints. Three to be exact. Two of the footprints led from the honey oak floor that surrounds the rug toward the side of the bed that she still thought of as her husband's. The third of the three footprints led in the other direction, back toward the hardwood floor on the room's perimeter.

Someone, she thought immediately, had stepped toward the bed, pivoted, and stepped away. She thought that the person must have stepped closer in order to open the drawer on the nightstand on that side of the bed.

The footprints on the shag were large. She had no doubt that they'd been made by a man's shoe. She told Hella that she'd squealed in panic, and terror, and rage when she saw the footprints. Certain of an intruder, and fearing that he might still be inside, she had, literally, run back out of the house. She called 911 from the sidewalk in front of her next-door neighbor's home.

Two Boulder police officers responded to the emergency call. She explained about the shag, and the rake, and the footprints.

They searched her home. They found no

signs of forced entry on doors or windows. The officers saw no indication that anything had been stolen or disturbed.

The officers escorted her back inside to try to determine if anything was missing. They had her check for missing prescription drugs or personal papers. Burning Man Lady saw nothing absent from her home.

The cops led her back to the bedroom. One asked if she would point out the specific footprints in the shag. Just to be sure. They lined up on the narrow perimeter of hardwood near the window. "There," she said. "See?"

She held up her phone. "I took pictures," she explained. She used the images on her phone to point out the outlines of each of the footprints. She then leaned over and identified the corresponding indentations on the rug.

She'd sent the pictures she'd taken to Hella. Hella sent the pictures to my phone. I was a little skeptical. If I used my imagination, I could convince myself that the shadows on the green shag rug were footprints. I could also convince myself that I was looking through a microscope at a terrain map of some novel type of fungus.

"What do you think?" I asked Hella.

"She believes that they were footprints."

"The cops, what did they believe?"

Hella said that Burning Man Lady didn't think they believed her. "At some point, she grabbed her purse and dug out the detective's card, the woman detective she'd been interviewed by on Saturday morning at the Boulder Police Department. Detective Davenport."

Lucy. Sam's partner. I didn't know Lucy well, but I knew her. Sam knew Lucy very well. He trusted her instincts. He trusted her with his life. I was curious to learn how Lucy had responded.

Hella continued. "She then told the two patrol cops about being raped on Friday. The ongoing investigation by the Boulder sheriff. She asked them to please call Detective Davenport and tell her about the break-in. They wouldn't. She then asked them to call the patrol officer she met the first morning. Um . . . his name is Heath Wade.

"Right in front of her, the older cop pulled out his phone and he called Officer Wade. He walked away. A couple of minutes later he came back. He said, 'Officer Wade and his partner are coming over. They suggested we try to reach Detective Davenport.' "

Hella said, "I was on the phone with her, learning all this, when Detective Davenport arrived. She said she had to hang up to talk with the detective. I haven't heard back since."

I retracted some of Fiji's leash. She reluctantly joined me on the hard-packed lane. I recognized that I'd allowed myself to become way too much in the dark in regard to Hella's patient's legal situation. I needed to get up to speed. Serious events were occurring for which I didn't have sufficient context.

I was completely aware I had a complicated potential conflict of interest going on. I had convinced myself — perhaps with too much facility — that even if all this hadn't happened across the lane from my home, I'd still be anxious to learn more details from my supervisee. I said, "Hella, before this gets any more complicated, I need to know the rest of the story from last Friday night. Let's get it done. Half an hour? My office? Yours?"

"You live out east, right? I live at the Peloton. Off Arapahoe? You want to come here? It's much more convenient than going all the way downtown."

"That sounds good. Send me directions so I can find your unit."

Seconds later, she said, "Done."

"I should be there within twenty minutes or so. Maybe thirty."

I cupped my hands and called for Emily. I tugged the Havanese away from her determined reconnaissance for prairie dogs. Emily joined up with us as we reached the clearing between the two houses. She was winded. She'd been onto something.

I said, "Foxes?"

Her ears jumped up to ready. She lowered her weight onto her rear legs, prepared to launch. Emily had been protecting us from foxes. Foxes that never bothered us.

Lauren wasn't happy when I explained that I had a supervision crisis I had to deal with in town. In all our years together as a couple, I could count the number of times I'd actually left home on an evening or weekend to deal with a practice emergency. The number was certainly smaller than ten. Most of those ten took place when I was a young therapist. Experience had taught me that there was almost always a way to deal with crises over the phone, and that that way almost always turned out to be more therapeutic than the alternative.

"You have to go in?" she said. "And it's not even for a patient?"

"It's for a patient, but it's not for my patient. It's my supervisee's. And it's not prudent to wait any longer. I hope it won't take long."

"I probably won't stay up," she said.

I told her I didn't expect her to. I said good night to the kids, got in my car, and drove out the lane.

15

Hella greeted me at the door.

She lived in a compact one-bedroom unit on the top floor of a building in a sprawling complex, near 35th — a mere long fly ball from the Boulder PD. She had a great view toward Eldorado. Moonlight still brightened the night sky, the jagged profile of the Flatirons forming a stark silhouette almost due west of her home.

She was wearing a baggy cotton sweater over a long jersey skirt. Her feet were bare. She pointed me toward a beat-up upholstered leather chair across from a sleek sofa that looked new. I sat.

She offered me something to drink. "Water would be great," I said. She poured two glasses from a pitcher with a built-in filter. Boulder's tap water no longer had the cachet it once enjoyed.

She sat across from me, folding her legs beneath her the way she always did in my office. “It’s small. I’m renting for now,” she said. “I’m trying to save for a down payment. Boulder is so expensive. Getting a practice started is so hard. Much harder than I expected. In this economy, I’m . . . I’m going slowly with things like . . . buying houses.”

I wondered why she felt a need to defend her apartment or her decisions about real estate. Were we in my office, and were Hella my patient, I might have explored the comment for further meaning. But Hella wasn’t my patient; she was my supervisee. I filed the impressions among the random information that would become raw material for understanding what happens at other times during the supervision process, either between Hella and her patients or between Hella and me.

One of those perspectives often becomes a mirror of the other.

“It’s nice here,” I said. “You have privacy and a great view. You must have terrific sunsets.”

“During the winter, yeah, if I’m home from work on time. During the summer the sun sets too far to the north. Thanks for saving me a trip back downtown. Once I’m in, I’m . . . in. This is so much better.”

Like psychotherapy, supervision is a relationship that has vague definitions; it is reinvented by every two people who participate in it. One constant, though, is that supervision extends the clinical, and thus legal, responsibility for the patient being treated beyond the therapist, to the supervisor. I was in Hella's apartment after hours because Burning Man Lady was — legally — my patient, too.

I said, "I need to learn what's going on with your patient and with the rape. And what's going on with her now, tonight, with the burglary, or whatever it was. I'm not comfortable not knowing the whole story any longer," I said. "Something you're probably already becoming aware of — when lawyers get involved with cases, they're like mice or roaches. When you see the first one, it never stops there. If your client has a lawyer, that means somebody else in her universe will have to have a lawyer, too. She's talked to the police. The police will talk to the DA. The DA means more lawyers, on both sides. And each lawyer has an associate, and pretty soon . . ." I shrugged a worldly shrug.

She said, "Where would you like me to pick up? I can do this with less detail, if that would help. You know, time-wise."

"No, given the situation, I want to hear

everything you have, but before we get back to what happened on Friday night, have you heard anything more about tonight? The break-in at her house?"

"Yes, she called me back after you and I talked. The officer came to her house. Heath Wade. And the woman detective came to her house. The one from Saturday? She came with her partner. A man."

Lucy Davenport's partner was Sam Purdy.

"They looked around. The woman detective suggested that my patient should spend the night with someone away from her house — with a friend or family. She called a girlfriend, one who hadn't been at that party on Friday. That's where she is right now. The detective said that she would have extra patrols drive by her house during the night to keep a good eye on it."

"Then the detectives thought that there was a break-in?"

"It's hard for me to tell. My patient said the woman detective took some photos of the shag in the master bedroom. Both detectives looked around. They all sat at the kitchen table and asked her some of the same questions the other officers had asked. She said that's about it. My patient hasn't been able to identify anything that's missing from the house. That complicates things, I imagine, for the police."

"It's possible the intruder got interrupted," I said.

My long friendship with Sam Purdy had taught me that routine residential burglary investigations are not a high priority with the police department. A full forensic response wasn't likely to happen unless a detective decided that this break-in wasn't routine. The fact that Lucy and Sam had responded at all meant that one of them, probably Lucy, wasn't convinced the break-in was routine.

"How are you doing with all this?" I asked Hella. I intended that my sudden focus on her feelings be disarming.

She looked away momentarily. I thought her gaze had narrowed a bit when she looked at me again. "This is new territory for me, Alan. Completely new. All the cops, all the lawyers. You know, I've never even treated a rape victim. Not right after, anyway. I've seen women who had been assaulted when they were younger, and the old assaults came up in therapy. But this is new for me. My patient is terrified. She sounded more terrified tonight than she did right after the assault. After the assault her affect was flat for a while. Now she's anxious. She's scared. The break-in, the burglary, whatever it is, has really freaked her out."

"What do you make of that?"

"I guess it's the jeopardy. The sense that the trauma isn't over? Tonight she said, 'This isn't over. This isn't over.' I asked her what that meant and all she said was that she feared her lawyer was right."

"About what?" I asked.

Hella sighed. "On Saturday, he told her that if he was reading this right, the rape was going to be only the first way people were going to try to make her a victim in this case. He said it was his job to keep that from happening. That it's why he needed her to be so discreet."

"Do you know what he meant?"

Hella shook her head. "No. I still don't. I was hoping you would."

"Not yet." I sat back. "Why don't you finish telling me about Friday night? After she decided she liked the bed linens."

Hella closed both eyes gently. She crossed her arms across her chest, briefly resting her fingertips on her shoulders. She exhaled through her lips and folded her hands in her lap. *An affectation?* I was reminded of an actor or singer finding an emotional center prior to a fresh take. I filed it all.

"Everything?" she asked.

On more than one occasion, I've told patients that facts are crap. Mostly, in therapy, I believed that to be true. But at that moment with Hella, I wanted facts. I said, "Yes."

"She brushed her teeth with the brand-new toothbrush. She peed. She changed into the pajamas that were on the bed. She said they were a little small for her, but the fabric was so nice, she loved them. They were much nicer than anything she'd ever had. She found a tag in the top and wrote down the brand and the size — they were a six, she wears an eight — and she put the note in her purse. She was hoping she could find a pair and that they weren't too expensive for her.

"She was about to climb into bed. She heard a knock on the door. There was a short robe on a hanger on the back of the bedroom door. She pulled that on over her pajamas before she opened the door. She made a point of telling me she was dressed modestly.

"It was her host. He had changed from the clothes he had worn during dinner. He was wearing cotton pants, thin, like exercise pants, she thought. And a T-shirt. A tight T-shirt with long sleeves. He was barefoot, even though the house was kind of chilly.

"She mentioned that she thought it was odd that his shirt was so tight. She couldn't imagine sleeping in something that tight.

"He was carrying two small glasses. Little wineglasses? She didn't recognize what they were, what kind of glass. She said that kind of thing happens all the time with these friends. They have food, and drinks, and utensils, and gadgets, and things that she doesn't recognize. They serve her things she doesn't know how to eat. She said she always does what she can to disguise her ignorance. That's important to her.

"So, she was thinking that he was offering her something new to drink. After the other guests had left, the wine they had was the same wine that had been served during the party. It was served in regular, big wine-glasses.

"The man, her friend, told her that he and his wife weren't ready to go to bed. He wondered if, since she didn't have to drive anywhere, she would like to come back out by the fire and have a nightcap with them.

"She said she thanked him but told him she was tired and thought she'd go to bed, because she was eager to head back home early the next morning. He said something about how disappointed his wife would be

— that she so much loved to have company stay late after parties. How it was one of her favorite things.

"She told me that puzzled her, that she hadn't known that about her friend. After all the time they had spent together, she always thought the hostess was the one person in the group who was most ready for parties to end. Reluctantly, she agreed to join them in the family room. The fire in the fireplace was almost out." Hella sipped some water. "And the man's wife wasn't there.

"I've talked about this with you before, Alan. At least I think I have. There's a smaller social group she is part of — a group of friends who were all at the housewarming. She considers them . . . above her. I don't say that to be condescending to her — my patient is a sincere, down-to-earth, unpretentious woman — but it's how she perceives the situation. Her friends are all wealthy — she makes them sound very wealthy, but I don't really know how to judge that. And they are all accomplished people. Successful in their careers, their lives. They're sophisticated. They've traveled to a million places, eaten at every restaurant around. They know other important people. They go to cool events. They have season tickets everywhere. Sports. Theater. They go on trips together and stay at each other's vacation homes.

"My patient is a young widow. She works a full day in an office. Struggles to pay her bills. Dinner out, if it happens, is Chili's or Applebee's. When she was initially drawn into this group with her husband — they were invited after her husband had started giving a couple of the wives golf lessons — she tried to fit in by being as accommodating as she could. She bakes well. She would always bring cakes, or scones, or cookies, or something for her friends. When any of her new friends asked her for a favor that she felt she could do, she went out of her way to try to do it. Always. As a group, and as individuals, they were all so generous to her and her husband with invitations and dinners out. The men included her husband in their golf games. They all went fishing. You get the picture. She always felt an obligation to try to reciprocate. She *liked* being able to reciprocate. She liked that she could do something her friends appreciated.

"I almost forgot — after her husband died, two of the men even helped her decide how to invest his life insurance money. She feels very indebted to them for that — she has no expertise with that kind of thing.

"That night? She didn't feel she could say no to something as simple as an invitation to stay up a little past her bedtime and have one final drink with her host and hostess by the fire. She felt as though she couldn't turn it down."

"Okay," I said. Hella's assessment of the relationship dynamics felt spot-on to me.

"She went back and sat down on the same chair as before. After she and the host talked for a while — they talked about maybe running the Bolder Boulder in the spring, among other things — she remembers asking him when his wife would be downstairs to join them. She doesn't actually remember if he answered. She thought he changed the subject, that he said something about the port. That's what they were drinking. Port. He told her it was made in California by a winemaking friend he'd met through Francis, um, crap — oh, God, the *Godfather* director guy, what's his name? I'm terrible with celebrity names."

"Francis Ford Coppola," I said.

"Him. Some friend of Francis Ford Coppola made the port from . . . Zinfandel grapes that the host had grown on his land in Napa. Do you know wine? Do I have that right? Or does that sound completely stupid?"

I had friends who knew wine. Peter, who died while living in the house across the lane, the house where Hella's patient had sipped the port in question, could have answered any questions about Napa and Zinfandel and port. I had no doubt that Raoul, who'd been at the same housewarming, could have told a charming story or two about the process and the people. Me? Not so much. "I know what I like, Hella. I'm not an expert."

"At some point he asked her if she liked it. The port. This is where things start to get really fuzzy for her. She doesn't remember replying to his question. She doesn't even remember whether she liked the port or not.

"She thinks he poured a second glass. So one of them must have finished the first one, right? She doesn't remember whether the second glass was for him or for her.

"The next thing she remembers is an image. When she first went back out, she sat down on the same big leather chair she'd been on before. Earlier, the host and hostess had kind of cuddled together on the other one.

"The image, the visual memory, is of a man standing above her. The guy is wearing a cap of some kind. She said it was a light-colored cap with a pattern. Flat on top. And it was tight. Not like a ski cap. Because she remembers being on the chair, the 'above her' part of the image confuses her. She thought she might have slouched down in the chair she was on. Or she may have been on a different piece of furniture in the house and she just doesn't remember moving. She even mentioned it's possible that a man was standing on the arms of the chair. She's not sure. She doesn't know how the man in the image could have been so 'above' her."

I was confused. "It was the same man? The man who gave her the port?"

Hella's expression made it clear to me that her patient was having trouble with that detail as well. "I asked her that. She's sure it was her host. But she doesn't actually *remember* that it was him."

She waited to see if, or how, I would react. I was in therapist mode. I kept my reaction to myself. Plenty of research has demonstrated that eyewitnesses often fill in blank spaces in their memories. They just do.

Hella said, "But the image she describes is of a man standing above her, with the cap thing. That's clear in her memory. She's adamant about it, that she didn't imagine it."

Hella, I sensed, was expecting me to

disbelieve her. Or challenge her. At face value, that made no sense. Hella knew the story she was telling; I didn't. Which suggested to me that at some point in the narrative, Hella's patient had expected the same — she'd expected not to be believed by Hella. I filed it.

Hella continued. "She says that the man who was hovering above her had pulled down the front of his pants. The pants had an elastic waistband. He pulled them down, and he'd pulled his genitals out over the waistband so that the elastic went back *behind* his scrotum — actually, behind . . . everything. So, his genitals, everything, were completely exposed. Above her."

Hella looked at me. "And, she says, he had an erection. When he was standing over her."

I did my best not to react.

"She remembers that the man was talking to her. While he was there, above her. Always talking, never stopping. In this monotone-like, calm voice. She called it 'hypnotic.' She remembers thinking it all felt surreal to her. *Artificial* is the word she used. He kept repeating her name, over and over and over. Other things, too, but she doesn't remember the other words he was saying."

"Any affective memory?" I asked. "For her?"

"I asked her the same thing. She said she felt 'separate' — as though it wasn't really happening to her. Dissociated, I guess. She says that she was there and she wasn't there, she was in the room with the man and she wasn't. She remembers trying to move her arms and having the sensation that they weren't even attached to her body.

"She isn't sure what room it was, whether they were still by the fireplace when all this happened. She says that she remembers at one point having a thought that they weren't alone, that someone else had to be hearing everything. What was going on. How embarrassing it was going to be that his pants were down and that he had an erection.

"She was afraid of being, I don't know, embarrassed. Of getting caught with him. She said that."

I said, "She remembers a fear of being discovered?" That was a far cry from hoping to be discovered and rescued.

"Yes," Hella said.

I got the impression that Hella didn't see the same disconnect that I was seeing in her patient's story. I wondered what that meant. And I wondered about the quality of her patient's recollections. What part of the story was memory and what was confabulation.

"And she says that was the last thing she remembered. At that point. Until the next morning."

"God," I said.

Hella looked beat up. Physically depleted.

She stood in front of the sofa. She stretched her neck, raising her chin so that her eyes faced toward the ceiling for a few seconds. "This is exhausting," she said. "For me, right now. This is the first time I've done this, told this story to anyone. It is so hard for me to say it out loud, to you, right now, that it helps me understand how hard it is for her to be living with what happened to her."

There were lots of things I could have said right then. I chose to say nothing at all. Some of what I might have said might have been soothing to Hella. Some of it would have offered her an opportunity to get some distance from her patient's experience. Most all of it would have gotten in the way of the work she and I needed to do. And that would be the most serious supervisory sin.

Hella sat back down. This time, her legs were out to one side, not curled beneath her. The nails on her big toes were painted a starkly different shade than the nails on the other toes. The big toes were a medium pink. The little toes were all dark burgundy.

She sipped some more water. "She woke the next morning at six twenty or so. There was a clock on a table by the bed, that's how she knew.

"She says she tried to remember what time she'd gone to bed, to figure how long she'd been asleep. But she couldn't do the arithmetic. It wasn't that she couldn't remember what time she went to bed, it was that the simple arithmetic was stumping her. She couldn't figure out how many hours were between eleven thirty or whatever and six twenty. That's how disoriented she was feeling when she woke up.

"The surroundings puzzled her initially, too. The room, the bed, the linens, the pajamas she was wearing, everything. The smells.

"She stressed how foreign the room smelled to her. Not bad, not noxious, just not familiar. She said that for a second, she was even thinking she was waking in the hospital. I'm not sure what that means, or if it's important, but when she woke up she was acutely aware of the way everything smelled."

Hella looked at me. She was giving me a chance to add some commentary. I didn't. I waited. She recognized that I was waiting. "She said it took her a minute or two to create a context that would explain where she was. The big party, the drafting tables, the drinking, the staying over. She said until she got there — until she figured it all out — she felt frightened. Her heart had started racing. She was panicky. She said everything felt dangerous to her until she remembered why she was there.

"She initially thought that she was feeling so frightened because of the disorientation, because she didn't know where she was. Not — at least not right away — because of anything that had happened to her. She didn't yet have any memory of what had happened to her." Hella looked me in the eyes. "Does that make sense?"

"Does it to you?" I said.

Hella nodded. "Completely. I don't think I buy that most of her fear was because of the disorientation of waking up and feeling lost, Alan. We've all done that. It's not that foreign of a sensation. The where-am-I panic goes away pretty quickly. I think, even if she didn't know it consciously, she still must have had a sense that she'd been violated the night before. That's what she was reacting to emotionally — that's why she was so frightened. It wasn't just the disorientation.

"The fear she was experiencing must have been awful, I think. Those first few minutes? She was disoriented, sure, but she had just been raped, right? She had to be trying to find a way to make sense of all that, even without conscious awareness or memory. How she was feeling? I can only . . . imagine."

"Okay," I said. The simple word was intended to reduce friction.

Hella went on. "Right away, she said, when she figured out where she was, she wanted to go home. Just get out to her car and go home. Her purse was on the bedside table. She grabbed it to make certain her car keys and her phone were there. That's all she wanted to know. That she had her phone and she had a way home.

"She grabbed the phone to check for messages. But it wasn't turned on. She immediately thought the phone battery must have died for some reason, because she never turns it off when she's away from home. Never. She made a big, big point of that.

"She hit the power switch and the phone started to come on, right away. It powered right up. The battery was fine. She said she immediately thought, *Someone turned my phone off.*"

"Right away?" I asked. "Her first explanation was that someone must have turned off her phone?"

"Yes," Hella said. "That was it. She said she tried to remember something from the night before that would explain it any other way. A conversation with someone about the phone. A problem with the phone. Some reason that she might have agreed to turn it off overnight. She couldn't remember talking about it, or thinking about it, with anyone. So she was sure that someone had gone into her purse — that's where she keeps it — and turned her phone off. Because she knows she wouldn't have done it. That freaked her out."

Hella filled her cheeks with air, and she sighed. She said, "And there's more."

In my business, there usually is.

16

"When she got the phone powered back up, it was set to vibrate, not to ring. She maintains she doesn't do that. Because she keeps it in her bag, she missed calls when it would vibrate. She said she's the one who's always embarrassed when her phone rings at the wrong time. At a movie, in church."

I wanted to be sure I understood. "Someone switched her phone to vibrate, and then someone turned it off? That was her conclusion?"

"Right."

"But that person left the phone in her purse? She could have turned it back on at any time? Does that make sense to you?" I asked.

Hella said, "Someone did not want her phone to ring."

Hella's reply lacked any confidence. I said, "Okay. Someone did not want her phone to ring. Keep going. Why?"

Hella exhaled audibly before she said, "He — her host — didn't want to be interrupted while he . . ." She raised her eyebrows. "Raped her."

I said, "Or whoever raped her didn't want anything to interrupt her sedation after he raped her. Or both. I'm thinking either, or both."

"I didn't think about that, Alan." Hella involuntarily tightened the muscles in her jaws. I could see tendons twitching at her temples. She pulled her painted toes under the tent of her skirt and tucked the fabric beneath her feet. "After she checked messages — there weren't any — she says she listened for sounds in the house, indications that anyone else was already awake upstairs, or maybe even out in the kitchen. She told me she said a silent prayer that she was the first one up. She wanted to get dressed and get out to her car without seeing anyone.

"She got off the bed to change into her clothes. And immediately, she had to catch herself. She was dizzy. She grabbed on to something, a chair, to steady herself. When she was finally able to stand up straight holding on to the chair, the dizziness passed, at least momentarily. But she said that standing there she became aware that the pajamas she was wearing felt funny. The bottoms felt, you know, wrong. She tried to straighten them with one hand while she held on with the other. She was thinking they'd gotten twisted during the night. But when she looked they were on her straight, that wasn't the problem.

"That's when she remembered that when she put them on the night before, she thought they were too small. *That must be it, right?* she told herself. *Why they feel so funny. They're the wrong size.* No big deal. She started to take them off to get dressed to go home. She took off the bottoms first. As she pushed them down off her waist, you know, leaning over so she could step out of them, she saw the tag. On the waistband. But the tag was in the front, not in the back.

"She knew she wasn't thinking clearly, but she also knew that wasn't right. That the tag shouldn't be in front. And she thought, of course, *That's why the pajamas feel funny.* But seeing the tag in front also caused her to remember that she had written down the brand of the pajamas the night before. It was like each little fragment of memory, each clue about things that happened the night before, gave her another little fragment of memory that she could use to connect to the next one.

"She'd written down the brand because

she liked the pajamas. Wanted to see if she could find a pair in a store. But to do it, to find the tag, she'd had to unbutton the whole top and take it off so she could see the tag that was sewn into the neckline. She was sure she would have been able to tell if she'd actually put on the bottoms backward, with the tag in the front. If she had, she could have just looked down to read the tag or, had she noticed the bottoms were on backward, read the tag as she took them off to turn them around." Hella took a deep breath. "I think I am making that sound more complicated than it really was. Her conclusions make sense to me, Alan. Am I thinking about all this correctly?"

"Sounds fine," I said.

"Anyway, she's puzzled by all of it. She knows it doesn't add up right. She can't figure out why she slept with her pajamas on backward. At that point, she isn't considering any . . . alternative explanation.

"And she's still puzzled about what happened with her phone. Altogether, she's feeling disoriented, she's still woozy, and now, with the phone thing, and the balance thing, and the pajama thing, she's thinking that she may still be a little drunk, or maybe a lot hungover.

"She spots the robe and remembers putting it on to go sit by the fire the night before. It's tossed on the end of the bed, not hung on its hanger on the back of the door. She says that's not like her — not to have hung it back up. She told me she's one of those guests who puts everything away, leaves everything clean and neat.

"More pieces of memory start returning. The robe caused her to remember her host knocking on the door and his insistent invitation for another drink.

"And then she remembered sitting by the fire with . . . her host . . . him . . . and the drink he gave her. She describes a dark liquid, a small wineglass; she wouldn't remember it was port until later. She remembers his wife never coming back downstairs. She tried to remember how much she'd had to drink. At that point she was thinking one little glass, or two.

"She maintains that none of it is like her. She drinks socially, wine with dinner, a margarita with a friend, a beer after golf, that sort of thing, but she's not a big drinker. She says she can't recall the last time she was really drunk. She said it was probably just after college, during the first few years of her marriage."

"Does that coincide with what you know about her?" I asked. "Her drinking habits?"

"Yes, absolutely. She has some relationship issues, Alan. Self-esteem problems, sure. She's half-lost, remember? But substances aren't one of her problems. She's not a big drinker.

"So then she takes off the pajama top, sees her bra where she left it — it's on a chair by the bed. She pulls it on, and she reaches for her underwear, which she'd placed beneath the skirt she wore to the party. The skirt was nicely folded on the same chair, just the way she thought she would have left it. Her panties were where she left them.

"But before she could put the underwear on, she gasped, and she froze. She held her breath. Her mouth hung open and she thought, *No!* Then, *NO, NO, NO!*

"She said, 'No.' Out loud. She was actually afraid she'd said it too loudly. She covered her mouth. She said that's when she knew."

My breathing grew shallow.

"Alan, she's really clear about all this, the details of getting dressed that morning. There was no doubt in her voice when she told me this part of the story.

"She stood up. She still hadn't touched the panties. She was standing in front of that chair near the bed. Her feet were about a foot apart. And she reached down with her left hand — she's left-handed — and she touched her vagina. She felt herself. Slowly. Carefully. She started to cry, she said. Her eyes just completely filled with tears. She could feel her chin quivering. She said, 'I was crying like a little girl.'

"She says that at that moment she was completely sure that somehow, some way, she'd had sex the night before. Intercourse. And that she didn't remember any of it happening. At all."

I was hesitant to interrupt, but I couldn't make sense of the story as Hella was telling it. I tried for a clarification. "The rapist didn't use a condom? He ejaculated inside of her? And she felt the presence of semen the next morning?"

"No. Not exactly."

I waited. Hella's discomfort seemed to redouble. "What exactly?" I asked. "What were the sensations she felt with her fingers that indicated she'd had . . . intercourse — that she'd been raped, vaginally — the night before?"

Hella said, "She could just tell. She said she tried to remember what had happened. Desperately. Any detail. Anything about it. At first, she couldn't find a trace of it in her awareness. Nothing.

"Her breathing sped up like she was hyperventilating and she started feeling woozy again. She stepped backward and she lowered herself down to sit on the edge of the bed. To try to steady herself." Hella's face blossomed into an expression of deep compassion. "She missed the edge of the bed, Alan. She misjudged the edge when she was sitting, and she barely grazed the mattress as she fell down hard. She ended up banging her spine against the sideboard of the bed frame and then she fell even harder still against the floor.

"She sat there on the floor, where she fell, she said, for a few minutes. She was weeping. She was hurting from the fall. She was desperately trying to remember what had occurred the night before.

"The fact that she'd had sex and that she didn't remember it? She couldn't quite believe that could really happen. And her wooziness was really concerning her, especially after she fell trying to sit down. But she couldn't recall anything at all that helped her make any sense of it, and that was terrifying to her. She had no memories of sex. Of being romantic with anyone. Of being intimate with anyone. Of being forced. Of being hurt. No good sex, no bad sex. No rape, no assault on her that included sex.

"Just this absolute certainty that she'd had

intercourse the night before."

In a neutral voice, I asked, "Do you understand that certainty, Hella?"

Hella said, "Let me finish this, please. After a few minutes, she pulled herself to her feet. She threw back the bedclothes and examined the sheets. She was looking for stains, dried wet spots, anything that might indicate that something sexual had happened on the bed. But she didn't see a thing. She even looked for hair. Body hair. Pubic hair. She found nothing.

"There's a long mirror on one wall. She looked at her body. For bruises, or scratches, or hickeys, or anything. Nothing, she saw nothing. But her back was already turning bright red from the fall, where she'd hit the sideboard.

"She took off the bra. Examined her breasts for marks. Nothing.

"Suddenly she felt unsteady again. She said that was the first moment when she considered that she might have been drugged. Right then.

"She sat on the bed. That time she didn't miss it. She forced herself to try to go through every detail of what happened after she had agreed to spend the night. She thought she might remember taking something. You know, a pill, something for a headache. Anything that might explain how off she was feeling. That's when she started remembering more and more little pieces of what happened out by the fire.

"She remembered him pouring the second glass of port. She says she started crying again when she suddenly recalled the image of the man with the cap standing over her with his erection not far from her face. She said she stayed with that memory as long as she could, trying to find more detail, to remember more. She forced herself to concentrate on it. Because . . . she wanted to see his face, she said, not his dick. Those words — she used those words."

I had a dozen questions, but I was determined not to intrude. I was wondering how long Hella could stay with this story.

"What she did next I didn't really understand at first, but she explained it later, and it's kind of . . . horrifying . . . to me." Hella took a deep breath.

I said, "No hurry. Take your time."

"I'm okay," she said, as though she were convincing herself. "Sitting on the bed that morning, she closed her eyes tight, and she slowly began to open her mouth, with her lips pressed up and down so that they covered her teeth. A half inch at first, then an inch, then a little more, and then a little more than that. Before she got her mouth all the way open she felt a familiar, sharp pain shooting upward in her face. It was in her jaw, on the right side, below her ear, and then up into her skull. 'Like a hot spike,' she said.

"And that's when she really, really started to cry. She fell facedown onto the bed and forced her face into one of the pillows on the bed so that no one else in the house would hear her sobbing."

Hella stopped to compose herself. She sipped water. Opened her eyes wide. Closed them tight. She said, "Okay. I'm okay. She has TMJ, Alan. She's had it for years. She gets terrible jaw pain in certain situations. Eating certain foods. A tall sandwich. Corn on the cob. A hard piece of fruit or candy. One of the things that causes the pain is . . . performing oral sex. On a man. She says she almost never does it. It was a problem in her relationship with her husband. A big deal for him. She'd actually talked to me about that before, about the fact that oral sex causes her such jaw pain, about the conflict it caused in her marriage.

"For her? The pain she felt that morning was absolute proof to her that she'd . . . performed oral sex the night before. She was completely befuddled by that. The intercourse? She said she could imagine a possible circumstance where she would, maybe, choose to do that. Have sex with . . . a man. She missed . . . that.

"But she could not imagine a circumstance where she would choose to perform oral sex on someone that night. Or . . . any night. She said it just would not have happened. She couldn't think of any circumstances that would cause her to *decide* to do that. The pain afterward is too excruciating for her. For days, it hurts her to eat. She gets headaches for a week, sharp pain in her ear.

"Alan, at this point, she tells me she's thinking a lot of things. I haven't written them down anywhere. I just haven't. I know I haven't written them down because I think someone might use them against her, not to help her. I don't know what to do with what I know. I could use your guidance about all of this."

I hadn't been writing anything down, either. Hella could see that clearly. "Tell me," I said.

"Her first thought after she recognized she'd had sex — intercourse — the night before was, *What did I do?* As though she might have done it intentionally and forgotten. That was her initial reaction. Then she said she thought, *What is my friend going to think?* She meant his wife. See, initially, she was reacting as though she was responsible. She assumed she was responsible.

"And then she became worried about the consequences. *Oh my God, I'm not on the pill. What if I'm pregnant with his baby?*"

I had a question for Hella. I was wondering if — during those initial moments when she was trying to sort out her responsibility for what had happened — her patient was already certain that it had been her host who was responsible for the sexual contact. If she was, how was she so certain? Did she remember something? See something? Smell something? Was it simple process of elimination? Or had the certainty come later?

I waited.

Hella went on. "She said she even tried to calculate her menstrual cycle, but she was so upset she couldn't remember the first day of her last period. She still couldn't get her brain to work right. Her memory. Her concentration.

"Then she said it all hit her, all at once. What had happened to her the night before became clear. She said she felt like she was suddenly immersed in the reality. The words she used were 'I was dunked in the truth. It was like a baptism.'

"She thought, *Dear, dear Lord* — those are her words, not mine — *I was raped.* Just like that. No 'What if I was raped?' Just, *Dear, dear Lord, I was raped.*

"She said her very next thoughts were, *He raped me. He drugged me, and he made me give him a blow job, and he raped me.* She used his name, Alan. She said his name to me then. *My own goddamn friend raped me.*"

"Her host?" I clarified.

"Yes."

"With conviction?" I asked.

Hella hesitated. "Yes."

I came back around to one of my questions from earlier. I asked it. "Did she have a specific memory, Hella? Of the rape? Of the oral sex? Of the rapist? Or did she reach a conclusion because of what she felt the next morning?"

Hella didn't answer.

"Did she identify her host because . . . he was there?"

Hella's breath caught momentarily in her throat. She coughed. She narrowed her eyes as she looked at me. She shrugged. She shook her head. She made a perplexed face. "He was the only man in the house, Alan."

I kept my tone idling in neutral. "Was it memory? Or conclusion?"

"I don't . . . know. She said that at that

moment she knew her friend had raped her. And had drugged her. I didn't question that. Should I have questioned that?"

I reviewed the pieces that felt factual. She remembered her host serving her the port. If she had been drugged — and I assumed a toxicology screen would determine whether that was true — it seemed likely that the drug was delivered in the port. If that were true, it certainly meant that her host had drugged her.

The rape? It seemed obvious that the same man who drugged her would be the prime suspect responsible for raping her.

I said, "I'm not saying you should have or shouldn't have questioned her. Your role with her isn't as an investigator. I'm trying to help you see that something that your patient was saying is still, apparently, unclear — even to her — yet you seem to be comfortable encouraging her to adopt a specific explanation as final. I'm wondering if that is the best way to help her through this ordeal. Do you see what I'm saying? Do you feel you need to agree to accept a certain version as true in order to help her?"

"What's the alternative?"

"Accepting that she is telling you what feels true to her."

Hella pondered the distinction. "I guess I

want to believe her. I think I *do* believe her. There was nothing insincere about what she was telling me."

"Why do you want to believe her? What's that about?"

"I need to be supportive of her. Of what she's been through. Don't I? Because it was so apparent to me at the end that she believed that she'd been assaulted. And drugged. By her *friend.*"

"Then believe that. Believe that she believes it. But in these circumstances, with the facts that you've described, believing that she believes it is a very different thing from believing she knows exactly what happened. It sounds to me as though she was desperately trying to make sense of some horrendous circumstances. Anyone in the same circumstances would have felt similar desperation. You need to be available to help her with that, too. The doubt, if it's there. The desperation to find certainty, if it's there. She found an explanation that helped her make sense of the memories she has currently. Is it the right explanation? Perhaps it is. Could there be another one? I don't know. But I don't think you know either. I'm trying to help you see that you have latitude here as her therapist, and that you need to make sure that you allow that latitude to be of the most possible help to your patient."

"You don't believe her?" Hella asked.

I leaned forward a little. "Is it important that I believe her, Hella? Is it important that you believe her? Is that how you see this, clinically?"

She opened her eyes wide. My questions were completely baffling to her.

I said, "What's going on here? Between you and your patient? Between you and me? She wants you to believe that her construction of events is accurate. You apparently want me to believe you that her construction of events is accurate. See the process? The parallel?"

"I don't know what you want me to do next. I don't get — I'm not sure what you're telling me to —" Hella sat back, turned her head away. She looked out the window in the general direction of the Flatirons.

"What?" I asked.

"It's kind of ironic. I was just reflecting on what she said next. What she was thinking about after she realized she'd been raped. And forced to have oral sex. And after she knew she'd been drugged. She said she started thinking about TV shows. *CSI* and *Law & Order.* Do you know them?"

"I know of them."

"She watches them all the time. She said that's what she started thinking about. Those shows."

"Anything in particular?"

"Yes. She said, 'I know nobody is going to believe me.' "

"Because?" I asked.

"Because, she said, that's what happens on the shows. When they do cases like this. She said, at first nobody believes the victim." Hella turned back to me. On her face was a tenuous smile. "And apparently that's what happens in supervision, too."

17

I was tempted to give Hella a version of my "patients lie" soliloquy. At one point or another, all of my supervisees heard it from me.

I consider the reality that patients lie to be an essential truth about psychotherapy. Patients lie frequently. Some, of course, more than others. Most of the time, the lies are irrelevant to anything but the therapy and, from a therapeutic process perspective, are often as valuable, and sometimes more valuable, than an initial recounting of truth. But the truth for young therapists to remember is: patients lie.

Occasionally, the stories patients tell are just that, stories. More often the stories are true, but some details are false. Every lie has permutations. The intent behind every mistruth is different. Some are unconscious, some are inadvertent. Some are flat-out sociopathic.

But I decided it wasn't the time for that speech with Hella. I didn't think that Burning Man Lady was lying to Hella. I didn't even think she was lying to herself. Nor was I seriously entertaining the possibility that her story was just flat-out untrue. Neither, unfortunately, was I sure that it was entirely true. My concern was that Burning Man Lady was stretching the facts that she did know in order to cover the void that encompassed all that she did not know.

We all extrapolate, every day. As an exercise in truth-seeking, it is a reasonable strategy. In therapy, especially the kind of therapy of discovery that I do, factual issues like these shake themselves out over time, usually revealing important facets of the character and emotional state of the patient doing the shaking. Only in rare circumstances do I feel any short-term imperative about sorting truth from fiction in therapy.

But the story Hella was telling me about Burning Man Lady wasn't only about therapy. It was also about felonies: a rape, a drugging, maybe a burglary. And already about cops and lawyers. An accused. Soon, courts, maybe, and jails.

I had a question or two that I hoped would clarify for me how things were stacking up on the veracity scale. I started with the one that felt like it might be simplest to answer. I was wrong, it turned out, about the simple part.

I asked, "Does she know if the man who raped her wore a condom?"

Hella's sudden glance at me was a few degrees shy of a glare. I didn't think she liked my question. The fact that she didn't like my question was undoubtedly as significant as the answer she might provide.

Hella said, "She did not . . . find semen that morning. When she . . . examined herself. He either wore a condom, or he didn't ejaculate inside her. Or it's possible he didn't ejaculate at all. I've done some reading. That happens . . . during rape."

Hella was right; it does happen. Although it was clear that Hella and I needed to discuss the dynamics of rape — that it's a crime of violence and domination, not a crime of sex — I didn't want to get sidetracked right then with a tutorial on the behavior of rapists. "Yet the next morning she was sure she'd been penetrated vaginally — probably against her will — hours before? Was there an indication other than semen?"

"She said she just knew. That she could tell."

I sat in silence, allowing Hella a moment

to digest the assumptions buried in those simple declarations.

I eased off the accelerator, tapped the brakes, and slowly depressed the clutch. I allowed my voice to find neutral. I said, "How do *you* feel about your patient's assertion, absent memory, that she had engaged in intercourse — without her consent — the night before?"

My rephrased question changed the climate in the room. The atmosphere altered suddenly, as if a low-pressure ridge had blown into the apartment and parked over the compact kitchen. Hella looked as uncomfortable as she had during our entire conversation. Maybe even more uncomfortable. She squirmed. She swallowed. She opened her mouth twice to speak before she finally managed to say, "I feel that she was telling the truth, Alan."

"That's not my question, Hella."

More silence. I gave her time. I knew she was determined to outwait me. My time was not unlimited. I said, "You seem comfortable accepting your patient's assertion that she knew she'd had intercourse — nonvolitional intercourse — despite having no memory of the act, and despite the absence of any semen or other . . . evidence."

Hella was ready. "I think she's being . . .

objective about it. What she remembers. She maintains she can tell." Hella then nodded her head, as though she was pleased with her reply.

"Still doesn't answer my question, Hella."

"She only remembers what she remembers."

"And that is where I keep getting lost," I said. "The *objective* part about what she remembers. Can you help me with that? So I can understand your certainty about her . . . certainty."

I suddenly felt a different doubt about the woman's certainty. Was the certainty something women would know, would be familiar with, but that I wouldn't know? I tried to remember whether I had ever had a similar conversation with a woman before. About whether she could tell hours later that she'd had intercourse with a condom-wearing man. I didn't believe that I had.

This could all have been about my ignorance. I backed off my confrontation and asked for some information. "Hella? Can you provide any guidance to me? I'm ignorant about this. I'm sorry. I need to understand it better." I was also thinking that Hella needed to understand it better.

I expected her resistance to take a respite as I backed off. I was wrong. Hella turned red. I waited as the red faded to pink, then as the pink began to fade to something cadaver-like. I wondered again if I'd inadvertently crossed some line with my question.

"My blood sugar is low," she said. "I need something to eat."

She rushed to the kitchen and went straight to the refrigerator. She poured and chugged a few ounces of orange juice. I watched her use a big french knife to whack off a chunk of hard cheese — Parmigiano, maybe. With her back to me, she ate the cheese in quick, small, bunny-like bites.

I pulled out my phone to check the time. It was getting late. I had a text from Lauren. I hadn't even noticed that the phone had vibrated in my pocket.

Much longer? my wife wanted to know. She'd sent the text almost thirty minutes earlier. **Fraid so** I replied before I hit SEND.

Good night she wrote back almost immediately. **Dogs need out.**

In my office, doing supervision or therapy, I never would have stolen a moment for a text exchange with my wife. I realized that I, like Hella, was taking advantage of the unusual circumstances of our meeting.

After a swallow, before the next bite of cheese, still standing at the counter in the kitchen, and still facing away from me, Hella said, "My manners? God. Can I get you something, Alan?"

"I'm good," I said. What I was thinking was, *I'd really love to see the replay. What just happened here?*

When Hella returned to the sofa a few minutes later, some color had returned to her face. She sat this time with her knees up, her legs pulled tight against her upper body, her arms around her legs. The bicolor toenails were peeking out from beneath the draped skirt. Other than crouching behind the couch and peeking at me over the cushions, it was the most protected posture I could imagine for her.

"Sorry about that," she said. "It ambushes me sometimes. My blood sugar. Sometimes it just drops, out of the blue. All my life. I'm sorry."

"You're okay?" I said.

"Yes, thanks. What you were asking? Your question? Earlier? Well, the truth is that . . . I don't know the answer," she said.

"Okay. Does that mean that the question of your patient's certainty about sexual activity on Friday night is an open one in your mind, too?"

Hella shook her head. "No, it's not. I think . . . she's telling the truth."

"What she believes to be true? Or what she knows to be true?"

Hella hesitated. With absolutely no assurance in her tone, she said, "Both."

"No filling in of blank spaces?"

"We all do that, don't we?" Hella asked.

"Again, doesn't answer my question," I said. The process was starting to make me spin.

"You want me to be objective?" The way she spoke the last word left it hanging in the air lonely and forlorn. I wondered where Hella was heading. She sighed.

To my ear, it was a frustrated sigh. I hoped that it was a sign that the resistance she was mounting with me was feeling some strain. She continued, "Actually, I can't provide that guidance. Not . . . right now. Maybe . . . I don't know."

I was unsure what Hella was telling me. But I had a sudden feeling that she was telling me something that was much more significant than the answer to the relatively simple question I was asking. In doing psychotherapy, and occasionally in doing supervision, there are innocuous-appearing moments that are actually laden with immense affective mass.

To an outside observer, those moments may seem inconsequential. But, sometimes in an instant, the emotional gravity in the clinical interaction goes from negligible to extraordinary. From one G to six G's. This was one of those moments. Because of Hella's innocuous words — *I'm not sure I can provide that guidance* — and her simple admission that she could not help me understand something that was happening between her and me, let alone between her and her patient, I suspected that my supervision with Hella was changing in an essential way that I didn't yet comprehend.

I couldn't predict what would happen next in the room. I suspected that the supervision session would turn out to be as much about Hella as a therapist as about her therapy of Burning Man Lady.

The stakes for me as a supervisor were high right then. Part of my role had nothing to do with Burning Man Lady's psychotherapy. A big part of my role as supervisor involved assisting Hella to reveal what she needed to reveal, so that whatever limitations or conflicts she was feeling in the current treatment wouldn't impact, or afflict, her care of future patients.

I absolutely needed to make the supervisory moment safe for her to do that. I decided to say what I needed to say, but nothing more. I said, "I don't think I understand, Hella. But I think this is a very important moment. Between you and me."

Initially, she seemed to be content with the silence that followed my words. We each waited almost motionless, our breathing so controlled that neither of our exhales would have budged a candle flame held in front our faces.

My expression was as neutral as I knew how to carve it. Hella's was not so neutral. Her countenance appeared wounded.

Supervision is not a relationship between equals.

The silence between us lasted a minute. Then another one. Before a third one was complete, Hella finally spoke. "I'm not ready to talk about that . . . tonight."

I waited to see where she would go.

Her vote was nowhere. She said, "I'd like to stop for . . . now."

18

I felt my phone vibrate again. Briefly. A text, or an e-mail. I didn't get many of either late in the evening. I knew that I couldn't ignore it. Given her health, Lauren had to be confident that she could reach me, especially when she was home alone with the children.

"Excuse me, I need to check my phone," I said to Hella. "Might be something with the kids."

The text was from Sam Purdy. **I said I'd let you know the time. It's now. Beer?**

I put the phone back in my pocket.

Hella said, "Kids are okay?"

"Yeah," I said. I paused long enough to allow a change of subject to feel natural. "How are you, Hella? Right now?"

"My blood sugar? I —"

"Not the blood sugar. The case. Us? The supervision? How are you?"

As a therapist, I rarely stooped to using

intentionally disarming earnestness as a blunt tool to hack away at defenses. But it could be effective. Time was tight; I knew Hella and I would not be meeting much longer that evening. If she shored up her defenses, even a little, she could outwait me. If she did, some of the poignancy of the supervisory moment would be lost. So I stooped, and I tried earnestness.

"Oh." Hella lowered her knees, sliding her feet to the side. She grabbed a pillow to embrace instead.

I felt a little cheap at what I was doing. The feeling passed.

"This is so hard, Alan. I'm so worried about this patient. About being there for her in the . . . right way." Her shoulders dropped. "I hope you don't think this is resistance, but I don't feel like I'm able to do any more tonight. Supervision. You said you needed to know some things. Was this enough? Do you . . . know what you need to know?"

It was low-hanging fruit. It would have been an act of kindness to leave it alone. I wasn't there to be kind. I said, "Do I?"

She shook her head in dismay at the opening she'd left. "I asked for that."

I nodded. "Intentionally, I suspect."

"No, not everything, probably," she said.

"But enough, I think. You know the story now. About Friday night, and Saturday morning, and about tonight — the break-in, if there was one. Where things stand legally.

"And . . . yes, I admit it appears that we may need to talk just a teensy bit more about . . . me. You know, just to provide some context." Hella smiled at her own joke. "I'm sure you can tell how much I'm looking forward to that conversation. I have some free time during the day on Wednesday and Thursday. Can we pick this up again then . . . maybe at your office?"

"Of course."

I capitulated. We spent a minute finding a time that worked. I said good night and walked out to my car. Upstairs, Hella was busy making emergency repairs to her defenses.

I leaned up against the driver's door as I texted Sam. **What are you thinking?**

Mountain Sun on Pearl.

That didn't feel right. Mountain Sun was too young, too hip, and too loud for Sam. I considered the possibility he was pulling my leg. **Really?**

At a table in back. Watching hoops.

Lauren and the kids were asleep. I could use some decompression time with my friend. A beer sounded great. **Fifteen minutes.**

So that if she woke, she wouldn't worry, I texted Lauren that I was having a beer with Sam. **No worries I** told her.

A simple geographical imperative had determined that in downtown Boulder I was a West End guy. Our offices on Walnut Street anchored me to the part of Boulder's original downtown that rests between Broadway and the mountains, more specifically to the few-blocks' radius from our door that allowed me to grab a quick bite or run an errand on foot and then get back in time to see my next patient. The other half of Boulder's nineteenth-century core, the part beyond 15th Street on the eastern end of the Downtown Boulder Mall, was territory that was not as familiar to me. That stretch of Pearl often felt like a different downtown, one I rarely visited without a destination in mind.

The differences in the adjacent neighborhoods weren't merely geographic. There were different types of stores farther east, catering to different types of folks. Different restaurants, different bars. A definitely different crowd, sometimes defiantly different, walked those sidewalks.

In the West End, Boulder's recent march to quasi-sophistication was crystal clear. The West End announced its gentrification in neon.

But ambling on the other end of Pearl it was still possible to spot abundant indications of what Boulder had been in the seventies and eighties — in the post-hippie yet still pre too-cool-for-school days.

Snarf's, for instance, was on the other side of the Mall. Snarf's sandwiches played anywhere there were people with appetites, but I didn't think the unique Snarf's ambiance would have thrived as well in the West End. Frasca and L'Atelier were the exceptions that proved the rule. The diners filling those precious east end tables nightly were a decidedly West End group. Go figure.

Even though I spent much more of my time in the West End, I often discovered that I was more at home with the enduring old Boulder that existed at the other end of the Mall. My Boulder memories fit those sidewalks a little better. The modern eastern edge felt more like the Boulder of Stage House Books and Fred's, of the Printed Page, of Shannon's, and of the original Pearl Street Dot's. It was the Boulder of Tom's Tavern long before Tom had cut windows into his dive, even longer before Brad Heap had imagined Salt.

I'd seen Mountain Sun dozens of times from my car, or passing by on the sidewalk on Pearl, but I'd never walked inside. I suspected the same was true for Sam.

"What are you drinking?" I asked as I scooted into the booth across from him. His eyes were locked on a big flat screen. The Mavs at the Lakers. His glass was almost empty.

Despite the economy the crowd was lively, and energetic, and young. Not at all Sam's kind of place. He liked to sup beer undisturbed by any backbeat. Especially if the backbeat had any acquaintance to hip-hop.

He looked at me and lifted his glass. "Found this place on Yelp. Nice, huh?"

I did not know what to make of Sam and Yelp. My suspicion was not diminishing. I said, "Great."

"This is Claymore Scotch Ale. The ale part I understand. I'm thinking the scotch part probably has more to do with the country than with the whiskey. The Claymore part? I'm on my second, and I'm nearing a conclusion that it has to do with the way these things make you feel like you've been sitting on a land mine the whole time you've been drinking."

Sam is not often loquacious about beer. I wondered what it meant that he was. "Good?"

"Yeah. It's why we're here. The hops and the hoops."

I doubted either was true. Sam could get interesting craft beer all over town. And where sports were concerned, he was all about frozen pucks, not hoops. He drank at bars where agreeable bartenders would tune in a hockey game for him. Time would tell why we were at Mountain Sun, or not. When there were serious conversational summits to be reached, Sam had a tendency to climb slowly and then retreat before he reached the peak. More often than not he ended up sliding back down as soon as he began slipping on scree.

A waitress — some people wear their Boulder-ness so visibly that it is as obvious as a brightly colored outer garment; she was one of those — stopped at the table with two grilled cheese sandwiches, each partially buried by a mound of french fries. Sam said, "I ordered for you. The sandwiches have tomatoes in them. That's for our hearts."

"Something to drink?" she asked me. She had a touch of glittery makeup on the lids above her pale eyes. Maybe some eyeliner.

I pegged her as waiting for the ski resorts

to gear up so she could spend her days doing some serious boarding. For an underemployed recent grad, being a ski bum had to be more alluring than slinging Scottish ale and grilled cheese sandwiches.

"A round of what he's drinking, please," I said, pointing to Sam's glass.

If someone had asked, I might have admitted that I'd had a tough year. One of the ways I kept any self-pity in check was by comparing my tough year with my son Jonas's much tougher year, with Lauren's awful year, or with Sam's I-can't-believe-all-the-bad-shit-that's-happened-to-him year. Sam's bad year was actually getting to be multiple years in duration. He'd suffered through a divorce, the breakup of a couple of relationships after his divorce, a suspension from the police force for misconduct, some traumatic something in Florida during a vacation trip that he wouldn't discuss with me but that I thought had somehow involved an attractive fed named Deirdre something.

He'd also reunited with the second of the women who'd broken up with him after his divorce, but the economy had forced them to maintain a long-distance relationship while she struggled through a difficult pregnancy in California. The pregnancy had ended with a long stint of bed rest and a tragic stillbirth late in the eighth month.

Sam was still in Boulder. Carmen, his girlfriend, was still in Orange County. Sam was still recovering from his loss. Carmen, he'd told me once — I'd had to promise in advance not to bring it up again until he did — had retreated into a shell after the death of her baby. For her the pain from the stillbirth was, he'd said, "Twenty on a ten scale." He was still flying to California to see her a couple of times a month as his work schedule permitted.

Despite my offers, he'd declined to talk more about the stillbirth or the status of things with Carmen. When Sam had texted me that evening, I was hoping that he'd decided he was ready to let me know more of what had come down and how he was doing with it all.

Frankly, his timing wasn't great. My brain was stuffed. But if Sam was ready to talk, I was ready to listen.

The grilled cheese was tangy, crisp, and just the right amount of greasy. I couldn't argue with Sam's description of the ale.

"You solve your puzzle yet?" he asked. "About your neighbor and everybody being . . . you know, safe?"

I didn't expect Sam to go in that direction, not without some kicking and screaming by me. Based on our one short phone call, and on the brief caution he'd given Lauren on Saturday morning, I expected him to continue to be part of the great stone wall of law enforcement regarding what had come down at the damn housewarming.

The fact that he was initiating a conversation about the Friday-night incident suggested that whatever he was getting ready to tell me about his personal life had to feel even more distasteful to him. I decided to allow him to set the pace, fully cognizant of the fact that with Sam, I didn't really have a choice.

"No," I said. "And I'm not happy about it, either." I ate another fry.

"You shouldn't be," Sam said. "I wouldn't be."

"Yeah?"

"Yeah. It's bullshit that you don't know. Right next door? You should know what you're dealing with."

"You expect me to disagree?" I said.

Sam smirked. "Want to know what the problem is? What came down isn't about cops and DAs and crimes and suspects. Not really. The problem is that this is already about lawyers. Almost always — I'm talking the old days — crimes were about good guys and bad guys, mostly cops arresting bad guys and turning them over to prosecutors and judges. Now? Sometimes, somehow, it's only about the lawyers. On both sides. The suspects have lawyers. Even the vics have lawyers." Sam made a what's-that-about face. "The rest of us — the cops, the judges — we're just taxpayer labor for all the private lawyers."

I shrugged. I wasn't able to disclose to Sam that I knew that Cozy Maitlin was working with the alleged victim because I'd learned that information in supervision, and I had no right to reveal the existence of the supervision relationship to Sam. I cautioned myself to be careful with my friend. He was a good detective. His allegiances were usually exactly where they belonged. Which meant they were not always with me.

He lowered his voice. He said, "I'm not telling you this."

That got my attention. He waited for me to acknowledge what he'd said. I nodded.

"One lawyer is none other than Casey Sparrow. Though I don't know anything for sure, I would bet that this impenetrable wall of silence is partly her doing. I spy the hand of an attorney wizard. My experience over the years has convinced me that Ms. Sparrow is one of those defense attorney wizards."

"Casey is representing . . . whom? My neighbor?"

Sam said, "You know I can't confirm anything based on personal knowledge. It's not my case, and if it were, I couldn't talk about it. For the sake of damn argument, not that we're going to argue, let's just say I've heard rumors outside official channels that she is representing the accused."

I restated the obvious. "Casey is a defense attorney."

"That'd be true," he said. "An excellent one. I did say *accused,* I think."

"So there's a crime?"

"Alleged." Sam pronounced the word by chopping up the syllables. *A-ledge-ed.*

I decided to push the door open a little wider. "Is the allegation of a misdemeanor or a felony?"

"If it is indeed a true crime," he said, "that true crime would fall into the felonious category."

"Then . . . a felony happened — okay, may have happened — thirty yards from my front door. That's what you're saying?"

"That's not what I'm saying. Like I said, I can't *say* anything. That would be wrong. But you know the lawyer I'm talking about.

Her reputation? That tells you something, right? I'm just reading tea leaves. Making inferences. It's what we detectives do. Did you know that?"

I laughed. "So what's your inference, Mr. Detective?"

"Do wealthy clients hire Casey Sparrow to make misdemeanors go away?"

I weighed my reply; I didn't want Sam to know what I knew. I said, "Point. So, it's a felony. Damn it."

Sam said, "Wouldn't know anything at all happened from reading the paper, would you? That there's been an alleged felony out your way. No word in the press. Nothing online I've been able to find. Those particular tea leaves I'm talking about? Way I read them, and I repeat I'm far from perfect at tea-leaf reading, is that the lawyer wizard Sparrow somehow got an airtight lid on all this before anyone outside even knew there was something to put an airtight lid on."

Interesting. "When exactly did all this happen? When did Casey get the lid on?"

Sam shook his head. I took it to mean that he knew the answer to my question but he wasn't going to tell me. Casey's involvement had probably started early — sometime Saturday, maybe even Saturday morning, hours after the assault. But if my neighbors left town in that limo on Saturday morning, how could they have arranged for Casey's representation? How could they even have known at that point that they needed representation?

No later than Sunday, I decided. Casey Sparrow was on board by Sunday.

I knew a lot more about the events we were discussing than I was letting on to Sam, but Sam's story was confusing me anyway. "I'm sorry, Sam. I don't get it. I really appreciate that you're telling me this, I just don't think I understand the message that you have buried in there."

Sam's a big guy. His head is the size of a late-summer cantaloupe. His chest is broad. His shoulders and biceps are so thick and strong that his arms don't ever hang perpendicular to the ground. In the time I'd known him he'd gone on and off diets more often than a senior Southwest pilot's gone on and off 737s.

He leaned forward, plopped his elbows on the table, rounded those huge shoulders, and curled his forearms around all of his food and most of mine. Either he was protecting his dinner, or he was creating an enclosure suitable for revealing a confidence.

I'd poked my upper body into caves

smaller than the space he'd created for us. He gestured toward the flat screen. "See that layup?"

I looked up. "Kobe?" I said. "He's good."

"Mr. Kobe Bryant. Better than good. Great. Remember the rape accusations? What was that hotel? Up near Vail?"

Oh God, I thought. *Not that.*

19

I was hoping — okay, I was praying — that Sam didn't really want to rehash one of the most prominent criminal set pieces in Colorado's recent decade of notorious crimes.

I didn't want to talk about Kobe Bryant unless it had to do with the new basketball season. Actually, I didn't want to talk about the new basketball season if it meant I had to talk about Kobe Bryant and that hotel in Eagle County. I almost said that to Sam. But I didn't. I answered his question. "Cordillera," I said. "Above Edwards." When Lauren and I used to ski, and didn't ski closer to the Front Range, we could often be found on Arrowhead Mountain. I knew the slopes near Cordillera well.

"That one. Remember what came down? Between Kobe Bryant and that hotel employee. When was that? It was sometime after JonBenet was killed. The media people

— I use both words generously — who were hanging around annoying everyone in Boulder about the Ramsey grand jury ran to their vans, caravanned down 93, hopped on 70, and just started broadcasting Kobe stories from Vail. Didn't miss a beat. Two thousand and three, maybe? Was it that long ago? Man.

"Anyway, Kobe was arrested. For sexual friggin' assault. Actually *arrested.* Booked. Sheriff picked him up before presenting the results of the investigation to the DA, which is not something we would normally do here in Boulder. That's something to remember, Alan. But . . . the media was orgasmic. Almost immediately, accusations started flying in both directions. Lots of mud got thrown by both sides. Crap went on for a year.

"But Kobe just kept up the Kobe magic. Dishing. Playing D. Driving the lane. Hitting the impossible J. After a year of fancy attorneys jabbering on both sides — the accuser had her attorneys, too — everybody busy sending out their hot-shit investigators and planning all their lawyer wizard moves, the pretrial hearings finally got started. It was a true mountain circus. Lions and tigers and bears, oh my."

Sam attempted a falsetto for the *oh my.* It

didn't go particularly well.

"The judge does something then that nobody expects. He grants Mr. Bryant's attorneys' motion to allow testimony about the accuser's sexual behavior in the brief time period just before and *after* the incident in question. It was a big friggin' shock to people who thought Colorado's rape shield law would insulate her. The ruling meant the alleged victim was going to have to testify about her sexual behavior just before and right after her encounter with Mr. Bryant." He raised one of his shrubby eyebrows for my benefit. "There were press reports that the defendant's investigators had a witness who was going to testify that he had sex with the accuser less than a day after the alleged rape. That wouldn't look good to a jury. Right?" Sam shot both hands into the air. "It was a three-pointer at the buzzer for Mr. Bryant's attorney wizard.

"The accuser's attorney wizard can't let that stand, of course. They fire off a response almost immediately. The accuser files a civil suit against Mr. Bryant only weeks *before* the criminal trial begins. DAs I know tell me that is dangerous territory — I mean legally dangerous — for an accuser. Filing that civil suit at that stage of the case got my particular attention. Do you remember all that, how it came down?"

"Vaguely," I said, though I remembered little. I didn't know where Sam was going or what the recent events in Spanish Hills had to do with Kobe Bryant's dark Colorado legal legacy. I did know that I didn't want to revisit any of it. I was hoping there was a quick point. "Is this history lesson necessary, Sam?"

"You betcha," he said. "Well, this thing got bigger, faster. Even the Supremes got involved, but I won't bore you with that. Jury selection finally began — you know, just like it was going to be a real criminal case. Then, like hours or something before opening statements, the accuser — the alleged victim — informed the prosecutor that she would be refusing to testify at the trial."

Sam's face became a bad caricature of a weeping mime. "Turns out the Eagle County prosecutor was no dummy. For law enforcement, in your typical he said/she said acquaintance-rape case, the absence of victim testimony creates a serious problem, you know what I mean? Goes from he said/ she said to just, well, he said. My experience is that when only the defendant tells the jury his story, it pretty much guarantees an acquittal. So I'm not blaming the prosecutor for laying down his cards at that point. He knew his choices were limited to either subpoena the vic to testify against her will, or drop the criminal charges against Mr. Bryant. He dropped the charges. No argument from me."

I was hoping to save us some time. I said, "Is that what you think is going to happen here? With what happened in Spanish Hills?"

Sam ignored me. "Turned out that wasn't the end of the story. Since this was no longer going to be the kind of criminal case where the search for justice involves, you know, a courtroom, the lawyers for both sides wanted to do some, well, let's call it damage control. And their next move — both sides, go figure again — was to file motions with the court asking for the charges against Mr. Bryant to be dismissed 'with prejudice.' Do you know what that means, Alan? 'With prejudice'?"

My wife was a deputy DA. I knew. I said, "It means the same charge can't be refiled by the prosecutor in the future. What I don't know is why the hell would the accuser's attorney take that position?"

"Why indeed," Sam said in a self-satisfied tone. "Seems to me that at that moment the accuser took the sharpest arrow out of her own quiver, broke it over her knee, and promised never ever to fletch a new one."

Sam was one of the only people I knew who would use *fletch* in a sentence. I didn't tell him that.

"But the legal surprises were just beginning. At the time, I was thinking that Mr. Bryant would choose to slink away. No criminal charges left to fight? No future criminal charges to haunt him? Training camp about to start? I figured he would jet back to SoCal and take his with-prejudice ruling with him. Let his . . . superstar persona recover in the California sun.

"But no! He did what I consider a remarkable thing. He issued a public statement through — I'm not kidding — his accuser's attorney. Not *his* own attorney. *Her* attorney. To my way of thinking about these things, it was a most surprising moment in the history of alleged perpdom. For me, it was yet another dazzling three-pointer at the buzzer, but Mr. Kobe Bryant appeared to have shot this one into the wrong team's basket."

My mouth hung open for any number of reasons.

"Do you remember it? Mr. Bryant's statement?" Sam asked.

"Sam, I have only the vaguest recollection. I try not to pay much attention to —"

"Celebrities? Right. You're above that."

I looked at him with pain in my eyes, hoping, vainly, for compassion. "Exactly."

He smiled in an unkind way. "The public statement the accuser's lawyer read for Mr. Bryant wasn't your usual I'm-sorry-if-anyone-was-offended or I'm-sorry-if-my-behavior-was-misinterpreted celebrity non-apology apology. Nope.

"A little history. The order of events was crucial. Here's how it came down: First, the alleged vic refuses to testify, and then the charges get dropped. *With* prejudice. Then, Mr. Bryant apparently finds some . . . impulse . . . for public compassion, or he discovers some latent remorse, and he has his accuser's lawyer read that apology. *Kind of* an apology, actually, but I'll get to that later.

"Note the order. B came before C. Absolutely not C before B. Mr. Bryant didn't announce any public compassion or remorse before the alleged vic refused to testify, or certainly before her attorney wizards got the charges dropped with prejudice.

"Keeping track, Alan? With me?"

"Taking mental notes, Sam."

"Glad to hear it. And then *poof,* a surprise. A bit of, well, profound perplexity turns up buried in the middle of that public statement. See, the specific sequence of events, the B before C, allowed Mr. Bryant to announce, as part of that apology — I'm continuing to use the word loosely — that the criminal case against him had ended with *no money* having been paid to the woman."

Sam is generally careful with the English language, or as careful with the English language as a natural born Iron Ranger is capable of being. I asked, "Sam, you keep saying B before C. Where's A?"

"Good. Shows me you're paying attention. I like that. We will get there. I promise. May I proceed?"

"Could I stop you?" Sam didn't care a whit about my assent.

"No." He ate a french fry. I didn't think he chewed it. "I don't know how else to read the peculiar statement of Mr. Bryant's — and I've read it a few times, almost have it memorized — but he seems to have been asserting a most mystifying fact: that no money had been paid to his accuser prior to her decision not to testify. He seems to have been announcing" — Sam's face was wide-eyed — "that he had not induced the alleged victim not to testify by, well, bribing her.

"And since her attorney was reading the

statement, she, the accuser, must have also wanted the public to know she wasn't a bribed witness. Which is admirable behavior on both parts, yes?"

"Sarcasm?" I asked. I wasn't always sure with Sam.

"Personally?" Sam said, ignoring me. "Regarding Mr. Bryant? I thought it should be one of those 'goes without saying' things. I tend to think it's something we expect of our idols and superstars — they don't trip old ladies, they don't smother kittens, and they don't go around bribing potential witnesses in criminal cases — but maybe that's just me being old-fashioned. But said or unsaid, still, admirable behavior. So, I guess we give Mr. Bryant props for not bribing his accuser, yes?"

I made a mental note to go online and find Mr. Bryant's statement. I couldn't believe the statement actually said what Sam was maintaining it said.

Sam rotated his head side to side in a wide arc, as though pins were standing tall on each of his shoulders and he was determined to use his bowling ball of a skull to try to pick up the 7–10 split. He said, "You think I'm being facetious? We all know that Mr. Bryant had considerable personal wealth at that time in his life, a fortune that a lesser, more morally compromised accused celebrity rapist *might* have attempted to use to encourage his alleged victim's silence. Though, dear Lord, behavior like that would have been tawdry, wouldn't it?"

I laughed. "Did you say *tawdry?*"

"Other than that one time I was in New Orleans, where it just seems so natural a word, I get few opportunities," Sam said.

Sam had a master's degree in lit. In the time I'd known him, evidence of his fondness for language leaked out at unexpected times. This long harangue was like the mother lode. I said, "What you're describing — purchasing his accuser's silence — in addition to being tawdry, also would have been a felony, right? For both of them?"

"There is that. Which, I imagine, was as good a reason as any why the attorneys on both sides were intent on reminding the world in Mr. Bryant's statement that he hadn't, in fact, done it. The bribing-the-accuser thing. Though I continue to think that most people in his shoes would have been reluctant to bring the topic up at all. To me? It was kind of like walking out of your hostess's powder room at a crowded cocktail party and announcing in a loud voice that it wasn't you who had just taken a dump in there."

20

Sam was on his game. I was actually starting to enjoy myself a little.

"In the statement, Mr. Bryant clearly admitted misbehavior. He says he committed adultery. He admitted that sexual acts occurred the day in question in Cordillera with 'this woman.' He also freely acknowledged that, upon further consideration, he might even have misinterpreted the young woman's impression of what was, let's say, 'consensual.' Why do I choose to call it that? Because Mr. Bryant did. And who am I to argue with the accused in his own statement?

"So, Mr. Bryant admits he's a cad, but we all assume that celebrities are cads, don't we? Some of them, at least? Sure, we do. And, because Mr. Bryant apologized publicly — I continue to be generous with the definition of the word; a careful reading will indicate he doesn't *technically* apologize to the young woman, though he repeatedly states that he *wants* to apologize to her. I still don't understand what was getting in his way — what was keeping him from *actually* apologizing, and not just *wanting* to apologize — but that's me picking nits.

"The point is that we, the public, if we're so inclined, could have concluded, after hearing that public statement from Mr. Bryant, that the Laker superstar is a stand-up guy. He was someone who could apologize and admit that he was wrong — or at the very least, he is someone who could sincerely *want* to apologize and freely admit that he might have misinterpreted the whole 'consensual' component of his sexual compact with 'this woman,' whom he'd known for all of fifteen minutes."

Sam had ceased camouflaging his sarcasm. His eyes went wide. "Which is kind of like admitting being wrong, right? In Hollywood, anyway. Or Vail. Yeah?" Sam's grin as he paused was subtle. He didn't want an answer from me. He kept the charming smirk on his face for about five seconds before he added, "Since he knew that all criminal charges had been dropped, with prejudice."

I leaned back far enough that I could take a long draw of my beer without hitting Sam in the face with the bottom of my glass. I was hoping he'd concluded the Kobe Bryant retrospective. No such luck. Over Sam's shoulder, on the flat screen, I watched Kobe hit an impossible fall-away jumper over Dirk. The man had crazy talent.

Sam wasn't done. "In that same remarkable statement, Mr. Bryant revealed another important side agreement between the opposing attorneys. He says that his accuser had agreed not to use his statement of apology against him in the upcoming civil suit."

Sam sighed. I thought it might be at my failure to applaud. Any disappointment he was feeling with me turned out to be brief. He continued. "Now, there was an obvious inference to be made. Since the statement referred to agreements involving the upcoming civil suit, the easy inference was that Mr. Bryant's public statement was *actually* negotiated between his attorneys and the alleged victim's attorneys. Who else, after all, could have given Mr. Bryant the assurances he had received about the future introduction of evidence in the civil suit?

"More puzzles," Sam said, looking puzzled. "Why would the attorneys from the plaintiff's side be negotiating the components of a public-statement-slash-apology with the defendant's attorneys? And why would the plaintiff's attorneys be making agreements about what evidence they would not attempt to admit in a possible future civil trial? Although the charges had been dropped in the criminal case, the civil suit was, after all, still pending. At that time, it represented the alleged rape victim's last hope at justice."

I thought it was a great question. Legal ethics weren't my strong suit, but it seemed that the kind of agreement between the opposing attorneys that Sam was describing must have been a breach of something important. Or if it wasn't, it should have been.

Sam shook his big head again. "Ah, lawyer shit. Honestly, the can't-use-any-of-this-at-the-civil-trial part of the whole public apology was kind of a letdown for me. Why? That meant to me that Mr. Bryant already knew his jeopardy was kaput. E-vap-o-rated. It was like Mr. Bryant had the Get Out of Jail Free card in his pocket the whole time his accuser's attorney was almost-apologizing for him.

"It'd be like my kid saying, 'Yeah, I'm the one who shot the street hockey puck through the front window, Dad,' but only after he'd negotiated assurances with me that not only wouldn't he be grounded, but neither would he have to pay to have the pane of glass replaced." Sam caught my eyes and smiled in the kind of devious manner I wouldn't want to see on a cop's face were I a civilian in some kind of trouble. "Again, though, I'm probably picking nits."

I certainly hadn't remembered the segment of Bryant's statement about the upcoming civil suit. Something else for me to check on Wikipedia.

My level of interest was increasing but was also increasingly irrelevant. I was buckled into a ride of set duration with Sam. I consoled myself that Sam didn't often waste my time. Something relevant this way had to come.

"Know what happened next? After the peculiar statement with the almost apology?"

"Pins and needles, my friend."

His expression revealed disappointment with my sarcasm. But he raised his hands in sudden exclamation. "See, because of the quality choreography accomplished by the attorney wizards — I'm thinking on both sides, accuser and accused — nobody knows what happened next. Well, the choreographers do, obviously. The lawyers. But not us, not Joe Q. All the public really knows is that Kobe went back to L.A. on a private jet and played more Lakers hoops. Over time, he got his full-on celebrity back. Got his endorsements back, or maybe he got new ones, better ones. Fair to say — and this is more personal opinion than fact — he even seems to have gotten his mojo back." Sam glanced up at the TV, where Kobe was busy doing Kobe magic. "Man's on *SportsCenter* a lot. I know. I watch it almost every night. Play of the Night? Play of the Week? Mr. Bryant.

"And his pretty wife? Don't forget her. She's a victim in all this, too, right? Who knows, maybe she forgave him for what he did. Tabloids say she got a big ring for her pain and aggravation and humiliation. Mr. Bryant eventually got more rings of his own, too. Championship rings. And later on, he got himself an Olympic gold medal.

"The vic? I mean, if she *was* a vic. To be fair, we don't actually know that, do we? By 'we,' I'm talking Joe Q. Since there was never a criminal trial, or even a trial of the civil complaint, we don't know what really happened in that hotel room, do we? Other than adultery, I mean.

"Well, as far as I can tell, the alleged vic has disappeared. Hopefully — I'd like to think — voluntarily. Some cops have told me that they think the next time we see her will be when she shows up on *Oprah* or *Ellen.* Or as guest host on *The View.* But I don't think that's going to happen. I think the choreography that was put in place includes a prohibition against her ever performing in those particular venues. Anyway, for now? She's history."

I shrugged. The relevance continued to elude me. My fries were almost gone, which was even more of a tragedy.

Sam said, "Big picture? Ready? A cynic — you know, someone like you — might suggest that the entire order of events was . . . choreographed from the start. Not just the part we know about, the B before C. But also the crucial step, A, and the concluding step, D."

Finally, I was hoping. *The point.*

"I promised you I would get back to A, didn't I? So here goes. Remember O. J.? His acquittal?"

I groaned audibly. "Sam, please. No. Don't make me —"

He held up an index finger. "Not what you think. Only one small point from that dark hole. Promise. Mr. Goldman, the father of one of the murder victims in the infamous Simpson murder case, waited until well after the phantasmagoric conclusion of the criminal trial to file his ultimately successful civil suit against Mr. Simpson. You recall?"

"Yes," I said. "I do remember that."

"When it's done at all — the civil suit option — that's the way it's typically done. If a criminal trial ends with an acquittal, the victim or the victim's family will take their pleas for justice to civil court. Like it or not, fair or not, for aggrieved victims the civil suit, with its lower threshold for culpability, often feels like a final chance at achieving something resembling justice."

I could finally see where Sam was heading. I said, "But in the Cordillera case, the victim —"

"Alleged victim."

"The alleged victim in Cordillera filed her civil suit while the criminal charges were still pending against Mr. Bryant."

"Exactly," Sam said. "For whatever reason, the alleged victim's attorneys must have thought it wise to get an extra card in their client's hand early on. But why would they think that? Were they anticipating losing during the criminal trial? Or were they, perhaps, seeking more leverage? Maybe, but what could possibly be more of an ominous portent to Mr. Bryant than a criminal conviction that promised significant incarceration?"

Ominous portent indeed. My friend was on a roll.

"The answer to that is 'nothing.' Which leaves me to speculate: Had the young woman's lawyer wizards already decided that the criminal case against Mr. Bryant was about to . . . go . . . away? Had they already advised her, because the judge had ruled that her sexual behavior in the days before and after the rape was fair game in the trial, that she should never testify? We, Joe Q.," Sam said in the voice of an over-the-top documentary narrator, "are left to wonder. I mean, what do we actually *know?* Well, all we can do is look at the public record to observe the sequence of the steps of the public dance that the lawyer wizards choreographed for their respective clients.

"First, the stage is set with the dark prologue: whatever happened in the hotel suite in Cordillera. And then . . . criminal charges hang over the accused's head.

"That leads us to A, when that surprise civil suit got filed, then B, when the alleged vic refused to testify and charges got dropped, then C, when Mr. Bryant quasi-apologized, and finally D, when the civil suit is . . . settled. *Da, da, da, daaaa.*"

One of the surprising things about Sam Purdy is that he's a graceful dancer. I'd seen him bust it more than a few times. The man did not embarrass himself on a ballroom floor. He broke into a seated version of some dance moves right then. His shoulders swayed. He rocked his hips. "With me? It's a one, and a two, and a three." He paused, opening his eyes wide. His forehead is so big that for a moment the tableau looked like a couple of dark pool balls hard against the cushion of a pinkish flesh-colored table. "With a surprising little four thrown in at the end. All in all, a nice tight little legal shuffle. All choreographed, in advance, by . . . ?"

I applauded gently. "The attorney wizards," I said. I was finally catching on.

"Yessss. Not the court. No. Not the prosecutor. Not the cops in Eagle County, I can promise you that. Take it from me, cops don't know these kinds of steps. To learn these kinds of steps, you need lawyers. The more wizardy, the better.

"And, oh yeah, that civil suit the accused filed? The one that started before the criminal case ended, the one that miraculously went away as part of the attorney tango's final steps? Well, it turns out that the terms of that settlement — there had to be a settlement, right? — were never disclosed. I'm presuming that the alleged vic got a cash settlement of some kind. Big? Small? If I were a betting man, I'd put my money on big. But that's a guess. All details remain undisclosed.

"Now, thing is, I don't recall Mr. Bryant's attorney, or the accuser's attorney, reading another public statement at that point or holding a press conference to repeat the earlier contention that no money had been paid to settle the civil action. I actually went back and looked, but if Mr. Bryant or his attorney or her attorney released a second statement like that, I'm afraid I somehow missed it completely. May mean nothing, but I'm thinking if indeed no money had been paid to allow the civil suit to settle, it would have served Mr. Bryant well to issue another statement. From a purely public relations point of view. Experience has taught me that prominent people do pay heed to PR concerns."

He gave me a moment to disagree. I didn't.

He transitioned to full whisper. "Mr. Bryant's earlier statement that no money was paid to that woman? I'm thinking it became, well, inoperative once the civil suit settled.

"And this is going to shock you, my friend, but I am someone who has dark private moments when I'm known to question the purity of the human heart. I, and I do feel some occasional shame about this, I have even had moments when I've believed that the lawyers in that case — Mr. Bryant's lawyers and the alleged vic's lawyers — may actually have arranged the whole darn thing in advance. Every last bit of it.

"Well, maybe not every last bit. Not all the steps, of course. Not the sexual indiscretion. That was ad-libbed by Mr. Bryant. And the sheriff in Eagle County was solely responsible for his bold move — arresting the celebrity. We can all agree that it's not the same dance without those first notes being played.

"But the other steps? The civil suit getting filed, the alleged vic refusing to testify in the criminal case, the nobody-bribed-anybody thing, Mr. Bryant almost apologizing, the suitable interval ensuing, the civil suit flying away on that private jet with Mr. Bryant, the possibility that money finally did change hands outside the public view, and then . . . no further public statements or quasi-apologies.

"What if those steps were nothing more than the public evidence of an elaborate exit strategy concocted far in advance by lawyer wizards who are very good at dancing just this side of . . . some important line?"

Sam gave me a moment to reply. I shook my head, declining the opportunity. "Do you know that one of Mr. Bryant's own lawyers called the statement read by the accuser's attorney — her client's own statement — the 'price of freedom' required of Mr. Bryant by the accuser? She said 'freedom.' His own lawyer said fucking *freedom.*

"That's serious stuff. It causes me to question Mr. Bryant's sincerity. And it leaves me to wonder if the alleged victim actually knew when she told the DA she wasn't going to testify — and if Mr. Bryant actually knew when he had his adversary's attorney read that crazy-ass public statement — that all the attorney wizards on both sides had already determined that it would never go to civil trial. Maybe that they even knew the outlines of what a final civil settlement would look like.

"An authority as expert as Roy Black — You know Roy Black? He is himself one of those fancy attorney wizards. He said he suspects that just such a thing occurred. He actually called what happened 'dirty.' "

Back to the Internet for me. If Roy Black said that happened, well . . .

"Wow," Sam said, in what I hoped was

conclusion, "now that would be some major choreography, wouldn't it?"

Sam had no facts to support his theory, just supposition. His story sounded like a tale of lawyer wizards doing what clients, especially wealthy clients, paid their lawyer wizards to do. But there was an obvious question Sam wanted me to ask. He'd gone to a lot of trouble, so I asked it.

"Would that be legal? For the attorneys on both sides to get together and make all those arrangements without involving the prosecutors or the court?"

21

Sam puffed out his cheeks, leaving him looking not so much like a big chipmunk as an albino rhino preparing for a dive. He said, "Answering that is complicated. If one of Mr. Bryant's buds — you know, a member of his crew — With NBA players, is it *crew* or is it *posse?* Ah, who cares. If, say, an employee of his approached the alleged vic and suggested that she possibly, maybe, could enjoy significant monetary advantages down the road were she to refuse to testify in the upcoming criminal case . . . well, that would be witness tampering.

"If, behind closed doors, Mr. Bryant's lawyer wizards cooked up a slightly more vague but similar scenario with the alleged victim's lawyer wizard, it's . . . what? Is it witness tampering? Or is it damn good lawyering?" Sam said. "After all my years in criminal justice, I still get confused by those two, I admit."

I leaned farther into Sam's cave. Despite his campfire story, I remained uninterested in the cautionary tale of Kobe Bryant. Rich people and famous people have always had advantages in our legal system. My bottom line? If Mr. Bryant's accuser was indeed a victim of sexual assault, I sincerely hoped she had found a constructive way to sublimate her trauma. If the undisclosed civil settlement helped, so be it.

But there were things I did care about. I rehearsed my next words in my head, praying that I could do a reasonable impersonation of actual indignation as I spoke them. I said, "This story? I'm assuming that you are telling me this story now because there was a rape Friday night, Sam? Right across the lane from our house. Is that the point of your story? Are you telling me that nobody in law enforcement has even informed me that there is potentially an accused sex offender living next door to my family? I have a wife and two young children, Sam. The police have a responsibility —"

"No," Sam said. His voice was no longer a whisper. "I am telling you no such thing. Whatever happened across the lane from your home is not my case, it is not my jurisdiction, and I am in no position to reveal investigatory details or to confirm your speculation. Neighbor or not. But" — he lifted his index finger and briefly touched it to the end of his nose, leaving behind a toasted, buttery breadcrumb from his grilled cheese sandwich — "neither am I taking responsibility for any conclusions, however reasonable, you might reach on your own."

"You think my conclusion might be reasonable?"

"May well be. What I've been doing here this evening is a result of some reflection I did after my time in church last Sunday. The good reverend left me thinking about the great value that can come from speaking in parables. One man's experience, told properly, can be another man's life lesson."

I sat back as I pondered the Cordillera parable for any nuance I'd missed. "Sam, are you suggesting that no rape ever occurred in Cordillera? Is that it? That Kobe Bryant was somehow the victim in that fiasco? And that the same may be true here? Is that why I have nothing to worry about?"

"I never said you had nothing to worry about. And I don't know the answer to the was-Mr.-Bryant-guilty-of-anything-more-than-adultery question. I can tell you it was my impression in the end that the outcome that was negotiated had more to do with Mr. Bryant's future as a celebrity basketball star than it had to do with the alleged victim's circumstances, or with justice.

"When I do try to understand it? The Cordillera saga? I keep coming back to the attorneys' choreography. At the end of the day that case — a case at its heart about rape, a felony — was resolved without the involvement of the police or the prosecutors or the court. What started off as *The People of Colorado v. Kobe Bean Bryant* was ultimately resolved by some lawyer wizards who decided that" — Sam's voice changed in tone right there — "justice would best be served if the public never knew what the fuck really happened. Because of the agreements those attorneys reached behind closed doors, it's most likely that the rest of us will never know what happened between Mr. Bryant and the woman in that hotel room. Crime? No crime? Rape? No rape?

"People who cross paths with the alleged victim in the future will never know whether she was a victim of an assault or if she was a gold digger. Other women who cross paths with Mr. Bryant will never know whether to fear Mr. Bryant as a potentially violent sex offender or to sympathize with him as the victim of a well-played extortion. Which is, I imagine, exactly the way that someone wanted it."

"Mr. Bryant?" I said.

Sam finished his beer. "One has to decide, I think, who would have had the most to gain, or to lose, by any continued public disclosure of the facts of the case. Whose future would be most damaged by continued exposure? By an eyewitness's account, a second-by-second account, of the sexual, or violent, encounter that occurred in that hotel room."

"We're not talking about justice anymore, are we, Sam?" I said.

He wiped his mouth with his napkin. He missed the crumb on his nose. "Nah. Not so much. When someone is as prominent as Mr. Bryant, the accusation of sexual assault alone can cause a shit storm that will do as much damage as any truth-seeking prosecutor. Justice? It becomes a casualty, a secondary consideration. Protecting potential future victims? An afterthought."

I sat back a little. But I kept my voice low. "Sam, I do want to know what happened across the lane from my house last Friday night. Was there a rape? Is that what you're telling me?"

Sam sat back for a moment. When he leaned forward again, all the theatricality was absent from his delivery. "I do not know what happened between Mr. Kobe Bryant and the young woman in that hotel suite in Cordillera. Was it a rape? Or was it a consenting act between two adults? I do not know. The statements made by the two parties available in the public record are contradictory. And —"

"Like you, Sam, I don't know what happened in that hotel room in Cordillera. Perhaps though, unlike you, I won't lose any sleep trying to find out."

"You interrupted me," he admonished. "What I was about to say is that neither do I know what happened in the house across the lane from yours last Friday night. Was there a rape? I do not know. Was there some form of sexual communion between two consenting adults? I do not know that, either. When all is said and done, I expect that any public statements of the only people who were in the guest room in your neighbor's home will be contradictory."

Sam knew about the guest room. *Was that a slip, or was he telling me something?*

He said, "Let that fact sink in, Alan. You . . . may . . . never . . . know. You will likely never know." Sam gave me a good half minute to allow all the ambiguity to settle. "Reflecting on Cordillera for another moment? Technically? That was an accusation of acquaintance rape. Acquaintance rape is a bitch," he said. "I've investigated more of them than I want to remember. Sometimes I think I know what really happened between the two people involved. Other times, I don't. But truth? Truth is damn elusive.

"Down the road, I expect that if it turns out that what happened Friday night was an acquaintance rape, the rape kit may provide some illumination. But not confirmation. I certainly expect that if DNA is tested, those results could shed further light, too. A positive result on a tox screen? That could be a game changer, too. Hard to say — there are often arguments of extenuating circumstances in these affairs. A man could always contend that taking any drug found in the woman's system was her idea."

I said, "I've always gotten the impression that you could tell, that at some point during an investigation you made some determination about who should be believed."

"I wish," Sam said. "Sometimes the facts are the facts. Both the man and the woman tell basically the same story. One looks at those facts and says, 'See, I was raped.' The other looks at those facts and says, 'See, we had sex.' "

He sat back. "You know Devil's Thumb?" he asked. "Above Chautauqua?"

"South of the Flatirons? The big rock

formation? I do."

"Say you don't know the name of that big ol' rock. You're hiking the Mesa Trail and you look up at the big thing poking out from the Front Range, and somebody you're with asks you what the hell you think that rock looks like. What do you say?"

I was thinking it was a trick question. "It looks kind of like a thumb," I said.

"And?" Sam said. "What else does it kind of look like?"

I could feel the warmth of the beer. "I've always thought it looks kind of like a dick."

"Exactly," Sam said. "Same rock. Same angle. Same perspective. It's a thumb, or it's a dick. That's what the problem is with acquaintance rape. For one of the two people involved, it's a thumb. For the other, it's a dick. My experience is that there is no negotiating perception."

I thought he was waiting for me to disagree with him. I lifted my last french fry.

"It's likely that the events in the guest room at your neighbor's house took place out of sight of any witness's eyes. That would make it difficult for you, or for anyone, to ever know what went down. If the contention is acquaintance rape, and lab results indicate sexual contact, one of the two people is going to maintain what happened was rape. The other is going to maintain that what happened was consensual sex. Truth? Ha. Find it, I dare you."

"Truth is unknowable, Sammy?" He didn't like it when I called him Sammy. I blamed the beer.

"Forensic science may throw us a bone. But it may not. Usually doesn't. Rape kit may tell us that sex happened. Even, maybe, whom it happened with. But in your neighbor's house? I suspect that the fact that genitals were bumping won't end up in dispute. What will be in dispute is the mind-set and consent of the bumpees. Forensic science has trouble with mind-set. But . . . subsequent events are taking place, at least partly, in the public eye. That's where, I think, you need to focus your attention — on the things that happen next that *are* knowable."

"You talking about the lawyers again?"

"Yep. The lawyer wizards."

Sam was being patient with me. Back when I was a complete hockey novice, he was the same way as he tried, unsuccessfully, to explain the concept of delayed off sides.

"The reason you know so little now, and the reason you may never know much more than that, is because of the attorneys. That"

— he raised his glass in a mock toast — "is my lesson. This case is starting to smell a hell of a lot like that case."

I didn't see it. I told Sam that.

Sam said, "Attorneys all across the land learned important things from the Kobe Bryant fiasco. Any defense lawyer who studied that case from start to finish learned how to handle certain . . . delicate accusations against a . . . celebrity client. You want to know why this dance, the current one, is happening completely off the public's radar?"

I knew my next line as though Sam had provided me with a script. "Because that's the way the lawyers want it."

"Lessons to be learned from Mr. Bryant? Shut everyone up. Attorneys everywhere learned from the situation between Mr. Bryant and his accuser that the earlier they are able to get everyone — I mean everyone, the cops, the prosecutor, the media, the accused, the accuser — to shut the hell up, the better things will turn out to be for the celebrity accused, and if the accuser knows what's good for her, maybe even the better it will be for the accuser."

"I don't get it. What's the advantage for the alleged victim?"

"That's the second lesson to be learned.

The attorneys for the defendant make crystal clear to the accused the high price she will pay for pressing her allegations. Reputation? Mental health history? Relationship history? Drug use? Sexual history? Determined private investigators will find it all. And then some. A ruling from the bench that the accuser's recent sexual behavior could be admitted as evidence? The attorneys for the defendant will do everything they can think of to convince the accused that proceeding with criminal charges will guarantee mutually assured destruction."

"And then?" I said.

"Then each side will start assigning a price to going away."

"You're certain about this, aren't you?"

"Name me a celebrity in prison for sexual assault. Right now, today. I'm serious — do it. Off the top of your head."

I couldn't come up with one.

"Did Michael Jackson go to jail?" Sam asked. "For what he did?"

"No."

"You must have heard the testimony about him in bed with that boy in his house."

"Yes."

"From your perspective did that . . . behavior look like Devil's Thumb? Or Devil's Dick?"

I didn't answer. "He's dead, Sam."

"What? You're arguing statute of limitations? Tell that to Roman Polanski. For the record, the jury thought it looked like a thumb," Sam said. "There is no explaining juries sometimes." He drained the dregs of his beer. "Especially California juries." After five more seconds, Sam said, "Time's up. You think you can't name one because no celebrity ever took advantage of some woman, or some kid?"

"No. I don't think that."

"Name me a prominent politician who is in prison for sexual assault. Come on, quick." I shook my head. "You think it's because no politician ever took advantage of his position with some woman, or some kid?"

"No," I said. "I don't think that."

"Next category: sports heroes."

"Sam —"

"Okay, okay. My point is that justice doesn't catch up with the rich and famous very often. Certainly not in cases involving" — Sam hesitated as he searched for the right word — "sexual license. Usually the best that vics can hope to get is some measure of compensation. My point? The earlier everyone involved — lawyers on both sides, the accused, and the accuser —

recognizes that the danger to the accused is not prison time but a slam-down beating in the court of public relations, the sooner the real work of resolving differences begins. And more and more, that work happens in private, not in court. Justice be damned.

"The other night I met the patrol guy who'd had the first contact with the RP on this incident." *RP* is cop slang for "reporting party." "Name's Heath Wade. Good cop. I told you detectives are always looking for something that will tell us whom to believe in an acquaintance rape. Officer Heath Wade gave me a reason. Lucy had asked him to tell her about meeting the alleged vic for the first time. Everything he could remember."

"And?"

Sam said, "His words to Luce: 'Woman is either Helena Bonham Carter or she was telling me the truth.' I had to look up Helena Bonham Carter online, by the way. Turns out she's Bellatrix Lestrange. Harry Potter? Good actress. Heath Wade, the cop who was with the vic right after, he didn't see Devil's Thumb, Alan. He saw Devil's Dick.

"Do you recall the media beating that the young woman took in Eagle County? Her mental health history revealed? Her sexual history revealed? Old boyfriends discussing private moments? Her family under scrutiny? I would imagine that the alleged victim in whatever happened in Spanish Hills on Friday night might prefer to avoid being dissected like that, or . . . that her lawyer, Mr. Maitlin, might be determined to keep his client from being dissected like that."

"What you're saying makes sense, Sam. I can see why the lawyers want silence. Maybe even why law enforcement wants silence. But I don't see why everyone buys into the need for silence. Even Diane won't tell me what she knows about the housewarming. Diane gossips like she breathes." He nodded at that. "Then why the complete silence? Even from people who have no . . . s'mores on the fire?"

"S'mores on the fire?" He snorted, then averted his gaze for a moment, as though he'd spotted something near the bar that deserved his complete attention. I turned to look. Nothing there. When he looked back at me, he said, "Everyone who knows anything about Friday night — before, during, after — has a s'more on this fire. Libel? Slander? Allegiance? Public ridicule? Guilt by association? Nobody likes their s'mores burned to a crisp."

Sam began to stand up. I asked Sam if I

could ask him one last question. I told him I wanted a direct answer.

He said, "No promises."

"As a father, do I have something to worry about? Based on what you know?"

He considered my question for a moment. "Do you have more to worry about than you did last week? I doubt it. Maybe less, given the sunlight."

I watched his face for signs of equivocation. I didn't see any. I said, "Thanks, Sam." I stood up.

He let me take a couple of steps away from him before he added, "As a husband, though? That'd be a different question. If you asked it."

I spun. "What are you saying?"

"Your wife is an attractive woman. Way too pretty to have settled for you, by the way. She seems to hold your new neighbor in some professional esteem. Now, I'm no expert, but those things are on the ingredient list for the recipe for the kind of mess we've been discussing."

I tried to make my face blank until I turned away from Sam. Then I mouthed a profanity that involved my upper teeth grazing my lower lip.

Our waitress was passing by on the way to

the bar. “Something wrong?” she asked.
“No,” I said, lying.

22

Lauren was awake when I got home.

She hadn't stayed up for me. She had not chosen to stay awake because she was waiting to grill me about being out so late. Nor had she chosen to stay awake because she was desperate to have an intimate moment with me before the day ended.

The reason she was awake was so familiar in our world that it had become almost mundane. Lauren was awake because she was in pain.

While I was out having a beer and a grilled cheese sandwich with Sam, pain had jostled or poked or aggravated Lauren awake during the early hours of her slumber. She would have tried to ignore it at first, to overcome it by defying it, and attempt to return to the sanctuary of sleep. When that failed — and it usually did — she would have opened one eye and spied the bedside clock. Then she would have sighed as she calculated the number of hours of discomfort she would have to endure until dawn.

At some point that night she reached out, or more likely looked over, and discovered that the bed beside her was empty. How she'd felt about my absence I had no way to know. It was not the kind of complaint she would give voice to at that stage of our marriage. Until issues are worked through, infidelity changes the degrees of freedom for an offending spouse. Lauren and I weren't done with the working through.

As the aggrieved spouse, I had already decided that any advantage for me was illusory. For each of us there was an enduring price for her infidelity.

I wondered for a moment if Kobe, and Mrs. Bryant, felt the same way.

I'd already checked on the kids. Gracie was sound asleep down the hall, lying sideways in her double bed, having managed to wrap herself in her pretty duvet as though she were the protein filling inside some tropical, ginger-red burrito. When I'd gone downstairs, Jonas was, I thought, pretending to be asleep. I whispered his name into the dark a couple of times, encouraging him to engage with me. He didn't.

His sleep patterns worried me. His recovery worried me.

The fact that maintaining the pretense of sleeping had more value to him than any immediate alternative involving contact with me worried me.

I told myself to give it some thought when I wasn't so exhausted.

I entered the bedroom in my bare feet. Lauren was sitting up in bed, her knees clutched to her chest, rocking gently from side to side. The sway was measured and kept a certain rhythm, like a human metronome. It was the kind of rocking a mother would do to goad a cranky baby to return to her slumber.

The dogs were nearby. I knew they would both be on alert. Emily got up to greet me. She nuzzled me in the crotch a couple of times before she forced the considerable weight of her flank against my thigh, herding me toward the bed. Toward Lauren. Fiji was on her side smack in the middle of the big bed. She wagged her tail maniacally as I approached, rolling onto her back at the last second so that I would rub her soft belly. The long silk of her tail was tangled in the bedclothes.

I would disappoint her about the belly rub.

The only light in the room came from the moon and from a muted match in Kitchen

Stadium. Mario Batali versus some young guy with great hair who looked like he wanted to be somewhere without cameras, cooking something other than aubergines.

From the edge of the bed, I couldn't see Lauren's face. It was screened by her dark hair. She didn't speak. I didn't speak.

I knew her nighttime distress the same way I knew her distant cousins. We were related, but my knowledge was once removed.

When her deep, disabling pain erupted in the dark of night, I felt helpless. The dreaded aches covered territories in her legs and expanses in her long bones that didn't exist on any anatomical chart. There were never true culprits. No injuries. No bumps or bruises. Never any structures to identify, never any specific maladies to blame. The pain she experienced laughed at the puny efforts of ibuprofen. The pain mocked the maximum doses of Vicodin or Percocet. Lauren rarely bothered to take them at all.

The pain was in her head or in the trunk line of neural cable that was her spinal column — caused by the way MS had screwed up her wiring — but she felt the agony in her legs, so we acted as though that was reality.

Once I spotted her rocking on the bed, I

inhaled slowly, checking the room for telltale signs of cannabis. She hadn't been smoking. Occasionally, weed was palliative for her. Science didn't seem to know why. Other times it wasn't. Science didn't seem to know why that was true, either.

One night as I joined her as she toked on her bong on the deck outside the bedroom — a night the cannabis was working — I convinced myself that there were angels in heaven who liked the aroma of burning weed. It was as good an explanation as any.

I approached the bed full of trepidation.

Our marriage was balanced on some kind of edge. Was it a high-wire or a wide causeway? I didn't know the margins of error. Neither did she, I suspected. All I knew was that there had been nights recently when my compassionate touch hadn't been welcome, and there had been nights recently when I hadn't bothered to offer it.

Chronic illness is not contagious, but somehow it spreads. Maybe it's fungal. There were times Lauren's illness brought out the best, the most generous, part of me. There were times that it brought out more callous instincts. That night I checked my tank for reserves. I had none. Hella's story about the rape and Sam's sermon about yet another rape had, together, exhausted me.

Lauren was rocking herself as though the movement alone could take her someplace else. But it couldn't; I knew her tank was as empty as mine, or emptier.

I sat on the edge of the bed, reached beneath the comforter, and rested my open hand on the top of the foot of her left leg. She didn't cringe or pull away. That was a good sign. After a few moments of skin-to-skin contact, I gently extended her leg, bending the knee. She didn't stop rocking. She didn't resist me.

Next, I didn't so much begin to massage her leg as I began to caress it. I'd learned from numerous failures at amelioration that my goal wasn't to solve the mystery of her agony, not to try to find the muscles that needed release, nor to trace toward an insertion point, but my goal was to distract her central nervous system from its focus on her agony.

Simply, my goal wasn't massage. It was competition — to give her malfunctioning central nervous system a damn good game. An alternative. I had low expectations. I didn't expect to win. But if I could stir things up, maybe I could keep the match from being a rout. There were no guarantees. What worked one time failed the next.

I followed my instincts. That time, I began

with her ankle. I used some pressure, wrapping the joint with both hands, intertwining my fingers, and closing them around the bony structures like a vise. I tightened my grip, released it, tightened it again. In between, I used some strokes, too. Gentle ones. I allowed my fingertips to circle the round bones, over and again, and let the pad of my thumb trace the length of the ligaments and tendons that tied the joint to the rest of her lovely leg.

I used my fingernails to scratch lightly and the flat of my palm to confound whatever part of her nervous system might be paying attention. I etched letters on her flesh with my fingertips, spelling out my wishes for her and for us.

After a while, I moved down from her ankle to her foot and worked it, instep, arch, and heel. I compressed her toes, one by one. I focused on the sole for an extended time until I thought I could feel tension seep from her toenails. How could I tell? I just could. Maybe it was her breathing. Maybe it was the fact that Emily, the big Bouv, had finally closed her eyes. I then changed my attention to the long bones in Lauren's leg, confusing the scene further, I hoped, by coming from two directions. At once, I moved up her calf with my left hand, slowly, and down her thigh with my right hand, slowly, until both my hands arrived at her knee.

I used both my hands to surround the knee the same way I had her ankle. Intertwined my fingertips. My hands squeezed. They coaxed. I caressed her knee. I soothed it, scratched it, pressured it. Confused it. Confounded it.

Then I started the process all over with her right leg.

The whole endeavor took a good half hour. More.

The timer in Kitchen Stadium was still counting down when I was finishing.

Mario never seemed to lose his cool. His competition had been defeated long before a single dish came off the fire. The poor guy was going through the motions.

In the kitchen of life, I wanted to be Mario, not the guy who was plating the sauce that hadn't set up quite right. I wondered if Preston Georges had ever been in Kitchen Stadium. Had ever taken on Mario Batali.

Toward the end, as I was tracing the femur on Lauren's right leg, she leaned forward and grazed the back of my shoulder with her dry lips before she lowered her head to the pillow. A few minutes later, when I gently lifted the comforter back over her naked legs, her breathing seemed to have found the rhythm of sleep.

For some time, I sat where I was and I watched her.

Sam was right. My wife was a lovely woman. And yes, she was probably also a bit too enamored with the legal accomplishments of the currently famous man who was our new neighbor.

Maybe I did have something to worry about. Tomorrow.

I found sleep quickly. When the alarm jarred me awake the next morning, that fact surprised me.

Lauren fixed breakfast. The aroma of wheat toast and cheese and herb-crusted baked eggs in ramekins filled the kitchen. I hadn't been hungry when I got out of the shower. But the aromas had me famished by the time I made it to the kitchen.

Hot breakfasts weren't the norm in our house on hectic weekday mornings. Gracie — the one of the four of us least likely to pull her punches — asked, "So, is this like a pretend Sunday?" It earned a chuckle from her almost always taciturn brother.

When the kids rushed to their rooms to get ready for school, I said to Lauren,

"Thanks for breakfast. I appreciate it."

"You're welcome," she said, her back turned. "Last night helped. I was at the end of my rope." She was busying herself with the kids' lunches. Almost like it was an afterthought, she said, "Our neighbors will be home later today. Thought you'd want to know. Because of his issues with Emily."

My breath caught, just a little. "Gotcha. You don't think I should let her run at night?"

"Maybe not until we reach an understanding with them. Once they get to know her, you know, things might change. We have to remember that she can be a scary-looking dog in the dark. Perhaps a little neighborly give-and-take will help? Maybe they'll come around and appreciate the fact that there's a tough sheriff in town."

"Sure, it's worth a try. They've been where? In . . . Napa, or Sonoma? Do I have that right?"

"Napa. They have a second home. Hake is a wine nut. Owns some vineyards. Dabbles."

When did Lauren start thinking of Mattin as Hake? Huh. I bit my tongue, but I decided it would be weirder not to ask Lauren the next question in my head than to ask it. I said, "How did you hear they're coming home? Have they been in touch?"

Adrienne and Peter always kept us posted about their out-of-town plans. We had always done the same with them. We had keys to each other's houses. We picked up packages, collected each other's mail, watered each other's gardens. Responded to emergencies. Despite the initial tension with our new neighbors, perhaps they were reaching out a little bit to try to establish a similar routine.

Lauren was wiping the kitchen counter. She smiled at me, as though she was having the same kind of benevolent thoughts I was. "No, not with me, directly. Someone in the office . . . was in touch with Hake. That's how I heard."

I thought, *She didn't have to tell me that.* Lauren wanted me to know that the DA was still interested in whatever had happened Friday night.

Huh. "Something official?" I asked as I tapped the last of the coarse grounds from the french press into the compost bucket under the sink. The compost was for Adrienne's garden. Adrienne had been dead for what felt like ages. I continued to dump food scraps into her compost pile and to turn the black soil with a pitchfork. I didn't know why.

I was thinking that it was possible that a

prominent attorney like Mattin Snow might have a benign reason to be in touch with the Boulder County DA's office while he was at his second home in Northern California. But if the reason for the contact were benign, I didn't think Lauren would have offered me the tidbit about her office being in touch with him.

"Can't say," is how Lauren responded to my question about the nature of the DA's office's contact with our neighbor.

Lauren's "can't say" didn't mean that she didn't know. It meant that she was not at liberty to reveal what she did know. *She didn't,* I thought, *have to say that, either.* She could have left my query unanswered or white-lied me with a "don't know."

"Of course," I said. The dance steps were familiar. Lauren was leading, but we had rehearsed these steps often enough that I knew how to follow without tripping over her feet. By specifying what she couldn't tell me about work, she was informing me about her work in a completely deniable way.

My conclusion? Someone in the DA's office had asked Mattin Snow to return to town. Who? At the roulette table in my head, I slid my remaining chips to the spot on the felt marked "DA." But why did someone in the DA's office suddenly want Mattin to return to town? For an interview? I thought that was unlikely, even highly unlikely. He would decline the interview request. He was under no obligation to talk with Boulder County investigators. He was certainly under no obligation to cut short his vacation to satisfy the curiosity of the sheriff or the DA. The man was a prominent lawyer. He would know all that.

It had to be one of two other things. First, it could be about developments with forensics. Sam had said something the night before about pending forensics.

I didn't think the toxicology screen that had been done on Three-Wood Widow would be back so soon. The rape kit? After the few days that had passed, the most that investigators were likely to know would be whether or not viable DNA was present in the samples collected. The DNA results wouldn't be available.

Was Mattin being summoned back to Boulder to give a DNA sample for a potential match? Would he voluntarily comply? Or had the DA's office convinced the judge that they had probable cause for a warrant to collect exemplars?

That would be *holy shit* stuff. I didn't expect Lauren to tell me if that was true.

The other possible reason that Mattin would voluntarily return to Boulder? If someone was making a veiled threat to end the secrecy that marked this case. *Come back, or the accusations become public . . .*

I wasn't sure how much Lauren would tell me. "I wonder," I said to Lauren, "if Mattin coming back to town could have anything to do with Sam's visit out here on Saturday morning with the sheriff's investigator."

"Always possible," she said. "Some people are revered for a reason. They earn their reputations, you know? People consider them good guys because they are good guys. He has been a tremendously positive influence on many lives. Many women's lives."

Lauren was talking about Mattin. "You respect him?" I said.

"I do. And this . . . mess . . . makes him vulnerable. Not guilty. Vulnerable."

I found it an interesting choice of words. But her point was true. If Mattin were accused of acquaintance rape, all that he had done with the public to create and polish his image over his professional lifetime would be destroyed in a single news cycle.

I did not want to reveal to Lauren what I knew about the alleged rape or about my own growing doubts about how good a guy our neighbor was, or wasn't. I tried to sound both neutral and ignorant as I said, "I suppose, in any dispute, there will always be someone in the wrong."

"Exactly. And it's not always the one with the finger pointed at him. No one knows that better than a prosecutor. At least, an experienced prosecutor."

Except, I thought, *maybe a defense attorney.*

Lauren liked Mattin. She respected Mattin. And even though she hardly knew Mattin, she was telling me that she was inclined to give him the benefit of the doubt.

23

Traffic was nuts west of 55th. Some sewer project. I arrived at my office on Walnut minutes before my eight forty-five patient. That session ended at nine thirty. My nine forty-five was a late cancellation, so I found myself with the unexpected luxury of being free until ten thirty.

The late night with Sam was catching up with me. After my early patient left, I hustled down Walnut to Amante, determined to restart my engine with a triple shot. I carried the jet fuel back to my office and nursed it while I let Google educate me about the forensics of acquaintance rape.

Hella had told me that standard rape kit evidence had been collected at Boulder Community Hospital on the morning after the alleged assault. She also indicated that her patient had provided samples for a tox screen. I assumed that meant blood, but research broadened my horizons: the samples might also have included urine, saliva, and hair.

A text from Hella interrupted my research. **Have time for a quick consult today? Kind of urgent.**

I replied, **I'm free until ten.**

Need to show you something. Be right over.

Five minutes later Hella was sitting in my office. I was beside her on the sofa so that she could show me some photos on her phone.

She had already explained that she didn't want to forward them to me. She didn't have to explain why. "I saw my patient this morning at seven thirty. She told me she found this" — she pointed at the first photograph on her phone's screen — "in her purse last night. It was in a zippered pocket on the inside. She was switching bags, moving her things to a different one. She has this purse . . . thing. She spends way too much money on . . . bags."

"Value judgment, or pathology?" I asked.

"I'm still deciding," Hella said with a smile.

I wasn't too worried about the woman's purse fetish. I was more troubled that I was having difficulty recognizing what I was seeing on the screen of Hella's phone.

Hella could tell I was perplexed. "It's a small rectangle of aluminum foil, about the size of a large postage stamp. That's the edge of a thumbnail next to it. Gives it some proportion."

"Okay."

She moved to the next picture. "This is the other side of it. You can see that it's folded, carefully. This is the way she found it." Next photo. "Here it is open, unfolded. Those two things you see are —"

"Pills." They were round and white. Aspirin size, I guessed.

"Yes. She insists that they are not hers. She doesn't know what they are. Or how they got there."

I could guess what they were. And I could guess how they got there.

I reminded myself that I was Hella's supervisor. My role was circumscribed. Part of that role, however, was keeping an eye on Hella's countertransference.

"Okay," I said. "Tell me what happened between the two of you this morning."

"I touched them," Hella said. "She handed the foil to me, and I touched it. She told me to open it, and I did." I waited for her to reach the conclusion I had already reached. She wasn't far behind. "It was so stupid of me, Alan. I really regret that.

Touching it."

"What are you thinking?" I said. "Specifically."

"Fingerprints," she said.

"It's possible you might regret it," I said. "When your work enters the forensic realm with a patient, you need to make decisions differently in therapy. Lesson learned. What did you and she discuss?"

"She's no dummy. She wondered if someone had planted this in her purse. Some drugs."

"Because?" I assumed I knew the answer to my question. But assumptions and therapy are about as good a combination as drinking and driving.

"Of the rape. Her belief that she was drugged."

"Okay. When?"

She looked puzzled. "During the burglary?"

"Why," I asked, "not the night of the big party? An ounce of prevention by whoever drugged her? In case there was suspicion later?"

"God, I didn't think about that." Hella sighed. "She asked me what she should do. I let her try to figure it out, but she seemed . . . completely unable to problem-solve this. Finally, I told her she needed to show them to her attorney. Right away. He would know what obligations she had . . . about them. What she should do with them."

"Good call," I said.

Hella exhaled in obvious relief. "I'm so glad. She's probably there now."

"Okay," I said. "You handled it well, Hella. And you recognize what you could have done . . . more carefully." I stood up. "Wait, which purse were the pills in? The one she was moving her things from, or the one she was moving her things into? And was it the purse that she was carrying on . . . Friday night?"

"I assumed they were in the one she was carrying, but I don't really know. I see what you mean. That's important. Should I ask her?"

I weighed my next words with great care. "Even if you feel confident about her recollections — even if you're inclined to believe her — other people are making judgments, right now, about the veracity of your patient's story. Therapeutically, you need to remain aware of that."

Hella seemed defensive when she replied, "What reason would she have to lie to me, Alan?"

"I don't know," I said. "Sometimes patients lie to me and I never discover the motivation. There's another question you might ask —"

"Please," Hella said.

"— yourself."

"Oh."

"What reason would your patient have to tell you the truth?"

"You think my patient is lying, don't you?"

I shook my head. "I don't know. I'm trying to keep an open mind about what might have happened that night. I am encouraging you to do the same. Your patient acknowledges big gaps in her memory."

"She was drugged."

"And perhaps that is the explanation."

"You think I'm not . . . sufficiently suspicious?"

"Suspicious? I don't know, are you?"

"I don't know."

"She will be feeling great pressure, both internally and externally, to fill in those memory gaps."

"Jesus, Alan. Why on earth would a woman put herself through this if it weren't true?"

I almost said, "Duke lacrosse. Hofstra gang rape." But I didn't. I suspected that Hella and I would have discussions about those events at some point during the supervision of this case. During a quick curbside consultation about another matter, however, wasn't the correct time.

I said, "You like her. You liked her before the trauma. Your natural inclination is to care for her. But your *responsibility* with this patient, Hella, is to be therapeutic, regardless of the facts of last Friday night. As soon as you lock yourself into a specific version of reality — hers, or anyone else's — you limit the degrees of freedom each of you has in the therapy going forward."

"I have to think about that. I think there is some value in my support of . . . her."

"Please do think about it. The drugs she found in her purse? If they are not hers, someone has gone to great lengths to make it appear that they are. If there are fingerprints on them besides yours, they are probably hers."

Hella said, "He could have put them there that night. You're right."

"It's possible," I said. "But that would indicate he was concerned with being caught. If most of her story is accurate, I don't get the sense that her attacker is someone who operates that way."

Hella said, "She wouldn't show me the drugs if they were hers, would she?"

"Why not?" I asked.

"Why?" she asked.

"What conclusion did you reach when she showed you the drugs from her purse?"

"That she wouldn't show them to me if they were hers."

"There you go," I said. "She ended up with the result that is most in her interest."

"She's not that . . . devious," Hella said.

"Perhaps not. Or she is."

"You think she is that devious?"

"I think you're missing my point." I paused for effect.

Hella sighed.

"Have any of the forensic results come back?" I asked.

Hella nodded. "That's why I know she's at her lawyer's office right now. He set the appointment to discuss one of the forensic tests."

Two minutes after Hella left, my phone beeped with another text. I glanced at it expecting that she was asking me something or telling me something she had forgotten to ask or tell me earlier.

But the text was from Jonas. Jonas texting me from school was an infrequent event. **Forgot guy at house yesterday with survey stuff sticks with flags**

Jonas considered punctuation to be a bit

of a bother. I didn't have an ongoing text relationship with any other kids his age, but I thought his aversion to commas and periods might be generational.

Thanks I replied. **Good to know. Show me later?**

Most of Jonas's peers wouldn't have known, or cared, about the implications of a surveyor showing up on the property. Jonas wasn't most kids his age. His loss issues had left him hypersensitive to any signs of imminent change, especially indications of imminent change that he could reasonably interpret as monumental or out of his control.

Us he asked. In my head, I added the omitted question mark, aware that I was enabling his punctuation pathology.

No, the new neighbors I replied.

What r they doing

Not sure. I'll tell you what I know when I get home.

What time

About four thirty. I expected to be home by four, but where commitments to Jonas were concerned, my goal was to underpromise and overperform.

My house he asked. Again, I supplied the understood question mark.

In Jonas's world, "my house" was the one

in which he grew up. "Your house" or "the house" was the one in which he currently lived, with us.

I texted **That, or Peter's barn.**

Can they

Let's see what they're up to first. You cool?

Cool enough fgw

Fgw was Jonas's text shorthand for one of his mother's favorite little sayings. Adrienne often added the phrase "for government work" as an appendage onto her pronouncements. Sometimes the context would be clear. More often, not.

I doubted that Jonas really knew what the phrase meant. He employed it because it connected him to his mom. I suspected he would hold on to it as long as he felt the need. Like me and the compost pile.

I had a feeling that when Jonas showed me the surveyor's stakes, I was going to learn exactly where my half a hectare in paradise began and where it ended.

24

I got home before the kids were back from school. A woman was waiting on the front porch. She had short, dark hair and a narrow, sharp chin.

I didn't recognize her. I pulled to a stop beside her black Jetta. The shiny car had temporary plates and looked new. She stood as I got out of the car, tugging iPod buds from her ears.

"I was about to give up," she said. "It's starting to get cold out here. I wasn't really prepared for . . ." She let the sentence drift away.

The day had been mild for November, but the sun was just finishing its final dip behind the Divide, an event that occurred too early in the day in the autumn in those towns, like Boulder, that sit in the near shadows of fourteen-thousand-foot peaks. As a general rule, cold replaces crisp in rapid fashion along Colorado's Front Range shortly after the late-day shadows begin to spread in the valley.

The young woman was wearing well-aged jeans — I was pretty sure she had purchased them that way — a fleece vest from the Prana store on the Mall, and knit half gloves. Her feet were well protected in a pair of Uggs like ones that Lauren was coveting.

They were on her Christmas list.

The presence of a stranger on the porch meant the dogs were going nuts inside the house. Emily's bark, in particular, was full of alarm. When she was on edge, the sharpness in her bark was like someone bringing their hands together in a loud clap right beside your ears.

"Can I help you with something?" I asked the woman while my car was still between us. I was feeling a mite wary. Not too many strangers make it to the end of the lane. Even people who are hopelessly lost in Spanish Hills begin to recognize how badly lost they are before they ever stumble across the poorly marked entrance to our dirt and gravel path. If nothing else deters them, the big official-looking DEAD END and NO OUTLET signs by the mailboxes get drivers to reconsider their route.

"I'm Nicole. I was here the other night. With the caterers? Over at the other house."

She gestured across the lane to the big ranch house.

She had told me enough that I knew who she was, but not enough that I would understand why she had come back. I was slightly less wary and a tad more curious.

Nicole stuffed her hands in the back pockets of her jeans. She opened her eyes wide as she lifted both shoulders. "I was in the van. Were you the man on the lane, the one we almost . . . hit? Walking a dog?"

I was wearing my therapist expression. It's almost reflexive for me when I'm wary. I tend to wear it until I feel the ground beneath my feet stop shifting.

She kept talking. "I'm hoping to find — I actually came out here to talk to that man, the one who was walking the dog that night. The little black and white dog? Was that you?"

"Yes," I said.

"Oh good. Not good that we almost — I mean good that I found you. I guessed you must live here, since there are no other houses out this way. This far out, I mean, so close to . . . where we were working. Listen, I'm so sorry," she said. "That's why I'm here. To apologize. But I wasn't driving the van. That was —"

"Eric," I said.

"Eric," she said as she moved her hands from her jeans into the pockets of her vest.

"Yeah. You know his name?"

"I heard you yelling at him."

"He wouldn't stop the stupid van. I wanted him to stop to see if you were okay, if the dog was . . . hurt. I was so scared that he had hit the little dog. I wanted to go back and check, to see if you needed any help. But he wouldn't stop. He just kept on going."

"You were really yelling at him."

"I am so sorry. Are you all right? Please tell me you're all right."

"I'm fine," I said.

She lowered her voice, as though she were afraid to ask the next question. "The little dog?" she said.

"Would you like to come inside to meet her?"

A big smile erupted on Nicole's face. She had great teeth, either from enviable genes or fine orthodonture. I guessed the latter. A new car? Fancy clothes? A top-end set of teeth? Expensive boots? Nicole had access to money. I didn't think catering rich people's dinner parties would earn her enough to cover it.

"I would love that," she said.

"Come on in," I said as I stepped past her.

I unlocked the front door. Before I opened it, I tried to prepare her for the onslaught to come. "The big dog is Emily. She can be intimidating at first, but she's a sweetheart. I don't think you saw her the other night. The little one is Fiji, like the island. She was the one on the lane with me. Her goal in life is to eliminate prairie dogs from Boulder County. After that, the world. She dreams big."

The dogs, of course, were right behind the door. Emily barked twice more when she saw us but quickly made an assessment about the degree of present danger. Nicole, she decided, wasn't foe. Fiji kept barking. She wasn't as adept as Emily at making independent assessments of dangers. Or of the true threat posed by prairie dogs.

Nicole was clearly a dog person. She went right to her knees to greet the dogs. Jonas's puppy danced and licked at her chin. "I'm so glad this little dog is okay." Emily shoved the Havanese out of the way to hog Nicole's attention.

"Me, too," I said. I led Nicole toward the family room at the back of the house. As we walked down the short entryway, she grew speechless at the view of the Front Range at dusk framed by the big windows. The end of that day was blessed with one of those clear early-evening skies when the vista stretched all the way from Pikes Peak to Wyoming. Boulder was just beginning to sparkle to night-life in the valley below.

"Oh, wow," she said. "The sky. It's so pretty. It's . . . gorgeous. Oh . . . my . . . God." She pulled off her vest. "The city? No wonder you live up here. The other night was so . . . different. You can hardly see this view from the other house."

I'm accustomed to the reaction. I naturally give people a minute to adjust, to take in the wonder. I took Nicole's vest from her. It smelled like smoke and tobacco. I was pretty sure I felt the outline of a pack in the pocket. As I hung it on the coat rack near the door, I spied the top of a pack of Newports.

"You can see the view from upstairs across the lane," I said. "The view is special from the bedrooms upstairs."

"We didn't go up there."

"Why was Eric in such a rush the other night?"

"Oh, God, five things. Eric is okay, but sometimes he can be such an ass. That's number one. The party ran late — but they always do, especially when a chef is on site."

"There was a chef at the party?" I wanted to keep her talking.

"Yeah. Preston something. We just called him 'Chef.' Anyway, Eric had plans to meet a guy after — oh, what the hell, I don't care, Eric's dealer lives in Lafayette and was heading to Breckenridge and Eric wanted to meet up with the guy before he left for the mountains or he'd be dry all weekend. They were going to try to connect somewhere close by on South Boulder Road. But timing was a problem. He was pissed off at Chef and at his dealer and he was rushing to get back to town in time to score something. He had promised to drop me off on The Hill, which he didn't really want to do, but it's not like I could walk from here, right? He acted like it was a major inconvenience. Right after we got in the van he got angry at me because I refused to go meet his dealer with him — I don't do that kind of thing." She sighed. "That's most of it, right there. Really."

Nicole seemed chatty and lacking in boundaries. I hoped that with some gentle prodding, I could use her predilections to my advantage. I decided to do a little fishing. I said, "Please, have a seat. It was a pretty crazy night, I hear. All around. At the party, I mean."

"Tell me about it," Nicole said. She was dividing her attention between the dogs, a pair that would take as much affection as she would offer, and the evening sky, which from her vantage attracted a person's focus like a magnet finds iron.

I went silent, hoping she would fill in the conversation. She didn't. She was too distracted by everything else. I repeated my earlier prompt. "The crazy night? Is that part of why Eric was driving away like such a wild man? I mean, why didn't he turn on the headlights? What was that about?"

"To be honest, I didn't notice they weren't on either, not for a few seconds. I think that woman did get him going, too. She certainly got me going. She'd been so nice to us all night, and then after dessert was served . . . Really, all we had left to do was finish cleaning up after a buffet service for fifty. That's nothing for us. That's when the woman suddenly came into the kitchen and started hurrying us out the door like the darn house was on fire. Eric . . . uh, he didn't handle the change too great."

Mimi was in a hurry for the caterers to leave? I found that curious. In as light a voice as I could manage, I joked, "Was there a curfew or something? Why the sudden rush?"

"Your dogs are so terrific. What are they?"

Neither of the dogs are common breeds. I went into a familiar, for me at least, explanation of their lineage. After I exhausted her questions, I coaxed her back to her story about Friday night's hurried exit. "The sudden rush to leave? You ever figure it out?"

"You know, I still don't know what was up. Most of the guests were long gone. A few were still there. After we started packing up the van, she and the couple who hired us moved from the dining room into the big room and started sitting by the stone fireplace — you know where I mean?"

"I do," I said. I'd been there a few hundred times.

"Then a few minutes later, the hostess just seemed to snap. She hurried into the kitchen and decided that she needed us out of her house. She kept saying, 'Go, go, finish, finish,' in this hissing kind of whisper.

"Eric had no patience with her. 'We're going, we're going,' he kept saying. He doesn't like to be ordered around. She slapped a hundred-dollar bill on the kitchen counter at one point. She said she'd add another one if we were gone in ten minutes. 'Not eleven. Ten,' she said. A tip of a hundred bucks each? For that party? I'll rush a little, you know?"

"Did you guys make it out on time?"

"Chef got out before we did. But just by a little. He was a handful, too; God, Eric and

I were both so glad when he left — what a jerk. I hope you don't know him. Is he, like, your friend? Tell me he's not."

"I don't know him."

"Well, we made it. At the end we weren't really cleaning, but we just packed our stuff up and left. We didn't get her kitchen that clean. Not as clean as we're supposed to. But she said it was okay like it was, and we rushed out the door."

"With your big tips?"

"With the tips."

"What about the host? Her husband? Was he pushing you out the door, too?" Mattin's role during the evening remained a question to me.

"No, he stayed away from us, mostly. I mean, all night. She was managing the kitchen. He stayed with the guests during the meal. Oh, he took care of the bar and the bartender. The wine. Earlier, he had told us what wine to pour, that kind of thing. Gave us a sheet, so we wouldn't screw up. What glasses to use. What he wanted to breathe. The rest? His wife, or significant other, or . . . whatever she was. She has a humongous diamond, so I guess she's his wife. She's the one who was in charge of the food and the kitchen."

I was getting the impression that Nicole

hadn't recognized Mattin Snow. Given her age, and Mattin's likely fan demographic, that fact wasn't completely surprising. His media appeal was targeted more to capture the attention of Nicole's mother than Nicole. "You hadn't worked for them before? As a caterer? This was a first?"

She nodded. "Yeah. Chef said it was his first time there, too. Do you know how much he makes to do a spread like that? Unbelievable. What, some shopping, a few hours in the kitchen? Jesus, I wish I could cook." She laughed.

Keeping Nicole on track was taking some effort. "You had never met them before? The hosts?"

"No. Oh, I forgot, one weird thing — the guy? He was a complete Nazi about smells. Personal smells. When we arrived he asked me about perfume, if I was wearing any. He even leaned in and, like, smelled me. It was so . . . creepy. He asked Eric about cologne or body wash. I didn't tell Eric this, but at one point he was standing behind Eric and he leaned over like he was smelling near Eric's armpit. I mean, how odd is that? Eric would have gone bat-shit if he knew.

"Earlier? While we were still setting up, he caught Eric and me taking a smoke break outside. *Outside.* We weren't even close to the door to the house. He said he didn't want to see us doing it again. He said he did not want his guests to smell any smoke on our clothes while we served. 'Not with this wine. Not with this food. No way.' "

She was trying to imitate Mattin's voice and manner. I thought she did a reasonable job of it. I enjoyed the impersonation, which felt petty of me. I forgave myself. "So you guys couldn't smoke all evening?"

"It's not a big deal for me, I can go a few hours without a problem. Eric? It was making him pretty uncomfortable, I think. He's a couple-packs-a-day guy. Sometimes he even chains it. I think that's part of the reason he was such an ass at the end of the day. Nicotine withdrawal."

"I could smell the smoke in the van," I said. "As you guys drove by me on the lane. It was strong."

"That was Eric. I don't smoke in cars. It stinks up my clothes and hair too much. I opened my window even though it was so cold out. I was going out afterward — meeting friends on The Hill — I did not want to smell like smoke."

I was trying to think of a way to learn more about Mimi's motives for rushing the caterers away from the house. The motive that was jumping naturally to the top of the list was that she was aware of what was about to happen, and she did not want any witnesses present when it occurred. But I was having trouble believing that could be true.

Was she really complicit in what happened later on in the guest room? I had not even considered the possibility that she knew in advance what would happen to her friend that night. Could a wife really cooperate with her husband in planning a sexual assault on a mutual friend?

Without any trouble, I thought of a handful of patients I'd had over the years who were battered badly enough in their marriages to agree to participate in something like that. *Was Mimi a battered wife?* I knew it was possible.

I had to force myself back into the conversation with Nicole. "So, the hostess was hovering in the kitchen, waiting for you guys to finish and drive away?"

"Yeah, basically. Eric wanted to bag everything and go. I was worried that she would end up complaining to our boss about the cleanup we did, or didn't do. When we were almost finished packing up the van, I even took some pictures of the kitchen with my phone so that if she complained, I'd have some record of exactly what we did and what she told us not to bother with."

"She didn't end up complaining to your boss?" I asked.

"Nothing that came back to us."

"The bartender?"

"She left first. Thirty minutes earlier."

Fiji spotted an opening. She jumped onto the chair beside Nicole and climbed onto her lap. "Feel free to put her down."

"No, it's fine, she's cute." She let the puppy chew gently on her wrist — it was a sign of Havanese affection that I'd never quite understood — for a few seconds before she said, "Well, I am so glad that we didn't hurt you, or this gorgeous puppy. I was so worried."

"Me, too," I said. "Would've spoiled my night."

She smiled before she added, "Or that other guy. God, that one was really close."

25

What other guy?

My breath caught in my throat. I turned my head so I could check the time on the microwave. The carpool would drop off the kids in fifteen or twenty minutes. I didn't have much time to learn more about the other guy that Nicole had spotted on the lane Friday night.

"Can I get you something to drink?" I asked.

"Some hot tea?" she said. "That would be great. Whatever you have. I love mint."

I fixed the cup of tea as fast as I could. I was torn. The news of the presence of another man on the lane left me with a lot of questions for Nicole, but I didn't want her to perceive my curiosity, nor did I want her to still be at the house when the kids got home from school.

If Gracie knew Nicole was in our house, the world would know Nicole was in our house. Lauren would have no issue with Nicole's visit. But if Lauren ending up asking me some questions about what else I knew about that night, and more to the point, how I knew what else I knew about that night, I was worried the conversation could go in a troublesome direction.

I had absolutely no right to divulge to Lauren my supervision relationship with the alleged victim's therapist. I also did not plan to betray Sam's trust about the Kobe Bryant parable.

"Did you know we almost slid off that cliff? In the van? Could you tell?" Nicole asked. "Oh, this tea is good. Thanks. Is it Celestial Seasonings? Which one?"

"I can go check," I said. "If it's important." I really did not want to go check what kind of tea it was.

"Never mind. After we . . . passed you? Almost . . . hit you. Could you tell we almost flipped?"

"It probably felt like a cliff to you in the dark, but it's more like a steep slope in that section of road," I said. "But, yeah, I could hear your tires spinning. I could tell that Eric was going way too fast going into that turn; I did think for a minute that the van might roll over. It's a tough pair of curves in the dark. I was thinking he didn't even know the second curve was coming."

Nicole shook her head. "He didn't know the first curve was coming. I was barking at Eric to slow down. He was cursing at the road. We had just almost hit you and the puppy and he had just turned the headlights on, and we were just coming out of that second curve — that's the spot where we came closest to rolling, the end of that second curve — and suddenly there's this guy on the road. Just standing there. Out of nowhere. I mean, it was like, 'Hello, what are you doing here?' "

"The man was by himself? No dogs?" I asked. Some of our neighbors with homes near the beginning of the lane occasionally walk their dogs late at night. We see each other when I'm out with Emily and Fiji. But I rarely saw a solitary pedestrian heading in the lane that late at night.

"No. This man was alone. And I was worried about dogs by then. I would have noticed if he had a dog."

"Was he young? Old?"

"It was hard to tell, honestly. He was cold, all bundled up. It was windy by then. He had a hoodie under a jacket. The hood part was up over a stocking cap. The wind was whipping good. Maybe he had on a backpack, too. I'm not sure about that, but maybe . . . yes. I didn't really see his face." She sipped some tea. "Does it sound like it could have been one of your neighbors?" She smiled. "You think?"

A stocking cap? "No," I said. "Doesn't sound like my neighbors." The closest neighbors down the lane — they lived a few hundred yards beyond the S-curve — were a pleasant gay couple who tended to keep to themselves. Neither was predisposed to take solo walks on the lane late on a frigid weekend night, especially not in a hoodie and stocking cap, wearing a backpack. "I have no idea who you saw. How close did Eric come to hitting him?"

"Closer than we came to you. I mean, close. By the time the headlights swung around so we could see him, we were right on top of him. Oh, he was a smoker, too. He had a cigarette in his hand that went flying when he jumped off the side of the road. It actually started a little fire. That was weird, too. God, what a night."

"A fire?"

"I had screamed at Eric to stop after the guy tumbled away, or jumped away, or whatever it was. At the time, I thought we might have hit him. There was no *thunk* or anything, but he really went flying. I watched it in Eric's mirror. Eric finally did stop, maybe fifty yards farther down the road. I kept my eyes on the spot where the guy had gone down until I saw him stand back up. At the same time he stood up, I also saw smoke curling up from the dried grasses right behind him. Flames jumping. It was scary. But the man stomped it all out, kicked at the dirt. Then he turned to the van and flipped us off.

"Eric flipped him right back and drove away. He was all, 'What the F was the guy doing there in the middle of the night? That is so not my F-ing fault.'

"I kept my mouth closed. By then? All I wanted to do was track down my friends in Boulder and have a couple of drinks. Eric bitched the whole way but he dropped me off on The Hill and went off to find his dealer. I found my friends; we ended up hanging out for drinks over at The Sink." She shrugged and smiled. "My night got better."

People Nicole's age had been hanging out with friends for drinks at The Sink on The Hill in Boulder for decades. "It was quite a night for you," I said. I had one more question I wanted to ask. I tried to find a sideways manner of posing it. "Did Eric meet his dealer on South Boulder Road?"

Nicole hesitated before she said, "No."

I didn't believe her. "Did the guy you almost hit call the police? Did Eric get in any trouble?"

Nicole looked at me suspiciously. "No, I mean . . . no. Why would he? We didn't . . . hit him. Just came close."

I could have explained that a charge of reckless driving doesn't require the actual impacting of a pedestrian. Running a couple of them off the road would probably be sufficient legal grounds. But I didn't think the lesson would have served any useful purpose. I said, "You know how people can be sometimes. I was just curious how bad the evening got for you guys."

What I really wanted to know is if Nicole had talked to the police about the housewarming, if any investigators had tracked down the caterers to interview them about what they might have seen inside earlier in the evening. I also wanted to know if the police or the sheriff knew about the man that Nicole and Eric saw on the lane, or about Eric's rendezvous with the dealer. Nicole didn't spot the intent of my questioning.

"Did you call the police on us?" she asked me. "Because a woman called me. A detective."

I held up my hands. "No, I did not. No. I

admit I cursed at Eric a little, but that's as far as that got. What did the detective want?"

"Just asked what time we left. Whether people were still at the party. That's all. You know, I should probably go. Midterms. Studying."

"Thank you," I said, "for coming back out here and checking on us. You didn't have to do that. I appreciate it."

"I felt bad. If it was just me, I would have stopped the van. Or I would have come right back the next day. But Eric said he'd get me fired if I got him in any trouble about his driving that night. So I didn't. Then yesterday? My dad told me that he didn't want me to work for the rest of the semester and he said I could quit my job if I'd also quit smoking. He promised to up my allowance to give me more spending money, and he said he'd pay for nicotine patches. Pretty good deal, huh? So I quit the job. And I've quit smoking. It all worked out. I'm really, really glad you're okay. But I have to go."

I needed some way to reach Nicole if I had more questions about the events of Friday night.

I said, "You ever do house-sitting gigs?"

"Seriously? Up here? I would so love it." She turned *love* into a multisyllable word.

"Dogs, too?" I said.
"Absolutely. I adore your dogs."
I handed her a pen and paper. "Give me your number. We're always looking for reliable people to help us out when we leave town."
I would no more give Nicole the keys to my house than I would ask Kobe Bryant to take my daughter to the prom. As she wrote down her number, I imagined her head spinning with plans for the amazing party she would have in our house while Lauren and I were out of town.
She handed me the pad. "Please. I would love, love, love it. To help you, I mean. I almost owe you, right?"
"I will," I said. "Count on it."
I'm accustomed to people — patients — lying to me. I'm not accustomed to lying right back at them. I had to admit that I was kind of enjoying the banter.
I helped Nicole on with her vest. I asked, "How's the quitting going? Smoking? Is it difficult?"
"Good, good," she said. "I've been wanting to, you know, for a while. Quit. A lot of guys don't like it. Girls smoking."
I wondered why she lied. Reflex? Daddy transference? Or did she have a reason?

26

The dogs had been cooped up all day. They had to go out. I fumbled around for a working flashlight — the "working" part was key; I seemed to always find a couple of dead flashlights before I found one with charged batteries — and then I got the halter on Fiji. I allowed Emily to head out the door first without a lead. She stayed within shouting distance of me as I marched Fiji out the lane, through the second curve of the S.

Emily took off up the hill when I slowed the march so I could begin searching for a patch of crushed grasses and indications of a small fire.

Fiji seemed pretty excited by the fact that I was in the grasses and not on the lane. I think she was pretty sure I had finally capitulated and was assisting her with her prairie dog hunt.

Nicole's description of what had happened made my work easy. I spotted a wide swatch of flattened, dried grasses on the west side of the lane almost immediately. It was less than fifty feet from the northern edge of the S-curve. Identifying the square foot or so of charred grasses took another couple of minutes of searching. The cigarette had blown a good twenty feet south in the wind. I used one of the dogs' unused poop bags to retrieve a cigarette filter from the middle of the burned area.

I had a suspicion that the charred butt would be a Newport. I didn't buy Nicole's story that the man she'd spotted on the lane was responsible for the fire. I was guessing that Nicole might have sparked it when she tossed her cigarette out the window.

In the distance, I spotted the headlights of a car turning onto the lane down near the mailboxes. *The kids' carpool,* I thought. I pulled my hands together and put out the clarion call for Emily to rejoin me. She didn't wait for the second call; I saw her bound down the hill from the highest ridge. I got her back on her leash about twenty seconds before a black Town Car rolled even with us on the lane. The car slowed to a stop and a back window opened halfway. Inside were Mattin and Mimi.

I leaned over and said hello, while I offered a silent prayer that the two dogs would be on their best behavior.

Mattin said, "I see the dog's on a leash. Very neighborly of you, thanks. We do appreciate it."

I feared that he had just seen Emily off-leash and that his gratitude was not only facetious but sarcastic. I decided my best bet was to ignore the comment. "Welcome home," I said. "Nice trip?"

Mattin answered. He said, "There are no bad weekends in Napa. I especially love the time after the berries are crushed. Everything has slowed down, the tourists are gone, the people are relaxed. The valley is full of hope about the harvest. Do you ever go?"

"Lauren more than me. She used to live in the City before we met. Do you grow grapes? Make wine?"

"We have some vines. Others make the wines. For me, it's a privilege to be even a small part of the process." He turned and smiled at his wife before he looked back to me. "Well, if you ever decide to make a trip to Napa, we'll introduce you to some friends who are winemakers. Changes everything, to meet the winemakers. Great people."

"Thank you. That's very kind. And neighborly."

Mattin smiled at me with his side-of-abus smile. The window rolled back up. And they were gone.

I wasn't sure what someone should look like after he's been summoned back to town to provide DNA samples because he's under suspicion of committing sexual assault on a close friend. But at that moment Mattin Snow didn't look like a man who had a worry in the world that extended beyond the end of my dogs' leashes.

"Good girl," I said to Emily. "Good, good girl."

I watched another set of headlights turn onto the lane. This time it would be the carpool. The dogs and I hurried back home.

Gracie walked in the door and asked who'd been smoking.

Diversion was my only hope with the kid. I got her a snack and she started her homework. I asked Jonas if he'd come outside and show me the surveyor's stakes from the day before. The dogs wanted to come. Grace wanted to come. I asked her to stay with the dogs. All three girls were unhappy with me.

Jonas and I were barely out the door when the garage door opened across the way. Mattin sped out the lane in his Cadillac sedan. He might have waved at us. His windows were tinted so darkly that I couldn't have said one way or another.

I waved at the car. Jonas didn't.

Jonas asked, "You want to see all of them? They go way up the hill. And way down the ravine. All the way out to the curve on the lane."

It was apparent to me that Jonas had covered the ground necessary to find all of the surveyor's stakes. It gave me a context for the extent of his anxiety about what might be going on.

"How about just the ones on this side, this end. Nearest the two houses and the lane. Those are the ones that we have to be worried about."

He jumped on that. "What kind of worried?"

I should have been more careful with my choice of words, but I'd already decided that I would tell Jonas what my concerns were about our neighbor's plans. Trust required it. "I am . . . concerned that the new owners of your old house will do some renovations. Remodeling, addition, new construction, something. I'm thinking any work they do will most likely be down here, close to us at this end of the lane. I say that because that's where the access is. That's where the utilities are."

"Utilities?" he said.

"Gas and electric. Wells. Septic — um, sewer. Phone. Access is the lane. They might have to get permission to extend it. I think whatever they decide to do — if anything — will be down here."

"I know what access is," he said. He was working something out in his head. "What kind of renovations?"

"I don't know. I'm thinking maybe an addition to the house. You know the story about the missing turret, right?"

He nodded. Peter and Adrienne had tracked down the original architectural drawing for the house. The first owner of the ranch had planned a grand turret on the southwest corner, but it had never been constructed.

"That'd be okay," he said. "If they wanted to build the missing turret. Mom always wanted to see how the house would look with the tower."

"I agree," I said. "That would be okay. I'm also thinking they might have ideas about what to do with your dad's shop. The barn blocks the views toward Eldorado from the first floor of their house. They might not like that."

"Can't they just go upstairs? The views upstairs are fine. You can see everything."

"You'd think they could," I said. "Just go upstairs. The Realtor who sold the house told Lauren and me that the new owners saw 'opportunities' with the house you grew up in. That must mean they have ideas already about what they might like to do. My friend Diane is a friend of theirs, and she said she heard that an architect is involved. That might mean they even have plans. You know, firm ideas. Maybe drawings. That's all that I know so far, kiddo."

Jonas took a couple of steps. Kicked at a round stone. "Can they do . . . whatever they want?" His voice told me he was imagining something awful.

I guessed it had to do with bulldozers. "There are limits. The county has land-use ordinances. Size limitations. Restrictions on what can be done with historic structures. They have to follow all those rules. And others. They can't put a store out here. Or an apartment building." I eyed him for a moment. Jonas's face usually told me little. "Is there something specific you're worried about?"

He took a few steps before he said, "I don't want them to knock anything down. Anything. Our house." "Our house" meant his old house. "Or Dad's shop. Can they do that? Just knock stuff down?"

"Maybe, Jonas. It's possible. But I don't know the exact answer to your question. I share your concern, though. I'm hoping that the house and the barn are old enough that they'd be protected historic structures."

"How old is historic?" he asked.

Great question. I told him I didn't know the answer. We could check the regulations online when we went back inside. The path he was leading us on led toward the ravine side of the old barn. The steep ravine to the south separated the hillside with our home on it from the scenic overlook that tourists used to gaze down on Boulder and up at the foothills and the Divide from the edge of Highway 36 on the eastern ridge of the Boulder Valley.

"Here," he said. He kicked at the dirt near a stake with a yellow plastic marker tied around the top.

I followed him as he marched thirty yards or so to another. "And here." He kicked again. He extended his arm at one more stake in the near distance. "And there." It was almost too dark to see it, but not quite.

"This might be our property line," I said, swinging my arm between the three stakes. "Ours. I mean yours, mine, Gracie's, and Lauren's. This could be the line that separates what's ours from what belonged to you and your parents."

"That's what now belongs to the new neighbors, right? Which means everything on this side is . . . theirs?" He faced toward the house where he'd lived almost his entire life and the wide-open hillside above it.

"Yeah. You and your parents had over ten acres. A small part of the original ranch, but a big, big piece of land. All the way from the ravine to the curve in the lane. And from the lane, up the hill almost to the ridge. That's a lot of land."

Over four hectares, I was thinking. If any kid knew about hectares, it would be Peter's kid. My kid.

"How much do you have?"

"We" — I made a point of including him, even if he wasn't yet inclined to do so — "have almost half a hectare. A little more than an acre."

Jonas was quiet for a moment. Then he asked, "What about the lane? Who owns the lane?"

"The lane is something called a right-of-way. It's shared access. Although somebody may technically own it — have a deed that includes that strip of dirt — nobody can build on it or block access to it. Not us, not them."

He was at least two steps in front of me.

He faced the ravine. "I told my uncle I didn't want him to sell the house."

As he was beginning to recover from his injuries and digest the reality of his loss after the bombing in Israel, Jonas had become very vocal about his resistance to selling his family home. Given the losses he had suffered, I thought rushing into a sale would be a huge mistake and managed to get his mom's brother to postpone the date the house would be listed to give Jonas time to come to terms with the eventual sale. His uncle relented once. But that was all.

I said, "I wish it hadn't been necessary."

"It wasn't necessary," Jonas said. "I don't need the money." He took a couple of steps. "Do I? Do I need the money?"

"No, Jonas. You don't need the money."

"My allowance is plenty." Although he had never asked how much money he had inherited — it was plenty, plus a zero or two — he was letting me know how out of control the universe looked from his vulnerable position in it.

All his money didn't make that view any better.

He walked me to the rest of the nearby markers. He kicked at the dirt near every one of them. If the surveyor's marks were accurate — and I had no reason to suspect they weren't — it turned out that we owned less of the land fronting the lane than I'd long suspected. Although I knew our lot was shaped like a slice of pie, it was a much more acutely cut slice than I'd remembered; the narrowest part of the slice was the section where our house, and more recently the garage, had been built adjacent to the lane. Most of our remaining half a hectare was on the steep slope that fell down below our house. It was a nice slope — the buffer it provided to our downhill neighbor's land was certainly welcome, but from the point of view of the possible future development of our closest neighbor's property, the actual demarcation line wasn't the best of all possible news for us.

The truth was that we didn't own much of the land that they might covet.

For the first time in my adult life, I found myself wishing I was the master of a larger plantation; Ahah was no longer a big enough chunk of Spanish Hills for me.

"You seen any other strangers out here lately?" I asked Jonas. "Other than the surveyor?" I was especially curious if he'd seen the solitary man walking on the lane on Friday evening, or seen him at any other time.

He spun away and took a couple of steps

in the direction of our house. "Nope," he said, his back to me.

"Are you sure?" I asked. I asked it because I thought, just maybe, he'd hesitated before he'd said *nope.* I could usually read Gracie with 90 percent–plus accuracy. Which, frankly, was nowhere near good enough a percentage to give me any parental comfort. Jonas? Not even close.

"Pretty sure," he said. He skipped a couple of times, doubling the distance between us. It wasn't unlike Jonas to get jittery and physical in a geeky way when he was anxious about something. Was our previous conversation about the uncertain future of his original family home responsible for the anxiety he was displaying? Or was it the question I had just asked him about whether he'd seen any strangers around lately?

I am an experienced psychologist. I should have been able to figure that puzzle out. But I couldn't tell. I tried again. "Nobody walking out here by himself recently?"

"Why? You see somebody?" He didn't turn around.

"I did not," I said. "I'm just trying to understand this whole situation. The new neighbors. What they're up to. Any new information will help. An architect, maybe?

Photographer? Contractor? Everything and anybody you notice will help us sort out what they might be doing. Like the surveyor. That was a great catch."

"Gotcha," Jonas said.

"You'll tell me if you see anyone?"

"Yep." He sprinted toward the house. "When's dinner?" he yelled.

I was about to tell him that Lauren was bringing something home, but he was already out of easy earshot.

27

Lauren was running late. She'd called and spoken to Gracie while I was outside with Jonas. Gracie informed me that I was supposed to do dinner.

"Things are okay with your mom?" I asked my daughter.

"Cool, cool, cool. Work, work, work," Grace said dismissively, letting me know clearly what she thought of my question. My daughter was ready for me to walk away. I didn't walk away. "That's it," she said, verbalizing her stance, in case I'd somehow missed it. When I capitulated — the alternative required parenting energy and enthusiasm that I lacked — and started to walk away, she added, "What are you making?"

I told her I didn't know. Dinner hadn't been on my radar.

"Can we have coq au vin?" She pronounced it *cocoa vinn,* like it was the nickname of a wiseguy named Vinnie who had a thing for hot chocolate.

Until recently, she'd called the dish "purple chicken." I considered her use of mangled French to be true progress. "Are you kidding? That takes hours."

"I don't care. I had a snack. Who was smoking in here?" she asked, her nose wrinkled in disgust. "And tell me again why we can't use calculators for our homework. And how come calculators don't show their work? It makes no sense."

She didn't want answers to her questions. She only wanted to sprinkle salt into my parental wounds. "Gracie —"

"Dad . . ."

I sighed. I shook my head. I opened windows on each side of the house and prayed for a cross breeze.

Lauren didn't drag herself in the front door until almost eight. The kids were fed. They'd each retreated to their private spaces for some alone time. I could tell the moment I saw Lauren that the day had been much too long and taxing for her. She looked like she'd been dredged in flour, fried, and fricasseed in red wine.

Like cocoa vinn.

While she hobbled off to spend some slow-motion mommy time with each of the kids, I chopped some spinach leaves, grated some Parmigiano, and crisped a little sliced ham for a frittata. I took great comfort from the fact that when I was in need of an emergency meal, I was always minutes away from a serviceable frittata.

Lauren started her meal by leaning back on the kitchen chair and cradling a glass of wine. I was about to tell her about Nicole's visit and the revelation about a man on the lane the night of the housewarming when she said, "Ready for this? Hake hit a bicyclist today, Alan. That's where I've been. The whole office is in turmoil."

"What? When?"

"Late afternoon, early evening. On Broadway, near Table Mesa. It was a bad accident."

"Is the cyclist all right? Helmet?"

"Transported to Community by ambulance. Yes, helmet. He's in surgery."

"God. Do you know who it is?"

"I didn't hear a name, babe. It's a guy. And he was . . . in club Lycra."

Shit. I knew the recreational road bike community in Boulder well. I'd been part of it for many years. If the injured cyclist was one of us — and since he was riding in club Lycra, he may well have been — I probably knew him. And possibly knew him well.

"That's not all. The worst part, maybe? Hake drove away. From the scene."

"Really?" I was dumbfounded. *How could he be that stupid?* "The man is a lawyer, for god's sake."

"He only left for a minute. When he got back, he told other people who stopped to provide assistance to the bicyclist that he wasn't sure what had happened at first, didn't realize that the sound he'd heard meant he'd hit someone, and he just continued around the block while he tried to sort it out in his head. He said when he pieced together what might have happened and began to be concerned that he might have hit a pedestrian, he got back there the quickest way he could, which was by . . . going around the block."

"Yeah? Does that . . . sound right to you?" It sounded contrived to me.

"There are witnesses. The time frame fits. He was only gone from the scene for a minute or two and came back from the same direction he'd been driving before, like he'd driven straight around the block. But still . . . he drove away from an injury accident, Alan. That's a . . . problem."

"Is that hit-and-run?"

She two-shoulder shrugged. "Sure it is. Doesn't mean it will be charged that way, but yes, he's vulnerable. Hake drove away from an injury accident."

"Was it his fault?"

"No determination, but it sounds like it. Witnesses say the cyclist clearly had the right of way. Hake's car swerved toward him. A small impact that forced the bike into the front end of a car that was just entering the roadway from a gas station. Witness statements have Hake talking on a cell phone when it happened."

"Talking, not texting?" I asked. Absurdly, it was illegal to drive while thumbing a ten-character text in Colorado but completely acceptable to drive while punching a ten-character phone number into the same device. Our legislators had determined that certain forms of distracted driving were just fine. Others, not.

"Talking."

The accident sounded like a potential legal nightmare for Mattin Snow. His second legal nightmare in a week. "Is he in custody?"

Lauren swept her open hand up into her black hair, running her fingers all the way to the crown of her head. "Get this: He was on the way to see Casey Sparrow about that . . . thing last Friday at his house. He was driving to her new office on South

Broadway. He called her from the scene. She told him to shut his mouth, of course, and got there seconds after the ambulance arrived. She followed the patrol car that ended up transferring him to 33rd Street.

"We got called in immediately, because of the . . . pending issues. I covered some other things for Elliot, but I left the office before it all got sorted out. Elliot is probably still over at the Public Safety Building while the police finish the investigation. They'll have to decide what to do about Hake. Everyone's falling over each other trying to figure out how to frame this. For the media, I mean. The politics of this alone, if you think about it . . . What a mess."

I couldn't stop thinking about the injured cyclist.

"To get back to your original question, I don't think Hake will spend the night in jail. Casey won't let that happen. I doubt that the DA or the chief wants it to happen. Not until there's a resolution on the other matter. This is one big can of worms."

The "Elliot" Lauren was mentioning was Elliot Bellhaven, the first deputy DA, Lauren's boss. Once, her friend. Lately, not so much. "Where does Elliot come down on the . . . drama you guys have been dealing with about our neighbor? Before tonight?"

"I think he sees it like I see it."

Lauren had seemed to be skeptical from the beginning about the acquaintance-rape charges and was not a fan of her young colleague's management of the case, but I wasn't sure exactly how she saw the events of the previous Friday.

"Which is how?" I asked. She had finally started making a dent in the frittata. "Never mind. Eat," I said. "We can talk about this later."

Between bites, she said, "No, I want to answer you. I think it's time for me to give you a better sense of what's been going on, but I think I should say the things I have to say when . . . we're a little less likely to be interrupted. I don't want the kids to overhear some of this."

From her bedroom, Gracie yelled, "Overhear what?"

I was trying to convince myself that my sense of dread about Gracie's still distant, but ominously looming, adolescence was nothing but parental fearmongering on my part. It wasn't working. I dreaded my daughter's coming adolescence.

"Point taken," I said. I'd left some toasted multigrain bread on the counter. I stood to get it. "I saw him come home and then leave the house. Mattin. Earlier this afternoon. It was a little after four, maybe. I was on the lane with the dogs when a Town Car came by and dropped him and Mimi off from the airport. The car stopped for a second — we talked briefly, about his trip. They both seemed to be relaxed, in a good mood. Mimi was quiet. Emily just happened to be on her leash, which was lucky. Then a short while later I saw him drive away. By himself. That was it."

"In the sedan or the SUV?"

"The Caddie."

"That's what he was driving when he hit the bike. Did you smell any alcohol? I mean earlier. When the Town Car stopped?"

"No, I didn't. And I was pretty close to him, too — a couple of feet away. I had to lean down to speak with him while he was in the car. Didn't they test for alcohol at the scene?"

"I haven't gotten a straight answer about that. Casey Sparrow may have intervened before the test was complete."

I shook my head at the mess. Refusing to take a sobriety test was a big problem all by itself. "This isn't going to stay quiet," I said.

Lauren nodded. "Before I left work, my secretary showed me a breaking news alert about the accident that was already up on the *Camera* website. They had Hake's name.

The fact that he drove away. They already had a couple of witness interviews. The networks and tabloids will pick it up, too. They probably already have."

Boulder is considered by many to be a cycling mecca, but the natural tension that exists on public roads between bicyclists — whether those riders are commuting, recreating, or training — and motorists is as pronounced in Boulder as it is anywhere. It might be worse here because there are so many bicycles on our town's roads.

The fact that a car had hit a cyclist and that the cyclist was injured was not going to remain secret. Not for an hour. Not in Boulder. The cyclist grapevine would be all over it. Especially if the injury was serious. Especially if it appeared the motorist was at fault. And had driven away from the scene, however briefly.

And especially if the motorist was a celebrity.

I wanted to go back to something Lauren had said earlier. "You said Mattin hired Casey to represent him about . . . the Friday-night thing? Is that news? Or has she been involved all along?"

"No way for me to know. I got the sense that we didn't learn about her involvement until —" Lauren stopped herself, took a deep breath, and smiled at me gently. "I should finish eating this. Let's get the kids to bed. Then I'll tell what I can tell you. How's that?"

"Sounds good," I said.

"Why are the windows open?" Lauren asked. "It's getting a little cold in here, don't you think?"

"Someone was smoking," Gracie called out from her room.

"Someone was smoking?" Lauren said.

"No. Long story. We had a visitor," I said as I stood. "I'll tell you later. I'll close the windows, then I'm going to go across the lane and check on Mimi. I want to make sure she's okay. God knows what she's heard about the accident. This has to be a miserable situation for her. Tell the kids I'll be in later to kiss them good night."

"That's really sweet of you," Lauren said. "Checking on Mimi. I mean, considering. You know."

She'd said it like she meant it. "I'm a nice guy," I said. "I haven't had any trouble with Mimi. Anyway, she's Diane's friend. I won't be long."

"You are a nice guy," Lauren said again, as though one of us needed convincing.

"You'll be okay?" I asked.

"I'm fine. I can get the kids ready for bed."

28

Lights set on security timers had illuminated the interior of the big ranch house since the couple had left for California. As I crossed the lane, I noted a different pattern of lights on inside. I considered it a reliable indication that Mimi was home. I knocked on the door loudly enough that I was confident the pounding could be heard from the kitchen in the middle of the house.

No answer. I knocked again, a little more forcefully. I added a few extra knocks, too. Still no answer. I tried the bell. I hadn't heard any sound when I pressed the button, so I was thinking that the bell probably wasn't working.

The doorbell had been cantankerous for years. It worked sometimes. It failed sometimes. Right around the time Peter was murdered, Adrienne had been bugging him to find the short in the wiring. Peter never got around to it. Much later, after she'd recovered from her loss and forgiven him for, as she put it, "boffing the nanny," the randomness of the doorbell became an ongoing amusement for her. She liked to think that God was determining on a case-by-case basis if she would know, or should know, whether or not she had visitors.

Adrienne and I had long disagreed about God's omniscient perspective over us all; I still didn't think God was at all interested in whether or not I was able to announce my presence at my friend's door. Or about much else I did.

Adrienne disagreed. She wasn't sure God cared about everything she did, but she was convinced God had a thing about her doorbell. But that was before Israel. She and I never got a chance to discuss her feelings about God's grand design after that. The doorbell was never fixed.

I gave Mimi a full minute to respond. I pressed the button again, just in case. Again, no answer. I stepped off the porch and wandered over to the garage to see if the family's second car, a big SUV, was inside. It was.

My next logical step would have been to call Mimi on the phone, but I realized that I didn't know any numbers for her. No cell number. No home number. No e-mail address. We just weren't the kinds of neighbors who exchanged numbers or spare keys.

As I turned to shuffle away from their garage, my hands in my pockets, I spotted a pair of headlights weaving through the S-curve on the lane. The lights were moving faster than they should have been moving. Had Mattin been released from custody?

It wasn't his Cadillac. I smiled when I recognized that the approaching car was a familiar Saab convertible. It belonged to my friend Diane.

She pulled to a stop between the two houses. She killed the engine but left the headlights on. The Swedish electronics beeped some disapproval at her about something, maybe the headlights. Diane didn't care. She was immune to beeped cautions. She hopped right out of the car.

"You heard?" I said.

She nodded and gave me a quick hug. "Mimi isn't answering her phone. I decided to come over to . . . be with her. She's been through so much, Alan. I mean, nonstop crap, for years, stuff you don't even . . . stuff you can't imagine. She just doesn't deserve this."

"When I heard what happened, I came over to see if she needed anything. Wanted some company. A ride to be with her husband." I shrugged. "I knocked, tried the bell. So far, she hasn't answered the door. It may be that she just doesn't want to talk to me."

In a teasing tone, Diane said, "Ohhh, why wouldn't anyone want to talk to *you?*"

"Really?" I said, only a little hurt. "That's where you're going with this?"

"Kidding. That was very sweet of you, Alan."

"What did you hear?" I asked. "About what happened in town."

Diane said, "I got a call from Helena — she's another friend, an electrical engineer. I don't think you know her. She and her husband were there on Friday night, too. Helena is the one with Gwyneth Paltrow's hair? Does that help?" I shrugged. "Any-hoo" — Diane was cognizant that she was veering a little outside the lines — "she's the one who told me that Hake was in a traffic accident. She didn't know any details for sure. She thought it was something with a bicycle. People are injured, but Hake is okay. He's being interviewed by the police. That there's a possibility that it could turn out to be a problem for him. That's pretty much all I know."

"That's pretty much what I heard, too," I said. Diane would have plenty of time to learn how much worse the situation might turn out to be. Not only for her friend, but also for the injured bicyclist.

My phone vibrated. I said, "Just a second," to Diane. The screen displayed a forwarded text from a cycling buddy. The cyclist grapevine had gone active. All the text said was that there'd been a hit-and-run on South Broadway with a car and a bike. The injured bicyclist was Rafael Toronado. He was critical.

The text was also a plea for witnesses to the accident. And blood donors. B negative. *Jesus. Shit.* My heart sank. Rafa — everyone had called him that, as long as I'd known him — was more than an acquaintance, less than a friend. We rode together occasionally, rarely by design. At the end of the day — actually, well before the middle of most days — I couldn't keep up with him on Boulder's roads. I had a prayer if I could draft him in the flats, but he was a true animal in the steep hills, where my quads always failed me.

If you rode with Rafa, you inevitably ended up in the steep hills. The man had titanium quads. Rafa liked to joke that it was my will, not my quads, that failed me. Once he said, "Quads can be trained. But determination? That's what the mountains test, Alan. Your determination. You have it in your heart, or you don't." He'd pounded once on his chest with a closed fist before he zoomed past me up Left Hand Canyon.

Rafa was gregarious, generous, and well liked in the cycling community. He wasn't known as a provocateur around vehicles. The fact that he was the apparent victim of the hit-and-run would make things even more difficult for Mattin Snow.

"What is that?" Diane asked.

"A text. It's nothing important," I said to Diane. I put my arm on her shoulder and walked with her toward the big house.

"People always tell me that about texts. That's why I don't like them. They're always unimportant. If video games are always unimportant, why bother?"

I was tempted. I controlled myself. I said, "What do you think we should do next?"

"I'll call again," she said. She hit ten buttons on her phone. I bit my tongue about speed dialing. "Now that she can see my car out here, maybe she'll answer."

"It's possible that someone — another friend — took her to the police station, right?" I asked.

"I think I would have heard about that. Did you see a car pick her up?"

I could tell Diane was skeptical. "No, but —"

"Did Emily go nuts?"

Emily always let us know when a car came down the lane. Usually her alert came in the form of a deep-pitched *woooo* sound that was like a practice bark. In Bouvier-speak, I'd learned to take the sound to mean she wanted me to look out the window and make some human judgment. I almost always did what Emily wanted me to do. It was part of our canine/*Homo sapiens* pact.

"No, she didn't hear anything. Does Mimi text? She has kids, right? She has to text. Give me her cell number, I'll text her."

"Okay," Diane said reluctantly. She gave me the number. I texted a simple, **Are you doing ok? Do you need anything? Please call Diane on her cell.**

I showed Diane the message.

"That's on her phone? Right now?"

"If the network gods are cooperating, yes."

"How does she know it's there?"

"It makes a sound when it arrives. Tells her to look."

"My phone makes sounds all the time. Maybe I'm getting texts."

Again, so tempting, but I didn't want to get lost in a tech tutorial with Diane right then. "Yes," was all I said. "I'm sure your phone does beep sometimes."

Diane said, "Don't be condescending, Alan. You know I hate it when you're condescending. Have you checked the outside doors? Walked around the house?"

"No," I said. "I haven't. I didn't feel right about —"

"Well, I feel fine about it. Shall we?" she said. She took my arm. She was dressed as though she had come directly from the office. She was wearing heels. Sensible heels, but heels. We started on the ravine side of the house on the south exposure, where the lower-level walk-out entrance had been cut into the slope over a hundred years before. On each side of the solitary door to the basement was an awning-type window that probably dated from midcentury. High above the door, on the main level, were the windows of the current kitchen.

Diane tried the door. It was locked. "Where does this door go?"

"It's actually kind of interesting. Peter told me the history once — his understanding was that this was the original kitchen level of the house."

"It's not interesting, Alan. Don't kid yourself. Just tell me where this door goes."

"The basement. Once, the kitchen. The family that owned the ranch had a maid, and a cook, and all the food preparation was done down here, not on the first floor." I increased the pace of my talking to a rapid clip, wary that Diane would again interrupt. I thought the story was interesting. "A long time ago — after the Second World War — the kitchen was moved upstairs. Now" — she rolled her eyes — "this is the laundry room, utility room, and — oh — in back there's a gorgeous wine cellar that Peter built in a space that was originally used as a root-cellar-type thing. Perfect temperature for wine. All the way in back, beyond that, there's another storage room with the original dirt walls, too. Mattin didn't show you the cellar during the housewarming? It's something."

"No," Diane said. "I must have missed that part of the tour. Maybe next time."

She wasn't being sincere. Diane didn't like old, if old meant anything that approximated creepy. A tour of the cellar? A room with dirt walls? She would demur.

She looked up at the windows above. "What was originally where the kitchen is now? Upstairs?"

"A conservatory. That's what Peter said."

"Ooooh," she said. "Fancy. Are we talking the greenhouse kind of conservatory or the music kind of conservatory? Elizabethans?

Or *Clue?*"

"The music kind, I think. The woman of the house did recitals and things. Peter had an old photograph of her way back when from the *Camera* playing a Steinway, something called a Centennial Grand." I shrugged. I didn't know pianos.

"How refined," Diane said. "And to think she could have wasted all that time she'd spent practicing and playing doing something unimportant, like . . . texting."

I laughed. We continued around to the back of the house. Diane paused at the corner and pointed up. "What are those windows? On each side? Is that the" — she took in a little extra air, as though she anticipated needing reinforcements — "guest room? Right . . . there?"

"It is," I said.

Diane went to take another step, but I kept my feet planted. I hoped Diane would say more about the guest room. In our previous discussions about the Friday-night party, she hadn't mentioned anything to me about the guest room. I was convinced Diane knew things that I wanted to know, too. About the guest room.

She didn't offer a thing.

The house's foundation had been cut back into a section of the hill that rose gently, rather than precipitously. Peter had taken advantage of the natural features by constructing an expansive, multilevel, heart-redwood deck that climbed up the hill to match the angle of the slope. Two sets of french doors provided exits to the deck from the big family room addition on the back of the house. Although the house blocked any view of Boulder and the Indian Peaks — both due west — the mountain views to the northwest and southwest from the terraced deck were special.

I led Diane up a few stairs to a portion of the big deck that was nearest the house. It was pretty dark. She did the actual peeking through the windows. I was good with that; I figured that of the two of us, she was the one who would be less likely to be shot as a Peeping Tom.

"It's obvious someone's home, or has been home," Diane said. "There are things out on the counter. Cheese. See the cheese? But I don't see her."

I didn't see the cheese. Diane tried the handles on each of the french doors. Locked.

"They're home from their trip, Diane. I saw them get dropped off this afternoon. They use a car service." That was a gratuitous dig. I regretted saying it.

"I know they're home," she snapped. "Mimi and I talked already. We're going to lunch tomorrow. And sometimes Raoul and I use a car service."

I touched her wrist to get her attention. "Are you worried, Diane?" I said. Diane knew me well; she knew that I was asking a question about her friend's state of mind. And her friend's impulse control.

Diane wasn't ready to go there. She said, "She could be in the bathtub, right? That would explain it."

"It's possible," I said. "But Adrienne had Peter put a phone by the tub. In the old days, before cell phones? It was a big deal between them for a while, kind of funny. He teased her about wanting extensions at all the toilets, too. It was so she wouldn't miss emergencies when she was on call."

My friend Adrienne had been a urologist. A fine doctor.

"I've been calling her cell, not her home number. She might not hear that in the bathroom." Diane located the home number — she found it in a cute little leather, handwritten phone book, with tabs for all the letters of the alphabet, that she kept in her purse — dialed the number into her phone, and hit send.

I almost offered to load all the data from

her little book into her phone's memory for her. I didn't. The gesture would not have been appreciated.

I could hear a phone ringing, not only from the speaker on Diane's phone, but also from inside the house. "It went to voice mail. It's possible the ringer could be off in the bathroom," Diane said.

"I don't know, Diane, it made a lot of noise in there. I could hear it." I repeated my earlier question: "Are you worried about Mimi, Diane? I barely know her. Are you worried, right now? I'm talking about her state of mind."

"Her state of mind?" She pondered my question for a moment. She turned to face me and looked me in the eyes. "Here's what I think. I'm in that phase of anxiety where I'm still convincing myself there is probably a simple explanation for the fact that she appears to be home but is not answering her phone or coming to the door. A simple explanation that I just happen to be missing. That's the kind of worried I am. Do you ever do that?"

"All the time," I said, allowing Diane room to manage her anxiety. "Does the process work any better for you than it does for me?"

"Not usually. Her state of mind? I came

out here, didn't I? All the way from Lee Hill. Hell yes, I'm concerned."

"Can you be more specific?"

"No." She sighed. "I don't think being more specific is a good idea. What about the other side of the house? Over there? Are there any more doors over there?"

"At the back, on that side, there are more windows into the family room. Pretty much the same view of the inside we have from right here. The rest of the first floor of the house at this grade is the attached garage up front. It was added after the war when the kitchen was moved upstairs. We could check the garage to see if any of those doors are unlocked."

We did. They weren't. I said, "And we should probably check the barn. Peter's shop." I had once discovered a body hanging from the rafters in Peter's shop. It was not an experience I wished to repeat.

Diane said, "Mimi wouldn't go in there. She told me that she'd never been in there. It's not her kind of place. She's not an 'old barn' kind of girl. We're what? A couple of miles from civilization? For Mimi, this is like homesteading in Irkutsk."

"I think Irkutsk is a city, Diane. You can't homestead in a city."

"Alan — don't. Irkutsk is both city and

countryside. And for the record — but I didn't tell you this — she has a thing about skunks."

"Everybody has a thing about skunks. Do you know anyone who likes skunks?"

"I'm making a point here."

I translated. "The move here was Mattin's thing?"

"You could say that. If it weren't for the view, she wouldn't have agreed to move out here."

Lucky for us, I thought. "Regardless, Diane, I'll feel better if I check the barn doors. You want to wait here? Or come with?"

"I'll go with you, but I won't go in."

The big barn doors were padlocked the way they had been padlocked almost every day since the time I found the body. The two smaller access doors — one on the south side and one on the north — were both dead-bolted and padlocked. I couldn't think of an uncomplicated way to padlock oneself inside a barn. Diane was going to be spared the indignity of having to enter.

"Told you," Diane said. She insisted that we walk around the back of the house one more time before we give up our search for Mimi. We were just turning the corner below the guest room windows when I heard what I thought was the sound of footsteps. I grabbed Diane's arm and I stopped.

I'm no wilderness seer. In the dark, and that night was getting darker by the moment, I couldn't tell human footsteps from coyote paw-steps or brown bear paw-steps. Raccoons, I knew from experience, could make quite a racket.

I guessed the sound had come from somewhere behind us, but it could have been from the ravine.

Who, or what, would be in the ravine? I had a plethora of fears: A pack of coyotes. Or a solitary cat. Or a brown bear, especially a mama looking for her cubs.

The reality was that I wasn't sure which I was more wary of at that moment, human visitors or critter visitors. But I was certain that I wished I'd brought Emily with me on this errand.

"Did you hear that?" I whispered to Diane.

"Yeah," she whispered back. I didn't need to hold her arm anymore. She was gripping mine with some ferocity. "Are you worried, Alan?"

Her voice told me that she was worried. But I knew what she was asking. She wanted a reality check. My thoughts had left the extended family of possible critter visitors and moved on to the possible identity of the solitary man that Nicole had seen walking on the lane late on Friday night. "Yeah," I said. "As a matter of fact, I am."

I pulled out my phone and texted Lauren as fast as I could. **Find the kids. Stay away from the windows. Get your Glock.**

29

Diane whispered, "What's a Glock?"

I thought about lying to her. Diane was not someone who would have her accelerating anxiety diminished by the prospect of adding a .9mm firearm to whatever soup we were in. I whispered back, "Lauren has a . . . handgun. Those threats she had a few years ago from . . . that guy? I suggested she get it ready. Just in case."

Diane stood on her tippy toes and put her lips near my ear. "Lauren carries a pistol? And just in case of what? Do you do this every time you get nervous? I thought eating all the chocolate I have stashed in the bottom drawer of the refrigerator was an unhealthy response to anxiety."

Diane made me laugh. I said, "Whatever — whatever — happened here Friday night after you left the housewarming thing has me spooked. I admit that. But right now, I'm just being . . . prudent."

"After we left? How do you know what happened after we left?"

Shit. I thought of saying "I don't know" but that would have been a lie. More to the point, Diane wouldn't believe me. "Just an assumption," I said instead. Though I quickly realized that was a lie, too.

"I get prudent sometimes, too. Never once has my prudence involved a handgun. Typically involves things like balancing my checkbook instead of relying on the bank."

"I don't have a gun, Diane. But Lauren does. And fortunately, she's the one of us who knows how to use it."

"And tonight, she's going to use it for what?"

"Probably depends what that noise was we heard."

"You guys need weapons to live out here? We live in the mountains and I've never once grabbed a pistol."

"Raoul has rifles."

"For hunting."

"Would you feel better if Lauren had a rifle?"

"No, I'd feel better right now if we were out front, where there is some damn light. Can we do that?"

We doubled back past the door to the walk-out portion of the basement. I tripped over a stone and fell to one knee. Diane was holding my arm so tightly she almost tumbled down with me. Diane leaned over me and said, "I always thought your daughter was named after you."

"What?"

"Grace?" She extended her hand to help me up.

"Cute." My other hand came to rest on something cold. I looked down and saw the shine of a new key. A house key. It had probably been stashed under the stone I just tripped over. I showed it to Diane. "What do you think? You want to go in?"

"Have you heard that sound again?"

"No, but then we haven't been very quiet, have we?"

"Let's get a flashlight first," she said.

"Or we could just turn lights on as we go. We're not trying to sneak up on Mimi, are we? We're trying to find her."

"Point. Is there an alarm?"

"Adrienne didn't believe," I said.

Diane sighed. "I'm not asking if she worshipped them. Just whether she had one."

"No," I said.

I texted Lauren that it had been a false alarm and that all seemed cool. Diane and I were going inside the house to check on Mimi.

I got a text back almost immediately. But it wasn't from Lauren. It was from the cyclist grapevine.

Rafa has a subdural hematoma. Concern about brain damage. We need a lawyer for Kari. Anyone? Still need blood. B-neg?????

The subdural was bad news. Kari was Rafael's wife. She wasn't a rider. But, by all accounts, she was a sweetheart.

"Unimportant?" Diane asked.

"Yeah," I said as we entered the basement level of the house.

Diane flipped on every light switch she saw. She also flicked on a table lamp and a floor lamp. I'd seen operating rooms with less illumination. I didn't say anything.

She waited in the part of the basement that had been the original kitchen, while I went off on my mission to search the darker, more primitive rooms dug into the hillside in the back of the basement. As I headed off down the doglegged hallway past a room with bunk beds, Diane said, "Don't skip any storage rooms that have weird doors or any rooms that have train sets in them."

Diane was making overt JonBenet Ramsey finding-the-body references. They weren't particularly welcome. I didn't say anything. But I didn't skip any storage rooms, either. I searched all the rooms. No train sets. One weird door, but every old basement has at least one weird door. I encountered a solitary surprise — Peter's temperature-controlled wine cellar, a magnificent space he had designed and hand-built to hold and display a few dozen cases' worth of his prized wine, had maybe twenty bottles in the slots nearest to the door. That was it.

Not much wine, I was thinking, *for a wine nut who has a second home in Napa.*

"Nothing back there," I said to Diane as I rejoined her in the room nearest the door. "Weird rooms. But it looks like it always looked. Just less junky."

"Alan," she said as she placed her fingertips on each of my cheeks, "we're not scouting for *Dwell,* we're looking for Mimi."

Although I assumed it was a dig, I didn't know what *Dwell* was, something I wasn't about to admit to Diane. She'd begun pressing buttons on the wall of the old kitchen that was opposite the door. The wall was close to the center of the room. No lights came on. She asked, "What do these do?"

"Nothing. Peter told me they'd been part of the second iteration of a dumbwaiter for the original kitchen. To move stuff up and down to the dining room and a sitting room on the second floor? It's defunct."

"What was the first iteration?"

"Ropes? Pulleys, I guess? It was the nineteenth century. The frontier."

Diane said, "I can't imagine." She pointed at the door adjacent to the wall with the dead buttons. "I didn't go into that room."

"It's the laundry," I said. I walked in. She followed, comfortable that any danger would assault me first. Over my shoulder, I said, "Quasimodern — maybe mid-nineteen eighties. I think you'll be okay in here." My first impression was that it was much more orderly than it had been during Adrienne's time in the house. The old washer and dryer — harvest gold — were still in place.

Mimi was not inside serenely folding towels.

The old wiseguy I had treated named Carl Luppo, the one who left us as caretakers to his miniature poodle, had once told me a story about how he and his gangster buddies had transported recently dead bodies by stuffing them into appliances. "You move a refrigerator into a building," he'd told me, "nobody pays much attention when you move a refrigerator back out of the building."

Small bodies, he'd added, could be transported inside washing machines or dryers. I had assumed at the time that those bodies would require some dismemberment in order to fit into the smaller spaces. Despite my unease, I had confirmed those suppositions with Carl. Dismemberment was not a topic that made him queasy.

I checked inside both the washing machine and the dryer. No bodies, no laundry.

"There's a laundry chute," Diane said. She was examining a curved sheet-metal pipe that terminated above the kind of canvas bin on wheels one might see in a small commercial laundry. The canvas bin was empty. "I told Raoul I wanted one in the new place."

"One what?" I was having trouble letting go of the image of an armless, legless torso stuffed into the front-loader.

"A laundry chute."

I said, "Your new place is a condo. It will all be on one floor, Diane."

"Maybe it could be something pneumatic," she said. "That would be cool."

Diane was determined not to learn how to text. Her mobile phone was older than my daughter. She continued to e-mail as though it were 1999. But she was interested in having a compressed-air cannon installed in her new home so that she could launch her husband's used underwear to her new laundry room.

I shook my head as we climbed the stairs from the basement to the main floor.

Diane remained in charge of turning on lights. She continued to overperform. I did the snooping. Since I was looking for something the size of an adult woman, my task wasn't that difficult.

Some big boxes had been stuffed into the back of the walk-in pantry in the kitchen. A couple of them were large enough to hide a body. I lifted one — it was too light. The second one, I opened. It contained a big ornate hanging pot rack. Wrought iron.

The only area on the first floor that gave me any emotional pause was the guest suite. I was reluctant to go inside. And I was also anxious to go inside. When I did open the door, I felt instant dismay.

The room had been freshly painted. New art on the walls. New window coverings. None of that surprised. What caused my breath to go shallow when I gazed into the guest suite was the fact that the bed was stripped to the bare mattress. No mattress pad. No sheets. Nothing. A few more steps revealed that the adjacent bathroom was devoid of hanging towels or any other linens. There were no bars of soap in the shower or at the sink. No throw rugs or bath mats were on the floor, anywhere.

I sniffed the air. Both rooms reeked of chlorine and Lysol. I opened a small linen closet. It, too, was empty.

Diane stood in the doorway while I did my poking around.

"Is this the way Mimi would usually leave a guest room?"

"Not really. She's fussy, but this is a little over the top. She probably hasn't gotten around to it since she got back, that's all."

I wondered whether Diane was being disingenuous or whether she really didn't know that one of her friends had spent the night in the guest room. "Has Mimi had guests already?" I asked.

Diane walked out of the guest suite without replying to my question. Her explanation about the sterile appearance of the room seemed vague. Something wasn't adding up for me.

I found no one hiding under the bed — I stayed behind and checked — or stuffed in the wardrobe. The bathroom was unoccupied.

As I rejoined Diane near the fireplace, she looked at me for a second before she looked away. She said, "That took you a while."

I nodded. "I'm trying to be thorough. I thought that was the point."

She said, "Okay," while she made a face that made it clear that she didn't believe me.

We went up the stairs to the second floor. The upstairs rooms weren't difficult to search. The only bedrooms the family had moved into were the master bedroom and the study/office. I opened a big linen closet that faced the hallway outside the entrance to the master bedroom. The closet was neatly stocked with bed linens and towels.

No Mimi.

As she climbed more stairs, Diane was growing more comfortable with our adventure. After she finished in the master suite and told me the office was "clear," she wandered into Jonas's old bedroom. "What's this?" she called to me.

From the hallway, I responded. "A special place that Peter built for Jonas. Adrienne called it his cubby. Peter called it a knothole. Jonas loved hanging out up there."

"How do you get in? It's too high off the ground. Especially for a little kid. He was a little kid back when Peter was still here."

Peter and Diane had a history I'd never learned about. I would ask Diane someday. But not that day.

I joined her in Jonas's old room. She was standing in front of the knothole. On the other side of the room, a couple of dozen moving boxes were piled along one wall, but no furniture had been moved into the room.

"There's some secret passage opening in the closet. Peter built it all himself. Jonas has never shown me how to get in. I've never pressed him on it."

I reached up and pulled back the curtains so Diane could see all the details of what Peter had built into the knothole. "It's empty," she said.

"It's a special, private place Jonas shared with his father. Or at least his father's memory. There's also a secret compartment of some kind hidden on the side with those shelves."

Diane was shaking her head. "Must be a boy thing."

"It's like having an indoor tree house. A special cave. Look at the wood, Diane, the way all the grain comes together. The joinery. It's great cabinetmaking. Jonas used to keep all his little-boy treasures hidden in there. It was — is, really — a very special place for him."

"Okay. Great kid place, I get it," she said. "But a secret passage? Really?"

"That's what Jonas told me."

"He wasn't pulling your chain? You can be kind of gullible, Alan."

I considered defending myself, but didn't. I could be kind of gullible. One rule of clinical practice that I'd learned the hard way was that the more skillful the sociopath, the less I should be his therapist.

Diane, of course, started digging around in the closet looking for the entrance to the secret passage. She was pressing on the walls, stamping on the floor, feeling along the molding and trim for hidden switches. Her efforts were futile.

"Come on, we're done in here. No Mimi," I said after giving her half a minute to solve the puzzle of Peter's secret switches. "Let's turn off some of the lights you turned on, lock up downstairs, and go." She agreed.

I walked Diane to her Saab. She said, "You've been home since they got back from the airport, right?"

"Yes."

"And neither you nor Emily heard a car come down the lane? Right?"

"Right."

"Her car is here, but she's not here. How did she leave? She's not someone who would walk out of this neighborhood. She has to be around somewhere."

I thought about the conundrum. "What if she left earlier with Mattin? He may have dropped her somewhere on the way to wherever he was heading when he got in the accident. He might have planned to pick her up later."

"I didn't think of that," Diane said. "But that doesn't explain why she's not answering her phone."

"It could be in her purse on vibrate. The battery may have died. Stuff like that happens all the time. It's technology."

"Which means she may not know why Hake hasn't picked her up. She may not even know about the accident."

"That is possible, too," I admitted. "Unlikely, but possible."

Diane pulled her phone from her pocket. She said, "No, it doesn't make sense. She would have called one of her girlfriends if Hake hadn't picked her up. If she couldn't reach him, if she needed a ride. Someone would have called me. It's the way . . . we do things. Us girls."

I wished I didn't need to ask Diane the next question, but I did. "You know how to use your voice mail, right? You would know if . . . your friends had tried to call you on your cell?"

"Yes," she said.

"I had to ask," I said.

"Whatever." She pecked me on the cheek, I thought to indicate her forgiveness, and lowered herself into the car.

At that moment, I was facing down the lane, toward the north.

"Diane, look," I said.

Emily began barking ferociously inside the house.

My guess was that Lauren still had the Glock nearby.

30

Someone was walking toward us on the downhill portion of the lane between the two bends of the S-curve.

Diane had pulled herself up to standing on the frame of the car door so she could see more clearly. She said, “It’s Mimi. That’s her coat.”

Even in scant moonlight, even from that distance, I could tell that the coat was dark, with a zebra-print collar. Distinctive enough to be recognized.

“So much for your theory,” I said. “It appears that your friend did indeed take a walk.”

Diane shook her head. “I don’t think so,” she said. Since Diane doesn’t like to be corrected, it would have been easy to write off her reply as defensiveness. I suspected there was more to it, though. She was struggling to make sense of an anomaly. She continued. “There’s some other explanation. This wasn't an evening jaunt on country lanes. That's not Mimi. She does not do that."

"Okay," I said. Despite the evidence to the contrary, I was trying to make it clear to Diane that I wasn't arguing with her.

She said, "Why don't you let me wait for her, Alan? I'll stay with her tonight if she needs me to. I think it would be better." She paused briefly, looking directly into my eyes. "If you, well, weren't here."

I laughed. I was appreciative of Diane's bluntness. And not only did I have no dispute with her judgment, I was relieved that my compassionate duty was ending. I gave Diane a quick hug, told her it had been fun, and hurried inside the house.

Lauren, of course, wanted to know what had just happened outside that I'd found alarming enough to call for firearm backup. Before I filled her in on my misadventures, I asked her for any news about Raphe. Or Mattin.

She shook her head, leaned forward, and kissed me lightly on the lips. She pointed at her laptop on the kitchen counter. It was open to the *Camera* website. "It's not good. He's apparently been hurt pretty badly."

That I knew from the cyclist grapevine. "Mattin?"

"My assistant just e-mailed me that Elliot

is still at the police station. So is Casey. Investigators are still at the scene. Nothing's been resolved."

"Is it a national story?"

Lauren nodded. "Drudge, E!, Huffington Post, TMZ. It's out there."

"Shit."

She smiled warmly and put an arm around my waist. "So, really, why did I need to be armed tonight? You find it kind of hot when I'm packing?"

It was the first sexual tease I'd heard from Lauren since I'd learned of her liaison in the Netherlands. Was it possible that the froth from that wave was finally receding into the sea? I kissed her, tracing her lower lip with my tongue. "Try me. But feel free to lose the clip first. My kinkiness has a limit."

"But it's so much more interesting when it's loaded," she murmured.

From down the hall, Gracie said, "So gross. Sooooo gross. Jonas!"

Lauren and I both laughed. I said, "I think I'm just spooked lately. Since Mattin and Mimi moved in, it hasn't felt right up here. The whole Spanish Hills vibe is different. My world is off balance. I miss Adrienne."

"I know," she said. "I know."

■ ■ ■ ■

The kids sensed the change in affective tone in the house. Jonas lived with his most personal grief almost every minute of every day. I was curious how it felt for him to see it up close in someone else. But he didn't ask what was going on, or wasn't quite ready to kick open that door.

Gracie asked, of course. She went through life with no query unasked, no comment unmade. I told both kids that a friend of mine had been hurt badly in a bicycle accident. I didn't mention the fact that our new neighbor was involved.

Gracie wanted details. Lots of them.

Jonas had only two follow-up questions. He asked if the guy on the bicycle had died, and if he had kids. I answered, my heart breaking for him a little more.

To my relief, both kids were cooperative about getting ready for bed.

I joined Lauren in our bedroom shortly after ten. She raised herself so she was sitting up against the headboard and stroked my neck while she ran her fingers through my hair. She didn't know Rafael. He was someone I saw socially only when he and I were both on the road with a hard saddle between our legs. She asked some questions about him. Got me talking about Rafa, and about Kari, and their two kids.

I didn't know Kari well, thought that I'd only met the two kids once or twice. It helped to talk, though. After a while, Lauren rolled onto her side and spoke softly in my ear. "I want to tell you what we know about the . . . problem after the party last Friday. The investigation . . . that the DA is doing."

"Okay," I said. "That's great. I would like to know. I've been worried . . . for you, for the kids."

She didn't tell me I had no reason to be concerned. She said, "This is one of those things I shouldn't tell you. Just so you're aware."

Lauren didn't often tell me things that she shouldn't tell me. I wouldn't say never, but it was close enough to never that I recognized the present moment as an exception.

"I appreciate it. I will treat it that way."

"Thank you. So far, everyone has done a remarkable job of keeping this quiet . . . while the investigation proceeds. If the fact that we're even investigating this gets out, it would be a disaster for Hake. Probably for the accuser, as well. But definitely for Hake."

If everyone else was unanimous in keeping things on the DL, I had to assume that Cozy was an advocate of keeping the investigation quiet, too. Cozy had a way of making his opinions known.

I was also recalling Sam's long parable about Kobe Bryant in Cordillera, and his insistence that in acquaintance-rape investigations involving celebrities, all interests can be served by silence. Except, perhaps, the interests of justice.

"Mattin's the focus of the allegation?" I asked Lauren, trying not to sound as disingenuous as I was being.

"Yes, he is. One of the female guests who was at the housewarming party accused him of rape."

I took note of the lack of mince in my wife's description. She didn't sprinkle any of the sweetness of *acquaintance* on top of the fire of the word *rape.*

"Rape? At an open house full of people?" *Was that too much?* I wondered. I did not like the thickness, or really the thinness, of the ice I was on.

"Diane hasn't told you any of this?" Lauren said. "I thought she might . . . because of your friendship."

"And," I said, "because she's a world-class gossip. I've tried to get her to talk, to tell me what happened. But she won't. Not about that night. Does she know?"

"I'm not sure what she knows. The timeline has her and Raoul already on their way home."

"She's been interviewed?" I asked.

"I haven't seen the file. This is being done discreetly but it's being done right."

"The alleged rape was the night of the housewarming?"

Lauren said, "It appears that there was sexual . . . contact between the guest in question and . . . someone . . . after the end of the party. In the house. The rape kit confirms that. Everyone seems to agree that the accuser was the last of the guests still present. So that is not in dispute. Neither is the fact that Mattin was the last male present in the house that evening. A bartender — a woman — the caterers, one male and one female, and a private chef, a man, had already left.

"The allegations the woman made involve alcohol, and drugs, and ultimately sexual contact with someone she knows that she perceives as assault."

"Mattin? Is she accusing him directly? You mentioned drugs. She's saying that he drugged her and raped her?" I was trying to inject some wonder into my words, cognizant that were I to rank my personal talents, acting would have been below singing, and right above levitation, at the bottom of the list.

"Hake is the accused. The accuser's memory had been . . . impaired by drugs. Rohypnol, actually. That is one of the few things we know for certain. The tox screen on her blood came back today. It was positive for roofies. Her BAC the next morning at the station was barely below .04, so she had been drinking. But the investigators don't think her blood alcohol would have been sufficient to make an issue of her consent. But with a roofie? Absolutely. Consent would be a problem."

Hella had told me that her patient had an appointment to see Cozier Maitlin that morning to review some forensics; it seemed likely that the meeting had been about the toxicology screen Lauren was talking about.

I said, "If this leaked —"

"If it *ever* gets out that Mattin Snow has even been linked to a sexual assault it would be a media firestorm. Not just in Boulder but everywhere. It would make tonight's bike accident look like nothing. Guilty? Not guilty? I'm not sure many people would wait for that determination to be made."

I remained troubled by the possibility that

Mattin was the accused solely because of process of elimination, because he was the last man — *standing* didn't seem like the right way to complete the idiom — present. Lauren wasn't providing much in the way of clarity on that point.

I said, "But Kobe Bryant survived similar public allegations after that thing in Cordillera. So did Ben Roethlisberger in Tahoe. Why not Mattin Snow? What's the difference?"

Lauren didn't follow sports. But I didn't have to explain what the two famous athletes had been accused of doing. "Oh," she said, "it would be different for Hake. Men follow sports. Women . . . follow Mattin Snow. The self-described 'defender of women's legal rights' accused of raping a woman? His own friend? In his own home? Athletes don't need credibility to throw their balls, Alan. But without his credibility? Hake has nothing. The allegation would consume him, and his family, instantly. His hard-earned reputation? Gone, facts be damned. That is precisely why everyone is so determined to keep this quiet until we reach a decision about prosecuting."

"Are there any mitigating facts?"

"There are two stories. There are always two stories."

"But . . . if he's admitting having sex with a friend of his wife's while they were all together in the house? That can't be good news for him."

"I can't tell you what Hake has or hasn't admitted."

I said, "Our visitor earlier? The one who smelled like smoke? It was one of the two caterers. She came to apologize to me about her colleague running Fiji and me off the lane. Get this — she told me they saw someone else on the other side of the S-curve before they got to the mailboxes as they were leaving the party. Does the sheriff know that?"

"Probably, but I'll check. The investigation is focused on Mattin for . . . good reasons."

Lauren and I still weren't looking at each other. My eyes were pointed toward the ceiling. Lauren remained on her side, her head near mine on the pillow.

"The bicycle accident won't help," I said. "It will draw attention to Mattin at a time when he doesn't want it."

"No, it won't help. Having his name associated with the accident will only make the possibility of a leak about our investigation more likely. The same media folks who build pedestals also dig holes. Give TMZ and the entertainment bloggers reason to start digging, and . . ."

They won't stop.

Lauren rolled on top of me and kissed me. She closed her eyes, something she had done every time we kissed since Holland. Something she had done relatively rarely before that trip to Holland. Our lips parted. I inhaled her scent as she pulled away. "You don't look at me anymore when we kiss," I said.

She rolled to her side.

"I can't," she said.

31

Diane's car was still in the lane when I took the dogs out at the end of the evening. Another car was parked beside Diane's. An unfamiliar one. A big Audi SUV.

Emily wasn't pleased with the continued activity in her domain. She circled the cars before she trotted off to complete her patrol.

The puppy didn't care about the traffic on the lane. Fiji wanted to search for prairie dogs. I gave her rope to see where she would head. She hopped off down the lane.

After less than a minute, my phone vibrated in my pocket. Diane. "Saw you out with the dogs," she said.

"Hey," I said. "How is Mimi doing?"

"She's beside herself. Way out of proportion. I've never seen her like this. Even during her divorce, she always maintained some . . . hope. She is absolutely despairing."

"Because of the accident?"

"Apparently. She's crying more than talking. She's reached her limit, I'm afraid."

"Mattin is still on 33rd?"

"Yes."

"Has he been charged?"

"I'm not part of that discussion."

"You really don't know?"

"I really don't know."

"Who does the other car belong to? Next to yours?" I said.

"Don't ask me that, please."

"I just did."

"I'm pretending you didn't, Alan." Diane sounded tired. "I'll be grateful if you pretend you didn't, too."

My curiosity about the big Audi doubled, of course. "Are you okay, Diane? You sound —"

"I'm all right. I'm tired, I'm frustrated. I may end up needing to spend the night in this creepy house. Or, wait — maybe I can get her to come and stay with Raoul and me for the night on Lee Hill. That might be better."

"Might be," I said. "Have you and she had anything to eat? Do you need me to bring you some —"

"It's spooky here at night. You feel that, sometimes? The Bates Motel vibe? I've never felt it over at your house, but here?

There's something not right in this house. An energy of some kind. I can't tell what it is."

"I never sensed anything when Adrienne was alive, but I have to admit that —"

"What about after she died?"

"I don't know. I've been feeling something lately. Like tonight, when we were inside."

"Whatever it is," she said, "I really don't like it."

I heard a loud noise in the background. "What was that, Diane?"

"Something banging in the kitchen. I heard the bicycle guy, the one Hake hit, is in surgery. That can't be good."

I agreed that it wasn't good. "I know him, Diane. His name is Rafael. He's Spanish, like Raoul. Rafa is a good guy. A respectful rider. A lot of people are hurting for him, and his family."

"I'm sorry, Alan. A friend?"

"A cycling friend. Wait." My cell was vibrating in my hand. A second call was coming in. "Hold a second, Diane? Okay? I have to get this." Before she could object — she would have objected — I clicked over to the second call. It was Lauren.

"Hi," I said. "What's —"

"Listen, please. Sorry for interrupting. A body was discovered a little less than an hour ago. I'm catching tonight. It looks like I will be going to the scene."

"Homicide?" I said.

"Patrol thinks so. Copious amounts of blood. Detectives are just arriving."

Although the murder rate had shown a significant spike in recent years, Boulder didn't get many murders. The investigation of an apparent homicide often meant all hands on deck. A prosecutor's supervisory presence during the initial hours at the scene was not uncommon.

I considered the practice an enduring echo of the law enforcement bell that had been so badly struck on the morning JonBenet Ramsey's parents discovered her missing from her bed. Sometimes institutions forget failures quickly. Other times institutional memory is stubborn. This was a case of the latter. The Boulder police were determined not to mishandle the front end of another important investigation.

"Okay," I said. "We'll be inside in a minute. I'm sorry you have to do this."

"You know what? I'm good," my wife said. "I'm ready to do this."

She was perceiving the investigation as a challenge, not a burden. I decided I would interpret that as a good sign.

I asked, "Where is it? How far do you

have to go?"

East to west, Boulder County stretches from the edge of the Great Plains to a high mountain plateau just below the final vault of the Continental Divide, from a little over a mile in altitude on the eastern boundary of the county to well over two miles in elevation on the west. If the murder were up near Nederland at the base of the Indian Peaks, it would mean a long, treacherous drive in the dark in mountain canyons.

"Not far. A house above Table Mesa," she said. "Near NCAR."

She spoke the acronym for the atmospheric research facility above south Boulder as *n-car.* The Table Mesa neighborhood below the research institute was a sprawling residential section of town almost due west of our home in Spanish Hills. For Lauren, getting to the murder scene would mean a short, straight shot down South Boulder Road. Curiously, on her way to the crime scene, Lauren would cross through the intersection near where Hake had clipped Rafa's bike.

"Is it near Devil's Thumb by any chance?" I asked, recalling Sam's irreverent analogy from the Kobe discussion. "That neighborhood right below the rock?"

Devil's Thumb was not only a prominent

landmark, it was also the name of a subdivision that bordered the abundant green space that Boulder had preserved along its mountain backdrop.

"Yes, the address is in Devil's Thumb. The house backs right up to the greenbelt. Why did you ask that? Do we know anyone who lives up there?"

"Maybe a patient of mine once. Sam and I were joking about the name of the landmark, the rock. Silly thing, about its shape. That's all. It's a coincidence that it came up. Hey, at least it's not too far away and you don't have to drive the canyons tonight."

"I'll stay in touch. Count on this running late."

Lauren hung up. I hit the flash button on my phone. "Diane, you there?"

She wasn't. I called her back. She wasn't answering. With anyone else, I would have texted an apology for having abruptly truncated the earlier conversation. With Diane, a texted apology wasn't, well, practical.

Emily came running to the clarion of the bellow from my cupped hands. As we turned back down the lane toward the front door of our house I thought I saw a flash of red hair on a tall woman stepping quickly down the front hall of the old ranch house.

Well, shit, I thought. The big Audi SUV belonged to Casey Sparrow, Mattin Snow's überlawyer. Or lawyer wizard.

Lauren was pulling out the lane as the dogs and I stepped up to the front porch. She waved.

I got the kids settled. Gracie appeared to have completed whatever cognitive and emotional processing she required about the bicycle accident. She picked a bedtime story for me to read to her that was an uncomplicated fable about a tough little dog who wanted to run with the big dogs. I loved the obviousness of my daughter's choices and almost always envied her obliviousness about the obviousness.

At bedtime, Jonas was on affective simmer, just beginning to process his reaction to the bicycle incident. He asked me if he could pass on a bedtime story. I told him we could. Jonas waited until I had turned off the light before he asked me how my friend was doing.

I told him the truth. Rafa was still in the hospital, in surgery. That I didn't know more. That I was worried about my friend.

Jonas wanted to know if the surgeon was a urologist. He also wanted to know if Rafa had a wife.

I made a shrink's translation of my son's second question. The first was easy; Jonas's mom had been a urologist. With the second question, I thought Jonas was trying to discover what would happen to his family if Rafa died. Specifically, he wanted to know if Rafa's kids would still have a mother. Or if the kids would have to find new parents, as Jonas had been forced to do.

I tried not to choke up. It took me a moment to find a way to reply, but I eventually found a story in my memory that would assure Jonas that the kids had a fun mother who loved them a lot. I told him that I'd watched Kari tubing with both kids on Boulder Creek the previous summer. The helmet Kari was wearing made her look like a turtle droid. The kids teased her about it the whole time. The story made Jonas laugh.

He rolled onto his side, facing away from me. I thought he was done with his questions about the accident. But he wasn't; he'd been steeling himself to step onto even more sensitive territory. He asked me if the guy in the car had hurt Rafa on purpose.

That one gave me chills. I told Jonas I didn't think so. I thought what had happened had been an accident. They happen.

"Nobody's fault?" he asked.

"Someone was probably careless. In that

sense, it was somebody's fault."

"Your friend?"

"From what little I know, it sounds like the driver of the car was . . . being careless."

"Mine weren't accidents," he said. "They were both on purpose."

He was talking about his losses. His parents' deaths. Adrienne had told me once that Jonas had gone online and read multiple accounts of his father's murder on the stage of the Boulder Theater. Afterward, he'd asked her a dozen questions about the day that Peter died. Details that weren't in news reports. A lot about the why.

Many years later, Jonas had been in Israel with her the day that Adrienne was killed by a terrorist's bomb. Since his return he had asked me dozens of questions about that. I had no doubt that he'd researched the incident online.

"Yes," I said. "Yours were on purpose. There are evil people out there." I leaned back against the headboard, with my left hand on Jonas's shoulder. I stayed there, unmoving, until his breathing convinced me that he was asleep.

I flicked off the light by his bed. On the way to the stairs, I tripped over his favorite sneaks, which he'd left strewn near the bottom of the stairs. The shoes were too small for him by far and completely worn out on one heel. His mother had bought them for him, though. Jonas wasn't ready to part with the sneaks.

Two discipline problems were apparent. One, the shoes had been tossed in the middle of traffic. And two, the kids both knew that outdoor shoes were supposed to stay upstairs by the front door. Lauren and I were in the midst of a concerted effort to sequester dirt.

In their defense, the kids argued — correctly — that most of the dirt in the house was transported inside by our dogs. The dogs, they pointed out, did not leave their shoes by the door.

Reality be damned, Lauren and I held firm, as parents do.

I made a mental note to remind Jonas in the morning about the dual transgressions. Jonas was a good kid. Probably too good a kid. He was such a good kid that I often caught myself wondering whether his occasional venial misbehaviors might be leading psychological indicators of something more significant. I paused a moment on the stairs while I pondered what the carelessly misplaced tennis shoes might be telling me. My parenting brain was as exhausted as the rest of my brain. I got nowhere with my musing.

Upstairs, the dogs were waiting for me in the bedroom. I texted Sam before I brushed my teeth. **Is Devil's Thumb yours? What are the odds of that happening now?**

Thirty seconds later, a reply. **Nope, mine is bigger. Ask around.**

Hardly. Is it yours?

Dominquez and Fratelli. They have Luce and me out following leads that will go nowhere. Not that I'm complaining. I like work. Work is good.

I thumbed back, **Lauren's up there. She was catching.**

Get some sleep. Warrants will take hours.

I couldn't sleep.

After about an hour of restlessness, I went to my laptop and checked for updates on the *Camera* website. Nothing new had been posted about the accident or about Rafa's medical condition. A text came in canceling the pleas for B-neg. I hoped that was good news.

I went out to the kitchen. For some reason I didn't understand, I desperately wanted a piece of cake and a glass of milk — I just did — but we didn't have cake in the house.

I settled for a cookie that Gracie had baked with Lauren over the weekend. It had way too many sprinkles for my taste. Shag-carpet-quantity sprinkles. I held the cookie over the sink while I performed a sprinkle-ectomy with my thumbnail.

To my surprise, the cookie beneath the candy wasn't half bad.

I spotted a note in a sealed envelope on the kitchen counter. On the envelope was a lowercase *a,* in Lauren's hand.

The note read, "My G is ready. You know where. Just in case."

In another world, one more responsive to fantasy, it might have been an erotic code of some kind. But it wasn't. The G she was referencing was not her spot, it was her Glock. When the hefty .9mm wasn't locked in the safe where it belonged — the location where I preferred it to reside — "where" was on top of the narrow tallboy in her dressing area in the closet.

"Ready" meant the gun was loaded, a status that made my breath go shallow, always.

I walked to the front door and looked out the window. Both vehicles I'd spotted earlier were gone. Casey Sparrow had moved on. Diane, I hoped, had gone home to sleep in her own bed with her husband. I was also hoping that Mimi had gone with her.

I wondered if Hake was going to spend the night in jail. Or at home.

The front porch lights were on in the house across the way, but the rest of the place was almost completely dark. The only light was a faint glow through one of the upstairs bedroom windows, as though someone had left on the central hall light.

I double-checked the locks on our front door before I turned to walk back to our bedroom. I tripped almost immediately. When I looked down, there was barely enough light to let me know that I'd just tripped over Jonas's beloved sneaks.

Huh. He wasn't asleep after all. He'd heard me trip over the shoes and carried them upstairs. I flicked on the overhead light. I noticed that the laces were covered in fine sawdust. *Has he been going inside his father's woodshop? How would he get in?* I didn't have ready answers to my questions. I kicked the shoes aside and continued to the bedroom, stopping first at the master closet, where I reached up and felt for the Glock hidden in the recess on top of the tallboy. It was there. By choice, I don't handle many guns. But each time I hefted Lauren's Glock, it was always colder and heavier than I expected it to be, or remembered it being.

For many people a loaded gun provides an additional sense of security. For me, a loaded gun is a loaded gun. Loaded with connotations as well as bullets. People comfortable with firearms tend to perceive guns as doing good things. People uncomfortable with firearms, like me, perceive them as being agents of fate.

Sometimes fate is kind. Sometimes not.

Recently, fate had been something of a bitch.

I finally fell asleep but woke when Lauren crawled into bed. I opened one eye. The digital clock read 3:22. She brushed her feet against me as she pulled the comforter over her. "You okay?" I said into the dark.

"Good," she said in a voice that said to go back to sleep, that she didn't want to talk.

Her feet were just-out-of-the-fridge cold. I mumbled, "If you want, you can put your feet on me. To warm them up."

She flattened the bottoms of her feet against my calves, which told me that she was lying in bed with her back to me. I felt a chill shiver through me all the way to my liver. "Thanks," she said. "You're so warm."

That's me, I thought.

Lauren got out of bed just in time to kiss

the kids on their way to carpool. I was almost ready to follow them out the door.

"You have to go in to work this morning?" I asked as I pulled on a coat. I knew she did. She had the prosecutorial side of a homicide investigation to manage. And, from an office politics perspective, she had collegial and managerial expectations to exceed. Lauren felt that everyone who mattered in her office was eyeing her for indications that multiple sclerosis had finally taken enough of a toll on her that she could no longer do her job. That would make her even more determined to prove them wrong.

"Absolutely," she said. "Any news on your friend?"

"He's in ICU."

"Sorry."

"How bad was it last night?" I asked. "In Devil's Thumb?"

"Some of the cops were saying last night that big crime scenes are a lot like movie sets. A lot of waiting around. I think I got back here around three, a little after. Getting search warrants is always slower than you imagine. We had to call Judge Delonis for the warrants. You know her?" I shook my head. "She must take sleepers — it was that hard to get her to wake up and focus on the homicide. She hung up on the detective three different times before he got her out of bed."

"What about the scene?"

"Truly bloody. As bad a stabbing as I've ever seen. Crime scene guys think it was a big knife. We didn't find it, though. Police will send dogs into the greenbelt today looking for evidence. Still have a lot of canvassing to do, too."

I made a face. "Domestic?" I asked.

"Didn't look like it. Guy lived alone. Appears he was surprised in his garage after the door came down. Significant spatter on the back of the garage door."

"He confronted a burglar? That sort of thing?"

"At first that's what we thought, but the more the detectives pieced the evidence together, the more it looked like the homeowner had been ambushed. No sign he was running away from his attacker. No initial face-to-face confrontation at all. ME tentatively put the first two cuts — a stab and a slash — as coming from behind the guy. Crime scene guys thought there was a short fight because there was one wound on his wrist that might have been defensive. As if — and it's not certain — he had been turning around. But everyone agrees he was already bleeding out by then."

"So it wasn't a burglary?"

"Hard to say. It could turn out that he interrupted it before it got started. Garage break-ins aren't uncommon — there have been a couple in Table Mesa in the past few weeks. Might end up just being a wrong place, wrong time thing. Intruder felt cornered, so he attacked. There's still a lot of evidence to sort out. Detectives and forensic teams will be there all day, I'm sure."

"You're good?" I said.

She smiled. "Yeah. I'm glad I went — I'm glad I showed everybody that I could go to a scene, do my part. The police did a good job. The warrants were clean. The scene was managed well. Forensic response was tight. Evidence collected by the book. I was pleased."

"Witnesses?"

"Immediate neighbors heard nothing. The fact that the house borders greenbelt complicates things. Provides unmonitored, unlit access to the property. We're hoping for something from the canvassing today."

I leaned in and kissed her. "Well, I have an early patient. Coffee's made. You think you're home for dinner?"

"I sure hope so. I plan to be home by midday."

I grabbed my keys and opened the door. I

remembered the big Audi and the red hair. I turned. "I think Casey might have been here last night. Does she have a big Audi SUV? Gray?"

"I think she does. She got it because it's big enough to hold all her dogs."

"She came by. I'm assuming to see Mimi. I found that interesting."

Lauren narrowed her eyes. "I do, too. Was that after Hake left the police station? Did she bring him home?"

"I didn't know that he was released. It's possible she brought him home, I guess. I didn't see him."

"Someone had to give him a ride from 33rd Street. His car was impounded. I think he left the police department around eleven. No media tried to follow Casey here? That's hard to believe if she had Hake in the car."

I hadn't considered the fact that Mattin Snow, post hit-and-run bicycle accident, would attract the various species of opportunistic press like horse shit attracts the various species of opportunistic flies.

"Casey was here before eleven. I didn't see other cars on the lane. It's possible I may have just missed Mattin. But I don't think I would have missed any other cars."

"Emily wouldn't have missed him," Lauren said. "She can smell Hake a mile away."

Emily misses little that happens in her parish. Especially when it involves potential adversaries.

32

The big house appeared deserted. As I pulled out of the garage, I saw no signs that anyone was home.

I took South Boulder Road west all the way to Broadway, which is not my normal route to my office. I wanted to lay my eyes on the intersection where Rafa had been hurt. Morning traffic cooperated, jamming the intersection and forcing me to miss the light at Broadway. While I was stopped at the signal, I eyed the area and imagined how the accident might have happened. It was easy to see that a simple swerve — two feet, three at the most — by a distracted driver on a cell phone could have caused the driver's car to swerve into the edge of the bike lane.

From the saddle of my bicycle I'd watched the same confluence of events occur a dozen times. Or a hundred. Most of the time an alert cyclist reacts in time to avoid the swerving car. Other times the driver recognizes his carelessness just in time to jerk back to his lane. The circumstances were routine and mundane. It could have been any cyclist in that accident. It could have been me.

I parked my car where our garage had stood adjacent to our little Victorian. I'd inherited the prime parking location because Diane considered the precise spot of the garage's tragic demise to be bad juju. I, on the other hand, considered the rectangle of reclaimed territory a newly created and most convenient parking space, juju be damned.

The clock visible from my desk revealed that my first session of the day was scheduled to start in six minutes. I was about to close my office door and use a few of those six minutes to try to collect my thoughts when my cell phone chirped with a happy sound indicating the arrival of another text message. The sound also served as a reminder to me that I had not checked the previous message, the one that had come in while I was driving. I read the second text. It was from Sam.

It read, **I think not.**

Really? I was doubly curious. I looked above the "I think not" text to read the message that had beeped at me during my commute to my office. That one was from Sam, too. **This is about to go public. Devil's Thumb vic is the cook from the party. Coincidence?**

It took me a moment to remember the ex–Pain Perdu chef's name. Preston Georges. I focused my attention on Sam's news. Someone who had been in attendance during the Friday-night housewarming in Spanish Hills was dead. Apparently murdered.

What might his murder have to do with the festivities, or the events that followed? I had nothing. I texted Sam. **Ideas?**

I'm a man of ideas.

He was, actually. I typed, **Relevant ones?**

It's not my case, remember?

Sam definitely had ideas, but he wasn't prepared to share them with me.

One eye on the clock, I cursed silently while I booted up my laptop so I could check the *Camera* website and my e-mail. The digital display on the far wall reminded me that only two minutes remained until I had to walk down the hall to retrieve my first patient of the morning.

I had two fresh e-mail messages. The first was from Hella. The message was too long for a text. She thought we should meet. It was urgent. She could be at my office at eleven fifteen, three fifteen, or four forty-five. She explained it was about "the DNA."

The DNA? It was way too early for any laboratory results to be available from the DNA samples that Mattin Snow had provided to the authorities — if indeed he'd provided any — upon his return from Napa the day before. Even initial DNA readings of quality samples from a laboratory willing to drop everything to test them wouldn't be available for days. I couldn't imagine what other DNA Hella might want to discuss with me.

The other e-mail was from Raoul. He, too, was thinking that he and I should meet. His concern was about the *Daily Camera* redevelopment project. That situation was urgent, too. He said things had reached a "tipping point" in due diligence and we needed a decision about including the Walnut property. He used the words *this morning.*

Ha! I thought. "We" hadn't even begun to discuss price or timing. Nor had I given any real thought to the ramifications of the decision to sell, such as where the hell Diane and I would relocate our offices. Lauren and I had not edged past the most preliminary of discussions about the financial consequences of selling Walnut Street, had not explored further the question of the sale of her rental home on the Hill or revisited the loaded possibility of packing up our family, leaving Spanish Hills, and moving to town.

The reality was that I had plenty to distract my attention without adding into the mix either Hella's pressing DNA concerns, whatever they might be, or Raoul's real estate development deadlines, not to mention the associated dominoes that would fall should those deadlines be met, or missed.

The condition of my friend Rafael was nearer the top of the list of my more pressing concerns. One eye on the ticking clock, I typed out a quick e-mail to a biking friend, hoping for an update about Rafa's health by the time my first session of the morning was over.

Also near the top of the list was the whole question of the death, apparently murder, of Preston Georges in his garage in Devil's Thumb, and the not-at-all-philosophical question about exactly where that felony might fit into the Friday-night-at-the-neighbors' mix of already perplexing felonies. Most imminently, a present responsibility would confront me, too. I had a patient who was about to walk into my office expecting, completely reasonably, my undivided attention.

My first patient that morning was a too-sweet-for-her-own-good forty-three-year-old mother of four whose upbringing had rendered her completely incapable of setting limits with the most important people in her life. The immediate consequence of her flawed limit-setting had to do with her own mother, a woman my patient had described as a demanding, intrusive, yet charming lady who was in the process of moving, both unbidden and unwelcome, to Boulder from Austin, Texas. Without any discussion with her daughter, the woman had placed a lowball offer on a house around the corner from her youngest and was currently awaiting a reply from the seller's Realtor.

The purpose of that morning's session, in my patient's eyes at least, was for me to tell my patient what to do to stop her mother from moving.

My take? My role was to be helpful, but slightly less practically so. Ideally, I would accomplish two things during the session that morning: to make a dent in my patient's characterological limit-setting problem through the miracle of insight. And to simultaneously provide her some guidance on the what-the-heck — my patient did not use foul language, even tame foul language

— might-she-do-about-her-mother-moving-in-around-the-corner problem.

This was bread-and-butter work for a clinical psychologist in general practice. I was expected to get it right. I wanted to get it right. But that morning my attention was getting stuck in a place that had nothing to do with that morning's reality. Instead, I was proving unable to keep my mind from focusing an unwarranted amount of energy on the chain-smoking, bad-driving caterer, Eric, and the unknown dealer he was trying to meet up with on South Boulder Road before the guy headed to Breckenridge, along with his stash, for the weekend.

I was particularly fixated on whether one of the items in inventory in that particular dealer's stash was Rohypnol, bootleg or pharm.

I was also investing too much of my limited energy into the identity of the mystery guy wearing the hoodie and ski cap that Eric and Nicole had almost run over on the lane after they'd just missed running over me on the night of the Friday-evening housewarming gathering.

I was trying to leave open the possibility that my mind's apparent associative hop-scotching might prove elucidative and become part of my creative process, but my thinking seemed to be producing nothing but disjointed, tangential musings.

At that instant a tiny light flashed red near my office door. The red light indicated that the overwhelmed mother of four, having completed dropping her admittedly unruly brood — limit-setting wasn't her forte as a parent, either — at school, had arrived in my waiting room, anxious to learn in forty-five short minutes a crucial life skill that she had completely failed to master in her previous forty-three years.

Later in the morning, at eleven fifteen, three consecutive sessions under my belt, the red light flashed on once more. Hella had arrived almost as soon as my ten thirty had departed. My next patient was due at eleven forty-five. Hella and I would have thirty minutes to puzzle out something useful about the mysteries of the double helix.

"What's up?" I said after we exchanged quick hellos. I sat first. "You said you had DNA questions. News. Something."

We hadn't met for supervision since the session that ended so abruptly at her apartment. Hella settled in before she replied. She kicked off her shoes and tucked her bare feet under the ample flows of her long skirt. She hooked the hair on the left side of her head behind her ear. She thanked me for seeing her on such short notice. "So much so fast with this case, Alan. I truly am sorry to bother you again, but I don't know what to make of all that's happening. I don't want to screw anything up. For her. I'm really hoping you can give me some guidance."

I was hoping that, too.

"Her attorney phoned my patient early this morning. He'd just received a call from the lawyer representing the man my patient has accused of assaulting her." She paused and stared at my face. "You don't seem surprised by that."

"I'm married to a lawyer. Attorneys talk to each other. A lot. I may end up being more surprised when I learn what they talked about."

"Okay. The other attorney — it's a woman — told my patient's attorney that she had received preliminary DNA results for her client."

I made a perplexed face. There was so much wrong with Hella's story. First, it was too soon for DNA analysis to be complete. Second, any results, when they were revealed to the accuser's attorney, should come from law enforcement, not from opposing counsel.

I said, "I'm no expert on this, Hella, but isn't that pretty rapid turnaround for forensic DNA results?" I was acutely aware that I had to be careful with the provenance of my knowledge. I was limited to discussing with Hella only facts that Hella might have shared with me or that might be in the public domain. Hella, for instance, hadn't yet informed me that Mattin Snow had been summoned back to Boulder by sheriff's investigators. That meant that Hella didn't know that I was already aware that the accused had arrived back in town only the afternoon before.

I had no way to ascertain if Hella even knew the accused was in town. Nor did I know if Hella was aware of the bicycle accident that had occurred the previous evening.

I reminded myself to be careful.

"It would be early, way early," she said. "Exactly. The police requested the . . . DNA samples only a few days ago."

I asked, "Do you know if they've been collected? And, if so, when they were collected?"

Hella said, "I think they have been collected. But specifically? If they were collected, it would be recently. Maybe as recently as yesterday."

That Hella and I were on the same temporal page with our facts made my subterfuge less taxing. I hoped. I said, "My experience with this sort of thing is limited — I think you know my wife is a deputy district attorney — but my understanding is that it typically takes a significant amount of time to get DNA results back from a forensic laboratory." Lauren frequently complained of how long it took to get routine forensic reports back from the Colorado Bureau of Investigation laboratory. "Lauren has explained that the CBI lab is always working off a backlog of cases and that it's hard to get something new to rise to the top of the queue. It doesn't seem possible that the —"

"I know. It's not like it is on TV." Hella smiled. "Nothing happens overnight. I checked online for all this information, Alan. Can I finish? Maybe save us some time. We don't have much."

"Of course," I said.

"Late yesterday, the accused's lawyer told my patient's lawyer" — in my head I translated that Casey Sparrow had told Cozier Maitlin — "that the accused had voluntarily provided his own samples for DNA analysis, collected under the videotaped supervision of an ex-FBI agent, for submission to a qualified laboratory. This all happened early on — the day after the police first made the man aware of the accusations against him."

My mouth hung open. I was that surprised. "Really?" I said.

"According to his attorney, the samples were collected and sent to a private laboratory for analysis. All at the accused's expense."

Wow, I thought. Mattin Snow did his own DNA tests. He anticipated the trajectory of the investigation, he knew what was coming, and he took evasive action. *He basically punted on third down.* A most inventive strategy.

Hella seemed to be waiting for me to say something intelligent about the news — not an unreasonable expectation in the circumstances. I said, "This is something new. I don't think I've ever heard of a potential criminal defendant doing his own anticipatory forensic laboratory work."

My initial reflexive response to the news Hella had shared was an urge to pick up a phone and ask my wife, the prosecutor, or my friend Sam, the detective, a pertinent question, or maybe two: Is it permissible for a criminal suspect to do a forensic examination on himself before the police get around to it?

And would the results be admissible in

any court?

I suspected Lauren and Sam's response to the first question would be that suspects and their defense attorneys are free to do almost anything they want with their biological samples and their own money as long as they aren't tampering either with evidence or with jury pools along the way.

To the second question, the one about admissibility in court, I felt certain that Lauren and Sam would reply in perfect two-part harmony. They would say, "Hell, no. No law enforcement agency or court in Colorado is going to care about the results of those independent tests."

Which, of course, raised the question: If the cops and the courts wouldn't recognize the outcome, why would Mattin Snow do it? If he knew the results would be irrelevant and inadmissible — and he and Casey Sparrow must have known that — why did he collect and then have analyzed his own biological material long before the sheriff's investigator or the district attorney had asked him to volunteer samples, or a court had compelled him to provide samples, for use in the *actual* sexual assault investigation?

Casey was smart enough to see how it might be useful, if it worked. She was certainly clever enough to plan the necessary legal moves. But was she trustful enough of her client to be willing to risk whatever the results of the testing might show?

I had to assume that Mattin Snow had been adamant with Casey that the laboratory results would prove exculpatory. But Casey was not trustful by nature. She certainly would not take her client's word about his own innocence or accept his assertion that the laboratory results would be exculpatory.

Clients undoubtedly lie to their attorneys as often as they lie to their therapists. In this instance, if it turned out that her client was lying to her, the impact of the anticipatory DNA tests would prove a thousand times more damaging for her client than would something like a failed lie-detector examination.

Why would Casey risk it? I wondered.

I suddenly had another question for Lauren: If the results of the independent test had turned out not to be exculpatory, would Mattin Snow and Casey Sparrow be required to share them with the prosecution?

The answer to that question, I thought, *might change things.*

The more I thought about Casey Sparrow

and Mattin Snow, the more credence I was giving to the likelihood that the DNA/ laboratory maneuver had been hers.

Over those beers the other night, Sam had preached to me that the primary legal lesson of the Kobe Bryant sexual assault case was that the earlier the attorneys could get everyone involved to shut the hell up, the better it would be for the future of the accused celebrity. And maybe even for the accuser.

Throwing exculpatory laboratory results — even nonadmissible exculpatory laboratory results — at the sheriff and the DA, not to mention at the accuser and her attorney, would certainly help shut them all up, at least temporarily. Once the prosecutors and the accuser were in possession of exculpatory laboratory data — even if the results would require replication before they could be used to further the investigation or be presented in court — it would be most reckless for either the sheriff or the DA to tarnish Mattin Snow's reputation by identifying him publicly as a suspect in a rape.

The exculpatory results would give everyone pause. Which would be a major tactical victory for Casey Sparrow.

Mattin Snow was trying to get everyone — everyone associated with the accuser, everyone in the sheriff's department, and everyone in the district attorney's office — to shut the hell up about what they thought had happened in the hours after the end of the housewarming.

Huh. I definitely had some more thinking to do.

I looked at Hella. She was clearly ready for me to become verbal again. I said, "Give me another moment to try to make sense of this? I'm trying to be methodical as I walk through it in my head. This is a —"

"But I want —"

"Please? Another minute?"

My conclusion about the underlying motivation for the strategy was simple: Mattin Snow must have felt a tremendous degree of confidence that the independent DNA analysis would prove to be exculpatory. Specifically, he was betting his future — personal and professional — that his DNA would not be a match for any of the DNA identified in the rape kit samples collected from the accused the morning after the alleged assault. He was, in fact, so confident that the laboratory would find no biological relationship — none at all, zero, ziggy, zilch — between any rape kit samples on the alleged victim and any samples he had voluntarily provided for the independent forensic examination that he was willing, literally, to bet his freedom on it.

How could he be that certain? The simple answer, the obvious answer, the only answer I was smart enough to surmise, was that Mattin Snow knew the results would not prove incriminating because he knew that he had not been present — and thus couldn't leave any stray DNA behind — when the alleged rape took place.

Which meant to me that Mattin Snow had not been part of any sexual assault on Hella's patient.

The psychologist in me gave that kind of confidence credence. By testing his own DNA, Mattin Snow was displaying self-assurance, pathological denial, or some kind of thought disorder approaching psychosis.

Which was it? That was the question.

Mattin Snow's sole motivation at this stage of the investigation was to prevent public disclosure of the fact that there *was* an investigation. It made sense, then, that neither Mattin Snow nor Casey Sparrow ever had any intention of sending a copy of the independent DNA testing to a Boulder County judge, or had any intention of arguing for its admissibility to a future court. The audience Mattin and Casey had in mind for the results of the DNA examination and comparison was extremely limited.

The data was intended to influence the very few people who held the power to decide if this investigation had merit, and the few people who would decide if the case ever saw the light of day.

Hella was still waiting for me to demonstrate that she had my attention.

"Ready yet?" she said. "You seemed to zone out on me there."

"Yes," I said. "I guess I did. I was considering the implications of all this. It's a lot to digest. Legally. Strategically, it's hard to make sense of it."

"Yeah — I — I totally — I don't even know what half this stuff means. I'm trying to be supportive of my patient as she deals with all this, but . . ." Hella closed her eyes. Her chin was quivering as she fought back tears.

That got my attention. "Tell me what's on your mind," I said. I realized I had not even given Hella a chance to do that.

"Okay, what my patient told me is that thus far only preliminary results are available from . . . from the independent DNA testing. I don't know what that means, technically. 'Preliminary.' I don't know if that refers to reliability or if it means that the results thus far are partial, that there are more to come. Do you know that?"

"I don't," I said. "I'll see what I can find out." I made a mental note to ask Sam or Lauren.

"I was afraid of that. Anyway, my patient said that these preliminary results were provided to the sheriff's investigator, to the deputy district attorney who is assigned to the case, and to my patient's lawyer. That's it.

"What's crazy for my patient's situation right now is that the preliminary results of the official rape kit — the one from Community Hospital — are known only to the sheriff and to the DA. Since no charges have been filed in the case, the results of the rape kit haven't been provided to either side's attorneys."

I said, "Which means —"

"It means my patient doesn't know what the sheriff was able to learn from the rape kit." I immediately saw where Hella was heading. She continued. "Which also means that the sheriff and the DA may know if the independent DNA results from the accused are, in fact, incriminating, or if they are exculpatory. But my patient doesn't know. And the accused doesn't know. Or he shouldn't know. Not for sure, anyway."

Wow.

"How crazy is that, Alan? That my patient, the woman who was raped, might be the last one to know what the science is saying about what happened that night?"

I asked, "So, what is her attorney telling her? Does he believe that the independent tests are incriminating? Or exculpatory?"

"Her attorney doesn't know. He hasn't been in this situation before, either. But he cautioned her that the other lawyer is good, and that she isn't reckless. He told her to be prepared for the possibility that, when the results of the rape kit are known, the independently collected samples won't match the rape kit samples."

I summed that up. "Her attorney expects the results to be exculpatory."

Hella sighed before she said, "Yes."

33

I reminded myself I had a job to do. My real job. I glanced at the clock. Too little time remained.

I said, "How's your patient, Hella? How is she taking all this? And how are you?"

Hella's eyes filled with tears again. "She is not doing well. She sounded devastated at this news, and she's started doubting everything. She's started to think even her lawyer doesn't believe her."

I paused before I said, "Everything?"

"Everything. Her memories. What happened. Everything."

Hella's maturity for a therapist her age had always been a strength. I was seeing some cracks forming. I didn't understand why. Nor did I have much time to learn why. "What would be most helpful right now?" I asked. "From me? We only have a few minutes." The clock behind her indicated seven more minutes, to be precise.

Hella turned her face toward the backyard. I didn't know what she saw out there. When I followed her eyes in that direction, I imagined a staging area for construction equipment and supplies. Haphazardly parked pickup trucks and vans. And a postage-stamp yard behind a huge new duplex.

Hella reached into her purse and removed her cell phone. I found it odd. I hadn't heard the thing ring, or vibrate. She tapped a few buttons. Then she cradled the device in her lap using both hands. Ten seconds passed, maybe more.

Without looking up at me, she said, "Please know that I don't want to show you this, Alan." I heard a sudden, sharp inhale. "I don't want . . . anyone . . . to see this," Hella said. "It was never my intention that anyone . . ."

She had something on her phone that she wanted to show me. I guessed that she had received an e-mail from her patient. Something ill conceived, written in a moment of weakness, something about the case that Hella was desperately wishing was not forever etched in her electronic records.

"This was . . . is . . . private." It was, I imagined, her patient's reasonable expression of doubt about some important fact related to the assault. But it was also something that Hella realized wouldn't look right in a defense attorney's hands.

That's what I was thinking I was about to see.

Hella said, "The whole thing is almost two minutes."

Two minutes? What?

She touched a control on the phone. Sound suddenly began spilling from the speaker. The volume was intense; it overwhelmed the tiny device. Hella adjusted the volume down. I heard music. Drums. Yelling. Chanting. *Chanting?* The thick, dense murmur of a crowd that is completely alive. Auditory chaos.

Hella watched the screen on her phone for about fifteen seconds before she leaned across the space between us and handed the phone to me.

I looked down. "Five more seconds or so," Hella said.

That's all she said. During those five seconds, I tried to make sense of the tiny image. Right away, I knew I was seeing flames, at night. A dark sky seemingly full of fire. In the foreground, and in the background, the blurred motion of many people dancing. Other people, in the foreground, standing, watching.

It took me an additional second or two before I was able to begin to comprehend the sum of all the visual noise. *It's Burning Man. This is Burning Man.*

The video was amateurish. The angle was low, from near waist level. The images were grainy, the light was inadequate, the focus inconsistent. I imagined a spectator with a camera phone mostly concealed in the front pocket of a pair of scruffy jeans.

The photographer was a guy. Not a nice guy. I recalled that Hella had spoken of an "expectation of anonymity" at Burning Man. No cameras. No photography.

So much for that. The five seconds Hella had alerted me about were ending. As if on cue, entering lithely from the left side of the screen, I saw Hella dancing, floating.

Her hair was up. She hadn't told me that about the night at Burning Man. She'd told me so many personal, even intimate details about her experience that night, but she had not told me that her hair was up. For a few seconds, I fixated on the benign fact that her hair was up.

And then I couldn't distract myself any longer. I watched Hella dance, almost nude, as she was lit by the hyperactive flames of a thousand fires.

She was wearing those familiar leather

boots. And the wedding veil she'd described the day she'd first told me about Burning Man. The veil, I remembered from her description, was eighteen feet long. I could see the weaves of grosgrain ribbon that represented fire rising from below to the earth, and from the earth to above.

I could see the veil trailing behind Hella like a predatory snake, or given the circumstances, like a fuse. It taunted the fire that was everywhere around her.

Hella danced with simple beauty and with captivating grace. What was apparent, and what was remarkable to me considering the chaotic intensity of the scene, and despite the fact that she was dancing among dozens, and that hundreds of others — including whoever was hiding the damn prohibited video camera — were observing, was that Hella seemed completely alone in that sea of fire and ocean of people.

For a moment, I looked nearby for a topless woman in a miniskirt whose head appeared impaled by a three-wood. The reason I was looking for her is because I thought I was supposed to, that she was the point of this video.

I didn't find her. My eyes returned to Hella.

Then, suddenly, I was done. I'd watched

long enough to register the nature of the video. To be entranced by the dance and appalled by the intrusion. I did not want to watch this private, intimate moment for even a second longer.

In a vacuum, things would have been different. I knew that. Were she not my supervisee, and were she not naked from the tops of her boots to the edge of her brow, I knew I would hardly have been able to keep my eyes off the woman dancing.

The performance that night in the desert belonged to her. Everyone else on that little screen was in the chorus. Or in the audience.

I asked, "Have I seen enough?" Hella's face was down. I was looking at the top of her head, the anything-but-straight line that marked the jagged part in her blond hair.

She thought about my question for longer than I thought it deserved before she said, "No. You need to watch until the end."

"Hella."

"Please."

I tilted the phone back into position. I watched more.

"Now," she said, "this part."

"Okay." I thought she must have recognized some transition in the music. That's how she identified the part.

"From the left side of the screen. See the woman?"

"Yes."

"That's my patient," Hella said.

She didn't have to tell me that. I could see it. *She was the one with the three-wood impaled in her head.* The woman's back was to the camera. The embroidered suns on the cheeks of her short jean skirt were stunning in their clarity. Her back was naked.

Her surgically enhanced breasts were not visible.

Suddenly she started to rotate, her shoulders cocked. Her head began to spin toward the camera lens, her hair flying. Her upper body rotated to follow.

That's when the video stopped. And the cacophony quieted.

Hella waited a few seconds before she reached forward and took the phone from my hand. She touched a control. Her head remained down.

She said, "I get up early, Alan. I like to spend some time with the day, with the dawn, before I begin to become productive. It's just who I am. I sit, I sip tea. I watch the light creep into the world where I'm living, I watch as the light becomes the day. One of the things I really like about the apartment where I am is that I get to watch what the transforming rays from the rising sun do to the Flatirons.

"The sun paints the rocks differently every day, and colors them, and transforms them. I love the irony it represents, that the sun, which is nothing but fire, has such a gentle effect on the beginning of my day. Despite its heat, it doesn't consume. It . . . illuminates.

"I try to let that happen to me, too. That gentle effect. So that I'm open to receive the light, the illumination." She looked up. At me. "This morning, during that time when I was alone with the dawn, I received a text message with this video attached. I didn't look at it right away, of course. I didn't even know it came in. But I think the time of day it arrived was important. Someone was telling me that they know about my relationship to fire.

"There was no real message. No words, I mean. I didn't recognize the sender's number. It probably doesn't matter who it was, does it? I mean, who sent it? I will probably never know."

The clock I could see over Hella's shoulder was marching toward the conclusion of our time together. I willed it to tick more slowly. If time weren't an issue, I probably would not have forced the next question —

I would have waited until a more natural moment. But time was an issue. I said, "You are thinking this . . . has to do with your patient?"

"Yes, I do. Of course. You don't?"

"I don't know what it's about. Other than a violation of your privacy. That it has to do with your patient is one possibility," I said.

"Possibility? I'm being warned, Alan. She's being warned. Come on, what other explanation is there? The video stops the moment she appears on the screen. That's a clear message. It's a threat that they will show what comes next. To defame her."

"They?"

"He. The asshole who snuck the camera into the theme camp. Whatever."

"Is it a threat? Are you that sure? This video is of you, Hella. The one who is being exploited in this is *you.*"

That fact alone had to be disconcerting to Hella. Was she in denial about this violation of her privacy?

"The clip stops," Hella said, "only when she dances beside me. That's what is important. This is the part of the dance when —" Hella fortified herself with an inhale. "Maybe five seconds later, ten seconds later, twenty seconds later — I don't know — she's about to dip her shoulders and shake her boobs in my face, Alan. And then do it again. Come on." The *come on* wasn't exasperated. It was a weak plea. "You really think the asshole who took this turned off his camera just as a second undressed woman waltzed into his frame?"

I had to admit that wasn't likely.

"How is her displaying her breasts to me going to look to a jury? How are those two shimmies going to look to a jury?"

"But that's not what is on this clip," I said. "Is it not important enough that someone took video of you when you had an expectation of privacy and anonymity? And that they somehow tracked you down to let you know they had it?"

"Of course it is. But that is not what this is about."

"Okay, what is this about?" I asked, my voice cushioned.

"Do they know?" she asked me.

"Do they know what, Hella?"

"That she's my patient? Am I supposed to pass along this . . . warning to my patient? Is that what this is?" Hella sounded small, almost defeated. She wasn't yet angry. I knew the anger would come. I hoped it would come soon. "Do I give this video to her attorney? Does he then give it to the DA or the sheriff? What happens now, Alan?

Is this how they get her to walk away?"

"I wish I had an answer," I said.

She poked at the screen on her phone. "If she continues with the case, how long until this video is all over the Net? How long does she have before this . . . private dance becomes public? Before the world's vision of her is defined by one crazy night in the Nevada desert? And then what? What happens next? After that? Are they going to play this at the trial?

"What happens to me, to my career, when this is played at the trial? And everyone I know thinks I dance naked with my patients?"

Without sufficient contemplation, I said, "There's not going to be a trial, Hella," I said. "There was never going to be a trial."

Her head snapped up. "What?" she said.

I realized then that Hella had been living in a reality in which her client's rape would lead to the kind of prosecution that involves courtrooms and trials. The kind of conviction that happens to defendants.

Wow. I realized I wasn't living in that world. I had come to believe that the only conviction that was on the table was the kind of conviction that means certainty, that this case was much more about persecution than prosecution, and that the main question to be resolved was the identity of the persecuted.

Would it be Mattin Snow? Would it be Hella's patient? Or would it be both?

And would it include Hella?

I softened my tone. "There was never going to be a trial, Hella."

"This isn't about a trial?" she said.

"No. If you're right about this clip, it's about the accused trying to make your patient go away, silently. Either with her tail between her legs or with a bank account full of money. But, if you're right, this video is definitely about making her . . . go away."

"Then this" — she touched her phone — "is blackmail."

I flashed on my conversation with Sam about Kobe and Cordillera.

I thought, *Or it's damn good lawyering.*

34

I resorted to cliché. I said, "Our time is up. We have to stop, Hella."

"Yeah," she said. "It's a good time. I'm fried."

I could feel the depth of her injury as though my fingers were actually probing the contours of the wound.

"You have a lot of decisions to make. About this video. We're not done discussing this. Would you like to talk later today?"

She looked me in the eyes. "I don't need to give this to someone? Like right away? Now?"

"There was no message attached? All you received was the video?"

"Yes."

"Then, no. Let's talk first, so you can make a clear-headed decision," I said. "Let's be deliberate about this."

"I'm relieved," she said. "I thought I'd have to . . ."

She didn't finish the sentence. "Then be relieved. We'll talk later. Come up with a plan that you can feel okay about."

She nodded. And shrugged. *Sure,* she was saying with the nod. *What good will it do?* she was asking with the shrug.

"What works for you?" I said.

Her voice lightened, just a fraction. "If I can't somehow turn back time?"

"Yeah, if you can't do that."

She hit some buttons on her phone, shaking her head. "I'm going to need to move something. I'll e-mail you later with times. Is that okay?"

"Of course. I'm sorry, Hella. You've been violated. I am so sorry."

"I know that. It's going to hit me at some point. Hard. I hope it's later. Right now I need to focus on my patient. What this means for her."

"You may not get to choose that progression. It's one of the things we can talk about later."

As she exited my office, she looked nothing like a graceful dancer.

I probably wasn't a good therapist to my next patient.

It happens rarely that I allow one session to bleed into the next, but it does happen. I knew my focus was fractured. Even as I tried to zero in on the words of the man sitting across from me — he was in the chaotic despair that often accompanies the first days following the end of a marriage — I couldn't stop replaying the details of the supervision session with Hella.

When the patient after Hella left, I had a text blast waiting for me from the cyclist grapevine. Rafael was awake. Still no visitors. But he was awake.

Some good news, I thought.

I forced myself to ponder the news that Hella had revealed *before* she'd shown me the video clip on her phone.

I reviewed what I thought I knew about the events after that Friday-night party. My vision of that night was almost entirely painted with the images provided by Hella's patient in the days immediately after the assault.

The perpetrator, in my view, had to have been my neighbor Mattin Snow. I could not see how it could be anyone else. For anyone else to be responsible, he would have to have been in the house. *Right?*

Right. But the results of Mattin Snow's independent DNA analysis suggested that my vision was incorrect. Had Hella's patient confabulated the entire event? I had trouble believing that was true. But the possibility had to be considered.

Had Hella's patient intentionally misrepresented what she knew to be true? Again, I had trouble believing that, based on what I knew. But that possibility, too, had to be considered.

Or had Hella's patient pieced together the fragments of memory she possessed into a narrative that was largely true but that ended up featuring a confabulated perpetrator? Had she in fact been raped, but had someone else raped her?

Who? How?

Raoul and I spoke by phone a few minutes after my patient left the office. Raoul was across town in the middle of a long meeting with the founders of a start-up who thought they had solved one of the fundamental problems that limited the life of batteries used in personal electronics. Raoul sounded excited. He no longer got excited about too much in the venture capital world.

I'd watched him on this road before. It had started years before with Storage Tech. And later at NBI. A couple of dozen other nascent companies had followed. A good half of them had become earning engines and household names. If the battery technology eventually proved itself in the marketplace, all would soon be wealthier than they already were. The innovators would get rich. The rich investors would get richer.

Raoul said, "They are setting up a demonstration for us. I have five minutes, maybe ten, until they are ready."

"Fine," I said. "That's all the time I have anyway. What's up?"

He lowered his voice, as though he didn't wish to be overheard. His tone became Midwestern American flat. All the spice and nuance of his accents and speech idiosyncrasies were gone. He sounded like he'd been born and raised in Indianapolis.

"We need the Walnut office to make the *Camera* project fly. I can't find a way around it. To keep Roscoe in the syndicate — if we lose Roscoe, we lose two others; all three are crucial development people. If we lose them, we're done as an entity. To keep Roscoe on board we must acquire the Walnut land so that he can build the duplex for his wife and for his sister-in-law and her kids. He knows Diane is a partial owner; he insists on that specific piece of land.

"The city planning department has also made clear that as part of our proposal we will need to provide them with assurances that we have access to nearby land for material staging and for worker parking during the extended construction on Pearl. The Walnut lot is barely adequate for that, in terms of size. We must acquire it. I can see no alternative, Alain. I'm sorry."

It's what I feared he would tell me. "Time frame?" I said.

"Start of business, Monday, for your decision. The syndicate is meeting at nine thirty. I know you have much to consider. And I'm not giving you much time."

"We haven't discussed price or terms, Raoul."

"If you agree to entertain an offer, I will have something formal prepared for you by this time tomorrow. The numbers will not be an insult. I know what you and Diane have been offered by developers in the past. I will make certain it is . . . enticing to you."

I said, "Okay. You heard about the murder in Devil's Thumb yesterday. Yes?"

"Yes. Tragic."

"That's become Lauren's case. She may not have much attention or energy to give to this proposal. I am making no promises we'll be able to meet your deadline."

Raoul's tone became softer in timbre and even lower in volume. He said, "Understood. I appreciate any consideration. We'll leave it there?"

"Fine."

"You know," Raoul said, the lovely lingual affectation instantly seeping back into his words, "we apparently ate his last meal. The last one he cooked . . . as a chef, for others. Preston Georges. It is so sad, what happened to him in his own home."

"I agree. I heard you had houseguests last night."

"Singular. Just Mimi. It's a difficult time for them. For the family. The accident on top of . . . There is much tension. It's hard for us to be in the middle. I keep telling Diane we have to try to be Switzerland."

"How's that going for her?"

"*Comme ci, comme ça.* In temperament, my Diane is not so Swiss."

That was the truth. I said, "Well, I need to go. Lauren and I will consider your offer, Raoul. We'll do it for you and for Diane."

"Gracias."

I e-mailed Lauren at work that Raoul and his LLC would be submitting an offer on the Walnut property for our consideration and that we would need to reach a decision by the end of the weekend. She texted me back that the "vic at Devil's Thumb" was the "chef from Friday" and that the homicide investigation was getting screwier by the minute.

Her decision to use a text message meant that my wife was apparently not eager for her editorial musings about the homicide to become part of a subpoena-able or discoverable permanent record. Over the years, she had taught me that e-mails were almost always archived. Text messages were often not so reliably discoverable.

In what way? I texted back.

My phone vibrated again within seconds. But the next text wasn't from Lauren.

It was from Jonas. **Whats soil analysis** he wanted to know.

What? It wasn't like Jonas to ask me school questions during the day. I replied, **We can talk tonight.**

Lauren at work

I supplied the missing question mark. **Yep. You cool?**

Yep fgw

For government work. The red light on the wall across my office flashed on, indicating that my next patient had arrived in the waiting room. I didn't even note that Lauren had failed to get back to me about what was so screwy about the murder investigation in Devil's Thumb.

After my last patient of the day walked out the door, I called Nicole. I said, "Hello, this is Alan Gregory. Remember me?"

She said she did.

I started lying. I wondered if she was still interested in house-sitting for us.

"Yes, when? Oh my God, yes. Yes."

I'd prepared a fictional itinerary for her. "We're going to Mexico for ten days, over Thanksgiving. Manzanillo. Right on the beach, if you can believe it. Will you be in town? Please say yes."

I suspected it was unlikely that Nicole would be in town. Most students at CU headed home, or elsewhere, over the Thanksgiving break. The reality was that it didn't matter to me where Nicole would be. We weren't going to Mexico over Thanksgiving. And there was no way I was ever giving her the key to my house. I just needed an excuse to ask her some questions about Preston Georges.

"Thanksgiving? No, my family lives in Seven Hills — that's outside Las Vegas. I'm going home for Thanksgiving. We always do this big feast. But I am so bummed. I would love to do it some other time."

She sounded truly disappointed. I was trying to decide whether she wanted access to my house for a blowout kegger or for a romantic weekend with some guy. I was thinking kegger. "I was afraid of that," I said, trying to sound disappointed. "Our neighbors told us that the chef you guys worked with up here — I'm sure you remember him — had given them a couple of names of good house-sitters. I guess I'll try one of them. I don't like to hire strangers, but —"

"Did you hear," Nicole said, "what happened to him? That he was . . . murdered? In his house?"

Garage, actually. I mouthed *thank you,* grateful that I didn't have to be the one to tell her about the murder. Nicole hadn't struck me as the type of person who stayed current with local news. "I did," I said. "Is that awful, or what?"

"Eric told me. He said they used one of his own knives. You know, to . . ." I hadn't heard that. I would ask Lauren. "He carried them . . . like, everywhere. His knives. He has — had — this leather . . . case thing for them."

"I didn't know that," I said. "I never met him. Who saw him last? At the party you did, I mean. You said he left before you guys?"

"Right before us. It was probably me, or Eric. Chef had gone in to chat with the last few guests. He came back into the kitchen just as we were finishing loading the van.

No, no . . . it was Eric, it wasn't me. Eric's the one who saw him last. Definitely, Eric."

"How can you be sure?"

"Because he hit on Eric as he was heading out the door. He called Eric off to the side, away from me. Asked him if he had plans later on. Whether he wanted to meet up somewhere in town. Right after the chef drove away, Eric was acting all offended. I told him to get over it."

"Is Eric gay?"

Nicole made a dismissive sound. "Hardly," she said. A second passed. She added, "I don't think so, anyway."

So Eric's not openly gay, I thought. I wondered how Eric felt about Preston Georges's advance. If his defensiveness that evening about the offer was as overt as Nicole was suggesting, I had another motivation to add to the list of possible explanations for Eric's recklessness at the end of the evening. He may have been having a difficult time dealing with the chef's flirtation. I also began to wonder if Preston Georges and Eric had actually hooked up later.

"So how long after the chef left did you guys drive away in the van?"

"Two minutes, maybe three," Nicole said. "We were basically ready to go when he left. Couple more things to carry out. Remember, we were hustling. The hostess wanted us gone. Eric wanted to go."

"Well, it looks like you're right, then. Eric was probably the last one to see Preston Georges alive . . . at work. One of my friends who was there heard that meal was his last professional gig. That it was like his last . . . meal."

"I'll have to tell Eric. It might turn out that he was the last guy Chef ever hit on." She laughed at that thought.

I told Nicole we had another trip out of town coming up in late January. I promised to call her to house-sit. She said that would be perfect for her.

All the lying felt as natural to me as breathing.

I had the information I'd wanted. If Nicole and Eric had come close to hitting that pedestrian beyond the second curve on the lane as they were leaving that night, then it was almost certain that Preston Georges, leaving only two or three minutes before, had seen the same man on his route down the lane toward the paved familiarity of South Boulder Road. When the chef drove out, the pedestrian would have been on a relatively straight stretch of the lane that ran for about five-eighths of a mile between the mailboxes and the first half of the S-curve.

Just beyond the NO OUTLET and DEAD END warning signs. And just past Peter's carved ALAN'S AHAH sign on the mailbox post.

That night the weather had been inclement. Cold air had been moving in. High winds were gusting from the north. It had not been a night for a leisurely jaunt in the neighborhood. That solitary pedestrian, stocking-capped and hooded, had to have recognized that he was heading down a road that led, almost, to nowhere. At somewhere around eleven thirty at night.

I was nearly certain that he had not been on his way to visit Lauren or me, or the kids. That meant that his destination had to have been the home of Mattin and Mimi Snow. Why? I had no idea.

I flicked my mobile off vibrate as I packed up my things to leave the office. Ten seconds later, the phone came alive with my latest ringtone riff.

The screen announced that the call was from Hella. I realized I had never received the promised e-mail that would let me know when she was available to continue our earlier supervision appointment. "Hi,

Hella," I said.

"Alan," she said, "I'm in . . . Cripple Creek." She paused for a couple of seconds, as though she wanted to allow me time to let the news sink in. "With that . . . patient."

Cripple Creek was one of three Colorado mountain towns with legal casino gambling. It's the one that's farthest from Boulder, almost ninety minutes south, in the hills behind Colorado Springs. Definitely a location that's way off the beaten path for a Boulder therapist at the end of a workday.

"Long story, but I think I am going to have to place a hold-and-treat on her. I've never done that. I didn't think I would ever do that. Have you done it? Can you walk me through it?"

"Not often, but yes, I've done it. Of course I will help. I need to e-mail you some boilerplate that you will have to find a way to get printed. You will then need to fill in the details about your concerns and describe your patient's history and current behavior. The key phrases to substantiate the hold are going to have to do with danger to herself or others and imminence of the risk. Do you understand?"

"Yes."

"Because of the pending criminal case,

you should choose to describe the recent events, especially the precipitating events, with great care. You'll need to be circumspect and assume that everything you write will see the light of day. Does that make sense?"

"Yes. Will you review it after I write it?"

"Gladly. You have a copy of your license with you?"

"Yes."

"You may need to show it to the police to get their assistance. You want to tell me what happened?"

"I don't know very much. Why she came here, to Cripple Creek, I don't know. She got a hotel room. The police are saying she tried to kill herself. Somebody restocking the minibar in her room found her. I don't have the details, but I think it was an overdose. How they got my name and number, I don't know yet. She's stable medically, but she was almost mute with me. I've only been able to meet with her briefly, but I wasn't able to get her to tell me any details about what happened. She's being transferred to a medical hospital in Colorado Springs. I'm afraid I'm going to be left with no option but to hospitalize her in a psychiatric unit once she's stable medically."

"Until she's able to convince you she's not a danger to herself, you have no choice. It may be exactly what she wants you to do. What are your thoughts if it turns out she did try to hurt herself, or kill herself?"

Hella didn't hesitate. She said, "I'm hoping it will turn out to have been a gesture. Low intent. Suicide wasn't even in the conversation when I thought about this patient, Alan. Not even a little."

I allowed Hella a moment to live with that optimism before I asked, "And your fear?"

"My fear? That the recent developments were too much for her, that her intent was high — that she meant to die — that the lethality of the method was high, and that she knew how to do it. And that she kept it all to herself. From me."

"It's a big leap, Hella, from a gesture by a patient not even contemplating suicide to a determined attempt by a patient intent on dying."

"You asked my fear. I'm afraid I missed the signs of how the stress has been accumulating for her since the rape. The news about the accused's DNA this morning? That may have been the final straw."

"I can see that," I said. "How are you doing?"

"I feel awful for her."

"Are you angry?"

"No," she said. Too quickly, I thought. "I'm afraid I missed something. That I could have prevented this." Hella's voice turned small. She said, "Know what else? I'm afraid I am about to learn that she received the second half of the same video that I got this morning. That's my fear about the actual precipitant for the suicide attempt."

Unbidden, my mind found the frame that would have come next when the video I'd watched that morning ended. That new frame began with Three-Wood Widow's hair flying in counterpoint to her spinning shoulders and torso. In my head, the scene played on. The woman I'd never met completed the spin, her body in profile as she turned toward her therapist, surprise and recognition lighting her eyes.

One of the two women in the frame was topless, the other almost nude.

One was wearing fluorescent Crocs, the other scuffed leather boots.

The woman in the jean skirt took one of Hella's hands, and because I knew her line, I could almost hear the sound as her lips moved and formed the simple words, "Hello, Doctor Zoet."

With wonder, I recalled a recent moment

when that peculiar collision of lives had seemed humorous to me.

35

I sent the necessary materials off to Hella.

The phone rang again. It was Lauren.

"Hi," she said. I could tell from the tone of her greeting that she was about to ask me for something she would rather not have had to request. I began thinking of places I could pick up something for dinner.

"What's up?" I said.

"I know I said I would be home early today, but . . . I'm still tied up. This homicide. I planned to be home to meet the carpool, but I'm not going to make it away from here in time. Is there any way you can do it?"

"What time?"

"Six," she said. "I'm so sorry I didn't call earlier. I completely lost track of time."

I looked at the clock across the room. Five forty. "It'll be close," I said. "I'll leave right now."

"It's just Jonas," she reminded me. "Grace

was invited to go home with Melody today. I'll stop by Melody's house and pick her up when I'm able to get out of here."

I had twenty minutes to get to Spanish Hills from Ninth and Walnut. On a good day, the drive took twenty minutes. But fewer and fewer Boulder rush hours offered good days. I rushed out to the car. Hoping to buy an extra minute, I crossed over to Baseline on Ninth before I headed east. The whole time I was kicking myself because I didn't have the carpool schedule with me. I didn't know who was driving that day. I would have felt much better if I was able to warn the carpool driver I might be a little late.

I called Lauren to find out the schedule. But Lauren wasn't answering. I tried Jonas. Neither was he.

As I drove south on Broadway, my eyes kept drifting to my right, easily locating the dark shape of Devil's Thumb silhouetted against the pink, striated sky. As the angle changed, the shape of the rock formation changed, too.

Sex, or rape? Thumb, or dick? Both, I thought. *It's both.*

I made it up South Boulder Road and across Spanish Hills to the mailboxes in a total of twenty-six minutes, which was later than I'd hoped, but it wasn't bad. I was consoling myself that the same traffic that slowed me down around 55th Street was probably impeding the progress of Jonas's carpool, too.

I stopped the car to collect the mail. The sun-dropping-behind-the-Rockies part of sunset was complete. That spectacle was always prelude to the final, more complex brilliance of the day, when clouds of orange and yellow and pink and gold pastels provided illuminated canopies to the lines of high clouds streaking from distant west to near west in lighter and deeper grays until the streaks disappeared into darkness. At the end of the nightly show, last light would recede inevitably in the west, like an ebbing celestial tide.

Our hilltop was already in deep shadows as I climbed back in the car and turned past the mailboxes onto the lane.

The far end of the lane was deserted when I pulled into the garage. The ranch house across the way looked quiet. I noted a different pattern of lights on inside than I'd seen the day before. An additional light was on upstairs, maybe in the main hall. Someone had been there during the day.

I peeked into our neighbor's garage as I walked to my door. The SUV was there. The

Cadillac was gone.

I begged the dogs for patience — they wanted out, and they wanted dinner; if possible, they wanted them both simultaneously — while I checked the carpool list that was posted on the refrigerator door. Chloe Cox was the parent who was driving Jonas home that day. Beside her name on the list, for a reason that eluded me, Lauren had penciled in "TM" and circled it.

I guessed that Chloe was supposed to pick up an extra kid on that day's route. TM, to be precise. Tamara Mendez, of course. Tamara ended up in someone's car a few times a month. Her occasional presence was causing a bit of consternation because Tamara's parents weren't part of the pool and never drove anyone else's kids. I was determined to stay out of that controversial quicksand.

I took care of the dogs while I watched for the headlights of Chloe's Pilot to appear near the top of the S-curve on the lane. After ten minutes of waiting, I began to suspect she'd already arrived and left, Jonas in tow, before I made it home. She probably called Lauren and left a message on her voice mail.

I called her. "Chloe?" I said. "It's Alan

Gregory."

"Alan, hi." She sounded completely unharried. I was impressed.

"Are you caught in traffic?" I asked. "That construction near 55th is a mess."

"No, no. I'm in for the night. Just fixing dinner for the kids. Kurt's in Dayton, or Cincinnati. Someplace. Des Moines? Maybe Des Moines. I think it's going to be a mac and cheese and carrot sticks night. You guys ever do that? Gosh, you probably don't. I shouldn't have admitted that I do that. *Errrrrr.* Oh well. What's up? These teacher meeting half days turn my world upside down. I'm such a creature of habit. You, too? Tell me yes. Please."

Teacher meeting half days? Oh. Shit. The "TM" penciled on the carpool schedule was for "teachers' meetings." Not Tamara Mendez.

I didn't have to think it through to know what we'd done. Instantly, the parade of parental errors was clear. My heart seemed to stop completely before it jumped and jerked the way manual-transmission cars do when you try to start the ignition after forgetting to first depress the clutch. I literally lurched forward half a step before I froze.

I assumed other sets of parents do it. Have moments, or hours, of mutual cross-contaminated child-rearing brain cramps. Times when assumption and routine and schedule somehow manage to supplant judgment and attention and adjustment.

Days when one parent's forgetfulness and distraction goes completely uncorrected by the other parent's mindfulness and purpose.

Lauren and I, I realized, were in the midst of one of those days. Jonas's school day had ended that afternoon at one o'clock. His after-school activities had been canceled. For teachers' meetings.

Chloe had probably dropped him off at home by one thirty or so. Jonas had probably given her a halfhearted wave as he let himself in the front door with the key that we insisted he hang around his neck. Chloe wouldn't have expected to see Lauren greet Jonas at the door. Not since she'd started using the cane. Jonas wouldn't have watched as Chloe drove away. That wasn't Jonas.

Jonas had texted me, though, when he discovered he was unexpectedly home by himself. *He texted me.* I checked my phone. He had texted me at two sixteen.

So he was home at two sixteen. The soil analysis question he'd asked me had nothing to do with his earth science class. It had everything to do with Mattin and Mimi Snow needing to know the answer to the mundane question that faces any Front Range homeowner considering foundation work. Our new neighbors were wondering if the land immediately adjacent to their house was burdened with expansive soils. If you're planning to excavate for a foundation along Colorado's Front Range, the presence of expansive soils is a crucial consideration.

While Jonas was trying to figure out why he was alone in his new house, he had been observing someone doing a soil analysis near his old house. The process of doing soil testing at depth required a drilling rig. A small rig. All the analyst had to do onsite was extract a deep core of dirt and clay, twenty feet, maybe more, for later assessment in a lab. The whole coring apparatus could probably fit in the bed of a pickup truck. It could certainly be towed by one.

Jonas wouldn't have intuitively known what the equipment was for. The truck must have had lettering on the door, or a sign. Something that included the words *soil analysis.* That's how he'd known what was going on. When he asked me about it, I had basically blown him off.

A fine piece of parenting on my part.

His second texted question to me, only minutes later, had been: **Lauren at work.** I had missed the meaning of that one completely.

My current translation? Jonas had thumbed that text just as he was beginning to get concerned that he was indeed home by himself and that his new parents had screwed up. He had been asking me for some guidance or some reassurance. Mostly, probably, he had been asking for some company.

Jonas didn't ask for much. My response to him? I had asked my son if he was cool. Four-hours-plus later, I was not feeling terribly reassured by his texted reply: **Yep fgw**

I searched the house, calling his name. Jonas didn't answer. His favorite sneakers weren't by the front door or anywhere down in his room. They were on his feet.

I called his phone. It went to voice mail. I texted him. And waited.

He didn't text me back.

I stepped out to the front porch and yelled Jonas's name. I did it again even louder.

I called Lauren. Her tone of voice, and her rushed, "Yes," told me how distracted she was by whatever was keeping her late at work. I assumed it had something to do with the homicide of Preston Georges. I forced my tone to float somewhere in the normal range as I asked, "Was today some kind of half day for Jonas?"

I was hoping — begging, praying — that she'd forgotten some other arrangement she had made to account for Jonas's free time that afternoon. A bowling party. A movie. Paintball. For one of his friends' mom or dad to pick him up, or . . .

As she heard my question, I could tell that Lauren had stopped breathing midexhale. In a fraction of a second her quick mind covered all the territory it needed to cover to understand the situation: "TM," Chloe, Lauren's own half day of work becoming a full day, plus. Jonas, alone.

"Oh no, Alan. Oh my God, is he okay? I totally for — Oh my God, what did I do?"

"I just talked to Chloe. She dropped him off around one thirty. She watched him go in the house, like always. I got home a few minutes later than I hoped, but I can't find him, Lauren. He's not around. He hadn't turned any lights on inside our house, which means he probably hasn't been inside since the sun went down. He's not answering his phone. Do you have any ideas where I should look?"

"Did he leave a note?"

"No."

"His dad's barn? Jonas likes it there."

"That will be my next stop."

"Should I tell the police?"

"That sounds . . . premature. Let me look around a little. I'll let Emily out to go after him, too."

"I'm on my way home."

"Please call Ralph and Topher. Ask them to keep an eye out on the lane for him. In case he's walking somewhere or coming back here. Topher is working from home these days. See if he saw Jonas at all this afternoon."

Ralph and Topher were the quiet couple who lived in a modern home at the other end of the lane, near the junction with the mailboxes. Ralph had been the listing agent for Adrienne's home sale. They'd known Jonas since he was a baby.

"Of course. I'll call them. I'm walking out the door right now."

Even if she were turning onto 6th as we spoke — and she wasn't — during late rush hour she was still a good twenty-five to thirty minutes from our home.

"And ask Ralph if he can find out what company might have been out today to drill a core sample for a soil analysis. The buyer's agent may have given Mattin the name of a company to do that work."

"Why is that imp —"

"I'll explain later. But it might be important. I'm halfway to the barn. Emily's there already."

"Is Jonas —"

"It looks locked. Dark. I can't see much through the windows. Hardly anything." I called out Jonas's name again. "Padlocks are on. I don't think he's in there. He has to know that I'm looking for him."

"Oh my God. Where's our son, Alan?"

"Emily just started circling down toward the ravine."

I never liked it when she headed that way. That's the direction that the cats and bears came from. Surprisingly, my heart didn't jump at the prospect of big cat and brown bear intruders. My muted sense of alarm informed me that wild predators weren't my biggest fear at the moment.

"Can you see her?" Lauren asked.

"Not anymore. It's way too dark down there."

"Oh my God."

I said, "I promised Adrienne I would keep Jonas safe. How could I . . . How the hell did I . . ."

"I'm at my car," Lauren said. "I'm going to hang up so I can call Ralph and Topher. Alan?"

"Sure," I said. I closed my phone. I was staring down into the blackness at the bottom of the ravine. The white noise of late rush-hour traffic on 36 provided the only auditory accompaniment. I had nothing to see, nothing to hear, and nothing to say.

I turned around to walk back toward the lane. After a few steps, I tripped over something. I caught myself. I didn't fall.

Right behind me, only twenty feet or so away from the southwestern corner of the old house, a series of four thin wooden stakes were taped together to mark off an area about two feet square. The stakes had been placed precisely where the foundation wall of the pioneer turret would be if it were ever built. I dropped to one knee to feel the ground between the four stakes. The dry Colorado clay inside the boundary was recently broken. The stakes had been set to mark off the spot where a drilling rig had taken a core soil sample earlier that day.

Our new neighbors were planning to build the missing tower on the ranch house after all. They were checking the quality of the soil in that location to ensure they would have no problems with a shifting foundation.

I put my hands together and blew the deep bellow that would call for Emily to return. Twenty seconds later, I had her back by my side as I walked up the steps to Mattin and Mimi's front door.

The damn doorbell was actually working. I could hear it clear as day.

36

No one answered the door. I used my mobile to call Diane. "Listen," I said, "I have a problem here . . . at home, with Jonas. Do you know if Mattin and Mimi are around? At home, I mean? Is Mimi still staying with you?"

Diane noted the seriousness instantly. "What kind of problem?"

"I can't find him. That kind. Lauren and I mixed up our after-school coverage plans today, and Jonas ended up being alone for most of the afternoon. Never should have happened, but it did. I just got here, and I can't find him."

Diane knew Jonas's history, and vulnerability, well. I didn't have to explain to her why the stakes were so high. "Shit, um — shoot. Mimi's still here. She's been with me all day. I couldn't . . . actually say where Hake is. There's some difficulty . . . there right now. Between them." She lowered her voice. "I'm not sure they're talking."

"So, no one is home at their house?"

"I don't think so, but I can't say that for sure. Do you want me to ask her? I'm happy to ask her. She's opening a bottle of wine."

"No, it's okay. Wait — Yes. Please ask her if anyone is home now or maybe was there this afternoon. Any . . . workmen, or visitors, or anyone who might have seen Jonas at any time after, say, one o'clock. That would be really helpful. To know if anyone saw him at any point this afternoon would be great."

Diane came back on the phone about a minute later. "Alan? She says that there was someone scheduled to do a soil test this afternoon. She'll try and find out the name of the company for you. If she finds it, I'll call you back. I'm afraid that's it. Have you called the police?"

"Not yet."

"It's dark, Alan. Pretty cold, at least up here. If he's outside? You need to think about calling the sheriff."

"Yeah." I hadn't thought it would come to that. But it was coming to that.

I heard a door open and close at Diane's end of the conversation. Diane's voice went to whisper. "I think Hake's downtown at the St. Julien. I'm pretty sure he's not sleeping at the house. I gotta go."

The fallout from the aftermath of the housewarming, and the fallout from the bicycle accident, were apparently taking a toll on Mattin and Mimi's relationship. That was hardly surprising.

I hit the doorbell one more time before I stepped from my neighbors' porch. Once again, I could hear the bell sing inside the house. In my experience, the thing working twice in a row was almost unheard of. Adrienne would consider it an omen.

I called for Emily to come with me. She ran directly to my side. Emily's a great companion. But obedient? On her whim. She was sensing my tension.

I thought I saw something move on the periphery of my vision. I stopped. Emily took an additional couple of steps in that direction, as though it had caught her attention, too. But she didn't bark.

Shadows covered shadows. I found them difficult to read. I wasn't at all sure what I had seen off to the side. Emily suddenly took off past me but stopped. Could it have been her shadow interrupting my shadow as the silhouettes stretched out in front of me and overlapped? Or had it been yet another shadow entering the montage from another location?

My impression had been that a fresh shadow, a new form, had been added to the mix of dark and light shapes that were projected onto the dust and dirt in front of me.

I spun around, half expecting to see someone standing on the porch I'd just vacated. But the porch was empty.

"Jonas?" I said. Then I said his name again, louder, while I scanned the old ranch house. Four light sources were responsible for all the overlapping shadows. A porch light was lit beside the front door. An identical light fixture was centered high on the gable above the garage door, to the north. A light in the middle of the first floor — I guessed it was in the kitchen — was sending off enough illumination to brighten the big windows on the front of the house. That light was generating some shadows. The upstairs hall light I'd spotted earlier was also sending enough illumination out the adjacent bedroom windows to cause barely perceptible shadows down below, between the two houses where I was standing.

I took a solitary step backward as I looked over my shoulder toward my home. As I changed my position, all the varied light sources caused the shadows behind me to move every which way. I stepped sideways and watched the shadows dance again.

That's all it was, I thought. *Shadow geometry. Just an alteration in the mix of shadows each time I moved.* I continued walking toward my front door.

Emily barked. I gasped, just a little.

The bark wasn't her throaty, *wooooo,* pay-attention bark. It was Emily's I'm-serious-damn-it, slam-the-Bible-on-the-table, hard-clap, I'm-talking-danger bark.

It was her where-the-hell-is-the-Glock bark.

I stopped again. I spun one hundred eighty degrees. I looked in the direction Emily was looking, directly at the ranch house. "Jonas?" I said.

Emily barked again. Once. The sharpness of her diction was stunning.

I saw nothing alarming. My eyes scanned left, right, up, down. At the house, at the shadows. Back at the house.

Then Emily erupted. The intermittent, solitary, holy-damn barks became a chorus of slamming Bibles. In rapid succession, the claps roared from her throat *rat-a-tat-tat* as though she had loaded a dozen of the fat holy books in a Gatling-gun-style slamming-Bibles-on-the-kitchen-counter machine.

One bark right after another right after the next.

Emily was not happy. I kept my eyes on the house, determined to find the source of any movement. The big dog was definitely seeing something I wasn't seeing.

I knew that it wasn't Jonas. Emily wouldn't bark like that if all she saw were Jonas. She would run to greet him. "Good girl," I said, releasing her. "Go get it."

The Bouvier jumped at the chance to confront the danger, launching herself into motion. I assumed she had a better idea what "it" might be than I did.

She had a destination ready. She took off immediately toward the side of the old house that faced toward the ravine. The side of the house with the walk-out basement door. In a split second the big dog was around the corner, gone from my sight.

The barking stopped soon after.

I was paralyzed in place for a moment. I was trying to decide if I should go inside and get the Glock. Or follow Emily, and the danger.

The shadows in front of me moved again. That wasn't an illusion. *How? What?*

"Jonas? Hey, Jonas? You there? Jonas?"

37

My phone was ringing. I reached into my pocket and touched the button to quiet it. When I pulled it out to see who'd called, my wife's photo was on the screen. I switched it to vibrate before I answered. "Yeah," I said. The call had only a small fraction of my attention.

"I'm on my way to the ER in Louisville, Alan. The girls were using Phyllis's sofa as a trampoline and Gracie hit the side of her head on the coffee table. She's okay. But she needs a few stitches."

I wanted to scream *Fuck!* Instead, I mouthed *fuck*. "No concussion? They're sure?"

"No concussion. Phyllis is there. She says the doctor says Grace is fine. Any sign of Jonas?"

"Still looking. Where's the Glock?"

"Right now? It's in my car."

Damn. The one day I want the thing at

home . . .

I lied. I said, "I just want to know it's in a safe place. You know, since . . ."

Since I have no friggin' idea where my son is. And since my dog is telling me that she feels danger from the pads of her paws to the roots of her fangs.

"Always," my wife said, reminding me how careful she was with her weapon. "We should think about calling the police, Alan."

"I know," I said. "I was just about to do that when you called."

"Okay," she said. "Well, it's time. What if he's hurt, you know if he fell or something?"

"As soon as we hang up, I will call."

I was about to hang up the phone when Lauren added, "I forgot. I talked to Topher. He said he saw a kid. One he'd seen before. Walking out the lane. Late this morning."

"Out? Topher used that word?"

"Yes. But he wasn't home all day. He spent most of the rest of the day with his sister, he said. Did you know she has melanoma?"

I didn't. But that was a tragedy for another day. "Thanks," I said. "Keep me posted."

My attention was fragmented. I was staring into the dark in the direction where Emily had disappeared. I was listening for any sound at all from any direction that wasn't the hum of white noise emanating from rush-hour traffic on 36. I was waiting for shadows to move.

I started hitting the buttons on my phone to connect with Sam Purdy. I would ask him to coordinate with 911 for me. The phone vibrated in my hand before I hit the second button. Diane's picture filled the screen.

"Yeah. What's up?"

"Mimi's in tears. There may be a . . . serious problem. With her family."

I didn't have time for Mimi's problem. "I'm in the middle of my own problem, Diane. I'm sorry, but we can talk after I find —"

"Shit," Diane said. Then, "Oh fuck — Damn it, I'm trying not to curse. Now somebody is at the door. Can you believe it? Raoul? Will you get that? We live in the middle of nowhere, Alan. People find us anyway. But don't worry, Raoul is going to get it."

I was worried about a lot at that moment. But I hadn't been at all concerned about Diane's profanity or who was at Diane's door.

Diane said, "Mimi didn't want to tell me any of this. I had to press her. She's afraid that —"

"Diane. I really don't have time for —"

"You asked who might be home at her house. Her son may be at their house. That's who."

What? Her son? I had to review what I knew about Mimi's family. When Diane had originally told me that her friends were buying Adrienne's house, she'd said something about Mimi having a couple of kids from a prior marriage. The older girl was a cheerleader at Kansas. Or Iowa, maybe. Missouri? I hadn't really been paying attention. At the time, it had seemed like information of infrequent utility. She was in the middle of a semester abroad, I thought. Singapore? Hong Kong? No, maybe someplace in Europe. I hadn't been paying enough attention. The only son was younger, a junior in high school at some boarding school for skiing wunderkinds in Routt County, up near Steamboat Springs.

I remembered thinking that I didn't even know there were boarding schools for skiing wunderkinds. In Routt County or elsewhere.

To Diane, I said, "Yeah. Okay. How is that a problem?"

"Hake isn't answering his phone. There had been some trouble between Hake and . . . her son. And between Hake and Mimi about her son."

"The skier? That son?"

"Yes. That son. Hake doesn't want him in the house. Mimi is worried that there could be a confrontation and —"

She stopped suddenly. The truth was that Diane was making me more nervous, which I wouldn't have predicted was possible. Whatever she had going on with Mimi certainly wasn't being particularly helpful with my search for Jonas.

Diane's voice was breathless. She said, "Raoul says the police are at the door. I need to go, Alan. They want — Oh my God. They have a warrant."

The call died.

I tried to make it compute. Why were the police at Raoul and Diane's with a warrant? What kind of warrant? *Search? Arrest?*

Emily barked once in the distance, bringing me back to the present crisis in Spanish Hills. I waited for more from her. But the single bark was all I got.

It hadn't been a Bible-slam bark, like earlier. The latest solitary bark had been different. A bark I had never heard before. Soft, at least on the edges. A high pitch at its peak.

A completely new word in her Bouvier vocabulary. A word, unfortunately, I didn't yet comprehend.

It wasn't the most opportune of times for

my dog to introduce a canine neologism.

I began taking measured steps in the direction of the bark. I hit the buttons to call Diane.

"Just listen, please. Call the sheriff for me. Tell them I have an emergency up here. I need to go, too. Emily is sensing —"

Just then, Emily came running around the corner of the house toward me at an awkward jog, as though she were running at a forty-five-degree angle. When she got to my side, I reached down to pet her with my free hand so I could get a sense of how winded she was, which might tell me how far she'd run.

My hand came back wet.

I had to lift my hand from the shadows to the light in order to confirm my fear. My hand was covered in blood. One look into my dog's dark eyes told me the blood was hers. She didn't really lay down next to me. She pretty much collapsed beside me.

"Do it, Diane. Now! Call 911. I need the sheriff. An ambulance, too. As fast as they can get here. Call Sam Purdy. Tell him everything. Please, an ambulance, Diane. Got it? And a vet. A vet, too."

"Alan," she said. "They are here with a warrant for —"

"Call 911. Please." I closed the phone.

Go to Jonas? Take care of Emily? I didn't know what I should do first.

I needed a flashlight and a weapon to go off in the dark to help Jonas.

I carried the eighty-pound dog inside. She stayed where I laid her on the rug in the family room. I ran to the first aid stuff, got a fat round of gauze and a big elastic bandage. I felt through my dog's thick hair until my fingers slipped into a warm wound on her chest on the left side. My fingers disappeared into the gash up to the first knuckle. I covered the wound with a fat fold of gauze and wrapped Emily's taut body with the bandage.

Fiji sat at attention right beside her friend.

I wondered if the half a minute it had taken me to compress Emily's wound would have been better spent searching for Jonas.

Please, please, please, I kept repeating to myself. *Please, please, please.*

"Hold on, girl," I said to the big dog. Fiji's eyes were as big as quarters. Her perky tail was down. Her ears were flat against her head. She looked befuddled, but she also looked like she knew in her heart that her world had just turned completely upside down, and that she had a job to do.

The creature she considered the most powerful animal in the world was down in front of her. I said, “Fiji, take care of Emily.”

I grabbed the big, black Maglite and ran back outside.

Jonas. I’m coming.

I really wished I had the damn Glock. I actually felt like shooting somebody.

I recognized at some level that I had just identified a good reason not to be carrying a .9mm handgun.

38

I sprinted across the lane, around the corner of the house, directly to the rock outside the basement door where Diane and I had stumbled, in my case literally, across the spare key.

I was working under the assumption that Jonas was in his old home. Why? I didn't know. But he wasn't a kid to wander the hills in the dark.

He'd been truly torn about the recent sale of the house where he was raised. He was very conflicted about any planned alterations.

The key wasn't where it had been. I lifted the stone — it weighed a good five pounds — with plans to use it to bust out the glass in the basement door. That, I figured, would be almost as effective as the damn key.

Though not quite so quiet. On a whim, I tried the doorknob first. The door swung open.

My conclusion? Someone else had used the key under the rock. The question was who. I had two candidates: either Jonas, or the asshole responsible for stabbing my dog.

I dropped the rock. I shifted the flashlight to my right hand. Hefted it. Swung it once at forty-five degrees, from high to low. From right to left.

If I didn't see Jonas, my target was going to be the side of the asshole's head. His ear was my bull's-eye.

I can do this, I told myself. I wasn't convinced. I whispered, "Jonas?"

Nothing. I poked my head into the laundry room. "Jonas?"

Nothing. I edged a few steps down the hallway that led toward the rooms at the back of the basement. "Jonas?"

Almost immediately, I heard the sound of footsteps on the stairs that led down to the basement. Someone was coming down. It was either my son or someone I didn't want to see. I wasn't feeling particularly lucky.

I could run, or I could confront the danger. I could go outside and knock on the door — or ring Adrienne's God bell — and try to engage whoever answered in some reasonable discussion about the whereabouts of my son.

The last option was winning out. But as I

retraced my steps toward the door, the first thing I saw coming down the stairs was the barrel of a revolver. *There,* I thought, *goes the ringing-God's-doorbell option.* I quickly backed into the laundry room, wondering why the man needed a gun to confront an eleven-year-old boy and praying there was no one already in the laundry room waiting to ambush me. The footsteps stopped. "Kid? Are you down here? Are you fucking down here? I swear, I'll . . . Come on, I saw you take that, kid. With my own eyes. I know you did. It's no big deal. I just want to know if that's the first time."

Take what? Has Jonas been stealing from the house? Jesus.

Despite my concerns, my heart soared a little with the man's threat. The odds that Jonas was still alive had just jumped considerably. I listened to two more footfalls as the man — the unfamiliar voice was a male's — edged farther down the stairs.

"Kid?" he said again as he tried unsuccessfully to make his voice sound less menacing than it was. That tactic might have been successful with somebody else's son. Not with my son. And not with Adrienne's. Jonas was already way too cynical. His menace radar was fine-friggin'-tuned. "Kid?" the man repeated. "I'd like to know how you got in here. Come on. This isn't the first time you did that? Right? I'm right? Just a few questions? Want to see what you have in there. Come on, come on. Talk to me."

The sound I heard next baffled me. It was a quiet noise — a quick *swish, scrape, swish.* All the component parts of the measure took no more than a second, combined. I couldn't place what they were. The progression of notes ended with a muffled thud. I could have sworn the thud had been right behind me.

Like *right* behind me. A pair of footfalls told me that the person on the stairs had taken two more steps down. I feared that he might have heard the same sound I had.

I turned my head slowly to check behind me for the source of the noise, trying to keep one eye peeled on the open laundry room door. The flashlight was high above my right ear. Locked and loaded.

Holy shit. Holy . . . shit.

"Kid? You know you've backed yourself into a corner, don't you? There are no doors back there. No windows. You have to come back my way. You ready for that? It's all us at the end, you and me. Why don't you just come out? Save us some fuckin' drama. Just tell me about your other visits. What else you took. I think you know what I mean, kid."

I did not know the voice. It wasn't Mattin Snow with its hint of the empire.

Nor did I know what Jonas would have been taking from the house.

I heard the sound of the man trying to move his feet quietly on ancient linoleum. The person on the stairs was no longer on the stairs. He was in the basement, with me. Probably only a couple of steps from the landing at the bottom of the stairs. I imagined him filling the opening to the narrow hallway that led toward the warren of rooms in the back of the cellar.

The good news? Yes, I could find some good news. The man was under the impression that Jonas was hiding from him in the rear of the basement. In the wine room. Or the old root cellar. Or in that creepy, JonBenet-ish room with the door with the bad latch. Back there, somewhere.

It was good news because Jonas wasn't back there.

Jonas was someplace upstairs. Specifically, he was someplace upstairs that was near an access door to the laundry chute.

The sound I'd heard behind me was Jonas dropping his favorite T-shirt down the laundry chute, to me. The shirt was faded green and adorned with a sketched profile of a free climber on the impossibly vertical face of a flat boulder. The shirt had the simple inscription I ROCK below the drawing of the climber.

Jonas must have heard me say his name when I poked my head into the laundry room, and he'd sent his T-shirt down as a signal to let me know where he was. He knew I'd recognize his father's old shirt.

I listened for the sound of distant sirens. The sheriff had to be getting close to the lane. Had to be. I didn't hear a siren. I pulled out my phone. With one hand, I typed **where r u.**

My thumb hovered above the SEND button. But I didn't press it.

I suddenly realized why Jonas hadn't been answering his phone. He had turned the power off. In this quiet house, the sound of a ringtone, or a text alert, or the distinctive buzz of a phone on vibrate mode, might alert the person who was after him to exactly where he could be found.

I killed the power on my phone for the same reason. Then I reached behind me and tapped ever so gently, three times, on the sheet metal on the inside surface of the laundry chute.

Jonas tapped back, just as gently.

From far in the back of the basement, I heard, "Damn it, kid. Come out. Let's talk."

I was wearing a beat-up pair of Toms. I slipped them from my feet. Then I made my move.

39

I was three steps from completing a remarkably quiet climb to the top of the stairs when my stockinged foot found a wide board that squealed like a cat that had just had its tail stepped on.

Subterfuge was no longer an option. I ran like hell.

"God damn it, kid. Those doors are locked. Double-keyed dead bolts, every one of them. I have the key. You don't. You're still trapped. Come on. Let's talk. We can work this out. Be better for you if you come out and show me what you have."

I flew up the stairs to the second floor, again trying to be as quiet as I could be. I wanted whoever was pursuing me to waste some time searching on the first level.

I did not know the intricacies of the laundry chute system in the house. Were there multiple access doors? Or only one? If there was only one, it would certainly be in the central hallway, upstairs. I ran there first. The linen closet that faced the hallway was bare. I did not see a chute door inside. I whispered, "Jonas."

No reply. I noted the hallway light. Had it been the upstairs light responsible for the moving shadows? Had Jonas been moving? Or had it been his pursuer?

I moved on to the master bedroom. I hadn't been in the room since Mimi and Mattin had bought the house. To my shock, the bedroom looked like a space out of a design magazine. It was completely decorated. Four-poster bed. Abundant linens. A plush sofa adjacent to the foot of the bed. Stuff — "accessories," Diane would say — everywhere. A flat-screen the size of a minor Great Lake on the far wall.

The walk-in closet in the master, another of Peter's finely crafted creations, was full of clothes. I spotted a hinged door on a lovingly fitted bench on one side of the large closet. I lifted the small door.

A laundry chute. Definitely. I lowered my head into the opening and said, "Jonas?"

He replied, "Cubby." *Of course.*

Another voice intruded. "I'm coming upstairs now, you little fuck."

As much as I'd grown to despise the man's voice, I appreciated the heads-up about his plans. I could hear his feet squeaking on the hardwood floor as he moved across the main level toward the staircase.

I hugged the hallway wall as I edged toward Jonas's room and his cubby. I had the big flashlight ready. I was feet from Jonas's door when I saw the top of a stocking cap. The man was making his way slowly up the staircase that was parallel to the hallway where I was standing. He was already about halfway up. I wasn't going to get past him in time to protect my son.

I held my breath. He took another step. He began to turn his head. In my direction. In the hand that wasn't on the railing, he held the gun. I thought of Emily's wound and decided he probably had a knife, too.

Time was up. I lunged across the hall toward the railing while I simultaneously began to swing the flashlight down as hard and fast as I could. I had already decided that I was cool with any impact location covered by the man's stocking cap.

In retrospect, the assault was a move that I wished I'd had an opportunity to practice. At least once or twice.

Momentum — mine — it turned out, was not my best friend.

The force of my leap across the hall,

coupled with the downward tomahawk motion of the heavy Maglite, combined with the sudden impact, just below my waist, of the rigid stairway railing, launched me over said railing toward the man on the stairs in the stocking cap as efficiently as if it had been my plan all along.

Catapulting over the railing headfirst had, of course, not been my plan all along.

And the move I ended up making was not a particularly graceful one. Still, in the microsecond that I was accepting that I was, indeed, launched, and cognizant that my best hope for doing something effective would be *before* I crashed into whatever surface the laws of physics determined I was about to crash into next, I was determined to do some damage — and hopefully not just to myself — with the swinging flashlight.

I continued to force the downward motion with my hand. Somehow I managed to impact my primary target — the stocking cap — with the flashlight. Hard? Not really. Hard enough? Maybe. As the man either collapsed from the blow or fell pulling away from it, his head swung away from the arc of the flashlight and came straight into my thrusting right knee.

I hadn't been aiming my right knee at his

head — other than the flashlight chop, none of my midair contortions could have been considered anything as intentional as "aiming" — but the concussion of his head with my right knee felt much more solid to me than had the initial impact of the flashlight with his skull.

He fell and tumbled down the stairs. My momentum carried me across the staircase until my right hip walloped into the railing on the far side of the stairs, barely escaping the indignity and agony of a forced landing with the opposing railing firmly planted between my legs.

Then I, too, tumbled down the stairs. I landed on top of the asshole. He was groggier than I was. My knee hurt, I suspected, more than his did. His head, I hoped, hurt much more than my knee.

I was desperately trying to find his gun. He was wriggling below me, more interested it seemed in collecting his senses than in finding his weapon.

The flashlight was gone. I couldn't spot or feel the gun. I knew I had to get back to Jonas. I wound up and hit the man as hard as I could with my fist. In his face.

He fell facedown. He stopped wriggling.

I was pretty sure I'd done some damage to my damn hand.

40

"Jonas," I said in a whisper. "It's Alan. Let's get out of here. Hurry."

He wasn't in the cubby. He wasn't in the closet. That told me he was between them in the hidden passageway his father had constructed as an entrance to the knothole.

In his muffled voice, I heard, "Closet's open."

One of the panels in the closet was indeed open. The entrance was a slot really, a mostly vertical space, not big in any dimension. I would have to contort my body to fit through it. I had no way to know how much room there would be to maneuver if I made it inside.

"Come on out," I said.

He hesitated for a moment before he said, "Okay."

From the hallway came a chilling threat. "I will . . . kill . . . fucking both of you."

The man from downstairs was not unconscious. Nor was he trying to sneak up on us. "I'm coming in," I told Jonas.

Jonas whispered, "He has a gun."

"Saw that," I said. I lowered my head and shoulders into the opening and pulled myself inside. The second my feet cleared the passageway Jonas closed the door behind me. The mechanism involved a motor. I could hear the hum. That's all I could tell about it in the complete darkness inside. I felt all around me. I was in a space about two feet by two feet by four feet. Jonas was on an even smaller ledge right above me. That ledge, I guessed, provided access to the cubby.

I felt Jonas's hand on my head. Then I felt his breath on my ear. He whispered, "He can shoot us right through the wall."

Probably, I thought. Jonas could feel me nod my head.

"Can you climb?" he said.

"Climb what?" I asked.

"Rocks," he said.

"What?"

Jonas said, "I think maybe we need a plan, boychik."

It almost made me laugh. It was something his mother would have said.

That's when I smelled smoke. The asshole, it seemed, had a plan. He planned to burn us, or smoke us, out into the open. Then he would shoot us.

I didn't see any immediate flaws in his plan.

But it turned out he was an impatient adversary. Twenty seconds later, maybe, he fired the first shot. I had to guess where he'd aimed. My guess, based on the noise and the reverberation in our hiding place, was that he'd aimed into the wall below the cubby. He'd surmised that the entrance Jonas had used to disappear into the hidden space involved a trapdoor of some kind. Not a bad assumption. Two more shots followed in quick succession into the same general location.

He'd missed us with those first shots by a good four feet. I was gripping Jonas's hand as tightly as I dared.

For a wonderful ten seconds, I thought the man was done with the shooting and that the only immediate mortal danger we were left to confront was fire. The eleventh second proved me wrong. The guy squeezed off three more quick shots. All three went into the back wall of the closet. One a little higher than the first, one a little lower.

The last one was two feet from my head. Max. I almost squealed.

I recognized a pattern. He was getting methodical, shooting bullets like a photographer shoots pictures, bracketing his exposures.

I recognized the modification to the asshole's plan: although he realized he could eventually smoke us out into the open, his current plan involved an option of shooting us in place, just before he cremated us in place. I couldn't find any holes in his plan from a killing-us perspective. I thought it would work just fine. Forensically, though? He was leaving way too much to chance. The crime scene guys and the arson guys would figure this out.

Of course, they'd figure it out way too late to do Jonas and me any good, but they'd get there. What did that tell me? It reconvinced me that the asshole trying to kill us wasn't Mattin Snow. He was too smart to leave this kind of trail behind.

The gun I'd seen in his hand earlier was a revolver. The man had fired six shots so far. Sam had told me once that most revolvers were six-shooters. If that one was a six-shooter, and the man had more ammunition, he would be reloading.

"Where are those rocks for me to climb?" I whispered to Jonas, desperate for an escape, hoping he'd been something approximating serious with his earlier question.

"Up," Jonas said. "Or down."

I had no idea what he was talking about. He took my hand and pulled my arm to full extension. I had to contort my body to allow him to pull it even farther. He finally closed my hand around an uneven protrusion on a wall about three feet from where I was sitting. I didn't know what it was that I was feeling.

"What?" I said. Jonas grabbed my hand and moved it over and up a few feet. I had to reach as far as I could to get my hand where he wanted it. He placed my fingers on another uneven protrusion. The second was the same sort of thing as the first. But a different shape. "What?" I whispered again.

"A rock wall. Goes up to the attic. Down to the basement. Dad did it."

I drew a blank at first. Then I got it. *Peter removed the old dumbwaiter and constructed an interior climbing wall from his basement to his attic? Of course he did.* I said, "Peter built a climbing wall in here?"

"Who else?" Jonas said. He said that with pride.

"In the dumbwaiter?"

"Yep. For me."

"Let's go then," I said. "You go first."

"I'm . . . afraid of heights."

Two shots pierced the wall just below the ledge where Jonas was sitting. Two more to the right. Two to the left. All in a period of ten seconds of abject terror.

The asshole had extra ammunition. He had started bracketing horizontally as well as vertically. The last two shots would have hit me if I hadn't moved to feel the rock wall.

He'd fired six more shots. He had to be reloading again.

To Jonas, I whispered, "You're not as afraid of heights as I am of guns. Hold on to my back. I'll do the climbing." To me, if there was an easy exit from the attic, up seemed safer than down — the man was firing into the wall below us. Up was also a much shorter climb — five feet versus twenty-five feet. Jonas tightened his arms around my neck. I began feeling for handholds and footholds in the dark.

I whispered, "Is there a good way out of the attic?"

"A door drops down into Ma's closet," Jonas whispered.

"We're going up then," I said. The gables on the old house had big vents. If I had to, I could kick one out.

"When Dad took out the dumbwaiter, he

extended the chute all the way to the attic. Same time he did my knothole. He thought I'd be a climber, like him. He wanted it to be something special just for us."

Peter knew damn well that Adrienne wasn't going to hang around in there.

I felt around me. The climbing wall was a square chute. I guessed it was forty inches on a side. It had footholds and handholds randomly placed on all four faces.

I can do this, I thought.

I had never been rock climbing in nature. I had never done an interior rock wall.

Jonas, of course, asked, "Do you rock climb?"

I thought about lying. It didn't seem like a good time for that. "I do now," I replied.

"Oy," Jonas said.

Oy, indeed. I was wondering if a twenty-foot-plus fall down a defunct dumbwaiter lined with fake rocks would kill us.

Frankly, I wasn't in love with our odds. My right hand was barely usable. I really had done some damage to myself when I punched the asshole in the face. In my life, I'd hit two men in the face. Both times had yielded great personal satisfaction. And both times I'd injured my damn hand. I was missing something, I figured, technique-wise. If Jonas and I lived, I would work on that. Take some lessons on how to hit adversaries in the face. Jonas and I could do it together. Gracie could come, too.

The climbing was slow, but I had plenty of adrenaline to provide buoyancy. I would get to the attic in five or six feet. *I can do this. I can do this.* My silent words were 20 percent confidence, 80 percent psychological cheerleading.

Jonas said, "Is that a siren?"

I listened. "Yeah. It is. That's great. Help is here."

Down below us, near where we'd started, I heard some loud concussions begin. Five or six of them, in succession. Like the asshole was kicking at —

Suddenly smoke filled the dumbwaiter core. Earlier, I'd been able to smell it, and even taste it. But suddenly I could see the smoke. Lots of it. We were being forced to breathe it.

The asshole was kicking holes in the drywall, or plaster, or whatever the walls were made of in Jonas's room. He was breaking down fire-protection barriers, making sure that the fire, and the smoke, would be able to move unimpeded into the parts of the house where Jonas and I had retreated.

Right below guns on my list of fears was fire. Snakes and bees were right up there, too, but at that moment? At the top of the list? Other people's guns. And fire.

The only good news I could think of? I was thinking the asshole might be out of ammo. The kicking stopped.

I reached up with my beat-up hand and felt a flat horizontal surface above my head. I pushed on it. It did not give. Not even a little.

"I'm there. How do we get into the attic?" I asked.

"I don't know," Jonas said into my ear.

"You don't know?" I whispered incredulously over my shoulder.

"I'm afraid of heights, remember? I've never been up here."

Jonas had a lot of his mother in him. A lot.

The irony that Peter Arvin — a rock-climbing legend in Colorado — would have a firstborn son who was phobic of heights would be something I would have to ponder some other time. "It feels solid above us," I said. "No opening. You don't know if there's a latch? A trick? Your dad liked tricks. Secrets."

"He did. But I don't know. I've never been up here. Feel for a knob or something carved."

More sirens below us. I thought I could

even hear some yelling. Help had arrived.

I tried to remember whether I had told Diane to get the fire department to respond. I didn't think I did. I'd said police. I'd said ambulance. Not good foresight on my part.

To take advantage of the first responders, all we had to do was get out of the damn dumbwaiter and get past the asshole who was waiting for us in the house with a gun. With or without bullets. The smoke was getting bad. We had to do all that fast.

"Nothing, Jonas. Can you reach your phone?" I asked.

He answered my question with a question. "Where's yours?"

"Lost it fighting the asshole."

"Mine's in my pocket. But I don't think I can . . . hold on to you with one arm."

"Sure you can. You ready to try?"

He hesitated. I waited. "Okay," he said finally. He pulled one arm from around my neck. I could feel his other arm quiver.

Seven, eight seconds later, he said, "Oops." I heard a thud. "Dropped it."

I sighed. "No worries. Hang on tight."

"Let's go down to the first floor," Jonas said. "I know how to get out there."

"Then that's our plan." I dropped my left leg down, feeling for purchase on a fake rock. Did it again with my right. I repeated the motions.

I was finding a rhythm. We soon passed the opening to Jonas's cubby, where I still feared the asshole was waiting for us with fresh ammo. We continued down.

The smoke wasn't quite as thick below the cubby as it had been above. We were making progress.

"You good?" I asked my son.

"Good enough for government work," he coughed into my ear.

My good hand slipped. My not-good hand was not so good. It slipped, too.

My feet were each on solid footholds. Jonas was on my back. As my hands slipped we teetered backward, not down, impacting the opposite wall with a deadening *thunk.* I waited for my feet to slip from their tiny ledges.

My toes ached in a way I didn't know toes could ache. My feet didn't slip. They were on one side of the dumbwaiter core. Jonas was hanging on my back. His legs were hooked around my waist. We were leaning forty-five degrees toward the opposite wall of the core. Jonas was pinned between my shoulders and the other wall.

I didn't like the position we were in. Literally. Or figuratively.

I said, "Still cool?"

"You're kind of heavy."

I thought the muscles in my back were going to explode. I figured they would explode a few seconds after my quads did, which would happen after my toes went off like a string of firecrackers.

I recalled Rafa's admonition about quads and climbing steep hills. How you either have the determination in your heart, or you don't. Right then, I had it.

"Don't let go of my neck. Feel around, find places to put your feet, Jonas. Just feel around."

Almost immediately he said, "Got one." I could feel him continuing to kick around behind me. "Okay, okay, got another one."

As he began to assume his own weight, I felt stronger and lighter. The load on my quads lightened. My toes? Still a problem.

"Get as steady as you can get on those footholds. Balance yourself."

"Okay."

"Now take your hands from around my neck and put your hands flat on my back."

"Alan, I —"

"Trust me. Please."

He put his hands on my back. "As long as you keep pressure on my back with your hands, you will stay pinned on that wall. Think about it. Does that make sense?"

He thought about it. "Yes. It does."

"Now push on my back. As hard as you can. Like you're trying to force me away. It will pin you even more securely."

Jonas was stronger than I feared he would be. Not as strong as I hoped he would be. But his pressure on my back helped me reach across the shaft to my left and right. I found handholds on each side.

My feet continued to stay in place on the far wall.

"As I move forward, in order to keep your hands on my back, you will have to lean forward, too. As long as you keep as much pressure on my back as you can, you'll be fine."

"If you say so."

I began to use my arms to pull slowly away from Jonas. I could feel his hands increasing the pressure on my back. "It's working," he said. He sounded surprised.

"It'll work," I replied. I was trying not to sound anywhere near as lacking in confidence as I was feeling. I moved my feet off the far wall onto footholds on the sides, slightly below where Jonas was standing. I moved my hands to the wall in front of me and braced myself to resume carrying his weight.

He kept his hands, and his weight, on my

back the whole time.

"Okay. Now climb back onto me, Jonas. When you have your arms locked around my neck, you can take your feet off those rocks."

"They're not really rocks," he said.

I knew that Jonas, like his mom, could get argumentative when he was anxious.

I was pretty sure he was anxious.

41

"Where we heading?" I asked.

"The pantry in the kitchen, where the dumbwaiter door used to be. There's a secret entrance in the back of the pantry. A closet for the closet."

I said, "Of course it has a secret entrance."

"Ma used to tell me that Dad would go into the pantry to get a box of cereal and then he'd completely disappear. Two minutes later he'd walk into the kitchen from the other side with a box of Froot Loops. She calls him Houdini."

I noted the present tense. At some times Adrienne was deader to Jonas than at others.

"She never knew?" I asked.

"Nope."

I was sure Adrienne knew. But it was a great story for Jonas to remember about his father.

"I looked Houdini up online."

"Show me later?" I said.

"Yep."

For the next ninety seconds, I continued to descend the shaft. We were both coughing and trying not to cough as Jonas felt along the walls for indications that we'd reached the back side of the magic pantry.

"Here," he said finally. "To the right. It's a ledge."

"You go. I'll follow you."

He scrambled off my back onto the ledge. I felt like I'd just shed a ton. "Is there room for me?" I asked.

"Come on," he said.

I squeezed in beside him. I could not feel either my fingers or my toes. The smoke was starting to burn my lungs.

"How does it open?" I asked, fearing that the answer would be that Jonas didn't know.

"There's a latch," he said.

"Great."

"But I can't find it. I thought it was . . . here."

The cavalry was arriving downstairs, in the basement. I could hear men and women yelling. Radios crackling. Someone said, "Too hot. Back out. Back . . . out. Wait for the firefighters."

At that moment, I couldn't think of a worse place to be trapped during a fire than where we were. Rescuers would never find us in this hidden, sealed shaft.

"Here it is," Jonas said.

"Terrific."

"I can't move it. But I found my phone. It was on the ledge."

Yes! "Do you have a signal?"

Seconds passed. The screen illuminated. "Nope," he said. "No bars."

"Let me try the latch." I contorted myself to reach past him.

"I've been here before. You pull it out," Jonas said.

"Gotcha." The latch was smooth and carved from hardwood to fit a hand like a glove fits a hand. Perfectly. But I could not get it to budge either.

"Are you pressed against the door, Jonas?" I asked. I was hoping the mechanism was a pressure latch and that the solution to the problem was simple.

"Yes," he said.

"Maybe that's the problem. I'm going to go back out into the shaft so you have some room to scoot away from the door. It should open right up then."

I did not want to go back out into the shaft. But I found footholds and I eased myself back out.

Immediately, Jonas said, "Got it. Only two

more steps to open it."

Two more steps? What the fuck, Peter? "Two more steps?"

"Dad liked puzzles."

Peter, I swear — The door swung open. Through the thick smoke, I could see a band of light down at floor level. Jonas tumbled out. "Stay close. Stay low," I said. "Breathe only down near the floor." I launched myself onto the ledge and then scrambled headfirst out the secret door into the pantry.

Suddenly, behind me, a loud *swoooosh* erupted but was instantly enveloped by an explosive roar. Bright flames rose like Satan's breath up the dumbwaiter shaft from the basement. Intuitively, I guessed what had happened. Someone in the basement had opened the old dumbwaiter door, creating a chimney effect in the core.

If that had happened five seconds sooner . . . I would have been rotisseried.

As I slammed the door closed behind us, Jonas said, "Holy shit. That was close."

The profanity surprised me. But, in context, I had no problem with it. I asked, "What's nearer? The front door? Or the french doors to the deck?"

"Same same." Another Adrienne-ism.

"We have to get out of here fast." The

front door was solid wood. If it had a keyed dead bolt on each side, as the asshole had warned us, it did us no good. We could get all the way there and still wouldn't be able to get outside.

The french doors in back were glass. Even if they were locked, we could bust our way out. "Help me find something to break glass," I said. "Something heavy and hard. A frying pan, a . . ."

We were working by touch, searching the shelves in the pantry. "What's this?" Jonas said a moment later.

I couldn't see it. I felt the shape of what he was holding. I said, "It's a sharpening steel. It's perfect. We're going to go out on our bellies toward the glass doors in back. You're leading. Go. I'll be on your heels."

The smoke was thick everywhere in the room. I thought I could see the bright lights of flames dancing from burning draperies on the walls. Even bigger flames were shooting up the outside of the house. The black smoke was billowing, drifting. The supply seemed endless.

Jonas crawled like an infantryman, leading us directly to a pair of glass doors at the back of the house. I passed by him right at the end, reminding him to stay down. I reached up to try the latch. The door was dead bolted, as the asshole had promised.

I couldn't stop coughing. Breathing at all was becoming a major concern. I kept telling myself we were almost out. I tried to say *I hope this is safety glass,* but I failed to get the words out of my throat. I put my lips next to Jonas's ears and rasped, "Move to the side. Cover your face."

I hoped Jonas did as I asked. I whacked the glass with the steel. Breaking the glass was much harder than I thought it should have been. It took me half a dozen blows with the heavy steel to get enough glass to break to make an opening that would allow us to fit outside. I helped Jonas scramble out onto the deck. I tasted a little fresh air.

"Get away from the house as fast as you can," I yelled.

He immediately collapsed as his lungs revolted in a coughing fit.

I could feel heat behind me. I turned my head to see a big upholstered chair erupt in flames. I started to follow Jonas outside.

Breathing a big gulp of what I thought was fresh air was a bad idea. It wasn't fresh. My lungs spasmed. I collapsed in the opening in the door in a fresh fit of coughing.

Through the drifting smoke outside, I watched a firefighter emerge. He was wearing one of those big firefighter's jackets. He scooped up Jonas and began to carry him away from the danger on the deck.

The fire department had arrived. *Thank God.* The relief I felt that Jonas was safe felt better than oxygen. But the firefighter was carrying Jonas in the wrong direction. He was heading up the hill *away* from the house. Not toward the rescue vehicles that would be parked on the lane in the other direction.

I heard someone yell, "Stop! Right now! Stop!"

It felt like bad advice. I decided I would stop *after* I made it outside the burning house.

"Stop! Put . . . that child . . . down. Now!"

I knew the voice. I knew the tone. *Lauren?*

"Take another step and I swear I will shoot. Put him down!"

I put all my energy into moving a few more feet. Just before I made it out through the opening in the french door, I realized I was slowly passing out. The awareness that I was losing consciousness, and my inability to do anything about it, was the strangest sensation for me. I felt as though I was heading down a slide at a water park, unable to influence my momentum. I would splash down when I would splash down.

"Stop! *No!*"

I heard a shot.

Through my cerebral haze, a second or two later, I heard a second shot. At least, I thought I did. Part of my brain was trying to convince the rest of my brain that the shots I'd heard were merely an echo of the shots that had been fired earlier inside the house.

The gunshots made no sense to me. Not then. *Help had arrived. The danger was over. Right?* Nothing was making much sense.

Fighting what felt like an inexorable slide to unconsciousness, I looked back toward Jonas. I didn't quite trust what I was seeing. The firefighter holding Jonas in his arms had one leg of his jeans turning from blue to black. No, not black. *Red.*

Why so much blood? Why is the fireman wearing jeans?

Jonas remained in the man's arms. Jonas's face was nothing but fear and soot. He was screaming and coughing. Screaming and coughing.

All around me, the house was painted in flames. Parts of the deck were on fire, too.

The firefighter took an additional step toward the stairs that would lead off the deck and up the hill. He tried to take another, but his next movement was more of a lurch than a step. He made one more lurching motion as he fell forward onto the decking, landing partially on top of Jonas.

No! I have to be hallucinating this. Maybe I'm already unconscious. This can't be happening.

The next thing I saw seemed more like an apparition than an event. Lauren emerged from the distance and entered the narrow frame of my vision. She was almost ghostlike as she hobbled through the smoke toward the distant part of the wooden deck. Her Glock was in her right hand. Her cane was in her left, but she was holding it as a weapon, not as a mobility aid.

She limped directly up to the fallen firefighter. Without any hesitation, she put the foot of her weak leg hard onto the man's throat. I mean *hard.* She was using all of her relatively insubstantial weight to pin the wounded man to the planks with the sole of her shoe. With the tip of her cane, she scooted a revolver away over the planked decking. It disappeared over the edge.

Then she used her leg to push the man off our son, and she helped Jonas to his feet. *Gotta be hallucinating.* She tucked her cane under her arm, and gripped our son as though she never planned to let him go. Her other hand continued to hold the Glock.

She had it aimed at the chest of the fallen firefighter.

I had no idea what was going on, but I was wondering how any of this was going to end well. Lauren shooting a firefighter had to be something that had unwelcome consequences.

The last thought I had was in the form of a simple question: *What the hell does any of this have to do with an acquaintance rape at a housewarming party?*

42

I was in the back of an ambulance, parked on the lane not far from our front door, when the roof of the old ranch house collapsed.

I didn't know how I felt about it, other than the relief I felt that Jonas and I were no longer inside. Lauren was next to me. She had a hand on top of my head, smoothing my hair. Her skin was dotted with soot and ash.

"The kids?" I asked. It felt as though all the sound I made was swallowed by the oxygen mask on my face.

Lauren said, "Grace is with Diane. She's fine."

"Jonas?" I felt a small hand grip my hand.

"Right here. Hi, Dad," Jonas said from behind my head. "I'm glad you're okay."

Dad. My heart healed. "You cool?" I asked.

Jonas said, "Cool enough for government work."

Oh God. "Emily? How is Emily?" Lauren's eyes closed briefly. My heart felt like it broke anew while I waited for her to reopen her eyelids. She didn't want to tell me. *Oh my God.* "Please tell me she's okay. Please, please, please."

"She's in surgery. Sam drove her to the emergency vet. She was cut badly. It's deep. She bled . . . a lot."

"I tried to pack the wound. I tried to — But I had to go find Jonas. I had to —"

She squeezed my arm. "I know. The vet will call us as soon as the surgery is over. Emily would have died without your first aid. She has a . . . chance at least. You gave her that. She's a strong girl."

I couldn't imagine losing her. I forced myself back to the moment. I gripped Jonas's hand. "You were great in there," I said. "Terrific. So brave."

I couldn't see his face. "I shouldn't have been there," he said. "I screwed up. Big-time. I wanted to see the plans. For the house. From the architect. I wanted to know what they were doing."

Of course you did. "You were great, Jonas. In that shaft? Unbelievable." The screwing-up part? The shouldn't-have-been-there part? There would be plenty of time for us to talk about that.

"You were, Jonas," Lauren said to Jonas. "Right to the end."

"Everybody else is fine?" I asked. I didn't even know whom else I was worried about.

"Well, you're not doing so good," Lauren said. "You inhaled a lot of smoke, much more than Jonas. They're going to take you to the ER. See what you might need."

"I'm fine," I said.

"No, you're not fine," she said. "You were almost blue when they pulled you out of that doorway."

I leaned in Lauren's direction, tilted the oxygen mask away from my mouth, and tried to whisper as I said, "Did I see you shoot that fireman?"

"Shhh," she said. "Later. We're not supposed to talk about that. The sheriff is only giving me a minute in here with you. Professional courtesy. It's a kind gesture; he could get reamed for it. But I agreed not to talk about what happened tonight until after I give my statement. I'll be gone for a while . . . while I'm being . . . interviewed."

I lifted my head far enough off the stretcher to see that Lauren was flanked inside the ambulance by a sheriff's deputy. *Oh shit.* I waved. She didn't wave back.

Jonas leaned over to my ear. He said, "It wasn't a fireman, Dad. Mom shot the asshole. In the leg. One shot. She's good."

I thought I heard two shots. I saw his revolver. I turned back to Lauren. "What? You? The asshole was a fireman? How did you know —"

"Shhh. I made a commitment to the sheriff. We can't talk about this. I promised."

The deputy made a zip-it motion across her lip. She said, "One more word, we're gone."

Lauren leaned over and kissed me lightly. "We'll talk later. I should go with the deputy now."

"Do you need Cozy's help? You should have Cozy's help."

"No," she said. "I'm good. I am good."

"Call Cozy, Lauren. Call Cozy." My voice, I thought, sounded like an old lawn mower motor with a misfiring spark plug.

"Jonas? You still have your phone? Look up this name online: C-o-z-i-e-r M-a-i-t-l-i-n. Tell him what happened. Tell him your mom needs him at the sheriff's headquarters."

43

After the wonderful experience of having the inside of my lungs filmed with a bronchoscope, the first familiar face I saw in the treatment room in the ER was Sam Purdy's.

"God, you look awful," he said. "You're going to live, though. That's the rumor around here."

"Hey," I rasped. "How's Emily?"

He nodded. Made a fist, raised his thumb. "Good. Well, fair. Actually, probably rotten leaning toward critical — I don't know much about dogs — but the vet thinks she's going to make it."

I mouthed *thank you.* I put my fist on my chest.

"Quite the scene up at your place. Quite the mess," he said.

I nodded. Messy in many ways.

"Your friend's house is gone. You know that?"

By "friend" I assumed Sam was talking

about Adrienne, not Mattin Snow. "I saw the roof collapse before they brought me here. Guessed it was gone. Arson?"

"Arson guys will be there in the morning. Arson's another one of those things I don't know much about. Why does it seem that just about every day of my life that list gets longer?"

I didn't have an answer. "Right now?" I asked, waving my hand between us. "You a cop or my friend?"

Sam stuck his tongue between his front teeth for a second or two while he considered the question. "Best for you to think of me as a cop right now. But a cop . . . with some discretion. How's that?"

Sam was telling me he would cut me some slack. "Jonas is okay?" I asked.

"Yes. Docs cleared him. Kid is like a trauma magnet, you know. You better keep an eye on him. He just lost his house. You wonder how much a kid can take."

"That's the truth. Grace? You see her?"

"Didn't actually see her, but I heard she got a few stitches in her head from being a kid. All reports are she's fine."

"Lauren?"

"Still sorting that out." He lowered his voice. "Guy she shot was definitely not a firefighter, but he didn't have ID on him.

Whether the shoot was justified . . . ? It's gonna be complicated."

"Guy is . . . dead?"

"Very. She shot him in the leg, which is good from a was-it-deadly-force perspective. But she hit his femoral artery, which is not so good from a surviving-a-gunshot perspective. He bled out at the scene."

"He had a gun, Sam. I saw it. He shot at her."

"Well, the sheriff hasn't found it."

"I know where it is," I said.

"If it's there, they'll find it."

"Diane told me that you guys went to her house with a warrant. True?"

Sam shook his head in dismay. He said, "Such a small town." Then he nodded.

"What kind of warrant?" I asked even though I didn't think he was going to tell me.

"Sheriff's business. Not up to me to say."

"But you know?"

"I know."

"Blink if it was a search warrant."

Sam didn't blink. *No shit?* "Who?"

"I'm not answering," Sam said.

"Mattin Snow?"

"I'm not answering, Alan."

"Makes no sense," I said. I wanted to explain to Sam about Mattin's private DNA analysis, but I couldn't.

"From where I sit, none of what happened tonight makes sense. Tomorrow or the next day? It's all going to make sense. You wait. That's how it works."

"You think?"

Sam grinned. "Okay, maybe the day after that."

"Does this all have to do with the damn housewarming?"

Before Sam could answer, an ER doc I'd seen earlier marched into the treatment room. She was holding a piece of paper. "Your pulse ox is steady. Low end of where we want it, but steady. Your blood work is improved. And this" — she shook the paper — "is decent news from the bronchoscopy. So we're going to let you go home, Mr. Gregory. You will need to follow up with a pulmonologist tomorrow or the next day, but we'll let you go. The nurse will go over your discharge instructions. You have someone available to take you home?"

"It's Doctor Gregory, actually," Sam said to the ER physician. Why he said it, I had no idea. I could hardly wait to find out.

The ER doc glanced at me, raised her eyebrows. "I did not know. Excuse me, *Dr.* Gregory."

I opened my mouth to speak but couldn't

think of anything to say that would undo the damage that Sam seemed intent on doing. The moments that Sam chose to become mischievous came out of nowhere. I rarely saw them coming.

"But don't worry about getting all professionally courteous and deferential with him," Sam said. "He's a Ph.D. That kind of doctor. History, sociology, economics. Something. Nothing to concern yourself with, doctor. Ask me, one of the problems with Boulder is that it has more Ph.D.'s than it has parking spaces. What good does that do any of us? Imagine what Boulder would be like if every spare Ph.D. suddenly became a meter-free space near the Mall."

He smiled at her, I thought, kind of flirtatiously.

She stared back at him, I thought, kind of astonished. I couldn't tell if Sam was flirting to flirt, which would be news, or if he was flirting only to mix things up, which would be Sam being Sam.

He said, "I'll be taking him home. I'm Detective Sam Purdy. Boulder Police."

"Wonderful," she said. She completed a graceful pirouette as she left the room.

Too bad for Sam, but it seemed that I had enjoyed his act much more than the doctor had.

■ ■ ■ ■

Sam drove me back to Spanish Hills shortly after midnight.

Everything on the eastern side of the valley smelled like fire.

Phyllis — Grace's friend Melody's mom — had agreed to stay with the kids until Lauren or I got home. Phyllis fussed over me a little. I thanked her profusely for her help with our kids and finally got her to agree to go home to her own.

The kids were asleep. Grace was, anyway. Jonas may have been pretending. I no longer had any confidence in my judgment about that.

Sam stayed while I showered away the soot and found fresh clothes.

I called the emergency vet. No news on Emily.

I collapsed on the sofa. Sam said, "You want me to stay?"

I shook my head. "I'm all right. Thanks. Go home to Simon." Simon was Sam's son.

"He's with his mom. So you know why you're getting a bill for a billion dollars, give or take, I called Cozier Maitlin for Lauren. Turned out that he'd already been retained, apparently, by Jonas. Cozy's with

Lauren now, with the sheriff. The meter is running."

"Thank you, Sam." He took a step toward the door. I said, "Your parable the other night, your Kobe Bryant story, wasn't only about lessons lawyers learned from what happened. It was also you lamenting how lawyer wizards are managing to hijack the criminal justice system. How they lock out detectives like you and prosecutors like Lauren. How they scoot past judges. In the end, Kobe Bryant and his accuser reached their own plea bargains, found their own version of justice."

"Yeah. Go on."

"The last victim of rape be damned. The next victim of rape be damned. Am I right?"

Sam looked back over his shoulder with eyes narrowed to read my face like it was a document with fine print and he was determined not to miss a word. Finally, he said, "Something like that."

I waited. He waited. I thought he smiled a little bit before he headed home.

The phone in the house rang as I was looking out the window at the space where the ranch house had stood for over a century. All that was left was a pile of charred rubble. Two of the three chimneys were intact. The top half of the third one had tumbled over. A wide perimeter around the rubble was marked off by crime scene tape.

Caller ID read "Maitlin LLC."

"Hi, Cozy."

"You guys should think about keeping me on permanent retainer. It's a better deal."

"I wish that were funny. My son now has you on speed dial."

"Smart kid, by the way. Basically, I went down and told Lauren to shut up. She should have known better. But I'm going to have to hand this off to another firm. I have some conflicts, unfortunately. Things you are better off not knowing."

I already knew about Cozy's conflict. I also knew what I was better off not knowing. I said, "That's disappointing, but I understand. I appreciate your stepping in tonight. Do you know who Lauren shot?"

"You don't know?"

"I don't."

"ID isn't certain, but we think it was your new neighbors' son. Her son, his stepson. Which means that Lauren shot a homeowner on his own property. Technically. Juries, especially out west here, tend to frown upon such things. It could get ugly, Alan."

"If the man is who I think it is, he tried to

kill us inside the house. Jonas and me. He tried to shoot us. Like twenty rounds. Then he set the house on fire. He shot at Lauren, too. Outside."

"The way the story is being pieced together by the authorities has you and Jonas as intruders in the house. Under Colorado law, he was entitled to try to . . . well, kill you. Under our progressive criminal code, he's even entitled to succeed in those efforts."

"He had a gun, Cozy. He tried to kidnap Jonas. I saw it all."

"So? He's allowed to defend his home. 'Make my day' ring any bells? He's allowed to use deadly force against an intruder. The gun hasn't been recovered yet. Right now? The way it looks? You and your son broke into your neighbor's house last night. Caused some significant damage. Those are felonies."

"My son was —"

"Just warning you, if things tumble badly for Lauren, this thing could get ugly. Same could be true for you. Don't minimize this. Understand me?"

"Yes, Cozy."

"I told the sheriff's investigator they could talk with you tomorrow at noon. I'll be there for that interview. In case you plan to waste any time rehearsing your lines, we will be declining to discuss the incident. The meeting with the sheriff will be brief. In the meantime, I will make some calls, find somebody good to take over the case for you and Lauren longer term. Probably be someone from Denver."

Jesus. "Thanks. Will Lauren be home tonight?"

"Any time now. She left here a few minutes ago. I wanted to catch you before she got there. She needs some sleep, Alan."

"Yeah. I figured."

"No, I mean it. Make her rest. I've not seen her this exhausted in a while."

I drew Lauren a bath. She walked in the front door seconds after I turned off the tap.

"How are you?" I asked as we embraced.

"Okay," she said as though she almost meant it.

I continued to hold her. "You killed a man. And you're okay?"

She gave it a few seconds' thought. She pulled back far enough to look me in the eyes. "Tonight? I shot a man to protect Jonas. I didn't shoot to kill. But it turned out he died. That's how it feels to me. Tomorrow, it may feel like I killed him. Let tonight be tonight, please?"

One of my clinical mantras was not to mess with a well-functioning defense. If denial would help Lauren make it through the night, well, hallelujah.

She had just lowered herself into the bathwater when her cell phone chimed. She grabbed it off the tub deck, looked at the screen, then at me. I was sitting across the room, on the closed seat of the toilet. "I have to take this," she said.

"Need privacy? Want me to leave?" I asked.

She shook her head. Into the phone, she said, "Yeah? You have something?"

Lauren listened for a good minute. The only question she asked was, "Voluntary?" At the end of the conversation, she said, "No, I never believed it. I'm not surprised. Thanks. I mean it. I owe you one."

She turned to me. "May I have some more hot water? Please?"

"You sure?" Lauren, like many people with MS, feared the consequences of raising her core body temperature. Baths were usually warm. And brief. Long, hot soaks were for other people.

"Tonight? I need it. I'm willing to take the risk."

I turned the tap. I raised my voice over

the din. "So, what's up?"

"It's good," she said.

"Really?"

She smiled. "Really. Let me enjoy my bath. Go check the kids again, please. For me? You have to wake Gracie. Make her open her eyes. See if her pupils are the same size."

"That should be fun," I said.

She laughed. "It won't be. But you have to do it. I'll tell you everything in bed."

Gracie's pupils were the same size. Let's say she wasn't exactly thrilled about demonstrating that fact to me.

Downstairs, Jonas was on his side, facing toward the wall. He was either asleep, or he wasn't. I guessed he wasn't. I whispered, "You want to talk, I'm here."

He didn't respond right away. I pulled a chair next to his bed so he would have a few minutes to reconsider. My eyes slowly adjusted to the darkness.

Two dark objects were resting on his bed linens.

One was a rectangular shape about the size of a paperback book. When I hefted it, it felt like it was made of wood. The other appeared to be his phone.

Even in the dim light I could tell the

phone was covered with greasy soot. And that it was open.

Jonas was the kid who always charged his phone at night. On his desk. *Every* night. He never left it sitting around open. I picked up the phone. Touched a button. The screen came alive with a photograph. I rotated the phone ninety degrees.

Is that — Holy shit, it is. Huh, I thought. *Huh.* I scrolled backward. I scrolled forward.

Jonas's breathing never changed.

There were eight photos from the night of the housewarming celebration. I realized immediately that the "taking" that the man had been accusing Jonas of didn't involve things. Jonas had been "taking" photos. The most recent few were from only hours earlier. Two showed partial views of a man from the back. In neither was his identity clear.

I waited in the chair for another ten minutes, offering my son a chance to choose to talk to me about the photographs he'd left for me to see. I also realized it was possible, maybe likely, that the chance he'd just taken was as much as he was able to risk that night.

I used the light from the phone's screen to examine the piece of wood he'd left for me. It had fresh, uneven, very rough cuts on all four edges. In the center of the small plank was an intricate wood carving only a few inches across.

I slipped my son's phone into my pocket as I climbed back up the stairs. I was already formulating plans, knowing that no one outside the family would ever learn what Jonas had seen after the damn housewarming.

In the light upstairs, I examined the carving. Three hearts coming together, overlapping like a Venn diagram. A large heart with a *P.* A medium-size heart with an *A.* A tiny heart with a *J.* In the area where they overlapped, the words *Us Forever.*

Peter had created the woodcarving for his son somewhere in the walls of the secret entrance to his son's knothole. Once the house was sold, Jonas had been determined to retrieve the carving for himself. I wondered how many hours over how many days my son had spent cutting it from the wall inside his secret space. What tools he had used.

I also understood where the sawdust on his sneakers had come from.

I sat at the kitchen island for a few minutes trying to decide what to do next.

Lauren was in bed.

"The call earlier?" I asked. "Someone from work?"

"Unofficially."

I almost said *Tell me.* But I didn't. I waited.

"It turns out the man I shot is Mimi's son from her first marriage. His name is Emerson Abbott. He's seventeen, Alan. A kid. I knew he wasn't a firefighter. I'd arrived home minutes after the first pumper got there. I watched this guy sneak out from behind our garage and grab one of those big jackets off the fire truck, pull it on, and jog immediately toward the back of the house. He wasn't dressed like a firefighter. He had on sneakers and a stocking cap. A hoodie. I knew something was wrong. I followed him as he ran straight to the back deck. Jonas was crawling out the door. I watched him grab Jonas, throw him over his shoulder, and start to run away. But not toward the ambulance. Up the hill."

I nodded. "He had a gun," I said.

She said, "Yes. I didn't see it at first. When I yelled at him to stop, to put Jonas down, he turned and shot at me. Wildly. But I saw the muzzle flash," Lauren said.

"He shot at us, too. Inside. Me and Jonas. A lot."

"God. The call I got in the bathtub earlier?

A friend in the office. After she was told that her son was dead, Mimi Snow confessed to killing Preston Georges."

That's what the warrant was. An arrest warrant. "Mimi was in custody?"

"For questioning. Yes."

"I didn't know. What was the motive? Why did she kill the chef?"

"The rape after the housewarming? She told the sheriff that was her son. She says she learned about it after. How? That part is not clear. Not yet.

"The son apparently wasn't even supposed to be in Boulder. Certainly not in Spanish Hills. Hake had forbidden it. Emerson wasn't allowed to leave his boarding school until Thanksgiving break. But Preston Georges saw him the night of the party — the same guy the caterer told you she saw walking in the lane. Probably. Georges stopped. He and the kid talked, apparently. So the chef knew that Emerson was in town. And at the house that night.

"After the rape investigation started, the sheriff's investigator talked to Georges. But they didn't ask him the right questions. They wanted to know what time he left. Who was still in the house. They never asked him about after, when he was driving away. If he saw anyone on the lane.

"He called Mimi after the sheriff interviewed him. Asked if she knew anything about a guy on the lane, if it was important. He described the kid. She knew it was her son but she played dumb. Georges revealed during the conversation that he hadn't said anything to the sheriff about it.

"Sometime later, when the accusations were made about the sexual assault, Mimi confronted Emerson about the rape. He admitted it. Mimi knew that the chef could recognize her son, place him there, on the lane, that night. She said she felt she had to do something to protect her son. She decided to kill Georges before he told someone he'd seen Emerson."

"God. So, the rape wasn't Mattin?"

I felt I had to ask. Not asking would raise flags I wasn't prepared to hoist.

Lauren shook her head. "Mimi said it was her son. He'd called her from the lane at the tail end of the housewarming. He told her he wanted to see the new house, too. She snuck him into the basement. Made him promise to stay down there until she and Hake left the next day for Napa. He must have come upstairs at some point. How he got the victim to take the roofie, we don't know yet. It will take some time to get the DNA results back to be certain, but if the rape kit confirms . . ."

"You think it was his Rohypnol?"

Lauren said, "Yes, but no one knows that for sure."

"Did Mimi say anything that makes it clear why her son was after Jonas tonight?"

"Nothing. Jonas may know the answer to that. If he doesn't, I'm not sure we're ever going to know. I suppose he may have seen Emerson before at some point. Coming or going down the lane. If Jonas has been sneaking around before tonight, maybe even inside the house. Emerson had apparently been in and out of the house since the night of the party. His mom knew he'd been around, but it was a big secret from her husband.

"Hake absolutely did not want him there. There was a lot of tension. Mimi said something about Hake being convinced that Emerson had stolen from him in the past. This is a guess, but I'm thinking that Jonas must have found out — somehow — that Emerson was around. The kid knew that Jonas knew. Maybe that explains what happened tonight. What do you think?"

I excused myself while I went to the closet to retrieve the wood carving that Jonas had left out on his bed. I showed it to Lauren. I said, "I found this when I was checking on

Jonas earlier. He left it out for me. This may be part of the reason Jonas was there. Right after I went into the house tonight looking for Jonas, I heard the man — Emerson, I guess — accuse him of taking something and wondering out loud if he'd done it before." I realized that by telling Lauren a partial truth, I was also telling her a lie. My facility at dissembling was beginning to trouble me. "Jonas had apparently been cutting this carving from somewhere inside his cubby. Obviously, it's something Peter had made for him."

Lauren's eyes filled with tears as she traced the carving with her fingertip. "Lord," she said.

I wasn't ready to show her the photographs. I thought about it. But I wasn't ready.

44

I rubbed Lauren's calves until she fell asleep. I wasn't able to join her in slumber. I spent a while wondering when the fact that she'd killed a man would become one of the things that kept her awake at night. *Within days,* I thought. A week at the outside.

I gave up trying to sleep just before dawn. I took Fiji outside with me as the sun was cresting the eastern horizon. Our house was still in the shadows of the rim of the valley, but first light was bouncing off the gazillion crystalline edges that are locked in the flat faces of the Flatirons.

Morning light revealed that an ember had caught the roof of Peter's barn on fire. The firefighters had apparently snuffed the outbreak quickly — damage was limited to about a dozen square feet just below the crest of the gable.

Fiji and I followed the perimeter of the

crime scene tape as we circled around to the back of the ranch house ruins toward the deck. It, too, had burned to a crisp. Peter's intricate planking was nothing more than a pattern of parallel lines of heart redwood charcoal. I scuffed a couple of lines in the ash at my feet. If I extended the lines, they would intersect in the area where I thought the investigators should start looking for the missing revolver.

I'd tell the sheriff exactly where to start searching when the first investigators arrived later on.

From my high perch on the hill behind the charred house, I was able to watch as a pair of headlights entered the S-turns on the lane. As the car got closer, I recognized Mattin's brooding sedan. He pulled it to a stop in the middle of the lane in front of the remains of his garage.

I didn't approach him. I waited for him to spot me. I was wearing a light-colored jacket and was standing in a sea of dark ash. It wouldn't take long for Mattin to find me in the landscape.

He walked up the hill with his hands in his pockets. Although neither of us was feeling an inclination to shake hands, he did nod a greeting my way, and he actually squatted down to greet Fiji.

She was having none of it. She backed away and barked at him. She usually saved whatever aggression she possessed for squirrels and prairie dogs. I was surprised to see that she had some true fierce in her. I almost said *Good girl* but caught myself. Maybe the puppy was growing up before my eyes.

"Where's the big dog?" Mattin asked.

"Not feeling well," I said. My teeth were clenched. I reminded myself to be cool.

He nodded. I wondered if he knew about Emily's injury. If he'd been responsible.

"Sorry about your house," I said. I didn't want my antagonism for the man to be blatant. Hake probably figured I hadn't yet learned about his wife's arrest or about his stepson's death. Or he didn't care one way or another about what I knew. Maybe the latter. I thought it better not to go down those roads unless he dragged me.

He sighed. "First time I've seen it," he said. "It looks like a . . . complete loss."

"Pretty much. But the firefighters managed to save the barn," I said. "It almost went up, too."

"Small favors."

He said it like he didn't mean it. In another circumstance I would have been tempted to argue with him about the barn's value. What it had meant to a hundred years of ranchers trying to scratch out a living on this dry prairie. To Peter. To Jonas.

"At the end of the day, it was all just stuff," Mattin said. "Sticks and bricks. It can all be replaced. Rebuilt. Restored. Improved."

I found myself amused that Hake was trying to appear philosophical about it all. Since we were omitting his stepson's death and his wife's arrest from our conversation, appearing philosophical about material possessions was a manageable chore for him. I was beginning to get the impression that Mattin Snow liked to play the wise man, the man who kept everything in perspective. I filed it.

"Well," I said, "maybe it's fortuitous that you still had most of your stuff in storage."

"Yeah," he said. "Maybe so." Mattin looked at me sideways, perhaps in recognition that, if I was fishing, I was fishing with a barbed hook.

I reminded myself, again, to be careful with him. He lacked neither smarts nor cunning. "Or maybe it's serendipity," I said. "Could have been serendipity." I meant it ironically but thought I was successful in keeping the coarser notes of sarcasm out of my tone. I was thinking specifically about the temperature- and humidity-controlled wine cellar that Peter had lovingly crafted in the basement. The wine cellar that Mattin had chosen to leave almost entirely empty prior to the fire, despite his twenty-five-hundred-bottle wine collection.

It was almost, I was thinking, *as though Mattin knew the cellar wasn't going to be a safe place for his treasure.* I was also thinking that it was possible I was chatting amiably with the arsonist responsible for setting the house on fire. But I didn't think I would ever prove that. *Oh well.* Proof is more important at some times than at others.

Mattin changed the subject. "Don't know," he said, "if you heard about the bicycle accident the other night. You ride, don't you? You probably know some of those people." He didn't wait for a reply. "Such an awful thing. Young man who was injured has a family."

Those people? The hair on my neck was erect. I couldn't think of any logical reason that Mattin would initiate a conversation with me about Rafa and the collision. "I did hear about it," I said warily.

The man's stepson was dead. His wife was charged with murder. His house was gone. And Mattin was choosing to goad me into a discussion about my brain-injured friend?

"One of my attorney's investigators got her hands on a surveillance video from a dry cleaner in the shopping center at Table Mesa. What a find. Speaking as a lawyer? Good investigators are better than gold. They're platinum. What a good one can dig up? The dry cleaner's video shows that the poor guy on the bike" — I gritted my teeth at Mattin's description of Rafael — "actually veered into *my* car after some woman in a Prius failed to stop as she was pulling out of the gas station. The bicyclist was avoiding the Prius and swerved right into my path. Pulled a license plate for the Prius right off the video. Me? I never saw any of it happen. Thank God for that investigator."

His tone was so self-satisfied at the developments that futility and anger were exploding within me. Mattin never saw any of it happen, of course, because he was talking on his damn cell phone the whole time.

Armed with her investigator's video, Casey Sparrow, Mattin's lawyer, would already be pointing her finger at the owner of the Prius. I didn't envy that driver. Casey was a red-haired bulldog. Her investigators were legendary for finding everything there was to be found. If the driver of the Prius had ever sneezed while driving, Casey would somehow end up with the used tissue, and with a video montage of the woman's history of distracted driving.

My mind drifted. I wondered if the surveillance tape was the only video Casey Sparrow's investigators had uncovered recently. If maybe they'd dug up some footage from a theme camp at Burning Man. *I'll never know,* I thought.

"Lucky for you," I said to Mattin.

"Luck? Good lawyers don't believe in luck. I'm a good lawyer, Alan."

For some reason, I thought that sounded like a threat, not a boast.

Mattin returned his attention to the charred remains of the house. "A lot of decisions to make now," he said. "Here."

"I guess," I said. "This" — I waved at the blackened residue — "is a blank slate. For rebuilding." I intended it as a provocation. I was confident he would bite.

"Almost," he agreed, biting.

The obvious exceptions to the tabula rasa in the scene in front of us were the barn, our house, and our garage. Mattin would have preferred, no doubt, that all those structures burn down along with the big ranch house. I wondered if that had been part of his original not-very-urban redevelopment plan.

"You know, when we rebuild, I might

push the new house a little farther up here, put the front door about where we're standing now. When you get a little higher up this hill," he mused, "it truly improves the view."

"I can see that," I said. From where we stood uphill from the burned mess, our house and garage fell just below natural sight lines.

In the odd pretense I was engaging in with Mattin right then, I could imagine feeling kind of neighborly and agreeable with the man about his prospects for making architectural lemonade out of lemons after his string of tragedies.

That is, if I didn't feel like kicking him in the teeth.

"Yeah," he said. "I do like it up here. This is . . . a much better place to build." He tagged on the first half of an old saying: "It's indeed an ill wind, you know?"

I should have thought more before I responded. I didn't. I blurted, "That saying? I've always had trouble with it. My experience in life is that there are plenty of ill winds that blow no good at all. But I'm confident that you'll do . . . the right thing here," I said.

Mattin dipped his chin in a dramatic pretense of humility. He inserted, I thought, a little deference into his tone, too. "I will try, Alan. I will certainly try."

He thought I was being sincere and compassionate with him. At another time, I might have chuckled at how badly he was misreading me. For a half dozen reasons, a few of them admittedly kind of pathetic, the way he'd used my name when he said "I will try, Alan" had truly pissed me off. The reality was that I didn't need much of an excuse to get more pissed off at Mattin Snow than I already was.

I realized that the man was preparing himself to be a public victim. A tragic figure who had lost his home, his stepson, and likely his wife, to prison. An object of sympathy, compassion, and endless curiosity. He would create the persona of a survivor — someone strong, someone who could move on. A phoenix.

My hand closed over the phone in my pocket. I ignored a silent caution that was screaming *Don't do it.*

I thought, *Okay, so much for agreeable.* The Mattin Snow Show *is so over.*

I pulled Jonas's cell from my pocket. Hit a few buttons.

Mattin tried to ignore what I was doing. I could tell he thought I was being rude, playing with my phone while we were having our neighborly chat about catastrophes, assorted other ill winds, and grand future plans.

Truth was, I was being rude. I didn't like it when people screwed around with their phones during conversations the way I was doing with Mattin right then. I didn't care, of course, about his sensibilities. Being rude was nothing compared to what I had in mind for Mattin Snow.

I held the screen out so that Mattin could see what I'd been up to with the cell phone. The picture I was displaying for him wasn't the most lurid of the photographs Jonas had stored on his mobile. But it was pretty damn incriminating.

Mattin glanced at it the way a casual acquaintance glances at proffered vacation photos he doesn't really want to see.

I watched his face as his eyes focused and his cortex made some initial sense of the image he was seeing. His jaw shifted a centimeter to one side and then a full centimeter to the other. He then brought his jaw back to center, as though his jawbone were a rudder, and after a temporary loss of control, he'd succeeded in bringing his craft back to straight and level.

He took a quick look at me, a fiery hot *what the fuck* flashing in his eyes. The flash disappeared quickly. He found his composure.

Mattin was good.

All he saw from me was my well-practiced psychologist mask. And maybe, if he was more perceptive than he'd already demonstrated, he could discern the barest hint of a smile in my eyes. He looked back down at the image on the screen for a few more seconds. He was inhaling slowly the whole time. Through his nose.

He lifted himself onto his toes. I thought the lawyer in him wanted to object to the court about the evidence I was introducing.

When he looked up again, he captured my gaze in a manner that I thought was intended to be intimidating. He thrust his shoulders back, pushed his chest out, and raised his chin. He leaned forward, closing the distance between us to mere inches.

I felt like retreating. I didn't.

His feet moved as he inched even closer to me. I held my ground while I endeavored to contain my sadistic glee at the box I had just created for him. I was truly curious to see what he would do with so little room to maneuver. I wondered whether he had a surprise or two for me.

In the exact same tone of voice he'd used to tell me that he was thinking about building his new house a little farther up the hill, he said, "That doesn't prove anything. Nothing. That . . is just a . . . dirty picture."

"Really?" I said. I had to keep from adding *Tell me.*

"It reveals nothing about consent."

I was impressed that he was able to maintain his composure so well. But his use of *consent?* That, I thought, was the magic Kobe Bryant word. Was Mattin one of the lawyers who had learned that lesson well?

Decorum was apparently the order of the day, so I kept my tone even to match Mattin's. I asked, "Does it have to? I mean, really? The dirty picture? Must it prove anything? To be . . . influential?"

I intentionally chose a neutral word. I'd silently ruled out using *devastating* in lieu of *influential.*

"I'm a lawyer. Trust me," he said, apparently unaware of the absurdity of the last suggestion. "That photo cannot be used against me. It shows consenting adults. Nothing more."

I wasn't sure what I'd expected — showing him one of the photographs that morning had been a bit of an impulse play on my part — but I think I expected better than that from him. Mattin had to see the flaws in his own reasoning. Then I realized that he was responding as though he was talking to another lawyer. Someone inclined to bargain about words like *consent* and quibble about levels of consciousness. Someone who knew the arcane rules that exist between gentlemen and ladies in these disputes.

And cared about them.

I allowed seconds to tick away, giving Mattin an extended interlude to ponder the depth of his dilemma. I used the time to choose a second photo for him to consider. The second photograph I displayed for him was the next in the series, an even more appalling indictment than the first. But it wasn't the worst of them.

I was saving that one. Just in case.

The second image I showed Mattin had him in tight exercise pants and a taut, long-sleeved T-shirt. He had pulled a surgeon's cap over his head. The hat was printed in an almost-cute sailboat motif.

His victim's pajama bottoms had been lowered to her knees.

I'm a road cyclist. During phases when I'm serious about my sport, I shave my legs. It's not a fashion statement. Following a, for me, inevitable fall from my bike, the subsequent road rash is less severe on well-shaved skin.

Mattin wasn't a cyclist. But the photograph made clear that he'd shaved most if not all the hair on his hands, feet, and lower legs. And his pubic hair, along with any hair that had sprouted on his testicles.

It was, to be sure, much more detail than I ever really wanted to know about the man's grooming. But my son's photograph revealed those details. The picture showed Mattin standing, his right foot slightly forward of his left, beside the young widow's chair. The waistband of Mattin's pants was pulled back behind his scrotum, displaying not only his partial erection but also his hairless testicles. He was leaning forward over the woman's upper body.

In this photograph, she appeared more than a little sleepy. Her eyes were at half-mast, as though they had already gone into mourning over what was being done to her. If pressed, *stuporous* is the word I would have used to describe her apparent level of consciousness.

The woman's face was about a foot away from Mattin's penis.

Devil's Dick, indeed.

In that photo, again, the kitchen in the background was unoccupied.

The man standing in front of me behind the crime scene tape that surrounded his burned-down house was a despicable, criminal assailant who apparently wanted to have a discussion with me about proof. And consent.

I waited until I was sure that Mattin had digested all the information in that second photograph before I said, "Not this one, either? So . . . it can't be used against you? See, I'm thinking that to do . . . damage, to have . . . influence, it doesn't have to be used against you in any . . . formal way. Not in a court of law. Not in any legal sense. I'm not a lawyer. So maybe I'm missing something about how these things work, lawyer to lawyer. But I would think just the circumstances depicted, and the lurid — is that the right word? — details in the photograph would . . ." I allowed him to finish the thought himself.

He physically turned away. From me. From the photo. From the reality. For those few moments, he faced due west. Toward the sunset, not the sunrise.

Whether he knew it or not, he was looking directly at Devil's Thumb.

"You?" he demanded.

I should have expected the question, but I hadn't. Of course he'd want to know if I'd been there that night. I wasn't there to answer his questions. I chose to be a statue.

He quickly tired of waiting for a reply. "Is this . . . blackmail?" he asked. The question was part accusation, part pure wonder.

"God, no," I said without any hesitation.

He took an additional step away. When he faced me again, a minute or so later, his eyes revealed a new level of fear and some confusion. He said, "What do you want from me? Not to build?" He scoffed audibly at that. His voice turned condescending. "Somebody is going to build here, Alan. Someone is going to build something nice up here, something modern up here, someone is going to soil your private little outdated paradise. And . . . someone is going to make you put your damn dog on a leash."

Wow. The man has a figurative gun to his head, yet he can't resist spitting in my face. Wow. Chutzpah, Adrienne. Chutzpah.

Knowing full well that my paradise had been fouled already, I waited to be sure Mattin was done speaking before I responded to his little tantrum. I was still feeling remarkably even-keeled. I said, "What do I want? Simple. Pretty much what I want from everyone. I would like you to do . . . the right thing."

He scowled. Then he scoffed, "I don't know what that means."

He was showing exasperation, and with the exasperation, some recognition of the extent of his vulnerability. I liked that. There have been times in my life when I would not have allowed myself to feel any pleasure from his vulnerability, but I was past that. I said, "Let me be perfectly clear: Personally? I don't want anything from you. Nothing. I will take nothing from you. Ever. The truth is that although I don't like you, I am not yet sure you have harmed me, or my family. I suspect if I gave you time, you would get around to harming us. But that is premonition, and thus, neither here nor there."

I raised the phone. "I do know for a fact that you have harmed others." Then I shut the phone and returned it to my pocket. "Your friend? In the picture? You want to argue consent with me? Go right ahead. It seems to me that you drugged her, and you raped her. You raped her. Someone you called your friend.

"You thought about it for a long time, too. This little set piece involved a lot of planning. Wardrobe, shaving, grooming. If this picture somehow gets public? Let's make a date — you and I can have the whole consent discussion then, and we'll see who lines up on your side. And who lines up on . . . hers."

He glared at me.

"I worry about other women before her, too. I assume there were others. I fear there were many others. This . . . looks practiced, definitely not a first-time production — you perfected this choreography on earlier victims. That's what I think."

He had become the statue. He didn't move a muscle.

"Your wife? Your stepson? Were they both victims, too? Or accomplices?"

I wanted him to defend himself with me so I could be cruel back to him.

He didn't. I was disappointed. I had a taste for a little blood.

"So what would I like from you, Hake? For all of your victims? For them, I would like you to do the right thing."

"What the hell does that mean?" he asked me.

"You can decide," I said. "I'll be watching."

I could tell that he wanted to insult me or hit me or kill me. Okay, he wanted to kill me. But he couldn't. Not there. Not then. He didn't know if we were being observed. Or whose photos they were, or how many copies existed. He certainly didn't know what the hell I would do with them next. Or had done with them already.

"If I do the right thing? I get those photos? All copies?"

"That would make this blackmail, Hake. I don't do blackmail. You want to make a deal? You got the wrong guy."

"Why should I trust you?"

"I don't recall implying that you should." I stepped away. "Let's go, little girl," I said to Fiji. "Let's go find us a big prairie dog town."

Fiji and I didn't go in search of prairie dogs. We drove over to the animal hospital on Baseline and we visited Emily.

She was conscious. She opened her eyes and wagged her nub of a tail when she heard my voice and grabbed on to the scent of her little sister. Fiji licked Emily's face quasi-maniacally before she curled up between the big dog's legs, resting her little head on her friend's foreleg. The big Bouvier sighed.

I scratched my dog's neck with one hand, while I placed my other open palm on her belly. I knew Fiji and I had only a few minutes to visit with her.

The vet assistant spent the whole time talking with me about the woods we weren't out of and about the serious risk of infection from the wound. About how close the knife had come to her lung.

I couldn't have found a better way to get the sour taste of Mattin Snow out of my mouth than those few minutes with my dogs.

Fiji and I brought home good dog news and bagels for breakfast.

As I put together a plate of Moe's bagels and opened the tub of cream cheese, I said to Lauren, "One of us needs to take Jonas to get a new phone. He lost his in the . . . confusion in the house yesterday."

Lauren said, "I'm taking the day off to spend with the kids. I'd love to do that with you, Jonas. It's a date? You know what kind you want?"

Lauren wasn't actually taking time off. She'd been placed on administrative leave while the shooting was investigated. That was a discussion we would have with the kids another time, apparently.

Jonas nodded at her. She smiled back.

He looked over at me with a blank face. The kid was so beaten down. I read his expression as the kind of flat gratitude a mistreated animal displays when he or she thinks the latest whipping has ended.

My heart was so heavy for my son that I feared I might need to put it in a sling just to keep it in my chest.

I didn't know what the rest of the day would bring.

But I knew this episode in our lives wasn't over.

45

To my continued amazement, the backstory about the rape remained the best-kept secret in town. Casey Sparrow was doing her job. Cozier Maitlin was cooperating with her. So much was at stake, yet so many huge egos were behaving and making nice. I found it remarkable.

Attorney wizardry, indeed. Every time I reflected on the deafening public silence about the rape, I found myself repeating things that Sam had said to me over beers and grilled cheese sandwiches during that Lakers/Mavs game.

Hella e-mailed me midmorning. She said she'd been trying to reach me on my mobile. I phoned her back from a landline.

She mentioned that she'd heard about the fire and the shooting on the news. I didn't know what it meant that she knew the headlines. Although Hella was aware that I lived on the east side of the Boulder Valley, I doubted that she knew precisely where.

Lauren's role in the shooting wasn't yet public. My name wasn't in the first round of news stories at all, but I feared that my involvement would be teased out as soon as reporters got around to searching public property records.

Mattin Snow's name was featured prominently in the initial news reports about the fire. I had no doubt that would set off alarms for Hella's hospitalized patient.

The reality I had to deal with? Hella would soon enough discover that I had become a player in the drama that was her patient's life.

Hella's patient was stable and was in the process of being transferred from Colorado Springs to Denver for continued psychiatric hospitalization. Discharge pressure from her insurer, and Hella's assessment that the acute danger was passing, would soon come together and argue for an early hospital release. In the next day or two — three at the outside — Hella would enter the uncomfortable clinical limbo that psychotherapists live with after a suicidal patient is discharged into outpatient care.

Hella told me she would be back in Boulder after she completed the hospital admission in Denver. We made an appointment for supervision for later in the week.

"We have a lot to talk about," she said.

I didn't disagree, but I knew some of it shouldn't wait. As the media continued to string together facts and rumors about the previous night, Hella would soon figure out what had happened, and more important, my role in what had happened. I didn't want her to learn those facts on the news.

"Before you go," I said. I filled her in. I told her that the man her patient had accused of rape was my new neighbor. That his house had burned down. That more details would likely become public that involved me and my family.

Twice, she said, "I can't believe this." Three or four times, she asked, "You knew?"

She challenged me immediately, demanding to know if, given my relationship with the accused rapist, I should have been supervising her patient's case at all. She asked, "Isn't this the very definition of a clinical conflict of interest?"

I answered her question, despite the fact that she'd asked it rhetorically. I said, "No. It's not."

Was Hella indignant with me? Not quite. She was edging up near that line, but she wasn't crossing it. At her age, in her shoes, I would have been asking the same questions she was asking. With even more attitude than she was mustering.

"It's . . . not? You have to be kidding."

I responded to her challenge. "How long have you been seeing her for therapy?"

"Six months maybe. Since last spring."

"How long have I been supervising your treatment of her?"

"The same."

"I met my new neighbor for the first time the week of that housewarming. We spoke for one or two minutes at that time. My supervision of your treatment of your patient predated any relationship with him, however tangential, by almost a full six months." I paused. "It's not my practice to cease providing clinical services, including supervision, to people because of a secondary relationship I might establish long after the clinical care has been initiated. That . . . would be unethical."

"And since?" Hella demanded. "Your relationship with him since?"

"He and I have exchanged hellos twice, in passing. That's it, until this morning. We did speak briefly earlier this morning."

"About?"

I'd anticipated this question. I'd decided to answer honestly but not fully. "We talked about the fire at his house. What might come next for him. Rebuilding. Moving on. We spoke for less than ten minutes in total."

"You didn't talk about his wife? What she did? His stepson's death?"

"He didn't bring those things up. I was trying to be . . . circumscribed with him because of the supervision. I am cognizant of the boundary issues involved, Hella."

"In your mind, ethically, you haven't crossed any lines here?"

"No," I said. "I haven't."

"Really?"

"If I knew then what I know now? I may not have supervised this case. But hindsight is perfect, and I didn't know six months ago that your patient's friend was going to buy the house next door and then sexually assault her."

Hella started to speak. She stopped before I could identify the swallowed syllable.

"At the time we started talking about your patient, I had no conflicts of interest at all. Even months later, I was confident that I had sufficient degrees of separation to allow me to continue to supervise your work. The man was an acquaintance. I felt I could manage the relationship with him as it existed. Keeping things like this separate is something that psychotherapists, like us, do every day. We work in a small town."

"And that works how? Those degrees of separation?" Hella asked me. She asked it skeptically.

It was a fair question. I offered examples. "I don't provide clinical care to the guy who cuts my hair. Or to his family. I don't provide clinical services to my neighbors, or to their families. But I would provide clinical care to someone who gets his hair cut at the same shop I do. Or to someone who is a friend . . . of my neighbor."

"This was like that?" she asked. "My patient was a friend of your new neighbor?" Still skeptical, I thought, but a little less so.

"Later on? Yes. That's what she was. At the very beginning? I didn't think I knew anyone involved in your patient's life. When it became clear that your patient was a friend of a new neighbor, someone I had just met, I considered the implications. I decided it did not pose an ethical conflict. Not . . . even close."

"She's also a friend of your partner, though. Diane Estevez? You must have learned that fact about the same time. What about that?"

"You're right. I learned that only recently, as well. You had not identified Diane and her husband among your patient's circle of friends until after Burning Man. Regardless, that relationship created no ethical dilemma for me. Diane sometimes refers her friends directly to me for psychotherapy. It's not a conflict; far from it. Boulder is a small town, Hella. The psychotherapy community? A little village. Lives intersect constantly in the work we do. You have to be prepared for that."

I could tell that my arguments weren't being persuasive.

Hella pulled out her best ammunition. "Okay, what about when you learned that my patient considered that new neighbor of yours to be a rapist?"

I chose to be vague. "I learned a long time ago that if I want a career with bright ethical lines, I shouldn't choose clinical psychology. From the moment I surmised that your patient was accusing my neighbor of rape, I intentionally did nothing to advance my relationship with him. I've been successful in that endeavor."

Hella got quiet for a few moments before she said, "I have to be honest. Going forward with this supervision? I am going to wonder whether your insistence that I remain open-minded — even skeptical — about my patient's version of events might have been influenced by the fact that the man in question was your neighbor."

"That is understandable."

"That's it? That's all you have to say?"

"It's understandable, Hella. Not accurate, but understandable. I'm comfortable with my role. I would have provided you the same professional counsel in this case whether or not he ever moved into my neighborhood."

"I am going to have to think about this. I may end up deciding to seek a new supervisor."

I said, "And that could be a valid response to your concerns about my behavior. When we meet later, we can talk about it."

"I need to get going," she said.

I said, "One thing to throw into the mix? The fact that you are considering changing supervisors right now may also be a way of avoiding the next big issue in your growth as a therapist."

"What's that? What are you saying?"

"The issues you were avoiding when we met at your apartment? At the end? That is what I'm talking about. But I would prefer not to do this on the phone. Can we talk about it when we meet?"

"No," she said. "We can't."

Okay.

Hella knew what she was avoiding. Her

retort, when it came, was at once meek and defiant. "I could do that work with my next supervisor," she said.

"Or . . . not. You know as well as I do that you're already licensed. You are not even required to choose a next supervisor. And I should remind you that you didn't exactly choose to explore whatever those influences are with me, in this supervision. Your resistance is . . . not insignificant."

"I really have to go."

I said, "You have a great rationale for leaving supervision. The courageous thing may be to stay." Hella killed the call.

Therapists, and supervisors, point out walls. We can't keep our patients, or our supervisees, from walking into them. Over and over again.

She e-mailed again two hours later. She asked me to call her mobile number as soon as I was free. I did. She was in Denver, walking to her car. She had just left her patient in the psych unit. Barring any changes, discharge would be in two days. But that's not what she wanted to discuss.

The lawyers had been busy. Casey Sparrow and Cozier Maitlin. That is what she wanted to discuss.

Hella's patient's lawyer had met with his

client for half an hour that morning.

Which attorney had offered what first wasn't exactly clear to Hella — who was not consulted about the decision — but there seemed to be agreement among all parties that Hella's patient was in no shape to testify at a hearing, let alone a trial. Without her participation as a witness, of course, proceeding with the criminal complaint against Mattin Snow would be most difficult. No criminal charges were likely to be filed.

I, of course, heard echoes of Cordillera. Sam the sage.

The tall lawyer, Hella said, was preparing a civil suit. The accused's attorney was preparing a confidential settlement offer. The attorneys were planning to meet in Boulder the next day to discuss the details.

Hella said, "She feels vindicated, Alan. Her mood has changed one hundred and eighty degrees. The fact that he is now eager to settle? She feels it validates everything she's said from the start."

"That's great," I said. But I was thinking about Kobe Bryant, and Sam's arguments about the way the criminal justice system gets hijacked by wealthy and prominent defendants, cooperating victims, and their choreographer lawyers.

Hella said, "You don't sound surprised. By the sudden settlement offer. I expected you to be . . . surprised."

"Surprised? Or chastened?"

"Chastened?"

"Remember, I'm the one who kept encouraging you to allow room for doubt about your patient's memories of those events."

"Okay," she said. "Maybe chastened, too. You can be chastened. I'm okay with that."

"You do sound surprised, Hella," I said.

"The DNA test the guy ran himself didn't match, remember? That gave me plenty of doubt, Alan. Why would he settle now? It seemed to me like this whole thing was turning his way. I am surprised."

"Maybe," I said, "he's just decided to do the right thing. Thanks for the news. I truly hope your patient can begin to heal now."

"I'll see you later in the week," Hella said.

Diane stopped into my office midafternoon. She was packed up to head home.

She said, "Hake has taken a leave of absence from the network. Don't know if you heard."

That's the right thing, too, I thought. I said, "Given the extent of the family . . . tragedy, I'm sure he needs some time."

Diane said, "He announced on his website that half the proceeds from his new book will be donated to the Women & Justice Project at the CU law school. That could be hundreds of thousands of dollars. Maybe millions, if the book takes off. His publisher thinks it will. Take off. All the publicity right now?"

Half? I thought. *Is half of the right thing to do still the right thing to do?* I would ponder that equation another time. "That's a nice gesture. Sit, please," I said to Diane. "How are you? This has to be hard."

She sat beside me. She said, "I can't believe all this. I thought I knew Mimi."

Diane and I talked about her friend for a while. About all she'd been through. The chronic emotional abuse she'd suffered in her first marriage. Her first husband's multiple affairs. Their ugly divorce. His remarriage to a thirty-two-year-old Pilates instructor from Santa Barbara. Her kids leaving home for school. Her kids and her new husband not getting along at all.

"And now this," Diane said. "Losing her son? Murder, Alan?"

I said something about mothers protecting their own. But Diane, it turned out, wasn't having as much trouble digesting the homicidal part of Mimi's behavior. What she was having trouble with was her suspicion that Mimi had been an accomplice, either before or after the fact, in her son's rape of their mutual friend. That, she said, she couldn't comprehend. She used the word *fathom.*

She didn't say it, but I suspected it was also something Diane feared she couldn't forgive.

I said, "After all these years doing this work? The things that a desperate woman will do to save a diseased marriage can't really surprise you. We see some awful examples in our practices every month. Every week."

Diane's shoulders dropped. "You're right, you're right." She exhaled until her lungs had to be empty. "There are women who allow their children to be abused. To be sexually abused, even. So, why not a friend? And a rape? That's what you're saying?"

"That's what I'm saying."

Diane leaned into me. I put an arm around her. "Hake told Raoul that if Mimi is sent to prison, he thought he'd move out of Boulder. Sell what's left in Spanish Hills. He didn't think he could live there."

"Talk about bad memories," I said. Diane had no way to know that the memories I was musing about weren't Hake's.

They were Jonas's.

"You could buy it, you know," Diane said. "Build something new, special, for your family."

"Don't think it's for us," I said. "Any decision we make will be based on what's best for the kids."

"Jonas," Diane said.

"Yes," I said.

On the way home from the office, I ran two errands. I picked up food for Rafa's family and dropped it at the house. Then I stopped at a framing shop on Pearl and made a special frame for Jonas's wood carving of the interlocking hearts. When I got back home, I hung his treasure at the foot of his bed, where he could see it during those times he was having trouble sleeping.

46

Raoul's real estate decision deadline was looming, so Lauren and I went out to dinner Sunday night to discuss selling Walnut. It was a conversation we didn't want to risk having with the kids in the house.

Okay, with Grace in the house.

Once we reached a grown-up decision, we'd bring the kids in.

My breath caught in my throat the moment I saw Lauren walk out of the closet after she'd dressed for our night out. Suddenly it felt like a date, not a business meeting. Her outfit was sexy. Her hair was sexy. Her eyes were sexy.

Sexy hadn't happened for us in a while.

I was off balance, in a good way, a way I hadn't felt in many years.

We returned to Salt. Lauren's idea. But first we stopped at The Bitter Bar, near my office, for cocktails. My idea.

I marveled as Lauren walked the two blocks between the bar and the restaurant. She set down her menu with certainty. She was going to have the chorizo clams and the lamb shank. She asked what looked good to me.

I said, "Besides you?" She smiled. "You look gorgeous."

"Thank you," she said, doing a good facsimile of demure.

I said, "I think a condo across the street looks pretty good, too."

Instantly, her violet eyes sparkled. Her lips parted just far enough that she could breathe through them. She wet her upper lip with her tongue while she waited for me to say more.

I told her I thought we should sell Walnut.

"Really?" she said. "And buy . . . ?"

"And sell Spanish Hills."

"Both?"

"And I think we should buy a new home for our family in Raoul's new palace across the street." Across the street was the *Daily Camera* site. "It's time for some changes. For us. For the kids. Certainly for Jonas."

Lauren was speechless. I felt that she was waiting for a qualifier. Something to poison the well. To disappoint.

I said, "I've been thinking about it a lot.

It's a hard choice, but I prefer the northwest corner, not the southwest corner. I want the mountain view, but I don't want to deal with the southern sun all year long anymore. North is better light, easier to manage, don't you think?"

A solitary tear escaped Lauren's left eye and migrated down her cheek. "Can we get it? Can we do that? What we want? Can we really afford it?" she asked.

"We'll have to see," I said. "I'm thinking we may have some leverage with the developers."

We made love later with the lights on and our eyes open.

Afterward, her head was resting on my chest. Her weak leg was bent over mine. It was heavy.

I said, "You know, I haven't spent a solitary moment tonight with the deputy district attorney."

"Yeah. That's been nice," she said. "Though I hear she's pretty good in bed."

I kissed the end of her nose. "She's still elsewhere?" I asked.

"Absolutely," Lauren said. Her voice often took on a sandpaper-and-honey tone after sex. It had it then.

I sat up beside her. She remained on her

side. I held her free hand in both of mine.

"Get her, please. I need to speak with the DA, now."

Lauren immediately sat up. Every cell in her body was suspicious. She said, "Okay. But you're beginning to make me nervous."

I handed her a pillow. "To cover your breasts?" I said. "I find them kind of distracting when I'm talking to the deputy DA." She blew me a kiss before she hugged the pillow to her chest.

I said, "I try, always, not to tell you how to do your job. You do the same with me."

She nodded. "That's true. We don't interfere. One of our strengths."

"But I *need*" — I stressed the word *need* with my voice and my expression — "to give you some work advice. Advice I hope you will consider seriously, no matter how wrong it may sound at first."

She frowned. "Is this a good idea? For us to —"

"Please. My counsel? No matter how good a case you think you have against her, you need to plea bargain with Mimi Snow about the murder of Preston Georges. You *need*" — I stressed the word the second time — "to offer her a deal, a reduced charge — or something — in order to get her to testify against her husband."

"Against Hake?"

"Yes."

"Why would I do that? Why would Mimi . . . do that?" She reached forward and placed a palm on my cheek, almost dropping the pillow from her chest in the process. "Alan, Hake is innocent. Just between us, we have . . . initial forensic results that clearly implicate Mimi's son in the rape. Reliable evidence. Trust me, the DNA results, when they come back, will clear Hake. I know you don't like him, but —"

I took her hand from my face and held it. "We don't need to argue facts. And I've said all I need to say to the deputy district attorney. For now."

Lauren said, "All right, but before you go on, you know that the homicide at Devil's Thumb is not my case anymore? I'm still on administrative leave, and I won't be returning to that case no matter what happens. You understand all that, right? I shot the accused's son. I . . . killed her son. I won't be involved."

"I know. But I also know how your office works. I know you have influence," I said. "You know you will have influence. This isn't the time for us to argue. I have more to say."

Lauren opened her mouth. She's a lawyer. About some things, she could always find time to argue. I touched a fingertip to the soft cushion of her lower lip. I said, "Shhhh . . . Next I need to say something to our son's mother. As our son's father. My wife can listen in. The deputy DA? She's not welcome in this conversation. Not even a little."

She literally pulled away. "Alan, I don't like where —"

"I preface this with a promise that I will never — *never* — repeat any of what I am about to say with anyone from law enforcement. Relative or not."

Lauren's eyes darkened. Her irises turned almost as black as her hair. She was imagining the walls that I was building. The divisions I was creating between her roles as prosecutor, mother, and wife. The stark boundaries I was insisting upon at that moment in the marital bed.

She took a deep breath. "This is big," she said. "Isn't it? What you're about to say. You know exactly what you're asking of me, don't you?"

"This is big," I agreed. "Huge. So big that if you decide what I'm asking isn't possible for you — if the role definition is something you can't live with — I will, reluctantly, stop right here, where I am. I will keep what I know to myself. I will live with a burden that I would much prefer to share with my wife, and with the mother of my children. For the good of our family, this knowledge should not be mine alone."

She shifted her weight, extending her weak leg out to the side. "I won't guess this, will I? What this is about?"

"No. You won't." She exhaled audibly before she climbed out of bed and walked, without her cane, to the closet. The steps she took were the least hobbled, and most determined, I'd seen from her since she left for Holland. She came back wearing pajamas. She tossed me a pair of sweatpants.

"Let's talk then," she said. "As parents of our children. As mother and father of our son."

I mouthed *thank you.* I pulled on the sweats. Then I reached behind me into the drawer of my bedside table and retrieved Jonas's old mobile phone.

Lauren recognized it. "That's Jonas's. I thought it was —"

I nodded. "Jonas's mom should see some pictures he took."

"When?"

"The night of the damn housewarming."

47

Lauren was the only person to whom I showed all eight photographs.

As she moved through the progression, her eyes filled with tears for the second time that evening. The look in her eyes when she returned her gaze to me was part horrified, part resolved. She asked, "Who has seen these?"

"That's a DA question. Not a mom question. Please."

She didn't vocalize her next thought. Her expression said it all. It was, *Why didn't I know about these before?*

I shook my head. "Can we have that conversation later? Please. It was still your case that night. The deputy DA's case. I didn't know if — I didn't think I could risk —"

She held up a hand to stop me. She swallowed before she said, "Okay. Okay. That's between you and me. We'll do that later.

Right now? Jonas cannot testify about this. About what he saw. It — He — We can't put him through that. We can't let that happen to him, Alan. Never."

"No," I said. "He can't. We can't."

"How did he — He had a way to get into the house, obviously."

"Yes. I asked him about that. Peter had installed a disappearing latch on one of the awning windows near the basement door. Press on some trim. Pull down on a lever that popped out. Then the whole window, frame and all, opened on a hinge. It was a secret entrance to the house. Jonas has used it all his life when he didn't have his key. And he's been using it to sneak back into the house since he moved in with us. Both before the sale and since.

"I think he's been going over there for a while, using some little handsaw, or some other tool, to try and remove the carved plaque from the wall inside the entrance to the cubby. The panel the carving is on is hardwood — very tough to cut. Without the right tools, it might take hours and hours for a kid to remove it. Jonas must have been afraid we wouldn't let him keep the carving."

"God," Lauren said. "We have so much parenting to do, don't we?" I nodded. She scrolled through the pictures again. The second time through was more deliberate. "These are in order?" she asked.

"Yes. The way he left them for me." I explained how I found the phone with the carving on his bed the night of the fire. "I've not talked with him about the photographs yet. I tried. He's not ready to discuss any of it. Not even close."

She looked me in the eyes. "He's going to need help," she said. "What he saw? My God. We have to get him some therapy. He has to see someone."

"I agree. We probably waited too long already. I misread him. His grief. His coping. I take responsibility for that. I will make those calls — I will find someone good for him." I almost added, *We need some help, too, Lauren. Our marriage.* But that conversation could wait a day. That night, we needed to keep our focus on Jonas.

She tapped the phone with her fingernail. "You have a story? That fits these pictures?"

She was wondering if I had managed to superimpose a narrative over the progression of images documented in the photographs. She wanted the graphic-novel version of the night's events.

Many of the details I knew came from my supervision with Hella. I didn't plan to tell

Lauren about my supervision of the victim's therapy. I didn't have a right to do that.

My wife was asking for a story. I could tell her the story. "Yes," I said. "I have a story that fits."

"I would like to hear it," Lauren said.

I hesitated, tempted to seek a final assurance that I was speaking only with my son's mother and not with the deputy district attorney. Lauren made my question superfluous. She said, "I need to know what my son saw. Everything."

At some point after almost all the guests were gone, Mimi Snow suddenly transformed herself from charming hostess to pack-up-your-things-now-and-get-out-of-here boss lady.

Her change in demeanor with the caterers was sudden and unexpected. Her cell records will probably confirm that the precipitant for the change was a phone call, or text, from her son. Emerson Abbott called or texted to let his mother know he had arrived on the edge of Spanish Hills. He'd be at the new house in minutes. Fifteen tops.

Maybe she'd argued with him, told him not to come, urged him to go back up to school. But Emerson was not an obedient kid. Discipline had been a growing problem since the divorce. He wasn't supposed to leave campus. Emerson knew he wasn't welcome in Boulder; his stepfather was adamant that he was not allowed in the house. Not until he'd cleaned up his act.

Lauren's eyes were asking me how I knew all that. I said, "Diane."

Mimi panicked at the news her son was somewhere nearby. The bartender had just walked out the door. She rushed the last few guests from the house. Then the chef, the caterers.

Moments before the chef left the house, he made a what-do-I-have-to-lose advance on Eric, one of the caterers. Eric shot him down. Eric was probably a jerk about it. That is Eric's nature.

Lauren asked, "You know all that, too?"

I explained about Nicole, the other caterer.

Preston Georges drove away in his pristine old Camaro. A few minutes later the two caterers followed him out the lane in their white van.

Eric was upset about a lot of things as he drove the big van away from Spanish Hills — he was nicotine deprived because Mattin didn't permit smoking in his zip code; resentful about being hassled to hurry to finish work by the party's hostess; offended, or excited, by the homosexual advance from the chef; aggravated at the possibility of entering the weekend without a chance to have his dealer replenish his stash; and irritated by his fellow caterer's insistence on being dropped off across town at The Sink.

Distracted about all those things, Eric almost ran over Fiji and me on the lane just before he entered the first bend of the S-curve.

Seconds later, he almost ran into another pedestrian as the van exited the second bend. The second pedestrian was a man in a hoodie and ski cap who was wearing a day pack.

Lauren said, "That was Mimi's son. That was Emerson."

Only minutes before the catering van almost hit Emerson on the lane, Preston Georges was the first to have spotted him. The chef was determined to find some companionship for the evening. He stopped his Camaro and offered Mimi's son a ride somewhere. Or maybe he invited him out for a drink. Or maybe, who knows, Preston Georges suggested something even more overt than that.

The young man declined. Maybe he, like Eric, was offended by the offer. He was a kid; maybe it even left him determined to prove his heterosexuality at the next opportunity.

Emerson kept walking toward his mother's new house. He lit a cigarette. Smoking was undoubtedly something else his parents didn't want him to do. When he dodged the caterer's van, he dropped the cigarette, which started a small fire adjacent to the lane.

I reached into my bedside table a second time. I handed Lauren a small zipper bag containing a charred cigarette butt and some burned grasses. "For what it's worth," I added.

Emily actually sensed some commotion down the lane before I returned to the house with her and Fiji. The big dog had tried to alert me that something was going on, but I didn't pay attention to her signals.

Only a solitary car, a little SUV, remained parked outside Mimi and Mattin's house as the dogs and I got back home.

I thought Jonas was asleep in bed — I had already checked on both kids before I went out with the dogs. I didn't check a second time. When I climbed into bed after the walk, Lauren reminded me that I had a meeting the next day with Raoul.

"I remember," Lauren said. "That's when

Jonas snuck out? After you came to bed? Is that what you think?"

"Yes."

I thought that's how it happened. Earlier in the evening, Jonas had overheard our discussion about the planned renovations, how the guests at the housewarming were being encouraged to offer their two cents' worth. He was curious. He snuck across the lane and entered the house through the special awning window on the basement level. He could still hear people walking and talking upstairs. He waited, hiding out in the basement. That's where he was when the young man with the hoodie and ski cap entered through the basement door. Mimi had probably gone downstairs to leave the door unlocked for her son. Or maybe she had told him on the phone where he could find the spare key under the rock.

The first photo in Jonas's phone is of Emerson Abbott walking through the basement door. Ski cap. Hoodie. Day pack.

Certainly, Mimi had told her son to stay down there and stay quiet. She must have warned him not to come upstairs under any circumstances.

Upstairs, Mattin was already busy trying to convince the sole remaining guest to spend the night in the guest suite. He was unaware his stepson was in the basement.

Mimi knew what her husband had planned with the young widow. Maybe Mattin had given Mimi a sign earlier in the evening. Maybe they'd planned the whole thing out in advance. Probably they'd committed the same felony before with other women.

Mimi might have initially resisted her husband's rape fantasies but at some point she lacked the will or the resolve to fight him. Along the way, she'd learned there were consequences to be paid for not going along.

"Do you know those consequences?" Lauren asked.

"The deputy DA," I told her, "should have no trouble learning that as part of the plea bargain negotiation."

Mimi did her part setting the stage. She prepared the guest room. Found pajamas for her guest, collected fresh towels, and retrieved a bottle of water for the bedside. The woman, the prey, continued to sit by the fire, drinking wine with Hake. Perhaps Mimi took her son a plate of food during the interval she excused herself to prepare the guest suite.

Jonas was likely still downstairs, listening to the interactions between Mimi and her son, watching only some of it from wherever he was hiding.

Mimi probably insisted that Emerson eat his meal in one of the primitive rooms in the back of the basement, where he couldn't be inadvertently discovered by Mattin.

Jonas scooted upstairs during the time period when Mimi was shooing her son into the back of the basement. Once upstairs, Jonas may have gone into the kitchen pantry. He knew that there was a hidden door behind the pantry that led to the shaft of the defunct dumbwaiter. It was another secret place his father had built. A great place for a kid to hide.

Or maybe Jonas went straight to the living room. Regardless, he ended up there, behind the sofa, on the other side of the freestanding fireplace that divided the family and living rooms. His position had him facing toward the family room. That's where he was when he took the second picture.

Mimi is back upstairs by then. The second photo shows Mimi, Mattin, and the young widow, by the fire, drinking wine. They are all still dressed in their party clothes. Mimi is sharing one big chair with her husband.

The young widow is in the other chair. She looks tired.

Mattin appears ebullient. I can easily

convince myself that Mimi looks distracted.

The third photo comes a short while later in the narrative. A slightly different angle. Jonas has moved a little, a foot or two. One of the two leather chairs is in the foreground of the frame. It's the one the young widow had been sitting on in the earlier shot, but it's empty. Both chairs are empty. In the background Mimi and Mattin are standing at the kitchen island. On the counter, off to the side near a bowl of apples and a tray of olive oils and vinegars, is an amber prescription bottle. In front of Mimi is a small stone mortar. In her right hand Mimi is holding a pestle. Mattin is at the narrow end of the island. He is cradling a tall bottle. I think it's port. He seems to be waiting for his wife to finish what she is doing with the mortar and pestle.

What she is doing is grinding a tablet or two from the prescription bottle into powder. For someone with even a little imagination, the photo documents that husband and wife, together, are preparing to drug their guest. Their victim. Preparing to dissolve the powder in the thick, sweet port.

"Would it dissolve?" Lauren asked.

I said, "They know. They've done this before."

"The woman is in the guest room at this

point," Lauren said. "Changing for bed."

"Yes. She was thinking the night was over. She was content."

Mattin gave her time to get changed and settled before he knocked on the guest room door. He invited her to come back out for one last drink. Maybe she resisted. But he was persistent. Maybe he said the nightcap was Mimi's idea. Maybe he said something about not wanting to disappoint his wife, who was eager for more company.

Jonas's fourth photograph is yet another picture of the two chairs by the fire. Mimi is absent this time. Both Mattin and the young widow are in different clothes. She has changed into pajamas and a short robe. Her ensemble is modest, but her feet are bare. She is holding the sole of one foot out toward the warmth of the fire. Mattin has changed, too. He is dressed as though he's heading to a Pilates session and he's thinking everyone will be impressed with the way he looks in snug clothing.

The picture shows the young widow on the same chair as before. She is sipping her doctored port. The glass is literally at her lips. Mattin is in the adjacent chair. There is fire in his eyes. Anticipation, maybe? All his attention is focused on his victim.

"Mimi is where?" Lauren wanted to know.

I said, "Unclear at that moment."

Perhaps she couldn't bear to watch the setup to the rape. Perhaps she was standing guard at the basement stairs, just beyond the frame. Mimi had to be terrified that her unpredictable son would do something unpredictable. She had to feel that she was in an impossible place, trying to protect her son from her husband and her husband from her son.

She knew she was protecting herself, too, from both of them. She also had to know that no one was protecting her young widowed friend.

The next photo in the series was the first one I showed Mattin the morning after the fire, just after I suggested he consider doing the right thing. I didn't tell Lauren about showing Mattin the picture.

The sedated young widow is still sitting in the big leather chair by the fire. But her robe is open. Her pajama top is unbuttoned all the way. Her breasts are exposed.

Her head is lolling back against the leather chair, her face tilted away from the camera lens.

Lauren asked, "Is she still awake at that point? Can you tell?"

"I don't know. Yes, no. I would say the drugs have started to take effect."

Mattin is sitting on the arm of the same chair as the woman. He's in the same outfit as before, but he has covered his head with a surgeon's cap.

With his left hand, the one that was not burned, he is holding the woman's right hand to his crotch. He is leaning forward and seems to be speaking to her.

Behind the victim and the rapist is an empty kitchen. Mimi is somewhere beyond the lens of Jonas's camera phone.

The photo that follows moves the story forward. Mattin has changed his position. He is standing beside the woman's chair. He has lowered the pants of her pajamas to her ankles. He has lowered his own pants, too, but only a few inches. He is well prepared for this moment. The cap with the sailboats. His pubic region is shaved. His feet and forearms appear hairless, too.

He is leaning down toward the young widow. She is looking in his direction, her mouth open. Her eyes are dull. She seems to be struggling to keep them open.

"Does he have his waistband behind his . . . scrotum?" Lauren asked. She was not believing what she was seeing.

"Yes."

The widow's face isn't far from Mattin's not-quite-erect penis.

"God," Lauren says. "God."

God, I thought, *was taking a break.*

I point out that the kitchen in the background remains unoccupied.

The next photo shows that things are starting to go very wrong for Mimi and Mattin.

"Some of this next part of the story," I told Lauren, "is speculation."

Mimi's son needs to use the bathroom. There wasn't a basement bathroom in the house. It had been an issue for decades. Peter was planning to install one around the time he was murdered. Adrienne had arranged to have two new bathrooms — one in the basement, one near the family room — included when she built the missing turret on the southwest corner of the house.

Mimi and Mattin were undoubtedly planning to make similar additions during their upcoming renovation.

But Mimi's son didn't know any of the plumbing remodeling plans. All he knew was that he needed a toilet and he couldn't find one downstairs. He listened for footsteps or voices upstairs, waited until he heard nothing, and climbed the stairs to the main floor to find a bathroom.

Jonas had moved a little by the time he took the next photograph in the series.

Maybe only a couple of feet — the angle is different from the earlier shots by a few degrees.

The foreground shows a continuation of the same horrific violation as the photograph before. But it's worse. Mattin is now standing on the arms of the chair, hovering above the woman's head and mouth, his erection in front of his oddly displayed testicles. This picture makes it even clearer that Mattin's pubic hair is shaved.

The background is different in this photograph. In the background is the kitchen, again. But it's no longer vacant.

Mimi is standing at the kitchen island. Her husband's rape of their friend is ongoing in the family room, in her clear view. She is not watching.

In the photograph she is looking, and pointing, across her body, in the direction of the basement staircase.

On the very edge of the photo, cut in half vertically, is the focus of her attention: a young man in a stocking cap and a Rossignol T-shirt. No hoodie. No day pack.

Her son, Emerson, is standing at the top of the basement stairs.

The shock in Mimi's face has the clarity of untracked snow. It's unmistakable. With her arm in motion, she is banishing her son back down to the basement.

But her eyes reveal that she is aware it is already too late. If Jonas's camera can find the young man in that frame, then the young man has already witnessed his stepfather's quasi-acrobatic sexual assault on the woman by the fire.

Mimi's son went back downstairs. Maybe he hesitated before he went. His bladder was still full. His anger? Only God knows how full that was.

Upstairs the rape, eventually, concluded.

Mattin's fantasy had its own sick progression. He didn't ejaculate in the widow's mouth. Either he didn't choose to, or he was too careful for that. Maybe his ejaculation was on her exposed chest. Maybe he didn't come at all.

If he ejaculated on her chest, he cleaned her carefully before he carried her limp body to the guest room.

Lauren said, "I'm sure Mattin was one meticulous bastard. Cleaning her was part of his ritual."

He must have had to support his victim's weight as he guided her to the guest room. Once there, he removed her robe, threw it on the chair at the end of the bed, and buttoned her pajama top. He may have taken an additional minute or two to goad her into allowing him to brush her teeth, or maybe into rinsing her mouth with antiseptic mouthwash. Maybe both.

Finally, he got her into bed.

He did one final review of his precautions. He was satisfied. He went upstairs to join his wife.

Feeling what? I cannot imagine.

Mimi's son waited in the basement until he no longer heard any noise upstairs. Maybe he waited a long time after that. He might have still been in shock from what he had seen earlier, or he might have been plotting how he could use any of it to his advantage.

He eventually climbed the stairs a second time, perhaps still in need of a bathroom. There was only one bathroom on the main floor. Emerson located it when he walked into the guest suite.

That is the last photo in the graphic novel. The young man is standing, now hatless and shoeless, in the doorway of the guest suite.

By the time Jonas takes that final photo, Emerson has already seen the sedated, sleeping woman whom his stepfather had just orally raped. In Jonas's photo, Emerson is looking back over his shoulder toward the family room. He is checking to see if anyone else is aware that he is there.

That is all that Jonas's photographs show. "That is all that our son saw," I told Lauren.

For the rest, we're left to fill in blanks.

Emerson decided that he and the woman were alone on the main floor. He stepped the rest of the way into the guest room. He closed the door behind him.

Jonas stayed on the first floor for a while. Or he didn't. We don't know yet what sounds he heard from the guest room. But Jonas knew the basement was empty. His path back out of the house was clear. At some point, Jonas made his way downstairs, and he went back outside. He scooted across the lane, around our house, and entered our basement on the west side.

Lauren said, "Where photography ends, forensics take over.

"Mimi's son Emerson raped the poor woman for the second time. He took off her pajamas, top and bottoms, and he . . . I don't know exactly what he did, but in the end, he raped her vaginally. He didn't use a condom, he probably didn't have one, but he didn't come inside of her. He ejaculated on her abdomen. He cleaned her off afterward. Like stepfather, like stepson. Maybe he used one of the bathroom towels to clean her. Even used soap and water. Eventually, he redressed her, but he was not as careful or meticulous as his stepfather. Emerson was a kid. He didn't really know anything about forensics.

"He made mistakes. He didn't clean her body well enough. He put her pajama bottoms on backward. He left behind traces of his own DNA. Two hairs. Some semen. One of the two rape-kit swabs that was positive for semen came from inside her navel."

Lauren knew things that I didn't know.

She continued, "Mimi and Hake woke the next morning to find their friend gone. They knew nothing of the second rape. Hake assumed the woman had left to go home none the wiser, her memories erased by Rohypnol. Hake assumed he'd gotten away with rape. Probably not for the first time.

"Mimi was not as confident that all the ends were tied up. She knew that Emerson had seen what her husband was doing the night before. She knew her son was asleep on a cot in the basement.

"But she didn't know what her son did in the guest room later on.

"Mimi knew her final steps in the precaution dance. She completely stripped and scrubbed the guest room and did a quick load of laundry before she and Hake left in the limo to head to the airport to fly to Napa.

"Sometime, later that day, Hake got a call on his cell phone from the sheriff's investigator about an allegation of sexual assault at his house the night before.

"Hake didn't know about the second rape. Neither did Mimi. He wondered what he might have done wrong in committing and covering up the first rape. He called Casey Sparrow. Denied everything to her."

It would have been tempting to conclude that Mattin was overconfident at that point, because that was the juncture at which he had decided to go all in. He volunteered his DNA for private analysis. But Lauren didn't know about the private DNA results. I couldn't tell her I knew that.

Lauren said, "But Mimi eventually guessed what had gone wrong — that the rape that had been reported wasn't the one by her husband. She confronted Emerson. He admitted what he had done. He told her everything, even about the chef seeing him earlier on the lane.

"For Mimi, the dominos had started to fall. She knew she was facing the prospect of losing both her husband and her son. She couldn't bear it."

I said, "She killed Preston Georges to

protect her family."

"And herself," Lauren said. "Ultimately, she was protecting herself."

48

I was suddenly in the dark.

Lauren revealed that the sheriff had retrieved the missing revolver from behind the burned house. Then she stopped talking with me about the ongoing investigations.

Hella had decided to change supervisors. When we met to discuss her decision, I called it resistance. She called it prudence. We agreed to disagree. I wished her well.

Sam was busy investigating a pair of vicious assaults that had taken place after hours near the Downtown Mall. I asked him once if he'd heard anything new about the rape. He told me it wasn't his case.

I knew that Mattin Snow hadn't been arrested only because the media wasn't screaming about it. If the DA's office was negotiating a plea bargain with Mimi Snow about the death of Preston Georges, those negotiations were ongoing well outside of my vision.

I'd stopped by Cozier Maitlin's office with a sealed Tyvek envelope containing Jonas's phone and eight-by-ten images of each of the photographs that Jonas had taken the night of the damn housewarming. On the outside of the envelope, I'd scrawled a cliché: "To be opened in the event of my serious injury or death." I'd signed it.

Cozy thought it was a joke of some kind.

I told him it wasn't.

He asked me if he could peek.

Someone from the sheriff's office took down the crime scene tape a week after the fire. It was the day of Jonas's second appointment with his new psychologist.

It was the day before Lauren and I would have our first appointment with our new couple's therapist.

The same afternoon, a demolition contractor stuffed a notice in our doorjamb informing us that final demo of the debris from the fire would take place ten days later.

I told Jonas he could skip school if he wanted to be there to watch the cleanup. He declined.

I wanted to be there.

I half hoped Mattin would show up for the final demolition. If the asshole were slipping back into denial, seeing me would certainly jolt him back into the reality that the face he was shaving each morning in the mirror was that of a rapist.

Just in case we had a confrontation, I'd arranged for backup. Sam had accepted my invitation to come over to join me in my ringside seats to the removal of all that remained of the old ranch house. I was feeling somber about it all. The feelings of loss I'd had at Peter's and at Adrienne's funerals haunted me anew. The complexities of all of Jonas's losses continued to stun me.

The first members of the demolition squad arrived midmorning. Their initial task was to stand outside their pickup trucks and drink McDonald's coffee. A caravan of heavy equipment rolled up soon after. I pulled a couple of lawn chairs out of the garage and set them up in front of Peter's barn. Despite a bitter fall chill under cloudless skies, and despite the fact that the festivities started a good hour before noon, I also retrieved a couple of beers from the refrigerator.

I was wearing a parka, my biking half gloves, and a good ski hat. When Sam arrived, I noted that he didn't even zip up his light jacket.

After one look at my outfit, he called me a wuss.

I didn't reveal that I was also wearing a base layer of long underwear. I wasn't in the mood to listen to another story about growing up on the Iron Range and how cold it could get ice fishing in northern Minnesota in January.

The next time he told me that story, I promised myself I was going to admit to him that I didn't even like walleye.

Once the diesels came to life, Sam and I reserved our conversational efforts for the interludes when the roar of the engines wasn't deafening.

During an early break in the heavy equipment action, he pointed toward the debris across the lane, where a winch was pulling Mimi's big SUV out of the rubble that had been the garage. "Didn't know that was in there," Sam said. Then, without any segue at all, he added, "Lucy told me last night there will be no charges filed, you know, after all. Courtney Rea has been keeping her up to date on the sheriff's side of things. Turns out they've become buds. Girlfriends."

The way he said "girlfriends" would have irritated Lucy were she with us. Sam knew that.

I raised an eyebrow. "Really? You're talking about the housewarming? Here? There won't be any charges? I did not know that."

"The evidence has all lined up behind a dead suspect. What are you going to do?" Sam said.

"I guess." Something about Sam's affect was making me uneasy. I set my beer on the dusty ground beside my flimsy chair. I tried to prepare myself for something I wasn't prepared for. I wanted both hands free, just in case.

"Cozier Maitlin has officially informed the DA's office that the accuser has decided not to testify about the alleged rape. If rape is what it was, of course. We don't know for sure there was a rape, do we?" Sam asked.

I felt like I was approaching a trap or a trip wire. But I couldn't see it. "We don't," I said.

"We do, though, right? Really. Know there was a rape." He stared at me. He wasn't looking in my eyes; he was watching my eyes. "But we don't, not officially," Sam said. "Mental health concern, I hear. For the victim. That's the reason for her not testifying. Since that's your neck of the woods — other people's mental health — I'm kind of wondering if you have any thoughts about it. Not testifying because of mental health concerns?"

My pulse was picking up speed. Could Sam know about my supervision role with the victim? I decided to play it as though he didn't. What choice did I have?

"Maybe the mental health concerns are valid," I said. "From what . . . I know, the woman must have been through a lot."

"What you know?"

Shit. "The rape," I said.

Sam was still examining my eyes. I was increasingly discomfited. "If there was a rape," Sam said. "Everything's alleged, you know." *A-ledge-ed.*

"Yeah? Even the kid's involvement? That's alleged?"

"You got me there," Sam said. "That's kind of confirmed by forensics. Back to the other — I think every rape victim would have mental health concerns about testifying. Don't you? Nature of the beast. Trauma being trauma. Many vics testify anyway. Some, I hear, even consider testifying to be therapeutic."

Sam said *therapeutic* in a manner that was packed with disdain.

"May be true," I said. I wished I had an app that would tell me where this conversation was heading. I couldn't see out ahead of us more than a few metaphorical feet, but I wasn't liking the current vector.

The heavy equipment provided a long break in the conversation. Thank God for excavators and dump trucks. After the next break in the action, I hoped Sam and I would start up someplace other than where we'd left off.

Sam had other ideas. When the noise dropped back to very loud, he said, "Lucy told me she's heard rumors about a settlement, too. Between the parties."

Wow. A settlement would mean there was a civil suit. If a civil suit had been filed naming Mattin Snow as a defendant, then the accusations against him would be public. At that point, his career and reputation would be gone. He'd have nothing left to lose. That freedom would make the man dangerous in completely novel ways.

If he had nothing to lose, why would he settle? I knew I was missing something crucial. Which I figured was just the way Sam wanted it right then.

The dilemma that Cozier Maitlin and Casey Sparrow had been busy confronting was how to settle a civil suit that couldn't actually be filed. Cozy's client, the victim, wanted a measure of justice from the still-living perpetrator of the rape — Casey's client, Mattin Snow. But if the rape victim filed her civil suit against Mattin Snow — a most public act — Mattin's career as a women's legal advocate was over. Even the faintest hint of the allegation would flatten him as completely as a direct hit from a meteorite. Any motivation he would have had to play nice — certainly to settle a suit with his accuser — would disappear.

Sam's Kobe Bryant story had taught me a clear lesson about accusations of sexual license with a celebrity: once the allegations were public, the accused Snow would have no choice but to begin a phase of mutually assured destruction with his victim.

I asked Sam, "What . . . parties settled . . . what?"

Sam nodded. If I had to translate the nod, I would have guessed it to mean, "Well played."

"The vic," Sam finally said. "And the family of the kid. The victim sued Emerson Abbott's mother and father, and his stepfather, for damages for the rape. I don't know the details, but some subset of that group, they're the ones who are settling."

Elegant solution, I thought. *Mimi and Mattin would pay their pound of flesh, the victim would feel some vindication, but Mattin's assault on her would never become public.*

Damn but these lawyers are good. Wizardy, even.

A truck filled with charred debris pulled away down the lane. Its empty twin backed immediately into the space that had been vacated. Across the way, the bed of a flatbed was starting to tilt down to await the arrival of the roasted SUV. I waited until all the backing-up *beep-beep-beep*ing stopped before I replied to Sam.

"I didn't know about the suit or the settlement," I said.

It was true. I hadn't heard. My usual sources were quiet. Lauren wasn't talking much about work at all, certainly not about the rape after the housewarming or the Devil's Thumb murder. And since Hella's supervision had ended, the legal updates I'd counted on during supervision sessions were no longer available.

"All just happened," Sam said.

"You have thoughts about all this, Sam? You seem to know a lot. Given that it's not your case."

"People talk to me," he said. "I'm a good listener. And I do have thoughts." He paused before he added, "You and Lauren, too."

I didn't know what that meant. "What?"

"No charges for either of you, right?

That's something, too, eh?"

From Sam's mouth, the Canadian *eh?* wasn't mimicry or unconscious affectation. It was intentional punctuation. He was getting my attention.

I thought, *Oh, so that's where you're going. But why?*

The fact that Lauren and I wouldn't be charged wasn't real news. Word that Lauren had been cleared in the shooting and that I wouldn't be charged in a break-in had dribbled out of the DA's office over the previous week. I thought the decisions had been communicated in a way that was intended to maximally irritate us. I blamed that on Elliot Bellhaven, Lauren's boss.

"My opinion?" I said. "I thought Elliot kept Lauren at the end of the gangplank longer than he had to, but I'm relieved that she's finally cleared. She was just protecting her son that night. You know that."

"No charges against you, either, buddy." Sam raised his beer in a toast. Or a mock toast. I was so off balance, I couldn't be sure. I didn't like that I couldn't tell what was going on.

I didn't raise my bottle to join Sam in the toast. "I was protecting my son, too. And my dog. I haven't been that worried about the system doing anything to me."

Sam sat quietly for a full minute. The machinery was active, but I thought the interlude of silence had more to do with process than cacophonic competition.

"You're saying no deals were cut for either of you?" Sam asked finally. "No lawyer wizard Merliny shit was involved?"

I decided to wait to answer him until the front loader finished emptying a shovel load of charcoal chunks into the dump truck. I could feel myself getting defensive. Or more defensive. "No deals, Sam. We just relied on facts. The sheriff investigated. The special prosecutor weighed the evidence. We were innocent. The authorities recognized that. *Fini.*"

"Fini?" he said. "This is going to end with you speaking French? Really? I can't tell you how disappointing that will be for me." He didn't wait for me to reply. "Most people of means don't like to leave such things to the whim of . . . the prosecuting authorities. They prefer playing with a deck that's been carefully stacked."

Here it comes. "By?"

"Lawyer wizards, preferably."

I looked at him, determined to try to understand what the fuck was going on. "What are you suggesting? Is there a question lurking in there?" I asked.

"So . . . no civil suits have been filed that I haven't heard anything about? No private settlements you want to share?"

"You talking about us? Lauren and me?"

"I am."

"No. No settlements." Sam's face revealed nothing. I said, "In fact, we heard that the homeowner, Mr. Snow, is putting this property back on the market. Given real estate these days, he'll probably take a loss. Since he moved into the neighborhood, he has taken . . . a lot of losses." I intended my reply to be a just-desserts punctuation mark.

Sam nodded slowly. But it wasn't an agreeable nod; it was a contemplative nod. He said, "I got to ask. Please don't get all offended. No money changed hands? I shouldn't be waiting for someone to stand up and claim that nothing was exchanged in return for anyone's silence? You know how that particular bullshit gets stuck in my craw."

"No." My discomfort and my defensiveness were joining forces. The sum of the parts was beginning to feel a lot like anger. I reminded myself that Sam was my friend. "What are you getting at? I don't like the implication of your question."

Sam ignored my protest. He asked, "There aren't any pending public statements from fancy attorneys I should be waiting for with bated breath?"

I'm thick sometimes. I had thought Sam and I were getting together as friends to attend a wake-slash-demolition. Part of the completing of the circle. A friendly effort to track down the always elusive, rare species that is closure.

Sam apparently had other ideas about how we were spending our time that morning. His plan felt more like interrogation.

Six months or so before, when Carmen was still pregnant, Sam had gone to a wedding in Florida and come back from the long weekend a different man. I couldn't put my finger on how, but my friend had changed.

This felt like part of that. Whatever that was.

"Really?" I said. "Cordillera? That's what you think this morning is all about? Not you and me? You're wondering if this whole mess has become another Cordillera? A Mr. Kobe Bryant, act two? And Lauren and I have starring roles?"

Sam turned his head toward me and smiled that smile of his I really didn't like. "Don't lose sight of what really happened up there in Eagle County. At the end, it wasn't about Mr. Bryant. Or his alleged victim. At the end, it was about attorneys who arranged a version of justice that they considered better than the version of justice the system — the cops, the prosecutors, the judges, the juries — might come up with."

"That's a powerful indictment, Sam."

"It is what it is. Other people, wiser people than me, were the ones who said it first. I'm just being agreeable, since — as we both know — that's my nature."

Ha. "But this, Sam? You think this" — I swept my arm at the mess being cleaned up — "is the same thing?"

"This here? This is nothing but rubble being cleared and carried away to the dump." He smiled at himself, pleased that I'd given him the chance to deploy that metaphor. Then he leaned forward, his elbows on his knees.

"What do we got? We got famous folk. Not as famous as Kobe, but there's at least one real-life true national celebrity around. Yes? Allegations of sexual assault. Check. We got a vic suddenly refusing to testify. Right? And potential felonies evaporating before our eyes. *Poof.* No doubt about that happening. Then, there's the aroma of big dollars." Sam sniffed the air. "And, of course, we have superstar members of the illustrious Colorado Bar. Proverbial lawyer wizards. Two or three of those at least.

"Add it all up and you gotta admit, Alan, minus a few hundred TV cameras, all the ingredients are right here and right now. For a replay, I mean. So to speak."

"I'm offended, I think. Are you really accusing Lauren of paying off Mattin Snow in order to avoid a felony charge?"

Sam tried to pretend he was trying to look innocent. He didn't pull it off. Not even close. He said, "It was his house. He could have decided not to press charges against her, or against you. But I'm not accusing your wife. Or you, for that matter," he said. He turned his big head my way, offering me yet another creepy smile.

"Me? You think I'm paying that asshole money to go away?"

"You know, you say that with such precious indignation, it's as though you believe it has never happened before. And you say it as though you wouldn't do it now, today, if you thought it was the only way to keep you or your wife out of prison."

A short round Hispanic man and a reed-thin Hmong woman were just completing tying down the blackened carcass of the SUV on the flatbed. They were throwing a tarp over it, cinching everything down.

I wasn't about to admit it to Sam, but if

things had come down the way Sam was implying they had come down — and Lauren and I were facing the ominous portent of incarceration — I would indeed have run to my nearest lawyer wizard and asked him or her to imagine me some justice that offered a different outcome.

I offered my friend a crumb. I said, "Point. I admit that. If I had to do it to save my family, I might. Okay, I would. So I'll spare you my indignation. But I will say it's not happening this time. Not with us. Not at all."

"Good," Sam said. "Glad to hear it."

"I'd feel better if I thought you believed me, Sam."

"Not my problem. What might make you feel better, I mean."

"I thought you were my friend."

"Don't act all injured on me. You and I have too much of the same dirt underneath our fingernails."

"What is it, then?"

"You may be surprised to learn this about me, my *friend,* but I don't always agree with what my bosses and the DA's office decide to do about charging people I think have committed serious crimes. I do my part. My job. I do the investigations. Sometimes I arrest the suspects. After that? The way it works, it's out of my hands."

I played along. "Really? You, a malcontent?"

"Yup, go figure. They decide to let some people walk even though I think I have all the evidence required to send them away. But even when I think they're wrong, I let it go. I believe my bosses and the DA are the ones who should be making those decisions. Why? Because that's our system.

"And sometimes it turns out — believe it or not — that I don't like how trials get conducted, what prosecutors do and don't do to bring justice to bear in criminal court. I let that go, too. Because I do believe that judges and juries and prosecutors are the ones who should be doing the people's bidding. So I keep my mouth shut. Again, I do that because that's our system.

"I live with it all. The good, the bad. Plenty of the ugly. Sometimes I'm happier than other times. But that's our system, and I go along."

I could've reminded Sam about one prominent exception to his going-along meme, but I wasn't feeling suicidal enough to bring up the solo trip he'd made late one night a year-plus back to a rented cottage on a ranch near Frederick, Colorado.

Sam hadn't forgotten Frederick. He'd

never forget Frederick. He was counting on the fact that I wasn't courageous enough to use it in our argument. Sam was right.

He timed a long draw of his beer to coincide with a determined dig into the garage rubble by the front loader.

I was waiting. I could tell he wasn't done.

"The way it works? If the public doesn't like how cops like me are protecting them, their community, then they're free to go to the polls and vote out the mayor. They vote in a new mayor, who comes in and cleans house. He — or she — appoints a new police chief. The new chief fires cops, picks new division chiefs, changes priorities in the department. Hopefully, it all works out better for the public.

"If the public doesn't like how a DA is prosecuting criminals, then they're free to go to the polls and vote out the DA. They elect a new one who will do it all differently. Hopefully, once there's a new DA, it all works out better for the public.

"And if the public doesn't like how a judge is handling criminal trials, the public can vote not to retain that judge. Doesn't happen often, but the public has that choice. If they vote not to retain, they'll end up with a new judge who will handle defendants and trials differently. Once again, maybe better.

Hopefully better for the public."

I watched one of the chimneys topple over after a nudge from the bucket on the excavator. It was incredibly anticlimactic. The excavator immediately reached down and grabbed on to the carcass of the old harvest-gold washing machine from the basement. Lifting it out of the junk made a lot of noise.

Sam asked if he was boring me. "Not at all," I said. "Please continue."

"But when criminal justice is outsourced — I like to think of it as hijacked — and left to the lawyers, to the private lawyers and only to the private lawyers, who exactly is it who ends up accountable to the public? Anybody at all?"

I couldn't tell if I had any lines in Sam's play right then. I decided silence was my safest option.

I'd guessed right. Sam went on. "What if the secret deals the lawyer wizards make don't work in the public interest? What then? For example" — Sam held up one finger — "because of the secret arrangements all the lawyer wizards made in Cordillera, we — the public — will never know if Mr. Kobe Bryant actually raped that woman in that hotel. Right? She said he did. He said he didn't. Maybe he did. And maybe he didn't. If he didn't, I suppose I can live with the outcome of all the fancy lawyering and secret deal-making and private justice just fine. But what if he did? What if he raped her?

"See, what I'm saying is that justice isn't only what happened between Mr. Bryant and that woman. Justice is a bigger thing. The public has a dog in that fight. An important dog."

He stared at me. I felt he was daring me to say something stupid. I didn't move a muscle.

"At the beginning? You were worried about your kids and your wife. Their safety if it turned out there was a rapist next door. Recall that? That's the public interest I'm talking about.

"Well, if Mr. Bryant did what the original indictment said he did, that would mean there is a rapist walking free, right? Today. And how shitty is that for the public? And if Mr. Bryant isn't a rapist, some other guy in some other situation who is a rapist has already gone free, or will eventually go free because of some other secret arrangements between some other lawyer wizards. Want to know how I know that?"

"Sure."

"Law of averages," Sam said. "You tell me, what is the public supposed to do when the law of averages catches up with all the secret arrangements between lawyer wizards that leaves men accused of rape walking the streets, free to pick out new victims?"

I considered responding. Then I reconsidered.

Sam went on. "I'm just asking. What is the public supposed to do when one of these private lawyer secret deals about testimony leaves a wife beater free to marry again, to get down on one knee and pick out a new victim and put a ring on her finger a few days or weeks before he reaches out and . . . breaks that finger? Hell, law of averages says it's already happened.

"I mean, what is the public's recourse when one of these secret deals about testimony leaves a *murderer* free to go on with his life, free to select a new victim?" Sam hesitated, then added, "Well?"

"Rhetorical question?" I asked. "Or has that happened, too?"

"Law of averages. If it hasn't happened, it will happen. Hardly rhetorical," Sam said.

"Okay."

Sam finished his beer. He long-tossed the bottle into a pile of rubble about to be scooped up by the front loader.

As if on cue, all the operators of all the heavy equipment killed their engines. It was break time.

Sam said, "If you're waiting for my point, and I know you are, it's this: as far as I know, there is no polling place the public can walk into to vote out the lawyer wizards. Is there? Am I missing something?"

Again, he wanted an answer. I shook my head at the "missing something" part.

"The way it is now? The way it looks like it will be going forward? If some accused criminal type can afford the fees, these lawyer wizards are absolutely free to go out and do it all again. What they did with Mr. Bryant — go into some pretty, private conference room where the public isn't invited and barter this in exchange for that. From where I sit it seems like what always ends up getting bartered is something that closely resembles testimony for something that looks a lot like money. But that's a guess. I've never actually been invited into any of those meetings.

"I guarantee you, though, that one of these lawyer wizards will end up, or has ended up, making a secret deal that leaves a rapist, or a wife beater, or a murderer, beyond the grasp of the real criminal justice system. And you know what? There isn't a damn thing the public can do about it."

Sam was making a big point. But in the

moment, the finger he was figuratively pointing felt personal and accusatory.

"You think," I said, "that there was some fancy lawyering like that going on here? With us?"

"I'm afraid I do, Alan," he said. "This one didn't end quite right. I don't have a good taste in my mouth."

"It's not the beer?"

I was aiming for a laugh. I got a chuckle. "It's not the beer."

"I suggest you wait, Sam, for this one to resolve completely. A week. A month. See what shakes out. See if justice — the public kind, the justice that leaves a good taste in your mouth — finds its way back into the equation."

I hoped my words turned out to be true. I didn't want the last lie in this tragic story to be mine.

Sam sat back, extended his legs. Crossed one ankle over the other. He said, "You know something, don't you?"

He said it as though he had trouble believing I knew something.

I said, "All I know is that there are still people out there determined to do the right thing."

He stood up, towering over me. He said, "Huh, you fucking know something."

49

Sam was right about some of the rumors he'd heard.

He let me know that the civil suit that had been quietly filed by the widow against the family of Emerson Abbott did settle, not only quickly but also confidentially. The rape victim immediately decided to move from Colorado. Sam told me he thought she was "gone before the check cleared." I suspected that Hella knew where she had gone.

I didn't know, nor did I care. I hoped she found a good therapist, and something resembling closure, wherever she landed.

I was wrong in regard to the time frame I had suggested to Sam about the meandering ways of justice. But not by too much.

Mattin Snow's arrest didn't come until two days before Christmas.

He was charged with two rapes. One victim was a thirty-seven-year-old real estate agent, a local, whom he and Mimi had met on a ski trip in Telluride the previous March. The rape had occurred in the couple's rented condo in the hours after the woman had been invited over for a nightcap.

The second victim was the twenty-two-year-old daughter of a Dominican woman who cleaned Mimi and Mattin's Boulder house, the one they'd lived in before moving to Spanish Hills. The woman's daughter had been filling in during the previous year's holiday season while her mother was recovering from surgery for ovarian cancer.

Both women recalled the circumstances of the assaults, which were almost identical. Neither recalled the rapes.

According to the charges, both rapes reportedly involved powerful hypnotics like Rohypnol, and each featured Mattin Snow's perverse dominance fantasies. The rapes also involved Mimi Snow. She, Lauren told me the night before the story broke to massive media fanfare, would be the primary witness for the prosecution.

Mimi's deal with the prosecutors? She had earned herself a reasonable chance of not dying in a Colorado prison. And an outside possibility that she might get to attend her not-yet-conceived grandchild's college graduation.

Lauren thought Mimi had also bought herself some peace of mind.

Casey Sparrow had Mattin Snow out on bond in time for midnight mass on Christmas Eve.

Sam's justice — the kind the public cared about — if it were to occur at all, would have a righteous adversary.

Casey Sparrow was most definitely a lawyer wizard.

On January third, our neighbor down the lane, Ralph, somehow managed to get the post of a for-sale sign to pierce through the crust of frozen earth on the land across the lane from our house.

That was the same morning the vet gave Emily the all-clear for full activity.

She immediately resumed making nightly rounds of her parish, with gusto.

That night, I allowed Fiji to run free with her big friend, at least on the open ground where I could see her clearly.

During Emily's convalescence, the little Havanese seemed to have totally forgotten about prairie dogs. She put all her energy into shadowing Emily and emulating the Bouv's good traits, which was most of them.

Fiji was trying to earn her deputy's badge.

ACKNOWLEDGMENTS

Thanks are long overdue to Boulder. So, thank you, Boulder, for — sometimes defiantly; reliably amusingly — being. I don't think this series would have endured had it been moored elsewhere.

I write in a quiet room with a sleeping dog by my side (thank you, Abbey). But my freedom to write is reliant on people who have been unwavering in support of my vision, such as it is, and who apply their substantial talents into helping me turn raw ideas into finished books. Brian Tart and Jessica Horvath were most patient, and their smart editing was especially crucial in helping me navigate some tricky terrain this time. Robert Barnett, Bonnie Nathan, and Thomas Hentoff offered unflappable calm and seasoned counsel for which I am exceedingly grateful.

For years Elyse Morgan and Nancy Hall have provided their astute vision as they critique early drafts. I thank them for that, and for their complete lack of guile in pointing out the errors of my ways (almost always absent any apparent glee). Jane Davis, too, is a valued early reader, but she is much more than that. My task would be so much more difficult without her invisible hand. I've counted on Al Silverman since the day he phoned me in 1990 (landline to landline, pre-email) and said he wanted to buy my first book. I still count on him.

I suspect that the family of any writer will recognize that the sometimes-endless hours he or she sweats at the keyboard are not the only source of the stress this life heaps on a household. The longer I do this, the more I recognize that, for me at least, the process of writing actually lasts all day — and sometimes all night — for months on end. What happens while I am at the keyboard is merely the writing-down. My loving gratitude goes to my family for tolerating all those present absences and for supporting this odd passion of mine for so many years.

ABOUT THE AUTHOR

Stephen White is a clinical psychologist and *New York Times* best-selling author of seventeen previous suspense novels, including *The Siege, Dead Time,* and *Dry Ice.* He lives in Colorado.

For more information, please visit www.authorstephenwhite.com

The employees of Thorndike Press hope you have enjoyed this Large Print book. All our Thorndike, Wheeler, and Kennebec Large Print titles are designed for easy reading, and all our books are made to last. Other Thorndike Press Large Print books are available at your library, through selected bookstores, or directly from us.

For information about titles, please call:
(800) 223-1244

or visit our Web site at:
http://gale.cengage.com/thorndike

To share your comments, please write:

Publisher
Thorndike Press
295 Kennedy Memorial Drive
Waterville, ME 04901